Against the Tide

Stephen Puleston

ABOUT THE AUTHOR

Stephen Puleston was born and educated in Anglesey, North Wales. He graduated in theology before training as a lawyer. Against the Tide is his third novel in the Inspector Drake series

www.stephenpuleston.co.uk
Facebook:stephenpulestoncrimewriter

OTHER NOVELS

Inspector Drake Mysteries

Brass in Pocket
Worse than Dead
Against the Tide
Prequel Novella– Ebook only
Devil's Kitchen

Inspector Marco Novels

Speechless
Another Good Killing
Prequel Novella– Ebook only
Dead Smart

ISBN-13:978-1523424177
ISBN-10:1523424176

:

In memory of my mother
Gwenno Puleston

Chapter 1

The summer mist was thick enough to bottle and it clung to his clothes, invaded his nostrils. He hesitated for a moment in the small yard alongside the cottage, allowing his eyes to acclimatise to the early morning gloom. Behind him in the kitchen the kettle boiled and he checked his watch – another night of poor sleep.

He grimaced as the first mouthful of tea stung his lips. Then he found some stale bread and dropped it into the toaster. It was going to be his last year digging bait, and scratching a living from fishing. But he'd said that last year and the year before that too. It was in his blood, like his father and his grandfather before him; the water and the sand, like some enchanting mistress, drew him back.

After his hurried breakfast he pulled the door closed behind him and stepped out onto the small yard, his Labrador at his feet. He gathered three plastic buckets and an old fork and made for the beach. Somewhere in the village a car fired into life. He drew heavily on the thin cigarette at his lips, feeling the smoke scouring his windpipe. On the bridge, he heard the sound of the sea lapping either side. He knew every inch of the shoreline, the bays and inlets. He knew when the tides would turn, when the water would fall, pulled out towards the sea and then rise, forced back again, filling the narrow inlet. He knew the name of every house and the history of every family, even the holiday homes. He knew the boats and their names and their foibles and their owners and often the fathers of the owners.

He stood and listened, resting one hand on his fork; the other held the ragged end of the cigarette as he drew on it one last time. He flicked the butt out over the water. He drew the zip of his fleece tight up against his chin before picking up the buckets. His dog brushed against his trousers, its breathing heavy and its tongue flopping around.

Looking down the bridge his thoughts turned to Uncle Richie who lived nearby at Bryn Castell, and with the mist thinning he could make out the silhouettes of the houses at the end of the bridge. Only another hour, maybe less, until the warmth from the sun would have burnt all the fog away. As a boy he'd sat for hours watching Uncle Richie tidying his nets, sorting his lines and gutting and cleaning fish. And when his uncle had drunk too much whisky he'd tell him how he could sense things, how he knew when death was at the door.

He tried to shake off a sense of unease and strode down onto the beach. The pebbles crunched under his feet and after a couple more steps the sand was soft under his boots. He stopped, set the buckets down and propped the fork against his leg before fumbling with the strap of a head torch. Eventually he had a narrow beam of light poking into the murkiness. There must be an easier way to make a living, he thought, not for the first time. He picked up the buckets and fork and moved towards the deep mud near the old ford. There he stopped and sank the fork into the soft mud and sand.

He'd work down with the retreating tide until low water in a couple of hours, before working back, ahead of the advancing tide, digging and collecting the worms he needed to make a living. Once he'd finished, the bait would be weighed, wrapped in newspaper and stored in a refrigerator. He had lots of regular customers, especially on the weekend, mostly men with 4x4s trailing fishing cuddies. By mid-morning, after a brief nap, he'd launch his dinghy to check the pots. If he was lucky there'd be some lobsters he could sell to passing tourists who without fail paid top price for fresh seafood.

He'd been working for a few minutes when he heard something behind him. He straightened up and tried moving his feet but the wet sand wouldn't release its grip easily. He made a half turn but saw nothing other than the fog gently swirling and caressing its way around him. He cursed at his timidity. His mind must be playing tricks. He whistled briefly for his dog but there was no response. He turned back to the work in hand.

Another sound, light steps on the wet sand – perhaps a stray dog had been drawn by the light from his torch. But there weren't any in the village and, besides, his own Labrador would have reacted. He raised his head and leant on the fork, making to turn around.

Louder now and closer. Much closer and regular. His chest tightened, his breathing shallow. Whoever it was wasn't going to give him a fright. He cursed the wet sand for stopping his free movement.

He tugged at his right foot, loosening it, and then he twisted as he straightened again, the light from his head torch bobbing around through the fog. A footfall, definitely. He looked up and opened his mouth, forming the words he would never speak.

Chapter 2

Ian Drake slowly tapped the end of a ballpoint upon the file of papers on the conference table in Northern Division headquarters of the Wales Police Service. It was his first day back after a few days' leave, but rather than feeling refreshed he couldn't shake off a jaded mood. He couldn't put his finger on what was wrong but the holiday felt wasted. His frustration deepened as he thought about the reports he had to write and the several hundred emails in his inbox that needed his attention, but instead he was listening to Andy Thorsen, a senior crown prosecutor who had called an early morning meeting specifically to suit his diary.

'I'll want all the statements cross-referenced for any inconsistencies,' Thorsen said for the third time in less than thirty minutes.

Thorsen looked more dishevelled than usual that morning. He had a tall forehead and eyebrows that danced around as he moved his eyes. His suit was grey and had lost its shape, as though it had been washed at a very high temperature.

A public order dispute in Bangor one Saturday night had deteriorated into a brawl that had resulted in various arrests for assaults, several police officers with broken noses and over a hundred statements. It had all left Drake sensing that the prosecution was destined to fail, a view reinforced by the reputation of Sergeant John Hollins, now sitting directly opposite him.

'I think you should explore the possibility that the defendants might plead to a lesser charge,' Drake said.

He knew Hollins was staring at him but he kept on looking at the prosecutor, waiting for a reaction.

'Don't you believe the evidence of your fellow police officers?' Hollins said.

'It's about the public interest.' Thorsen folded his

arms.

'I agree, of course,' Drake said, giving Hollins a sharp look.

Drake's mobile, switched to silent, vibrated in his pocket. He fished it out and, seeing it was area control, declined the call.

'All the lads on that Saturday night have given clear accounts of what happened. There's overwhelming evidence that the defendants are guilty,' Hollins was looking impatient.

'It's never that simple,' Drake said, putting the mobile on top of his papers.

Hollins sat back in his chair heavily. 'And what's complicated about seven police officers having broken noses?'

Hollins had joined the Wales Police Service after ten years in the army, bringing with him a military style to the application of policing. He probably enjoyed cracking heads together, Drake thought.

Drake leant forward. 'It's a matter of reasonable doubt, Sergeant.'

'Don't preach at me, Inspector.'

'Then you should know it's going to be embarrassing if this fiasco gets before a court.'

'They were drunken toe-rags who needed to be locked up.'

'Is that what you're going to say in cross-examination?' Drake glanced over at Thorsen, pleased that there was a troubled look on his face.

'We need to nail these guys.' Hollins leant forward over the table, fists clenched.

Before Drake or Thorsen could say anything more, the door opened. A tall woman came into the room. 'Inspector Drake. Area control is trying to contact you.'

'It's my first day back. Can't somebody else take

the call?'

'It's urgent, apparently.'

'We're done here,' Thorsen said, a pleased tone to his voice. 'If I need to speak to you again I can reschedule.'

An hour later Drake parked on the pavement behind a Scientific Support Vehicle. He turned off the CD player and the Bruce Springsteen track stopped mid-drumbeat. Looking in the rear view mirror, he pulled a loose hair into place and straightened his tie before leaving the car. He pressed the remote and the Alfa Romeo GT flashed. He glanced around, satisfied that he'd parked a safe distance from other vehicles.

Cars lined each side of the road leading to the bridge and as he walked alongside them, the mobile in his pocket began to vibrate. He fumbled for the handset and read the message from Sergeant Caren Waits – *be there in ten*. Her lateness could be infuriating but he'd come to rely on her more than he cared to admit, certainly to her. After reaching the bridge he noticed a stream of onlookers walking down from Four Mile Bridge, the village on the opposite side, some exchanging serious glances, others gesticulating with raised arms. He turned to his right and saw the crime scene investigators and uniformed officers huddled over the corpse. Behind them was a wide expanse of mud and sand, stretching into the distance, broken by a narrow channel of water that eventually pooled a few hundred yards behind them.

Over to his left were more mud banks dissected by the meandering tide and in the distance a shroud of heat masked the mountains of Snowdonia. The sun was warm on his shoulders. It had only been two months since his father's death and apprehension crept into his mind that he wasn't ready for a new murder case, especially as the counsellor had warned him that he might find it difficult to cope and that his little yet ever-present rituals, his need for things to be *just so*, might get more severe. He shook off his anxiety and walked off the bridge down onto the seashore. A flimsy blue-and-white tape fluttered as Drake ducked his head underneath. Soon his shoes were crunching on the pebbles at the high-water mark. A young constable with sweat patches under his arms approached him, but the look of mild antagonism evaporated once Drake produced his warrant card. Dry seaweed rimmed the shoreline, a salty smell hung in the air and Drake noticed a disused windmill in the distance.

A sergeant, standing near the body, saw Drake approaching and raised a hand in acknowledgement before making his way laboriously towards him. Drake stood and waited.

'Frank Watkins. Glad you're here, sir,' he said, his cheeks flushed.

'What are the details?'

'Male. Late forties, early fifties.'

'Any ID?'

'Ed Mostyn. He lived in the village.' He pointed towards the houses at the end of the bridge. 'Did you bring wellingtons?'

Drake shook his head.

'You can try mine.' Watkins sat down on a rocky ledge, and took off his boots. They were a size too small for Drake and they pinched his feet as he made his way out over the sand. Drake recognised Mike Foulds, the crime scene manager, standing over Dr Lee Kings, the local pathologist.

'Good morning, Mike,' Drake said.

Foulds nodded an acknowledgement. Kings stood up. 'Good morning, Ian.'

'What can you tell me, Lee?'

'Blow to the head. Probably knocked him unconscious. But massive blood loss from the penetrating wounds to the neck is the likely cause of death. I'll get a better idea after the post mortem.'

'Apparently the sergeant removed a fork when he arrived,' Foulds added.

'What? A garden fork? He was impaled with a fork!' Drake looked down at the bloodied head of Ed Mostyn. There were two puncture wounds on his neck and blood stained his clothes and face. 'Is there any reason not to move him?' Drake said to Kings.

'None as far as I'm concerned,' said the doctor, dislodging his feet from the wet sand.

Drake turned to Foulds. 'What do you think?'

'We don't have much time,' he replied. 'We'll have to move the body and then do a detailed search. But we'll need the help of the uniform lads.'

'How long have we got until the tide turns?'

'I was told that low water was at half past seven, so high tide will be about half past one. But the sea water will have covered the area well before that.'

Drake looked towards the bridge and noticed that the flow of water passing through its arch had already increased. The remains of some plastic bags and baked bean cans floated past in the narrow channel.

'Where does this water go?' Drake said.

'Fills this whole bay. Basically, it's a big lagoon that divides Anglesey from Holy Island and for some reason it's called the Inland Sea. The water is trapped between the bridge behind us and the main embankment.' Foulds pointed into the distance with one hand. He waved at the uniformed officers who moved towards them slowly.

They leant over the body and tried lifting it, but the water and sand pulled it back. A young officer pressed his boots under the corpse until eventually the body was lifted clear; a trickle of brown water dripped along the sticky sand as the four officers moved towards the shoreline.

Drake spotted the end of a Velcro strap in the sand and knelt down. He gave it a brief tug and pulled out a head torch, which he held between two fingers, examining it before stepping towards the high-water mark. 'Mike,' he said, holding up the torch.

Foulds dipped into his pocket, an evidence bag at the ready, and stepped over to Drake. Painstakingly they made their way back to the shoreline towards a group of uniformed officers who had been press-ganged into helping the forensics team. Foulds explained what he wanted to achieve – there might be a piece of clothing, some relic of the man's life hidden below the surface of the sand, a fragment of his life and his violent death that might give them a clue, a signal as to where to look for the killer. Drake guessed the exercise would be futile, even possibly absurd, but they had to preserve evidence.

As Foulds finished, Sergeant Watkins arrived alongside Drake. 'Mike tells me you moved the fork.' Drake nodded towards the scene.

'I wasn't going to wait for the CSIs to arrive – there were enough people gawping at the body as it was.'

'We'll need a statement.'

Watkins nodded and then jerked his head towards the bridge. 'The press have arrived, sir.'

'What!'

Drake turned to look at the bridge and saw the lights of a camera unit and three men standing together with clipboards and equipment. How did they find out so quickly? He struggled out of the wellingtons and laced up his brogues before walking towards the bridge, squinting against the summer sunshine. Anxious faces appeared in the windows of nearby cottages and when he reached the tarmac he caught himself looking towards the Alfa, checking for scratches or bumps. He noticed Caren getting out of her car and then half running as she made her way towards the bridge. Her hair was the usual tangled mess and her blouse full of creases. She had a rolling gait that reminded him of his mother; the result, he suspected, of living on a farm.

Behind him he heard the chatter of bystanders and a camera light came on, a bright shining glow. A voice shouted his name.

'Inspector Drake, Inspector Drake.'

Drake turned and saw the small man calling his name, his face vaguely familiar; he was dressed in a tight-fitting three-button suit, grey shirt and grey tie, and his clean-shaven head was shaped like a large bullet. He stroked a black goatee beard of perfect proportions. His head bobbed up and down as he tried to get Drake's attention.

Caren was by Drake's side now. 'So what's happening?'

'Ed Mostyn. Local man from the village apparently. You go and talk to the CSIs. I'm going to talk to this journalist.'

Passing cars had their windows lowered, faces staring towards the scene. In the distance the mountains were even clearer as the morning temperatures rose, promising another beautiful day. Two young boys with fishing rods were talking into mobiles. A group of retired men huddled together, exchanging serious glances, their dogs pulling on leashes.

Drake saw the journalist pushing his way past a woman with a young child.

'Calvin Headley. HTV News,' he introduced

himself.

Drake recognised the man's face from the TV news bulletins and guessed that one of the uniformed officers must have given the journalist his name.

'Can you give us a statement?' he continued. 'Do you know who the man is? How long has he been dead?' The light of the camera shone into Drake's face; he looked down at the journalist.

'This is off the record,' Drake began.

Headley motioned to the cameraman who switched off the light.

'I can't tell you anything at the moment. The investigation is just beginning. We've discovered the body and at the moment that's all I can tell you.' He turned away, but Headley followed him.

'Will you be setting up an incident room?'

Drake didn't answer.

'Where can I contact you?' he continued.

'You'll have to speak to the press office.'

'Will you be in charge of the investigation?' the journalist persisted, as he tried to face Drake, dragging the cameraman and sound recordist behind him. 'Can I contact you again?'

'Look,' Drake said. 'I can't add to what I've said already.'

The journalist turned away, disappointed.

Normally Drake would have taken Caren with him to speak to the person who'd found the body but she had been late and he was annoyed, more annoyed than he should have been. The reporter added to the irritation factor. Drake heard Caren's voice shouting instructions to the other officers, telling them how to do their job, so he decided to leave her to it. At least she would be out of his hair for a while.

His mobile rang and, dragging out the handset from his back pocket, he saw his wife's number.

Deciding that he needed more privacy, he crossed the road, walking away from crowd. There'd been another argument that morning and he didn't want everyone to hear his conversation.

'Hi,' he said.

'How are you?'

'Fine. Fine.' He cupped the handset closer to his mouth. 'I can't talk.'

'Where are you?'

'Near Holyhead, there's been a murder. I've got to go. I'll call you later.'

Sian had called on her mid-morning break from her GP surgery appointments. He often thought it would be nice to have a standard routine – knowing what was going to happen every day. Perhaps promotion to chief inspector would give him a routine, but then he'd probably miss the excitement of looking at dead bodies and watching CSI officers crawl over a crime scene in all weathers. He heard his name being called from the other side of the bridge. He waited for a car to pass and as he crossed the carriageway a uniform officer ran towards the bridge, shouting, his arms thrashing around.

Chapter 3

Drake marched over towards Foulds who was standing by a line of thick gorse that marked the boundary of an adjacent field. The CSIs stood aside once Drake approached, and he peered down into the hedge. Drake saw a length of timber and guessed it was over a metre in length, one end tarnished a deep red colour. He noticed shreds of flesh glistening at the edges. He gazed around the gorse bushes and then over to the field beyond, towards a farmhouse in the distance.

'We need to secure the scene, Ian,' Foulds said.

'Of course.' Drake wondered why the murderer had thrown the timber into the gorse bush. Perhaps the killer had been disturbed. Maybe he panicked, discarding it before making good his escape. But there might be some forensics on the timber – a microscopic piece of flesh was all they needed. Drake stepped back and glanced over at the bridge behind him. The tide had turned and water was advancing behind the CSIs and uniformed officers labouring over the mud, prodding at the damp surface with forks and their own pieces of timber.

'And we'll need a full search team,' Foulds added.

'Of course.' Drake reached for his mobile. After a couple of telephone calls he located the search team supervisor on duty that morning, a Sergeant Brown based in Bangor. 'DI Drake, Serious Crime. I need a full team for the search of a beach in Four Mile Bridge. A body was found this morning and what looks like a weapon was thrown into the gorse nearby.'

'On a beach, sir?'

'Low water is going to be later this afternoon. So you haven't got much time. I suggest you coordinate with Mike Foulds. And I want to control the budget on this one so don't call any officers on their rest days.'

The reply sounded vaguely disappointed.

'And bring metal detectors,' Drake said before finishing the call.

Caren joined Drake and they stood watching CSIs hauling boxes of equipment along the shore before erecting a tent over the gorse bushes – all under the expectant gaze of an increasing crowd of spectators on the bridge.

'Can't we close the road or something?' Drake said.

'Difficult, boss.'

'We could divert the traffic.'

'Can't stop people walking on the road.'

'Yes, but they might get in the way.'

He could see the headline – *Police overreact, village closed down* – and for what? He watched the television crew as they stared over at him, waiting, as though by some act of telepathy he could communicate with them.

'Who found the body?' Caren asked.

'John Hughes, the local shopkeeper.'

'What time was that?'

'About six-thirty.'

'He was up early.'

'Runs the post office. We'll need to talk to him.'

The water level was rising fast, and on the opposite bank Drake saw a small group walking along the shoreline, cameras in hand. 'Oh, for Christ's sake ...'

He tried to calm his irritation. A man was dead. There would be a grieving family. Maybe a wife and children – and some of the locals wanted to take photographs. Uniformed officers on the bridge could move them away, Drake thought before realising that the rising tide would see to that. He stood staring over the water and on the opposite bank an elderly man, holding the hand of a boy, no more than ten, looked over at them.

Drake wanted to shout at him. Tell him that he needn't acquaint his grandson with death at such an age. It struck him that his grandfather would never have done that and Drake recalled his childhood anger that his grandfather hadn't lived longer.

Caren, standing by his side, said something. He heard her but didn't listen.

'We need to see Hughes.'

'What?'

'John Hughes. The man who found the body.'

'Of course.' His mind focused.

They set off towards the bridge. He was making a mental checklist, telling himself he had to concentrate. There were glances and whispered comments from the crowd as they walked over the bridge into the village. Over in the distance he saw the rising water filling the narrow inlet on the other side. Small boats were bobbing up and down in the water. A man was pulling the oars of a dingy; fishing rods perched on one side.

Drake rubbed his brogues vigorously on the mat outside the shop and brushed down the trouser leg fabric, but he failed to dislodge all the mud and sand. It was one of his best suits too and he worried that walking around in mud would cause it real harm. He caught a glimpse of himself in the window – at least the button-down shirt and blue striped tie looked tidy. He pushed open the post office door and heard voices raised in conversation, marvelling at the events of the morning. *Ed's been stabbed through the heart. No, it was an axe. Who could have done such a thing?* Drake strode in, Caren behind him; a woman with a long face and a blue T-shirt turned to look at him. The conversations stopped abruptly. Five heads turned and five pairs of eyes bored into him

'Is the owner here?' Drake said, as a man with a thick moustache and a grey polo shirt came through from a side door. Slim and toned, he was under thirty with an enthusiastic look in his eyes.

'John Hughes,' he said.

'I'll need a word. In private.'

Hughes led them through into a small kitchen behind the shop, leaving a young girl in charge. As soon as the door closed behind them the voices started up again.

Hughes stood by a worktop and turned an open hand towards the pine table. Drake drew out a chair from underneath and sat down. He noticed a film of grease on the surface and then folded his arms. Caren sat down at the other end.

'I knew it was Ed straight off.'

'Why do you say that?' Caren asked.

'Ed digs for bait. Goes out at odd times of the day. Every week in the summer. Funny way to make a living. I told him many a time to get a proper job.'

'Why were you on the bridge so early, Mr Hughes?' Drake asked.

'I thought you'd ask me that.' He gave a smirk. 'Delivering the newspaper to Richie Mostyn at Bryn Castell – he's Ed's uncle. Same routine every morning. Regular as clockwork, me. Up at five when the deliveryman gets here. Then sorting the papers. I've got lots of regulars. I try and give them a good service.'

'Do you deliver to lots of houses?' Drake asked.

'No. Most people don't want to pay.'

'Which house is Bryn Castell?'

'The last cottage in the small row after the end

of the bridge.'

'Was Richie awake?'

'I don't think so. The fog was thick this morning. I haven't seen anything like it for years. You should talk to him.'

'How did you know Mostyn was digging bait this morning?'

'At first I saw Ed's dog running around like something demented. Then I walked to Bryn Castell and by the time I was walking back the fog had thinned and I could see the dog on the beach howling. I knew straight away something was wrong.'

'And did you find the body?'

Hughes's voice broke. 'I walked down onto the beach and I was almost sick. Never seen anything like it.'

'How well do you know Ed Mostyn?'

'Everyone knew him. His family has been in the village forever. He's ... I mean ... was a local character.'

'When did you see him last?' Drake asked.

'Yesterday. Comes in every day for his paper.'

'Do you know anyone who'd want him dead?'

'You need to talk to his sister.'

Drake left Caren to take a detail statement from John Hughes, who seemed pleased to be the centre of attention. Outside, the summer sunshine warmed his face. He walked back over the bridge, threading his way through the inquisitive locals staring at the CSIs. In the distance he saw a police car parked in front of the flickering blue-and-white tape that guarded the entrance of the narrow lane, half concealed by a massive rhododendron bush.

He walked over, ducked under the tape and

headed up the drive. Bits of twine and fishing cord littered the route towards the cottage and a smell of saltwater and rotting fish stuck his nostrils. Outside the property several lobster pots lay discarded in no apparent order; there was a bench with small tools, knives and more fishing cord. The line of ridge tiles sagged and the roof was covered in a whitish slurry, protecting the slates from the winter's storms.

Drake heard the sound of a movement from the rear. He prised open a gate that hung at one end of a fragile fence of rotting timber, marking the divide between front and rear. He passed a south-facing window and, looking inside, noticed two cannabis plants growing on the sill.

Drake saw the face of a uniformed officer peering out.

'We've been expecting you, sir,' the officer said, as he held open the door.

Drake crossed the threshold. 'Anything?'

'Haven't touched anything, sir. It's a bit of a mess.'

In the kitchen Drake recoiled in disgust. The smell of dead fish hung in the air. Packets of breakfast cereal lay flat on the table, spilling their contents. There was dust over every surface and dirty crockery was piled into the sink.

'Think someone's trashed the place, sir?'

Drake shook his head.

From the kitchen he opened a door into a narrow hallway and found a small sitting room at the front. It would have been impossible to fit another piece of furniture into it. In front of the television were two small armchairs covered with blankets that reminded him of the quilts his grandmother made. A faded image of Mostyn with three men in evening jackets and black ties was propped in a black frame, an alabaster figurine either side of it.

Drake saw a pile of newspapers under the side window and various magazines stuffed into a rack. It was obvious that Ed Mostyn planned to return. Leaving the room, Drake strode down the hallway before pushing open the door to a bedroom. He reached over and wrenched open a window to clear the muggy smell of sweat and bedclothes. From the kitchen he heard the sound of a radio crackling into life and the voice of the officer.

He gave the bathroom and second bedroom a cursory glance before retracing his steps and eventually headed out through the kitchen into the morning sunshine. He walked down to the bottom of the garden, pleased to be outside. A shed with two large wooden doors and a brass sign with 'Boson' engraved on it stood alongside the boundary wall. Beyond it Drake noticed the advancing tide filling the inlet, and over in the distance he saw the heat rising from the RAF base. He yanked open one of the doors, to reveal piles of fishing tackle and equipment. The cottage and shed all meant more work for the search team, more overtime for the officers involved and then complaints from the finance department about the budget.

Over his shoulder he could hear an officer talking to someone in the front yard. Drake turned and watched as a woman pushed her way through the gate in the fence, followed by the officer who'd been in the car at the bottom of the lane.

'You can't go in there,' he said, raising his voice.

She ignored him and carried on. When she saw Drake she stopped.

'Are you Inspector Drake?'

'And who are you?' Drake asked.

'Joan. Ed's sister.'

Chapter 4

Caren stood outside the post office, eyes closed, letting the sunshine warm her face. A telephone rang behind her in the shop and she heard the muffled fragments of one snippet of a conversation. A car horn startled her and she opened her eyes, squinting against the harsh sunlight. Her mobile hummed with a text message for her to meet Drake near Bryn Castell, so she made her way across the bridge and saw Drake standing on the pavement, deep in animated conversation with a woman she didn't recognise.

Drake had his hair a little longer than normal and Caren noticed scuff marks on his shoes that usually looked pristine. Drake had his hand on his hips, darting glances towards the bridge, a troubled look on his face. Normally, Drake had evenly balanced features that made him handsome in a neutral sort of way, but now his lips were drawn tightly together, his eyes narrowed. He was going to be rude to her very soon, Caren thought.

'This is Joan Higham,' Drake said, almost spitting the words out. 'She's Ed Mostyn's sister.'

'I'm very sorry for your loss,' Caren said.

It was difficult to tell her age – Caren guessed mid-forties. She had broad hips and a flowing skirt that made her look older. Wisps of white hair caught in the light breeze like faint strands of silk.

'I've arranged with Mrs Higham to see her tomorrow.' Drake spoke to Caren, but he made it sound like an order for Joan Higham to leave. But she stood glaring at him. 'If you'll excuse me, Mrs Higham.' Drake strode away, nodding for Caren to follow him.

After a few steps Drake turned to Caren. 'Dreadful woman.'

'John Hughes can't stand her. Apparently nobody likes her.'

'Did you get a preliminary statement?'

Caren nodded. 'Where are we going?'

'Let's go and talk to Richie Mostyn.'

Drake marched ahead of Caren, taking a quick look over towards his car and tilting his head as he examined it. Caren had, as always, glanced at the car as she passed it that morning; it was, or course, immaculately and enviably clean.

The row of old cottages was set back from the main road, down a narrow lane. The windows were small and the walls thick, and the broad roof of weathered slates seemed to be in better condition than many Caren had seen. They were buildings with a history of families toiling the land and the sea to make a meagre living. Passing a new Range Rover squeezed into a parking slot, she pondered how many were now holiday homes.

The front door of Bryn Castell was ajar and Drake shouted a greeting as he led Caren inside. From the rear of the house they heard a mumbled reply and, passing through a hallway lined with old black-and-white prints hanging on embossed dark-red wallpaper, they reached the kitchen.

Richie Mostyn sat in a wing chair in one corner. It was covered in an old throw and probably a lot of dust, if the exposed surfaces were typical of the rest of the house. Caren could see the pained expression on Drake's face as he scanned the room. Richie had a wispy grey beard and long thin strands of hair over his head. He wore a waistcoat over the collarless shirt and rolled the end of a cigarette through his fingers.

Drake had his warrant card in one hand.

'I've been expecting you to call.' Richie had a strong accent that rolled the words and gave them warmth that the circumstances didn't merit.

'You know why we've called?' Drake said.

'Sit down.' Richie nodded towards the chairs surrounding the small table. 'I was probably the last person to see Ed alive.'

'What do you mean?'

'I saw him last night.'

'What time was that?'

Richie began assembling another cigarette. Very slowly.

Impatience gathered in Drake's eyes. Caren doubted that after Joan Higham he had the persistence for a protracted conversation. A small terrier appeared from the hallway and scampered over to Richie before jumping onto his lap.

'My father's got two,' Caren said. 'How old is he?'

Tom looked up and gave Caren the barest of smiles. 'Five.'

'My father called his Waldo – after the poët.'

'Good name. This is Carlo.'

Caren hesitated. 'Could you give some background to the family? And perhaps tells us what happened last night?'

Tom finished rolling the cigarette.

'Ed was here last night. We had a whisky before bed.' He sparked an ancient lighter into life before leaning into it, and drawing on the cigarette. Smoke drifted out from his nostrils.

'Were you up when John Hughes delivered the paper this morning?' Drake said.

Richie shook his head.

'What time did Ed go home?' Caren asked.

Richie sat back and looked at Caren intently. 'Midnight maybe. Doesn't sleep well, runs in the family.'

'Did he tell you he was digging bait this morning?'

'Didn't need to.'

Drake moved uncomfortably in his chair and cleared his throat.

'What do you mean?' Caren said.

'It's a summer's day. That's what he does.'

Drake interjected. 'Who else would know that he'd be out first thing this morning?'

Richie shrugged. 'Everyone, I suppose.'

Drake stood up abruptly. 'Look, if there's nothing else, we won't take anymore of your time.' He took a step towards the door.

Caren was on her feet now.

'You should talk to Maldwyn Evans.'

'Who?'Caren turned to Richie.

'He had a hell of an argument with Ed two weeks ago.'

Drake glanced at Caren and then turned to Richie. 'Did you hear what happened?' Drake let too much aggression into his voice.

Richie gave a brief smirk.

Caren sat down and Drake, too, returned to his chair, dragging it nearer to the old man. 'I need you to tell me everything.'

Caren already had her notebook open and jotted the details as Richie spoke. After he finished he let his gaze scan around his room as though he was checking nothing had changed, that his world was unaffected.

It was mid-afternoon when Drake arrived back in his office and slumped into his chair, before surveying the tidy columns of Post-it notes on his desk. Order and neatness always gave him a sense of reassurance, but the sound of raised voices outside his office broke his concentration. He stood up and pulled open the door. Two administration staff were busy erecting an Incident Room board. Drake noticed Caren fumbling with some photographs on her desk, before walking over to the board and pinning up a photograph of Ed Mostyn.

'Quite a violent assault, boss.'

'Yes.' Drake stared at the wounds on Mostyn's neck.

'Somebody had a score to settle, I'd say.'

'Did you get anything from Hughes in the post office?'

'Bumptious little man. He pretends to know everything that's going on.' Caren folded her arms.

'Probably does.'

'Apparently everyone knows that Mostyn and his sister were hot tempered. They were arguing about some land they owned.'

'Joan Higham seemed cut up about her brother.'

'Crocodile tears.'

'We'll see her tomorrow.'

Drake turned when he heard the muffled conversations outside the Incident Room door. Detective Constable Gareth Winder was the first to enter, but once he saw Drake he abruptly stopped talking to DC David Howick, the final member of Drake's team.

'Boss,' Winder said.

'Good afternoon, sir.' Howick straightened his tie.

Drake mumbled an acknowledgement. He turned back to the board. 'Ed Mostyn was killed early this morning. The killer decided to make absolutely certain and impaled a fork into Mostyn's neck.'

Winder let out a faint whistle. 'Who was he?'

Drake turned his back to the board and looked over at the officers facing him. He could still remember when he was a junior officer and the detective inspector would bark orders, then swear and curse if he didn't do things on time. Winder was short but he made up for it around the chest and neck. Drake was convinced that Winder used some aftershave or gel on the skin of his scalp to get its glistening sheen. He'd loosened his tie a couple of inches and the bags under his eyes weren't as dark as they'd been lately. It had even occurred to Drake that Winder had been using make-up to hide the bags once he'd had a verbal warning about his timekeeping.

'House-to-house in the village is the first job for both of you.' Drake looked at Winder and Howick in turn.

'How many houses are there, sir?'

'Get a couple of the uniformed lads to help you.'

A brief look of exasperation disappeared from Winder's face and he sat down.

'After that you can start on Ed Mostyn's cottage, once the search team have finished. Go through all his papers, bank statements, files – all the usual stuff. Somebody wanted him dead.'

'Of course, sir. When is the search being done?'

Caren cut in. 'Probably tomorrow. They're doing the beach later this evening. And the cottage is disgusting.'

Howick raised an eyebrow.

Caren continued. 'No, really. It's foul. Smell of dead fish everywhere.'

Drake still couldn't escape the stench that had hit him as he had walked up the drive to the cottage, and, now, recalling its dirt and filth made his fingers itch to get clean. He pictured fish scales under his finger nails and fragments of fish bones clinging to the underside of his shoes. It was no use.

'Let's get on with it.' Drake marched out of the Incident Room to the bathroom down the corridor. He took off his jacket and hung it carefully on the hook on the back of the door. He had to let the water flow for a few seconds before it was hot enough for him to scrub his hands and nails.

He stared at his face in the mirror. He felt like a fool for believing that his counselling had given him control over the rituals that punctuated his day. It was simply not his choice to ignore them – even when, as they inevitably did, they drew him away from his duties. Increasingly, these days, he couldn't move on to his next task, until he'd obeyed his little internal instruction – no matter how small. His worry, one that he barely acknowledged, was that these interruptions, these *necessities*, would grow so big, would crowd into his life so much, that he'd end up simply sitting at his desk, unable to move, unable to function.

Drake made the journey back to Four Mile Bridge knowing that Superintendent Price would probably question his decision to be present for the search. The Scientific Support Vehicle had been replaced by two vans and three patrol cars. He pulled the Alfa near to the kerb and walked down to the bridge. The early evening sunshine was still warm and Drake guessed there would be a spectacular sunset.

He reached the bridge as a car in the middle of it slowed, its occupants staring out over the Inland Sea.

A group of youngsters milled around at the opposite end and Drake looked out over the southerly side. A couple of yachts were perched on fin keels astride long curving sandbanks set out in meandering loops between Anglesey and Holy Island.

Crossing the road, he leant on the wall and looked at the search team combing the sand. He counted a dozen officers; six had metal detectors and were scanning the surface with a smooth sweeping motion. Others had long-handled metal implements that prodded and poked at the damp surface.

He raised a hand to Sergeant Brown, the search team supervisor, who then walked towards the bridge. Drake remained where he was; at least from the bridge he had a good vantage point.

His mobile rang but there was no name to accompany the number. 'DI Drake.'

'It's Calvin Headley, Inspector.'

'Who?'

'Calvin Headley. HTV News.'

Immediately Drake's nerves were on edge. 'How the hell did you get this number?'

'Is it true that Ed Mostyn was impaled with his own digging fork?' Headley managed to mix incredulity with journalistic objectivity.

'Don't ring me on this number again.'

'Inspector, will you be the senior investigating officer? And I just wanted to know if the reports about Ed Mostyn are really true.'

Drake killed the call and then stared at the handset for a few seconds, cursing the journalist. He noticed Brown approaching and tried to ignore Headley's comments.

'How's it going?' Drake said.

'Slowly. We should get the sand and beach done tonight. But the gorse and all the heather and the paths at high water... Well that could take...'

'Have you got someone here all night?'

'Of course.'

Drake followed Brown down onto the shoreline. The cloudless clear blue sky was gradually being burnt ochre-red as the sun made its final descent.

'The lads tell me he was speared with a garden fork.'

Drake nodded.

Brown screwed his face up in disgust.

'Have you found anything yet?' Drake took his first step onto the beach again, grateful that he'd found an old pair of boots in headquarters.

'Some old cans and fishing hooks.'

They heard a shout from one of the officers, who was holding his headphones in one hand and waving at Brown with the other. The officer was leaning over a fork that he'd used to prise open the surface of the sand. By his feet was a small metal object.

Brown leant down and with gloved fingers lifted it clear, dropping it into an evidence bag. He gave it an inquisitive stare. 'Looks like one of those knives that fishermen use.'

'Might have belonged to Mostyn,' Drake said.

Brown turned to the officer. 'Carry on, we haven't got much time.'

The man replaced his headphones and switched the machine back on.

Brown and Drake stepped back to the high-water mark.

'We're using pulse induction detectors,' Brown said, as though he expected Drake to know what that meant. 'They're more effective on sand and wet surfaces.'

Drake watched as officers turned over the surface of the sand with various sizes of forks.

Occasionally one knelt down and dropped something into an evidence bag. And at the same time the water slowly crept up behind the officers. Drake hoped they'd find something of value.

Another shout, this time from a different officer with a metal detector, sweeping the area where they'd found Mostyn. Drake scurried over towards him, his pulse beating a little faster with expectation.

By the officer's feet, lying on the surface, was one end of a pair of sunglasses. The search officer knelt down and prised the frames clear of the sand. 'They look like Ray-Bans,' he said. 'Probably titanium frames. That's why I could detect them.'

Drake dropped them into an evidence bag and retraced his steps towards the gorse and dry sand.

Half an hour later the water had made it impossible for the search team to work and Drake gazed down at the plastic evidence bags. There were two rings, the Swiss army knife, an old metal comb, lots of empty food cans, some coins and the Ray-Bans.

Drake noticed Richie Mostyn standing on the bridge smoking a cigarette and staring at them. There must be something he knows and he's not telling us about Ed, Drake thought, sensing this had the potential to be an awkward investigation.

'We'll start on the gorse tomorrow,' Brown said, interrupting Drake's thoughts.

Drake had the house to search and a family to interview. The gorse and the fields would have to wait. 'I need your team to start on the house tomorrow.'

Brown blew out a lungful of breath.

'And then continue along the beach.'

The frustration was evident in Brown's reply. 'That's going to take far more time than I'd planned.'

'No choice. I need to start on Mostyn's place.'

Brown shrugged.

Drake considered talking to Richie again but he was nowhere to be seen. A band of fierce red light covered the horizon as Drake tramped back to the car.

Chapter 5

Drake had managed a few squares of that morning's Sudoku on the journey to see Joan Higham, but his mind couldn't focus after a poor night's sleep that hadn't been helped by Sian complaining vehemently that he was late *again.* That morning she'd accompanied a dark glance with an announcement that she wanted to *talk* to him.

Caren blasted the car horn at a tractor in the middle of the road as she threaded her way through the narrow lanes of Anglesey. The sound distracted Drake from the morning's domestic events.

'Not far now, sir.'

The farmhouse was set back from the main road at the end of a narrow track lined with beech trees, an unusual sight on an island battered by the south-westerly gales. Caren indicated and then turned down the lane, eventually parking near a flatbed van. A sheepdog ran out of a barn towards them, Caren leant down and the dog pitched its head as Caren stroked him. Drake didn't do dogs, or any domestic pet come to that; it was the hairs that fell everywhere – and then there was the smell.

Joan Higham appeared from the back door of the house. 'You don't like dogs then?'

'Well. I'm not …'

'He won't bite.'

Beyond the farmhouse Drake could see rolling fields and in the distance a dozen stationary wind turbines. Joan led them inside and motioned for them to sit around the table. Drake declined the offer of tea – coffee wasn't offered – but Caren asked for hers with two sugars. Outside they heard the whine of a quad bike and moments later the engine cut out. The dog barked, followed by footsteps on the concrete path outside until they heard the sound of boots being discarded in the porch.

'That'll be my husband, Dafydd,' Joan said

Dafydd Higham had a thick neck and the small, hard eyes of a poker player. Drake guessed that, in stockinged feet, he was five foot eight, maybe a little shorter.

'Good morning,' Dafydd said, reaching out a hand. He had a short brisk handshake.

Drake turned to look at Joan. 'What can you tell me about your brother?'

She cleared her throat. 'We own a piece of land that the power company want for the development of the new nuclear power station. Everyone thinks it will make us millionaires, but it's only small— we're not going to make more than few thousand pounds. But it's not our land they really want: it's the land owned by the adjacent owners, Maldwyn Evans and Rhys Fairburn. Without their land the development might not go ahead.'

Drake's attention sharpened at the sound of a familiar name.

Dafydd made his first contribution. 'Evans and Fairburn are livid. They tried to reason with him but...'

Joan nodded energetically.

'Can you give us details of the land involved?' Drake said.

'Of course.' Dafydd stood up and left the kitchen.

Caren turned to Joan. 'Do you have contact details for Evans and Fairburn?'

'Of course.'

Dafydd returned and unfolded a large map with various areas edged in different-coloured highlighters. He explained that Evans and Fairburn both owned land that they couldn't sell unless Ed and Joan sold their land first.

'We inherited the land from our parents,' Joan added.

'And Ed was stupid enough to stop the land being sold.' Dafydd folded his arms.

'Are you his next of kin?' Drake asked.

'I knew you'd ask that,' Joan said, drawing her hair back and then frowning at Drake as though she was challenging him to accuse her of murder.

'Ed had no children,' Dafydd said, adding, 'None that we know about.'

'And we have no idea if he made a will,' Joan said.

'So why did Ed decide not to sell?' Drake said.

'My brother fell in with that Gwynfor Llywelyn who persuaded him to object. Ed swallowed all the propaganda about the impact it was going to have on the Welsh language and on the environment.'

'Where can we contact this Gwynfor Llywelyn?'

'He's got an *artisan* bakery in Cemaes Bay. At least that's what he calls it.' Joan looked as dismissive as she sounded.

'How much money was involved for Evans and Fairburn?' Caren poised her pen on her notebook.

'Half a million pounds.'

Drake, startled by the sums involved, stared over at Joan, then over at her husband who stared back at him, his eyes dark and expressionless.

On the journey to Cemaes Bay they passed one boarded-up house after another; sheets of plywood were screwed to the windows, and pasted to one was a notice warning of regular security checks. Entrance gates left abandoned had rusted on their hinges in front of drives and paths overgrown with weeds. Caren guessed that the houses hadn't been pulled down, just in case the power station didn't get the go-ahead.

'Weird, isn't it, sir?'

Drake said nothing.

'Looks like something from a horror film set,' Caren added.

Drake was not himself that morning. He had said very little on their journey from headquarters and, more significantly, he had ignored most of the Sudoku in the morning newspaper.

They reached the brow of a hill and Caren pulled the car to a halt, looking down towards the nuclear power station on the edge of the coastline. The plant looked peaceful and calm, but the plans for the new station were controversial.

'We need to establish if Mostyn had a will,' Drake said eventually. 'Maybe there was something in his papers.'

A microlight appeared above them and slowly skirted around the power plant. In the distance Drake could see the long, wide pebbled beach at Cemlyn Nature Reserve. Caren drove on to Cemaes. Drake fell into a dark mood again and she wondered if the rumours about him and his wife were true. She'd met Sian a few times and on each occasion she had decided that she liked her less.

Caren found a small car park in the village and, once she'd reversed into an available slot, they made their way down through the main street. The sun was warm on their faces as they strolled down past the few shops that remained. They reached the bay and looked out over the seaside. Tents and windbreaks were dotted over the sand and children were splashing at the water's edge.

'The bakery must be down one of the side

roads,' Drake said.

'I never realised it was so pretty here.' Caren stood, looking out over the bay.

By a pub they cut down a lane, and between two old cottages, their white walls glistening in the summer sunshine, they spotted a notice indicating the bakery. The building had a small sign hanging over the door and two windows had been placed as far as possible into a recess in the walls. A bell sounded when Caren pushed open the door and entered the shop. She was surprised at how large the place felt. A low bench was dusted with a fine covering of flour. Various baskets with different shapes of loaves were piled on shelves behind the counter. There were handwritten labels advertising sourdough, hundred-percent wholemeal and a Polish rye bread.

A man with thick stubble walked from the back and looked at Drake, before giving Caren a warm smile. She guessed that Gwynfor Llywelyn would know all his regular customers and that he'd normally have spoken in Welsh, but it was summer and the village was full of tourists.

'What would you like?' he said.

Drake flashed his warrant card. 'Are you Gwynfor Llywelyn?'

'Yes, what's this about?'

Drake glanced towards the back. 'We're investigating the death of Ed Mostyn. Is there somewhere we can talk?'

Llywelyn lifted a flap at the end of the counter. Drake and Caren followed him through the bakery, the air thick with the smell of yeast and hot from the ovens that hummed in the background. A radio was playing from a small room and as Llywelyn pushed open the door Drake could make out the dying chords of an Eagles song. A girl with short hair and two rings in her right nostril was sitting by a desk, staring at a computer screen, various books of accounts in front of her. Llywelyn said something to her in Welsh and she gave Drake and Caren a brief nod before leaving; she was even thinner standing up than she appeared sitting down. A small white T-shirt clung to her body, accentuating her thin shoulder blades. Llywelyn leant against a filing cabinet, nodding towards the two chairs for Drake and Caren to use. Drake pushed one over for Caren and sat on the other.

'I understand you knew Ed Mostyn?'

'Who told you?'

Drake hesitated. 'Were you friends with him?'

'It must have been his sister.'

'We'll be talking to everybody that knew Ed Mostyn, his friends, girlfriends and family. What we want to establish is what your relationship was with him?'

'I met him a couple of times.'

'Is that once or twice or more?'

Llywelyn shrugged. 'He came to one of the public meetings and we got talking. He was interested in our campaign to stop the nuclear power station.'

'Where did you meet?'

'He came here.' Llywelyn looked at his watch.

'Did you ever see him at his house?' Caren asked.

'Once, that's all. Look, his sister is a right bitch. She came in here one day, shouting and cursing. She even lost me business, some of my regulars won't come in now.'

'Why did she do that?'

'She was complaining like hell about that land they own. She said it was my fault that Ed wasn't going to sell.'

'And was it?' Drake asked.

'Well, he's dead now, isn't he? And I have a business to run.'

Llywelyn made for the door and Drake stood up.

'And where were you on the morning Ed Mostyn was killed?'

Llywelyn looked around. 'It was first thing in the morning. Where would you think? I was here, preparing.'

'Can anyone vouch for that?' Drake said.

'Nobody.' Llywelyn crossed his arms and stared defiantly at Drake. 'There wouldn't have been any bread to sell unless I'd prepared. And you can check my sales for that day if you want.'

They retraced their steps towards the shop.

'Why are you objecting to the power station?' Drake said.

Llywelyn lifted the flap on the countertop.

'It'll mean the end of the Welsh language. Is that something you want?'

A customer pushed open the door and the bell rang. It had an old-fashioned metallic ring to it. Llywelyn smiled at the customer and then turned to Drake.

'You should come to the public meeting we have organised next week.'

Drake and Caren left. Outside, momentarily blinded by the sun reflecting off the gleaming whitewashed walls, Caren squinted and then raised a hand to her face before they walked back through the village.

'Let's check him out,' Drake said. 'I need to know everything about Gwynfor Llywelyn.'

'Awful place to work – inside all that dust and flour every day,' Caren said.

'Maybe he likes the creative side of making bread.'

'Bit of wild goose chase. What possible motive could he have?'

'Maybe Mostyn had told Llywelyn he'd changed his mind. Llywelyn loses it and decides to finish Mostyn off. Maybe even possible that Mostyn has made a will which Llywelyn doesn't want changed.'

'You're hypothesising, sir.'

'I know. It's dangerous.' Drake stopped outside a café. 'But half a million pounds is one hell of a motive.'

Chapter 6

After a hurried lunch Drake and Caren left Cemaes and headed back towards the power station. After parking in the visitors' car park they walked over to the main reception area.

All three of the girls sitting behind the desk had the same fixed grins, white blouses and jackets with small metal pins in their lapels that matched the corporate logo of the power company. It all looked clean and highly organised. They smiled at every visitor and joked amongst themselves. Drake picked up one of the company's glossy brochures from the table in front of his chair. He noticed various job titles: community liaison manager, project implementation director. And there were photographs with local councillors and dignitaries all smiling broadly. Drake slid the brochure back onto the tabletop as one of the receptionists glided towards him. Caren was engrossed in an edition of *Country Life*.

'Inspector Drake.' She gave his name an American twang that made it sound like a question. 'I'll show you through.'

They followed her to a door at the far end of the reception, where she punched a set of numbers into the security pad. There was a dull buzzing sound and she pushed the door open, holding it so that Drake and Caren could pass through. After two flights of stairs there was yet another security pad by a door with a sign: Senior Management. She turned her body to hide the numbers that she tapped onto the screen. She gave them a weak smile after finishing.

A large oblong table dominated the room. Framed aerial photographs of various power stations lined the walls, but Drake didn't have time to read the descriptions of each before the door opened.

'Mark Rogers,' the man said, holding out his hand.

His handshake was firm and brisk. He had a strong jaw line and it was difficult to guess his age – mid-forties, Drake thought, a couple of years older than him. After pulling out chairs from underneath the table they sat down.

'I'm investigating the death of Ed Mostyn.'

'Yes, of course. The staff explained. How can I help?'

Drake found it difficult to make out his accent, probably from somewhere in the south of England and definitely a private education.

'Ed Mostyn owned land with his sister that's needed for the power station. He didn't want to sell it. That must have caused a major problem?'

Rogers folded his arms together and gazed through one of the windows. 'It wasn't helpful, certainly. The development is a major part of the government's economic policy. There's a lot of pressure to make certain that everything is dealt with smoothly.'

'So the politicians in Cardiff are all in favour?'

Rogers gave Drake a surprised look and moved forward slightly in his chair, resting his hands on the table. 'This level of development is a matter for the government in London. The Welsh assembly in Cardiff is irrelevant.'

'But you still need planning consent?'

'Of course. And we need to make certain that we have all the land that we need.'

'And there were others affected by Mostyn's refusal to sell.'

'Rhys Fairburn and Maldwyn Evans – both local landowners.'

'Do you have their contact details?'

'I can email them.'

Drake reached for a business card that he slid over the table. 'So if Ed Mostyn refused to sell the land he jointly owned with his sister, what was likely to happen?'

'Difficult to tell.'

'Could he be forced to sell?'

'Ah …let me put it like this. We would prefer not to have the adverse publicity that a compulsory purchase order might generate. We'd probably find a way around it.'

'So Evans and Fairburn wouldn't get the money involved.'

Rogers nodded slowly.

Half an hour later they approached the blue-and-white crime scene tape fluttering gently as it hung across the entrance to the beach. Hopefully the search team could return to the gorse and the surrounding fields in the morning, and for a moment Drake worried that he was already over budget.

A young uniformed woman police officer stood by the mobile incident room that was parked in front of a converted chapel in the middle of Four Mile Bridge. As Caren parked, Drake saw the figure of John Hughes emerging.

'I think we might do a quick background check on him,' Drake said to Caren, as they watched him talking to the uniformed police officer.

'But he found the body.'

'I know, it could be the perfect cover. He knows suspicion would fall on him so he pretends to have found the body to throw sand in our face.'

They left the car and Drake strode over to the large blue truck emblazoned with the logo of the Wales

Police Service, leaving Caren with her mobile pressed to her ear, instigating a check on Hughes. Gossip had circulated around Northern Division that the designers had charged a six-figure sum for something that most officers thought their teenage children could have completed for the price of a takeaway meal and a large bottle of soft drink.

'Hello, Mr Hughes.' Drake smiled at the police officer, whose name badge read 'Yvonne Gooding'.

'Good afternoon, sir.'

Drake gave her a cursory nod of acknowledgement.

'I hope PC Gooding here has been looking after you?'

'I'm glad you called round. There's something you should know.' Hughes leant forward, giving his voice a conspiratorial air.

Caren had finished on the telephone and joined Drake and Hughes.

'Not here.' Hughes beckoned. 'Come down to the post office.'

The shop was empty, the chatter from the day before having long disappeared. Closure seemed imminent, Drake thought, as he noticed that the vegetable selection included a tray with two ageing onions, four overripe tomatoes and a fridge compartment with only half a dozen yogurts on offer. Most of the customers probably shopped at one of the nearby supermarkets.

'Around the back,' Hughes said.

It was the end of the afternoon, the second day of the investigation was drawing to a close and unless Hughes had something very constructive Drake knew his patience would fray. He had seen self-important men like this before and invariably they had nothing but gossip to offer.

In the kitchen Hughes waved regally towards the chairs by the table. 'There's been a lot of talk.' Hughes drew a hand over his mouth and paused. Drake waited, knowing he was expected to inquire. 'People have been talking.'

Drake sensed Caren wriggling in her chair.

'Ed Mostyn owed a lot of money, to a lot of different people.'

'To who exactly?' Drake said.

'A farmer called Rhys Fairburn to start with and—'

'And who told you about this?'

'It's confidential.'

'In that case there's nothing I can do.' Drake stood up.

'But there's more.'

'Look, Mr Hughes,' Drake slowed his voice. 'I can't rely on gossip. If you've got concrete evidence it's your public duty to inform me.'

Hughes looked taken aback, uncertain exactly how to respond but he soon regained his composure. 'People come to me and talk to me. They trust me, they rely on my good sense.'

Drake pushed the chair back. 'If you're prepared to give a statement, then talk to Police Constable Gooding. She can arrange for one of the CID team to attend.'

'But I thought I could talk to you...'

Drake moved towards the door, Caren a step behind him. 'The mobile incident room will be here for the next few days. We're interested in hearing from people that can provide us with definite information.'

'There's something else...'

Drake stopped by the door and looked over at Hughes.

'There was somebody else around first thing

yesterday morning.'

'Who?'

'He's a regular. Always comes down to the shop first thing.' Hughes darted a glance towards the window.

'Why didn't you mention this yesterday?'

'Don't be stupid. Somerset didn't kill Ed. He's not that sort of person.'

'And what sort of person is he?'

'Well, he lives up at the Hall – his family are the local aristocracy.' Hughes was gathering confidence. 'Somerset de Northway always comes in for his newspaper – *The Telegraph*, and he'd been into the shop while I was out delivering to Bryn Castell.'

'How do you know?'

'The paper wasn't on the counter.'

Drake stared at Hughes, wondering if there was anything else he wasn't telling him. 'It's a pity you didn't mention this yesterday. What's de Northway's address?'

Caren jotted down the details and they left Hughes in the kitchen. By the time Drake and Caren had returned to the mobile incident room Winder and Howick had arrived and were both deep in conversation with Gooding.

'Anything from the house-to-house enquiries?' Drake asked Howick.

'Nothing much yet, boss. There was nobody about. I spoke to one woman whose husband works shifts at the power station. He was the only one around at that time of the morning. And everybody knew Ed Mostyn.'

Winder gave a brief hollow sort of laugh. 'He was either loathed or loved.'

'I found the same,' Howick said. 'People either liked him, thought he was a nice character, or they thought he was a drunk and a layabout.'

'I've had a lot of people wanting to make statements,' Gooding said, offering a clipboard to Drake, which he scanned quickly.

'Are all these addresses local?'

'Yes, sir.'

Drake was scanning the details when the search team supervisor arrived at his side.

'We'll be finished in the morning,' Brown said.

'What's taking so long?'

'Place is full of shit, sir.'

A dull ache attacked Drake's back and he stretched, hoping it might help. For the first time that afternoon he thought about Sian and felt uncertain as to the reception he'd get at home. Tomorrow morning there'd be another early meeting with the team and more dark stares from his wife. A message bleeped on his mobile. It was Superintendent Price – *case review and update in an hour.* Drake stared at the screen, then at the faces surrounding him and wondered what time he'd get home.

It had been a month since Superintendent Wyndham Price had returned from a six-month secondment to the West Midlands police force, and the new initiatives instigated by him had resulted in more meetings, more management memoranda and less time on police work. Emails from Price encouraged greater transparency, more 'joined-up thinking' and, whenever he could, he emphasised that everyone should be 'working smarter', which was a particular favourite of his.

Hannah, Price's secretary, gave Drake a warm smile that made her cheeks pucker. It had been obvious, even to Drake, that she had been pleased when Price returned. There was more enthusiasm in her voice, her high heels were back and she used significantly more perfume than during his absence.

'He's waiting for you.' Hannah nodded at the door.

Drake knocked and in response to a shout he opened the door, which slid over a thick pile carpet. Price had a telephone propped against his ear and was exchanging banter down the telephone. The certainty of dealing with Price, who knew about his past, was somehow preferable to the cold objectivity of his temporary replacement Superintendent Lance. Price waved his free hand towards the chair in front of his desk. Drake sat down and soon enough Price had finished.

'So, bring me up to date?'

'A body of a man called Ed Mostyn was found on the beach near a village called Four Mile Bridge. He makes a living from digging bait. He was up really early. Somebody decided to impale him to the mud with his own fork.'

'Angry wife? Jilted girlfriend?'

'It's probably somebody very determined.'

'And very cold-blooded.' Price straightened in his chair, leant forward and stared at Drake.

'And how have you been since your father's death?'

'It's not been easy.'

'I want you to know that I read the report from the counselling service.' Price stopped, as though he were uncertain exactly what else he should say. 'How are you coping?'

Drake didn't want to tell Price that since his father's death things had got worse. The WPS would want to know that he was getting better; that he was managing his compulsions and that the intrusive thoughts that drove his them were abating. The counsellor had warned him that after his father's death he might feel his obsessions worsening.

'My mother's still grieving and the family are only coming to terms with things slowly,' Drake said, without answering Price.

'It's important for me to know that I can rely on you. If there are more difficulties then... well... I don't need to spell out the alternatives.'

Drake could feel a bead of sweat forming on one side of his temple.

Price continued. 'If you need support from the counselling service or if the WPS can be of assistance, then you must ask. And I want you to know that you can talk to me whenever you feel it appropriate.'

Drake was unaccustomed to the sensitive touchy-feely response from Price – it was obviously something he had learnt in the West Midlands. Price fumbled with the papers on his desk and hesitated, as though he was searching for something.

'I've had a call from Assistant Chief Constable Osmond.'

Drake immediately thought it was about the counselling and his pulse beat a little faster.

'He's heard about the death of Mostyn.'

Initially Drake was relieved, until he wondered why an ACC was interested in a routine case.

'He explained that Mostyn owns land needed for the nuclear power station.' Price paused to look over at Drake.

'That's right. But I only spoke to the power company's representative this morning.'

'Well, our political masters are obviously well informed. The case needs to be handled carefully and with the *utmost circumspection*. His exact words.'

And we don't normally, Drake thought.

Price continued. 'There's a special adviser going to be here next week.'

'Special adviser—'

Price held up a hand. 'I don't know any more. Looks like somebody in both the UK and Welsh governments wants to be kept informed.'

Price stood and for a moment Drake remained seated, all clarity smothered by the reality that political interference was the last thing he wanted.

Chapter 7

Drake woke early after another night of poor sleep. He exchanged the barest of conversations with Sian before leaving for headquarters. A distance had grown between them that the long hours he was working made wider. Sian's announcement that she wanted to work full time had left little room for discussion and meant that Helen and Megan spent more time with their maternal grandmother than Drake would have liked.

On the drive to headquarters he listened to a discussion on the radio about the latest energy policy and how fracking was going to reduce bills. He fidgeted with the controls of the radio and retuned it to the Welsh station, wanting to ignore the programmes dominated by news about England. There was a report about a Mid-Wales football team, a subject that left him cold so he switched it off as he arrived at headquarters and parked the car.

Which radio channel does a special adviser listen to? Drake thought, as he marched over to his office.

He was the first to arrive and the Incident Room was quiet. His office had the sweet smell of furniture polish still drifting in the air. The bin had been emptied and the monitor wiped clean. The photographs of Helen and Megan stood by the telephone and once he'd sat down he moved them a couple of centimetres. It was the comfort of an established routine that made his obsessions tolerable – at least to him. He paused for a moment, hoping that the inevitable interference from Cardiff wouldn't make his work any harder.

He heard the thump of the Incident Room door against a wall before he heard the voice of Winder, deep in conversation on his mobile. Drake got up and wandered out of his office. Winder dropped a bag of pastries onto his desk and then started giggling down the telephone before noticing Drake and stopping abruptly, explaining to the caller that he had to go. Since a recent conversation with Winder about his timekeeping the young officer was one of the first to arrive and the comments that Caren and Howick often made about Winder playing computer games until the early hours had been less frequent. It occurred to Drake that Winder had a new girlfriend, but the opportunity to ask him was lost when Howick breezed in.

'Good morning, sir.'

David Howick wore a white short-sleeved shirt, a fraction too big in the collar and a grey suit, its jacket folded neatly over his right arm. His straight brown hair was combed into a neat parting. After failing his sergeant's exams a period of disappointment had followed, during which his attitude and appearance had deteriorated, but now he was back to looking neat and tidy.

'Dave,' Drake said, before walking towards the board just as Caren arrived.

Pleasantries exchanged, Drake stood before his team, having pinned to the board the names of persons of interest, maybe even possible suspects.

'Ed Mostyn was killed from massive blood loss caused by an injury to his neck. He owned a piece of land jointly with his sister that he was refusing to sell to a company that wants to build the new nuclear power station on Anglesey. And his refusal was preventing two other adjacent owners, a Maldwyn Evans and Rhys Fairburn, from selling their land.'

'How much were they offering?' Howick asked.

'Evans and Fairburn stood to make half a million,' Drake replied. 'Although Mostyn's sister, Joan

Higham, said that they were only going to make a few thousand.'

Winder let out a brief whistle. He had his hand in the bag of pastries, fiddling around for his breakfast, and Drake regretted not having reprimanded him about his eating habit when he had the chance. 'Why the hell didn't he want to sell?'

'His sister thinks it's political and she blames Gwynfor Llywelyn, an anti-nuclear activist, for persuading Mostyn not to sell.'

'Where do we start, boss?' Winder said, before biting into a Danish pastry.

Drake gave him a dark look before continuing. 'I'm going to see Maldwyn Evans with Caren later this morning. I want the house-to-house finished today. And then get started on background checks on Evans, Fairburn and Llywelyn.'

'And John Hughes? Caren said. 'The man who found the body.'

Drake hesitated. 'Yes.'

'Is he a person of interest?'Howick asked.

'Might be.'

'He's one of these know-it-all characters,' Caren said.

'He did mention a Somerset de Northway as well,' Drake added.

'Sounds like someone from *Downton Abbey*,' Winder mumbled through a mouthful of food.

'Who?' Howick said, sitting up in his chair.

'De Northway lives in Crecrist Hall and is an early riser. He was in the post office when John Hughes was delivering the paper to Richie Mostyn. So we know he was around. But first I want to work on these other names.'

Drake thought about mentioning the special adviser but decided against it. 'Let's keep this simple.

There's somebody out there who knew or guessed that Ed Mostyn would be out digging bait and they had motive enough to kill him.'

It was early afternoon before Drake and Caren found number thirty Trem-y-Mor. It was a small bungalow in a cul-de-sac in Llanfairpwll, the village nearest to one of the bridges over the Menai Strait. The concrete roof tiles of the house had yellow streaks and down one valley the lead was stained green. The neighbouring bungalows had the same worn-out feel of properties that needed money spending on maintenance.

Drake opened the door, pleased to be out of the car, having convinced himself that the farmyard stench from Caren's vehicle would stick to his four-hundred-pound suit. He strode up the path towards the front door and rang the bell. From inside he heard a woman's voice. It sounded old and the face that appeared at the door confirmed Drake's first impression.

'Detective Inspector Drake and Detective Sergeant Waits,' Drake said. 'We're investigating the death of Ed Mostyn. Are you Mrs Evans? Is your husband in?'

She was short – no more than five feet four – with auburn hair that hadn't seen a hairdresser for months. There was a tired look in her eyes.

'Enid Evans, come in.'

Standing in the small hallway Drake could feel the heat of the house envelop him. It would only be a matter of time before he'd have to unfasten his shirt collar. The dry, pungent smell of old skin lingered in the air.

Caren turned up her nose as they walked

through into the sitting room. Maldwyn Evans struggled to his feet. He wore a faded sleeveless sweater, despite the warmth, and a grey tie with navy stripes. Every window was closed, there were piles of magazines on the table in the middle of the floor and a paper rack overflowing with fading copies of the local newspaper.

Evans was a couple of inches taller than his wife, with small hands and a narrow chin. His skin was a pallid colour, as though the constant heat in the house had dried it so that every healthy fibre had been destroyed.

'I believe you knew Ed Mostyn.'

Evans nodded, very slowly, as if he was pondering the meaning of every letter.

'Maldwyn went to see him,' Enid said.

Evans held up his right hand in a regal fashion as though he were commanding his wife to be silent. 'He wasn't going to sell the land,' Evans said. His thin reedy voice complemented his frame perfectly.

'Without Ed and his sister agreeing to sell their land you stood to lose a lot of money,' Drake said.

'I went to see him. I wanted to tell him about my circumstances.' Evans managed to roll every vowel and emphasised the 'r' that made him sound like the old farmers Drake remembered from his childhood, who hardly ever spoke English.

'You wanted to get him to sell the land?' Caren added.

Evans nodded again.

'What did he say?'

'He laughed at me,' Evans said. His eyes stared at Drake, a stare that said more than any words.

'Is that causing you a financial problem?'

Evans rocked back and forth for a moment. 'This bungalow is owned by the bank, as is all of my farm.' Evans then stared through the window. Evans's skin pulled tightly against his chin as he talked. 'Some of the land is rented out but it doesn't cover the interest. If the land is sold we might be able to clear the debt and keep this place. You can get all the details from Dafydd Higham, my accountant.'

'Did you argue with Ed when you met?'

Evans leant forward slightly. 'What do you mean?'

Drake wanted to ask what exactly was difficult about the question. 'An eyewitness has told us that you had blazing row with Ed Mostyn. Told him that *you'd fucking sort him out unless* he sold the land. And that he didn't *deserve to live* and that he was a *disgrace to his family*. Is that true?'

Evans shook his head slowly.   'I never shout at people.'

There was a moment's silence before Enid spoke. 'Ed Mostyn was an evil man. He wanted to destroy us. And our family and everything.'

Drake looked again at Evans who had closed his eyes.

'Where were you on the morning that Ed Mostyn was killed?'

'I was in bed. Of course.'

Enid Evans nodded her confirmation without being asked.

Drake had just reached the car when the telephone rang.

'Boss.' He recognised the sound of Howick's voice. 'We've just arrested two girls.'

'What?' he reached for the handle of the car door.

'They were making a scene outside Mostyn's

place.'

Caren was already sitting in the car.

'What did they want?'

'Complaining about Mostyn. Seems he had lots of girlfriends.'

'Take them to the station in Holyhead. We'll be there in half an hour.'

Drake looked at his watch– the conversation he'd promised to have with Sian that evening would have to wait. He stepped away from the car and dialled Sian's mobile, his mouth drying around the edges as he composed another apology.

'Don't tell me,' Sian said. 'Something's come up.'

'I need to go and do two interviews in Holyhead. I—'

The line went dead. Drake stood for moment before tucking the mobile telephone back into his jacket. The afternoon was hot and he tried to remember what Megan and Helen were doing that evening. Perhaps the girls had some activity that he should have attended but he simply couldn't remember. Sian had said something at breakfast but his mind had been a blur.

He couldn't understand how day-to-day occurrences could disappear into a haze while his focus on each vital ritual was pin-sharp. If only he could work out how to reverse the situation, at least his domestic life might be simpler.

He pulled the car door closed behind him. Caren gave him a brief smile and for a second he speculated what she might have heard and what she thought might be happening. Even Drake knew how gossip could travel around Northern Division. From underneath his jacket on the rear seat he pulled out the day's newspaper and found the Sudoku page.

'Gareth and Dave have arrested two women in Mostyn's house.'

Caren gave him a puzzled look.

'We'll go to Holyhead and do the interviews.'

Caren started the engine and drove towards the main road. 'So what did you make of Evans, sir?'

Drake's mind was already on the bottom rectangle of the puzzle.

'What century was he in?' she continued.

'Bit old-fashioned, maybe.'

Caren turned onto the A55 and accelerated west. 'He was *really* odd.'

Drake let his eyes slide down and then across the columns. Relaxation inched closer as he solved two squares.

'Maybe losing all that money drove him off his head,' Caren continued.

'He looks too weak to have used that piece of timber.'

'But he could have used the fork.'

Drake tapped the pencil on the side of the paper. Caren signalled to overtake a line of trucks all with European number plates. Soon they were speeding over the causeway into Holyhead, past the closed aluminium smelter, and on through the town towards the police station. The narrow streets and one-way system took them away from what remained of the shops that the large out-of-town supermarkets hadn't killed off.

After parking they stood by the rear door, staring up at the CCTV camera monitoring their movements. Soon enough the door opened and Caren led the way into the custody suite. Before his promotion to CID, Drake had been a custody sergeant at Holyhead, dealing with the daily grind of drunk drivers, petty thieves and drug dealers. But instead of walking through into custody they took the stairs to the canteen, where Howick and Winder were nursing half-empty mugs of tea. A couple of community support officers sat at the far end and two road traffic officers maintained a loud conversation about the fortunes of Liverpool Football Club.

'Coffee, boss?' Caren asked.

Drake looked over at the counter, hoping that he could see a decent brand of coffee but all he could see was a large metal tub with a tall spoon protruding from the top. 'No thanks.'

Drake pulled up a chair opposite Howick.

'So, what happened?' Drake said.

Caren arrived at the table and sat down.

'These girls arrived at the house as the search team were finishing. They demanded to be let in. Then they got mouthy and Sergeant Brown called us. Only then they got worse and we had to arrest them.'

'What was their explanation?'

'One of them is an ex-girlfriend. She said that Mostyn had promised her some jewellery. She was going to search in the cupboards in the kitchen. And then she demanded access to look for her old clothes.'

'Where are they from?' Caren asked.

'One of the villages in the middle of the island,' Howick said.

Winder turned to Drake. 'You'll need to see them both together, boss. They've both got one hell of an attitude.'

Drake read the time on his watch, knowing that there was little chance of him getting home for a calm mature conversation with Sian. Instead he had to interview two women who'd probably curse and lie.

'Let's go,' he said to Caren.

'Do we treat them as suspects?' Caren said, as they walked down the flight of stairs to the custody

Stephen Puleston

suite. She continued, answering her own question, an annoying habit that Drake had become accustomed to. Yet in an odd way he was finding it comforting. 'But we've got nothing to suggest that they had anything to do with the murder.'

Drake stood in front of one of the interview rooms and turned to Caren. 'Have you got your notebook?'

He straightened his tie, adjusted the cuffs of his shirt and unbuttoned his jacket, before turning the handle of the door. Both girls sat by the table and gave Drake hard defiant stairs when he entered.

Drake checked his notebook. 'Which one of you is Donna Jones?'

The smaller of the girls with neatly cut blonde hair responded. 'That's me.'

'So you're Joanna Barnes?' Drake said, looking at the other girl.

The girl moved slightly on her chair. 'Yeah.'

Long curly red hair cascaded over her shoulders, which she adjusted with a quick flick of her right hand. She pushed out her chin, pursed her lips and fiddled with her hands on the table. Drake sat down; a heavy smell of stale tobacco hung around both girls.

'Am I under arrest or something?' Barnes said.

Drake opened his notebook at a clean page and placed his biro in the centre. Then he adjusted it a couple of millimetres. 'What do you know about Ed Mostyn?'

'That slime ball promised me that ring.'

'Were you his girlfriend?'

'Yeah. It's worth at least two grand. That's what he said.'

Drake picked up the ballpoint, took the top off and wrote a few words on the notepad. It had the desired effect of distracting Barnes's attention.

'How long had you been going out with Ed?' Caren said.

Barnes shrugged. Then she flicked back her hair again. 'A year maybe.'

Drake underlined his notes with a flourish a couple of times. He looked up and saw Barnes swallowing, and then he wrote another sentence of notes.

'And I want my clothes and there are photographs I want back.'

'Clothes?' Caren said.

'Yeah. I left a lot of stuff in the wardrobes.'

'Can you prove the clothes and photographs were yours?'

Donna made her first comment. 'You tell them what he did.'

Barnes clenched her fist. 'He took photographs of me, naked.'

'Where did he keep them?'

'On his laptop. And I saw other girls too.'

Drake lowered his voice. 'Other girls?'

'Yeah. He was a bit of a perv really. Liked looking at pictures of young girls.'

'Where did he keep the laptop?'

Barnes shrugged and a look crossed her face that spoke of an immaturity that none of the carefully applied make-up and hair colour or painted nails could hide. 'Can we leave?'

Drake couldn't remember a laptop on the inventory from Mostyn's place – something else to check. He stood up, replaced the top of his biro and tucked his notebook under one arm. 'We need to speak to someone first.'

Drake and Caren left both girls looking terrified. The custody sergeant was a man who needed to lose two or three stones in weight. He held a handkerchief in one hand, mopping away the beads of sweat forming over his brow. Behind him a news programme was playing on a small television.

After he'd listened to Drake the sergeant asked. 'So what do you want me to do?'

'Give them a gypsy's warning and let them go.'

Behind the sergeant's head Drake recognised the face of Calvin Headley on the screen. 'Turn the sound up,' he said.

The sergeant found the remote and pointed it at the screen.

'*It has been twenty-four hours since the badly mutilated body of Ed Mostyn was found on the beach in Four Mile Bridge, a well-known local beauty spot. Mostyn, who was a popular local figure, had lived in the village all his life.*'

Headley dipped his head and the screen switched to an interview with one of the villagers, who was suitably shocked at the events, then back to a headshot of the journalist.

'Isn't that outside the station ...?' Caren said.

Behind Headley, Drake could make out the dark shadows of the Holyhead police station.

'*In this fast-moving inquiry police sources have refused to confirm the details, but it is believed that two women are helping the police with their enquiries.*'

Chapter 8

Drake sat by the kitchen table eating breakfast when he heard Sian's footsteps on the stairs. He read the time, knowing that he shouldn't be late. He chewed on a second piece of toast as she pushed the door closed behind her, pulled out a chair and sat down. She was wearing the thin dressing gown he'd given her as a Christmas present the year before. It occurred to him that perhaps she'd lost some weight; she looked thinner than normal and paler, too. Her blonde hair was already neat and it framed her delicate features perfectly. She clenched her jaw and her eyes darkened with determination.

'I wanted to talk to you about the girls. You know we had that discussion about their schooling.'

It had been over a month since Sian had made it clear that she wanted to move Helen and Megan to a new school that didn't teach the girls through the medium of Welsh. Their conversation had descended into a difficult standoff with recriminations flying and had ended with Drake feeling resentful that Sian wouldn't support him in wanting their daughters to be bilingual.

'The school I was telling you about does some of its teaching in Welsh.'

A piece of toast suddenly stuck to the top of his mouth.

Sian continued. 'My Mum says—'

'And what's she got to do with it?'

'She only wants what's best.'

'And you think I don't.'

He reached for the coffee mug and tightened his grip.

'You're taking this too personally.'

'And how else am I supposed to be taking it?

We agreed about the girls' schooling.'

She placed one hand over another on the wooden tabletop. 'I'm not so certain any longer. The new school has an excellent record. My Mum knows the headmaster and lots of my friends send their children there.'

Drake left the last of the toast and pushed his plate to one side. 'You'll probably prefer me not to speak Welsh to them.' He drained the last of the tepid coffee and plonked the mug on the plate.

'You're just impossible to speak to.'

'You've already decided. I haven't been consulted. And your mother seems to know more about it than I do.'

'It's not like that.'

Drake got up, marched over to the sink and with a flourish stacked his dishes into the dishwasher. Sian crossed one leg over another.

'You'll still talk to them in Welsh and there's all your family.'

He glanced at his watch again. He'd insisted the team get in for an early briefing. 'I've got to go.'

'This is for the best, Ian.'

'Can this wait?'

Sian shook her head slowly.

Normally a Saturday morning gave Caren the opportunity for a leisurely breakfast but Drake had made clear that he expected the team to be working. She stood in the kitchen looking out over the nearby field where Alun was moving fence posts. She had missed him badly when his driving job had meant long periods away from home, but now that he'd found a job with a local company she had begun re-evaluating her life. Caren flicked on the electric kettle, her thoughts distracted by how she could avoid working on a Saturday in the future. Maybe she could get a transfer to a station as a custody sergeant, but the prospect of working in a stuffy custody suite with no windows, where the drunks would vomit on the floor and drug addicts howl in the depths of the night, was unappealing. Then there were other squads. The economic crime officers were always relaxed and they never had any dead bodies to look at. And a transfer back to uniform would seem a backward step.

She and Alun had talked about having children, but their conversations had petered out somehow. There never seemed to be a good time for a discussion about their plans. If they did start a family the possibility struck her that she might be able to work part time. She laughed to herself at the prospect of what Superintendent Price or Drake might say to such a request. On reflection, working with Drake had certain attractions and in the last two years she had become accustomed to his way of doing things. There was a certain comfort in the familiarity of his routine and in the way he liked things done, even if he could be rude and abrasive. And during all the time she'd worked with him, he had never once tried a flirtatious comment, which she'd put down to the fact that he was married to an ice maiden who'd frozen his emotions.

She decided that she'd have to talk to Alun first. Realising that the kettle had long since boiled, she clicked it on again and then made tea, accepting that she was going to be late. Alun wandered in, discarding his boots in a pile by the back door.

'I thought you had to get to work?' he said.

'They can wait.'

He smiled at her. 'The boss wants me to work extra hours next week.'

The family discussion might have to wait, Caren

thought.

'Will you be away?'

'No, but I might be late back most nights.'

'I've was wondering about asking for a transfer.'

Alun sat down. 'I thought you were enjoying working with Ian Drake.'

Caren poured tea into two mugs and set one down in front of him. 'I want regular hours. And if we want to start a family, then ...'

Alun reached a handover and touched hers. 'Now that I'm more settled maybe we could think about it again.'

'But we never really talk about it.'

'I know the alpaca business took more of my time than it should have done. But I've got a regular job now. Let's talk about it when we've got more time.'

'I'm thirty next birthday. My Mum had two children when she was my age and well... that old body clock is ticking.'

'I know. But I've only just started this job.'

'I want to think about my options.'

'I thought you wanted to make inspector?'

She hesitated and looked over at Alun, knowing that he really didn't know what was in her mind. 'Things change.'

'Let's talk about this later.'

Never, you mean.

Caren took a mouthful of hot tea and Alun shifted uncomfortably in his chair until he finally got up. He turned towards her. 'Toast?' he offered and she shook her head.

'I need to get going,' Caren said eventually, when the tension in the kitchen became something she couldn't break with a wise comment or remark. Standing up, she avoided kissing Alun who sat at the opposite side of the table. He mumbled a farewell through a mouthful of toast and she left.

She pulled the back door closed behind her and walked down to her car, throwing her bag onto the passenger seat. She buzzed down the window and let the hot summer air freshen the inside. The tourists would be streaming down the Conwy Valley that weekend and it struck her then that Ed Mostyn had no one to mourn him. No wife or children and even his girlfriend had wanted to steal from his cottage.

After half an hour she indicated for the junction to Northern Division headquarters and parked alongside Drake's Alfa. She gave the alloys a second glance, noting that they glistened. She couldn't imagine anyone wanting to scrub their car wheels clean.

On her way to the Incident Room, Caren bumped into Winder carrying two mugs of tea.

'Making tea, Gareth?'

'I'd make you one ... Only the boss is already complaining that you're late.'

She held the door open for her colleague but even so he managed to spill drops over the floor. Drake looked over and grimaced as he noticed. He gave Caren a brief smile and turned back to the board.

Howick was sitting by his desk and gave Caren a nervous frown.

'The most significant event so far is that we have evidence that Mostyn had a laptop. I checked this morning and it wasn't on the search inventory,' Drake said.

'So we've got a thief as well,' Caren said.

'And we need to establish when he had it last.'

'Must have been something incriminating on it,' Howick said.

'Joanna Barnes's photographs, to start with,' Caren said, adding, 'and other girls too, apparently.'

Drake stared at the image of Mostyn pinned to

the board. 'We can start on Mostyn's papers, bank statements etc. ...etc. ...We need to know everything about him: friends, and neighbours – all the usual stuff. And look out for a will or a copy. There must be something. And if not, then start contacting local solicitors next week. The search team picked up some personal effects in the sand near the body. They found a knife, some rings, a comb and a pair of Ray-Bans.'

'Any forensics yet?' Howick said.

Drake raised his eyebrows in surprise. Howick nodded his understanding.

'It'll be impossible to trace that sort of stuff,' Winder said.

'Local chandlery shop and ironmongers might sell them. It's not your average Swiss army knife,' Drake said.

'Might be available on the Internet,' Howick added.

'It's all we've got for the time being, unless we turn up something from his belongings. We should have the forensics' results back early next week. In the meantime we're going to see Rhys Fairburn.' Drake glanced over at Caren.

Any lingering hope that she might be able to finish early was dashed and she smiled at him weakly. Caren was convinced that Drake wasn't himself. In fact he had been out of sorts all week. He'd even worn the same shirt two days running and she was certain he'd worn the same red striped tie twice that week.

Drake said little on the drive to see Rhys Fairburn, which the satnav had told Caren would take fifty minutes. He spent time staring at the Sudoku page of the newspaper, occasionally scribbling a number down and, after forty-six minutes, she pulled into the drive of

Rhys Fairburn's farmhouse. A south-facing patio area at the side of the property was having a conservatory built on it and a tall man with thick black hair was giving directions to a stocky man in a T-shirt advertising the name of a local builders merchants. He broke off when he saw the car and walked towards them.

They left the car and met him as he stood under a couple of wind-battered plane trees.

'Rhys Fairburn?' Drake said, producing his warrant card as Caren did the same. 'Detective Inspector Drake and Detective Sergeant Caren Waits. We're investigating the death of Ed Mostyn.'

'I thought you might call. You'd better come inside.'

He led them round to the rear of the property. A three-year-old Mercedes estate was parked next to a 4x4, a couple of years older. The buildings at the back of the property looked well cared for, the slates were new, the gutters were clean and the windows recently painted.

Fairburn undid the laces of his farm boots and threw them into a pile in one corner of the small porch.

After a couple of steps down the hallway Fairburn pushed open the door of an office and sat behind a small desk, leaning over it as Drake and Caren sat down. A small bookcase was pushed against one wall, its top littered with a set of framed photographs. Caren spotted one with Fairburn, a woman his age and three more with younger faces that Caren guessed were his children. Another two photographs had Fairburn smiling at the camera with three men in a black-tie dinner. Even though he was clean-shaven and his hair cut neatly, Caren recognised Ed Mostyn and the puffy face of Maldwyn Evans looking uncomfortable in a dinner jacket. The final face was a younger and leaner Dafydd Higham.

Fairburn had a round face and a clear complexion made healthy by working on the land. His volume of hair was all-natural, Caren concluded, although it looked unnaturally dark. 'Do you want some coffee or tea?'Fairburn sounded unconvincing as a host.

'No thanks,' Drake said. 'How well did you know Mostyn?'

'I've known him a few years. I wouldn't say we were close friends.'

Drake continued. 'He was preventing you from selling your land to the power company. So he must have caused you a problem.'

'I don't need to sell the land to survive.'

'But having the money would be helpful.'

'Well, of course it would. I have a successful farm. We manage over five hundred head of cattle and sheep and I've got regular contracts with a big supermarket. And I've got three small convenience stores.' There was something rather too confident about Fairburn that Caren found unsettling. He had a too-good-to-be-true manner and he'd smiled regularly each time Drake had asked a question.

'Is it true that you lent money to Ed Mostyn?' Caren asked.

Any confidence that Fairburn had built up soon evaporated as his eyes darted around. 'That was a long time ago.'

'What was the money for?'

'He got himself involved with a business running a fishing trawler. The whole thing was a disaster.'

'Are you going to claim against Ed Mostyn's estate?' Caren asked.

Now Fairburn gave her a wintry glare.

'Where were you on the morning that Mostyn

was killed?' Drake said.

'Same place as always at that time of the day: in bed. And I'm sure my wife will confirm that.'

Drake fell into a dull mood as they made their way back to headquarters, his thoughts dominated by Sian's possible reaction that evening. Caren had tried to start a conversation in the car on the way back and he had nodded and agreed when appropriate, but mostly he wanted her to stop her stream of comments on the case so far.

He pushed open the doors to the Incident Room and watched as Winder pinned various photographs to the board. Drake walked over towards him, past Howick sitting by his desk. He was wearing a bold checked shirt with a red tie that made him look like a second-hand-car salesman.

'I googled the name of Joan Higham,' Winder said. 'She's had her face in the newspaper. As did her husband. She's a local county councillor and the chair of a local charity helping the homeless.'

'And her husband?' Drake said.

Howick piped up. 'Another upstanding member of the community with his own accountancy business. Employs half a dozen people. Sits as a magistrate and he's secretary of the local Cambrian Club.'

'What's the Cambrian club?' Winder said.

'It's a dining club. You know, businessmen and professionals. They meet for dinner and do good work in the local community. It's a bit like the Rotary Club except that it's only in Wales.'

'Is it only for Welsh speakers then?'

Drake interrupted. 'No, Gareth. Anyone can join.' He looked over at Howick. 'And Maldwyn Evans?'

Howick rustled some papers on his desk and

found a photograph. He stepped over to the board. 'Evans aged eighteen,' he said, pinning a grainy black-and-white image to the board. 'He was charged with drink driving.'

'That's no bloody good, Dave,' Winder said.

'Why not? Better than nothing.'

'We don't even know if they are persons of interest yet,' Drake said. 'Somebody out there had a motive to kill Ed Mostyn.'

'Anything in the papers from the cottage?'

'Just started, boss.' Howick gestured to a pile of paper on his desk.

Winder made a face. 'And there's the smell of fish bait on everything.'

Drake cut in. 'Anything from house-to-house?' He watched heads shaking slowly. 'And anybody been to see WPC Gooding in the mobile incident room?'

'The guy from the local post office makes a nuisance of himself,' Winder said. 'He's full of bullshit. And I checked our records – there's nothing known about him. But I don't think we could rely on anything he's said. There was a crowd in the shop when I called, all listening to him like he was an Old Testament prophet.'

'Having someone killed in a quiet village isn't exactly commonplace is it, Gareth?' Caren said.

Winder pouted. 'He mentioned the name Somerset de Northway again. He told me—'

'I know. He gave us the details too. We'll need to talk to him next week. Any sign of Ed Mostyn having made a will?'

Howick shook his head.

Drake wagged a finger at both men. 'That's the priority for both of you next week. I want the house-to-house finished too.' He turned to the board and pointed at the name 'Maldwyn Evans' printed in bold font. 'We need the names of Rhys Fairburn and Gwynfor Llywelyn up here as well.'

Howick and Winder both wore serious expressions. Drake continued. 'Get a full financial check done on all of them.' He turned to Caren. 'In the meantime I want to know everything about Ed Mostyn. Bank accounts, credit cards.'

Drake strode over to his office and sat down. He noticed, from a certain angle, yesterday's dust on the computer monitor. The photographs of his daughters had been moved since the night before; they were no longer aligned as they should be, along a particular grain of the wood of his desk. He watched his hand reach out over the desk, moving involuntarily towards the picture frames. It was so easy and once he'd made the adjustment he could clean the screen and empty the bin and then concentrate on work.

He made an effort to pull his hand back and it stopped, suspended in mid-air until something pulled it away from him again. He closed his eyes. He forced his hand onto the desk and the pile of statements, the first of the paperwork that would dominate the inquiry.

Chapter 9

'Area control, sir.' The voice sounded detached, like the pre-recorded announcers at post offices. 'There's a report of a fatality.'

Drake stood up abruptly, pushing back his chair, which crashed against the radiator behind him. He finished the call and looked out into the Incident Room.

'Caren,' Drake shouted before making for the door and retrieving his suit jacket as she appeared in the doorway. 'There's a body been found a couple of miles from where Mostyn was killed.'

The traffic was heavy for a Monday morning as Drake powered westwards along the A55, the main dual carriageway that crossed the North Wales coast from Holyhead to the border with England. Springsteen's *Born to Run* was playing on the CD, but his mind was full of the comments Sian had made the day before about *where they were going* and that she was finding it harder to live with the constraints that his rituals inevitably brought into their home life. He followed Caren's directions before peeling off the dual carriageway. The car jolted to a halt at the roundabout at the top of the slip road and Caren pointed towards an exit.

'Are the CSIs there?' Caren said.

'No, on their way.' Drake crossed the roundabout.

'Then who's at the crime scene? Turn left here.'

'Uniformed lads.'

Caren reached for the satnav, punched in the postcode and waited, staring down at the LCD display. A voice gave directions and Drake obediently turned left down a narrow track towards an entrance to a farm. The road then forked right, over a cattle grid, the tarmac petering out into a track, a line of grass down its middle that brushed the underside of the car.

The track soon disappeared altogether and they found themselves on a rough, sandy area lined with potholes. Drake slowed and negotiated his way around the various holes until he saw a patrol car in the distance. He turned the satnav off and pulled up alongside the police car.

Once Drake had locked the car he marched over towards the shore. In front of a row of four cottages, their roof line sagging with age, stood a man in cycling shorts holding a helmet and talking to a uniformed officer, a mountain bike discarded on a sand dune nearby. It looked expensive, suspension front and rear.

'Good morning, sir. Constable Radcliffe.'

'Where's the body?' Drake said.

Radcliffe pointed beyond a mound of grass and vegetation, towards the sea. 'Constable Parkes is down there.'

'Can I go now?' the cyclist said.

Drake gave the man an intense stare. 'You'll stay until I say otherwise.' He strode down to the water's edge, Caren following behind him.

A voice shouted over at them. 'Here, sir.'

Parkes had sand dusted over the bottom of his trousers and a harassed look on his face. The relief was evident when he saw Drake. The body of a girl was lying face down by the edge of the beach, well above high water and sheltered by the dunes. She had long blonde hair cascading over her shoulders. Her jeans looked clean and well pressed. Her legs were curled slightly, making it difficult to judge her height.

'Is there any ID on the body?' Drake said.

'I haven't touched her,' Parkes said, faintly surprised that Drake had expected him to search a corpse.

The young officer stood to one side and Drake leant down. Behind him he heard the familiar sound of the Scientific Support Vehicle drawing to a halt. Fine grains of sand were already rubbing against his skin inside his socks. The thought of his car being full of sand for weeks, trapped in the carpet of the footwell, set him on edge. He wondered about booking a professional valet.

He snapped on a pair of latex gloves and turned the body onto her side, then searched through the pockets of her jeans. He guessed she was twenty, maybe younger. He hesitated when he saw the deep bruising around her neck.

Footsteps approached and then the voice of Mike Foulds. 'Good morning, Ian.'

Drake unzipped the girl's light-grey fleece and searched the two inside pockets.

'Who's the dead girl?'

'No ID as yet.' From the second pocket Drake found a small purse. He snapped it open and drew out a driving licence and a bankcard. 'Jane Jones, Tyddyn Du farm.'

Drake stood up and stared down at the body. He left Foulds and the CSIs to their work and strode away from the beach, Caren following in his slipstream.

Drake stopped next to Radcliffe and turned to the cyclist. 'Does anyone live here?'

'How would I know? I'm on holiday.' Drake couldn't identify the accent immediately – Midlands, maybe Birmingham.

'We'll need your details. Name and address.'

'Can I go then?'

Drake didn't answer; he was already striding towards the cottages, leaving Caren jotting down the man's contact details. The windows on the first cottage were dirty, obliterating any chance to see inside. The door was locked and when he thumped on it the place sounded empty. There was a low stone wall surrounding a small front garden and he walked round to the second property. Sellotaped to the door was a plastic envelope with the contact details of the Anglesey Wildlife and Environmental Trust printed in clear letters on a sheet inside. He found his mobile and rang the number. It rang out a couple of times until the messaging service clicked on, first in English and then in Welsh. Drake left a message, urgently asking someone to call him.

The windows of the next cottage were cleaner and Drake knelt to peer in. There were some implements and an old wooden settle. Caren was rattling the door of another cottage, its windows shaded by a net curtain. Drake stared up at the roof. Nothing had been done to the cottages for years. The pretty postcard image didn't last long once he'd looked carefully.

'Anything in the first two?' Caren said.

Drake shook his head. 'There's a contact number for some charity.'

'Place looks deserted.'

'We need to find out who owns them.'

Drake walked down towards Foulds and the CSIs working around the body. He passed cases of equipment piled above the high-water mark; his shoes sank into the sand as he approached the tent erected over the body.

'She was strangled,' Foulds said.

Two CSIs were scouring the sand; another searched the surrounding dunes and shoreline.

'Pathologist?' Drake said.

'On his way. We'll move her once he's finished.'

'Anything from the search so far?'

'Nothing and I'm not expecting any results either. There's sand everywhere. We don't have a chance of finding anything.'

Overhead two small training jets flew past. Drake returned to the cottages and strode up onto a large mound. He stood and looked down the inlet towards the sea; the tips of antennas and masts from the nearby RAF station could be seen in the distance. The sun was hot, and below him Drake saw the small pool formed by a curling finger of rocks jutting out into the inlet, an idyllic secluded spot for swimming. The CSIs had moved away from the shoreline, and in the distance was the small bridge near where they'd found Ed Mostyn.

He heard the phut-phut sound of an outboard approaching and he saw a small fishing dinghy pointing its bow towards a sandy section of the shore. Drake scrambled down from his position and walked over to where the boat had landed.

The fisherman was lifting lobster pots out of his dinghy laden with rods and buckets of bait and equipment. He stopped when he saw Drake. The man wore a battered red fleece over a T-shirt torn at the neck and a pair of faded jeans.

Drake produced his card. 'Detective Inspector Drake.'

'I know who you are.' The man stood dead still.

'A body has been found on the beach behind me.'

The man looked at Drake, said nothing, waited.

'I need to know who owns the cottages.'

The man moved a hand over his face, pulling at his nose. 'Who's been killed?'

'We haven't got a positive identification yet.'

'Man or woman?'

Drake wanted to believe the man wasn't being

deliberately obtuse. 'I'll need your personal details.'

'Why?'

'What's your name?

Drake scribbled down the details. 'So, do you know who owns the cottages?'

'Of course. Somerset de Northway.'

Chapter 10

Drake drove down several single-track lanes before realising each time that he was in the wrong place, forcing him to retrace his route back to the main road. Eventually he found the right turning. After a narrow entrance, the lane opened into a long straight road for about a hundred and fifty metres, with a ditch on either side filled with green stagnant water; an expanse of reeds covered an area to Drake's right. At the end of the track a small post with a crooked sign announced the entrance to the farm.

Tyddyn Du looked over a handful of small fields down to the shore. The house looked bleak; the window frames were painted a dark brown, now barely distinguishable from the walls. Outside was a row of sheds covered in corrugated iron with wooden doors, their red paint peeling and tired. What first struck Drake when he got out of the car was the smell. It was the usual smell of soil and earth, but also the harshness and acidity of diesel or petrol.

Drake walked over a path of large flat stones towards the rear door: it was dark blue and unusually large, and as he approached it was opened by a middle-aged woman, her complexion pasty, her long grey hair unbrushed and unloved.

'Mrs Jones?' Drake said. 'Detective Inspector Drake.' He held up his warrant card. 'And this is Detective Sergeant Waits.'

'Mildred … Mildred Jones. Have you come about Jane?' She looked tired and drawn. 'Come in.'

She led them through the kitchen into a parlour. Natural light came into the room from two small, deeply recessed windows, covered in thick net curtains.

'My husband, Ray.' Mildred gave a lank wave towards him. Jones was dressed in a collarless shirt and a dark blue serge waistcoat. The wrinkles on his brow were deep and wide, covering his entire forehead. He nodded. Drake resisted the usual courtesy of extending his hand, sensing an invisible barrier. Ray remained seated while Mildred stood with Drake and Caren in the middle of the room.

'May we sit down?' Drake said.

Caren found two chairs from the table and they sat down opposite Ray Jones. Mildred sat next to him on the old sofa, at the edge of the seat as though she was waiting to fall off. Drake cleared his throat and glanced at Caren. Her face had an intensity Drake had not seen before.

'I have some bad news. This morning we found a body on a beach nearby. We believe it might be Jane. I am most terribly sorry.'

For a moment Mildred just looked at Drake and then at Caren, before her eyes began to fill and then she started crying uncontrollably. Gulping for breath in between the blubbering, she clasped her hands to her face, saying nothing. Ray just sat there, a blank expressionless face; but his jaw tightened as his wife spoke haltingly between the sobs.

'I knew something was wrong. I just knew it,' she cried.

Ray lifted an arm over his wife's shoulder without moving himself any nearer to her.

'It'll be all right. We'll be all right,' he said simply.

She ignored him and continued to weep. Between the tears she tried to grasp a small glimmer of hope. 'Can you be sure it's Jane?' More sobbing. 'How do you know it's her?'But then a certainty prevailed. 'I told her to be careful.'

She covered her face with her hands.

Ray Jones turned to look at Drake. 'Jane had

some friends that we thought were a bad influence.'

Although Ray Jones looked towards Drake, he adopted an affectation of averting his eyes to an invisible spot on the ceiling.

'I know this has been a terrible shock. But we will need you make an identification.'

Ray Jones stared at Drake.

'I need you to come to the hospital.'

'What, now?' Ray asked.

'You can travel with me and we'll arrange for a family liaison officer to bring you back. I know it will be a difficult time.'

'We won't need any help, thank you,' Ray said as his head pointed at Drake, his eyes returning again to the ceiling. His voice was firm and the tone contemptuous.

Drake continued. 'The officer won't be in the way at all. I'm sure it will be of help.'

But Ray Jones was dismissive. 'No, thank you.'

'Do you have any other close family?' Drake asked. 'Any other children?'

Mildred answered Drake between sobs. 'Ellen lives in Litchfield. She's a teacher and Huw, he's away today.'

'I can arrange for a policeman to call and see your daughter.'

'No, that won't be necessary,' Ray Jones said. 'We'll call her.'

Drake was finding this hard going – harder than any other time. 'What about Huw – can we contact him somehow?'

'He should be back soon,' Ray said flatly.

Drake continued. 'If it's possible, could we agree to meet you at the hospital in two hours' time? In the meantime Sergeant Waits will write down our telephone numbers so that if you need to contact us you can do so.'

Mildred continued to cry, but the intensity was diminishing. Eventually Drake and Caren left the farmhouse.

'That was weird,' Caren said as they walked back to their car.

Drake looked over at the land surrounding the farmhouse; weeds grew in wild unkempt clumps all over the grass and fences lay broken. His grandfather would never have tolerated such bad husbandry.

'I've never seem someone react in such a way,' Caren continued.

Drake stood for a moment as he reached the car. 'I wonder when Huw will be home,' he said, thinking about Mildred. 'I hope he'll be of help.'

'Shall I ask them again if they want me to accompany them to the hospital? I can always wait until Huw arrives,' she added.

'I think that Ray Jones' reply was quite clear.' Drake opened the car and climbed in. He started the engine as Caren closed the door behind her. 'Let's keep an eye on the family at the hospital and then we can always send one of the liaison officers to the house each day.'

Time dragged as Drake and Caren stood outside the front doors of the hospital waiting for Mildred and Ray to arrive. Drake looked at his watch, regretting not being more forceful with Ray Jones and insisting that the family travel with them.

Drake saw Mildred first; she seemed to have visibly shrivelled. Ray walked to one side of his wife, the distance marking the relationship between them. Mildred walked with a slight stoop that Drake hadn't noticed in the house but Ray, despite his size, also appeared shrunken. When Mildred reached the door she appeared surprised to see Drake and Caren.

'What do we do now?' she asked simply.

'I know this will be difficult,' Drake told her, as he led them through the hospital corridors.

Drake was close to Mildred and Ray as they entered the mortuary. Ray kept his hands in his pocket; Mildred grasped a handbag tightly. The body lay on a table covered in a white cloth that the technician pulled away to reveal the blonde hair and features that made Jane recognisable. Drake was pleased that the technician hadn't revealed the bruising around her neck. Mildred's eyes filled with tears before her face collapsed into a contortion of emotion and she began to sob.

'No! No! No!' she cried repeatedly. She drew her body in and almost crouched as if in physical pain. Ray just stood there, hands in his pockets, staring blankly at the corpse: disengaged, almost as if the body before him was not his daughter. Mildred carried on sobbing. Drake stood at the opposite side of the table.

'*Pam fi? Pam fi?*' Mildred cried helplessly in Welsh, which Drake knew meant *why me?* Then she turned to Ray. '*Pam eis i allan nos Sul? Lle fi oedd bod adre.*'

The technician replaced the white sheet and Drake turned to Ray and Mildred.

'Sergeant Waits will take you home. We can make arrangements for someone to collect your car again.'

Ray spoke first, momentarily looking at Drake in the eyes before averting his gaze to the ceiling. 'We'll be all right. We don't need anyone.'

Mildred continued to sob, ignoring the offer of water from Caren.

'But I am sure it will be of great help. All the family liaison officers are specially trained. It can be a very difficult time for the family.'

Drake tried to sound as insistent as he could but Ray turned to him, the resolve evident in his eyes. 'Mildred and I will be all right. Huw will be home when we get back.'

Drake tried another tack.

'Could I at least send someone to help you tomorrow? The officer will be very sensitive. I know you will find it helpful. There will be a lot for you both to deal with – the funeral, the inquest and the investigation.'

Ray gave Drake a smile of disdain. 'No, thank you.'

They walked in silence to the main doors of the hospital. Mildred put her hand through Ray's arm. Drake and Caren carried on walking with Mildred and Ray to their car and watched as they drove away in the old Rover.

The sun was setting a deep scarlet over Anglesey as Drake and Caren stood in the car park.

'What did Mildred say inside the mortuary?' Caren said.

'She said that she shouldn't have been out the Sunday night Jane was killed and that her place was at home.'

'What's that supposed to mean?'

The mobile rang, but Drake didn't recognise the number.

'Inspector Drake, it's Calvin Headley. We're running a piece on the murder this morning. Do you have any comments about the case? Do you have any suspects? Is there really a serial killer on Anglesey?'

Drake's chest tightened.

'I take it you're the senior investigating officer. Can I refer to you by that title? Is there going to be a

press conference?'
Drake terminated the call and drove home in a rage.

Chapter 11

Tyddyn Du looked bleaker than it had done the day before. The roof was darker, the dried-up mud in the entrance of the barn harder and the water on the yard dirtier. The farmhouse seemed ugly and out of place amongst the natural beauty of the countryside.

Drake parked alongside a black Ford. Caren got out before him and looked around.

'It must have been an awful place to have been brought up as a child. It gives me the shivers,' she said.

Drake said nothing. He closed the car door and looked over at the farmhouse.

Drake noticed the back door opening. He squinted towards the woman standing on the threshold. 'This must be Ellen.'

As they approached Drake recognised Jane's sister as an inelegant combination of her mother with her untidy, greying hair and the strong facial features of her father. He stretched out a hand. 'Detective Inspector Drake and this is Detective Sergeant Waits.'

'I'm Ellen, Jane's sister.'

Inside in the parlour Mildred and Ray Jones sat together on the grey sofa. The bags under Mildred's eyes were a fierce grey, her eyelids heavy. Drake pulled two chairs from underneath a table and pushed one over at Caren. Behind him Ellen followed suit, the chair leg scratching along the quarry-tiled floor. They sat down and looked over at Mildred and Ray.

'We need to know more about Jane,' Drake said.

'My mother is very upset,' Ellen said. 'And she hasn't slept very much.'

Drake nodded. 'Can you think of anyone who would want to kill her?' Mildred reached for her handkerchief as her eyes filled with tears.

Drake continued. 'Did she have any boyfriends?'

Mildred sobbed a little, though seemed to be trying to stop herself.

Ellen answered. 'Jane had lots of boyfriends. She was very attractive.'

'Did she have a current boyfriend?'

A tremor passed over Ray Jones's jaw as he clenched it tight. Mildred dabbed a handkerchief to her eyes. She shrugged.

Drake could sense the reluctance to discuss Jane with a stranger, a reticence he found incomprehensible; his irritation intensified. Their daughter was dead and they wanted to keep up appearances.

'She'd been seeing Gwynfor for the past year,' Mildred said.

Ray Jones stiffened. 'We didn't approve of him.'

They slipped into another silence.

Drake badly wanted to raise his voice. They were mired into a taciturn truculence that he'd seen so often in the older generation. His father always said that the people of Anglesey were an odd lot and that living on an island made them insular and remote.

He reached forward and looked at them each in turn. 'My job is to find Jane's killer. I need your help.'

Mildred had stopped crying.

'I shall need Gwynfor's contact details.'

Ray had an utterly inscrutable look on his face.

'Gwynfor Llywelyn—'

'Gwynfor Llywelyn? Drake couldn't hide the surprise in his voice. 'And was he her current boyfriend?'

She looked at him uncertain at his response. 'I don't think so. But she could be secretive and …'

'Where did Jane go to school?' Caren asked.

Mildred replied, slowly at first, as Caren made notes. They heard about Jane, from her primary to secondary school and then her adolescence years and the arguments and tantrums. Mildred visibly relaxed as she talked.

'What did Jane do after leaving school?' Drake asked.

'I wanted her to stay on and get some qualifications,' Mildred answered.

'What did she do?' asked Drake.

'She began to train as a hairdresser. She did some day release in the local college. But all she wanted was to earn money and see her friends. She loved going out.'

Caren butted in. 'Can you tell me the names of her friends? We'll need to contact them. They may be able to help.'

'She went out with a group of girls on Sunday night,' Ellen said.

Mildred nodded and then gave Caren various names and addresses. Drake turned to Ray Jones who had sat impassively.

'Did you meet any of her friends, Mr Jones?'

Ray turned his head towards Drake but averted his eyes before answering. 'She never brought her friends home.'

Drake stared at Ray Jones, anticipating some eye contact that never came.

'How long had she worked at this salon?' Caren asked.

'About a year,' Mildred replied.

'And before then?'

'A couple of other local salons.' Mildred sounded flustered.

Ellen answered for her mother. 'Jane never

seemed to settle in one place. She complained that the other girls would get jealous and then arguments would begin.'

'Do you have the names of the other salons?'

'I can find them for you,' Ellen said.

By the end Caren had several sheets of paper with names, addresses and dates. Drake had witnessed a mother's grief and the reserve of a man who hated invasion of his privacy. Intruding into the immediacy of the family's grief was an inevitable part of his work but this family was more dysfunctional than most.

'Where were you last night Mr Jones?'

'Here.'

'And you Mrs Jones?'

Mildred's eyes opened wide and she blinked. 'I was out at a women's group meeting in the local chapel.'

Outside there was a roar of a Land Rover.

'That'll be Huw,' Ellen said.

'I'll go and see him.' Drake turned to Ellen. 'Perhaps Caren can look at Jane's room.'

Mildred and Ray frowned in unison. Neither said anything; they both looked blankly at him.

'Of course,' Ellen said, leading Caren towards the door to the hall.

Outside Drake noticed the warmth of the sun after the coolness of the parlour and squinted to acclimatise to the sun's rays.

Jane's room was north facing and cold but, more than that, it felt bereft of life, of human warmth. And then it struck Caren how utterly humourless the house really was.

'My parents are very old-fashioned,' Ellen said,

walking over to the window.

Caren was thinking about Drake and how he might have been a little more tactful. But he hadn't lost his patience and at least he'd been sensitive when asking for their help.

'Did Jane have any hobbies?'Caren scanned the room. It was absent of any sign that a young woman lived there.

'Going out – sometimes she'd go the local stables.'

'Did your parents approve?'

Ellen shook her head slowly.

'Were you close?' Caren opened the drawers of an enormous chest with two hands, hoping for evidence of perfumes or make-up or deodorants or jewellery.

'Not really. There was a big age gap. Enough to make us a different generation.'

'Did she rebel?'Caren looked into one of the drawers full of neatly stored clothes.

'My father isn't the easiest of people ...'

Caren didn't respond. She looked over at the bed. It had an ancient bedspread; even Caren's grandparents had a duvet. Caren noticed a large trunk with metal straps on top of an oak wardrobe with large doors.

'What's in the trunk?' Caren said.

'It came from my grandparents' home.'

Ellen stood, arms folded, as Caren opened the wardrobe and riffled through Jane's belongings. There was a small box on the bottom shelf and Caren reached down and opened it. Another box sat inside, which she opened to find yet another box. Inside it was a diary, some loose change and a key.

Caren stood up and held the key with two fingers. 'Any idea?'

Ellen shook her head.

Caren looked up at the trunk. 'Give me a hand.'

Together they manoeuvred the trunk to the edge of the wardrobe and then pushed it from below; judging it to be empty, Caren lifted it onto the bed. The key opened the lock easily enough.

They looked down into the hidden world of a young woman. Bottles of perfume, shower creams, face wipes and lipstick. As Caren moved an empty condom packet to one side she noticed Ellen catch her breath. Caren took out two small diaries and then her fingers touched an old mobile telephone. She placed them onto the bedspread.

'I'll need to take these.'

Ellen stood, her arms folded even more tightly.

Huw appeared unsurprised when Drake walked up behind him. He was hauling various sacks from the rear of the Land Rover.

'I'm Detective Inspector Drake.'

Huw didn't stop what he was doing. He had a narrow chin that jutted out prominently and eyes that had a hard piercing focus. A few days' stubble made his face look heavy and swarthy. He had broad and powerful hands like his father that he wrapped round a bag of feedstuff lying on the back of the Land Rover. There was no physical similarity to suggest Jane was his sister.

'I need to talk to you about Jane,' Drake said. 'When did you last see her?'

'Night she was killed.'

'Where?'

Huw walked off towards the inside of the barn. 'Here.'

Huw dropped the bag on the floor. He stopped

to open an old wardrobe full of blue and green one-piece overalls.

'Did you know any of her friends?'

'No, definitely not.' His reply was sharp. He was searching for a suitable pair of gloves from a drawer full of assorted sizes.

'Did you know Gwynfor Llywelyn – Jane's boyfriend?'

Huw stared at him. 'She'd finished with him.'

'So who was her boyfriend?

Huw shrugged.

Drake paused, noticing the dark colour of Huw's eyes. 'Were you close as brother and sister?'

'What do you mean, close?'

'Well, did you share confidences? Did you know about her life and she about yours?'

Huw looked perplexed, as though he didn't understand the question.

'She was a lot younger than me.' Huw walked out to the Land Rover.

Drake followed him, but after more monosyllabic answers Drake decided he wasn't achieving anything.

'Do you know Somerset de Northway? Apparently he owns the cottages.'

'Of course I do. Everyone knows him.'

Huw reached for a sack of feed that he manhandled onto his shoulder. 'He owns this place,' he said, tipping his head towards the farmhouse. 'And he's doing everything he can to get us out.'

Drake thought about his grandfather telling him about the struggle he'd had to buy his smallholding from the local aristocracy. 'What do you mean?'

'He's served a notice to quit on the basis of poor husbandry.'

'What's happening with that?'

'We'll fight it.'

'How much land do you have?'

'We have 120 acres of tenanted land and another thirty we own.'

Huw made for the back of the barn.

Drake walked up to the back door and stood outside ready to knock when the door opened and Ellen stood there with Caren.

'Ellen showed me Jane's room,' Caren said.

'I haven't been in it for years,' added Ellen quietly. 'There was something a bit unsettling about it.'

Drake thanked her again and they walked down to the car.

'What was her room like?' Drake said.

'Barren.'

'Did you go through all her things?'

'Everything was hidden away in a trunk.'

'All her personal stuff?'

'Her make-up and the usual things for a girl of her age.'

Drake found his keys and bleeped the Alfa. It was hot and the smell of warming leather filled the car. Grains of sand glistened in the footwell despite Drake's vacuuming the night before.

Driving away, Drake opened the window and let the summer heat brush his face. He caught a glimpse of Ellen in the rear view mirror standing, quite still, by the door.

Chapter 12

Caren left Tyddyn Du hoping that she'd never have to return. The place and the Jones family had depressed her and she kept thinking that if ever she had children her home would be full of happiness and fun and laughter. Her mood lightened the further they drove away from the farmhouse.

She reached for the diaries and flicked through the pages. They were for the last two years and scanning the entries made her remember her own teenage years. But she had been younger than Jane when her short-lived attempts at keeping a diary had petered out. Then she fingered the old Nokia – it was a handset she hadn't seen for years.

'I thought the CSIs found a mobile on the body,' Drake said.

'This is an old version.'

'Get Dave to have it checked by forensics.'

Caren turned the mobile through her fingers, wondering if there were numbers of interest or the record of messages still on the old telephone.

They found the first house on the list without difficulty. A pitched-roof porch as well as new uPVC windows, adorned with extravagant swirls, had been added to the ex-council house. Drake parked and Caren cleared her throat, wanting to suggest that she conduct the interview without actually sounding as though she didn't want Drake to do so. She'd suggested this on other occasions when she thought his approach would be too brusque.

'Let me talk to this girl, sir. She might respond better to a feminine approach.' Caren was already out of the car before Drake could mumble an acknowledgement.

Caren pressed the bell and chimes echoed

through the house. She heard a shout and the door opened. A woman with a perfect beehive of jet-black hair, a flamboyant pink blouse and a narrow pencil skirt opened the door. Her make-up cracked slightly around her eyes as she squinted at Caren's warrant card.

'I need to speak to Tracy,' Caren said.

The woman stared at Caren and then Drake before shouting over her shoulder. 'Tracy, the cops are here.'

There was the sound of movement upstairs and then footsteps on the staircase. Tracy had a round face and there was a reddish tone to her chestnut brown hair that she'd drawn back into a ponytail, and Caren immediately thought she must have been adopted. She wore a pair of faded jeans and a thin T-shirt. She needed no make-up. Caren and Drake followed the young girl into the front room.

Every surface was covered with miniature vases and fairings. There were runners on the carpet alongside the sofas and chairs. Sitting down in such order was daunting. Tracy's eyes were swollen and Caren guessed they'd been a lot worse.

'We're investigating Jane's death,' Caren said.

'I was the last to see her.' Tracy sat on the edge of the sofa, staring at Caren and then Drake.

'Where?'

'At that club in Rhosneigr.'

'Were you with anyone else?'

'There was a crowd of us. In the summer we always go there. There are boys from the sailing club and there are discos and a barbecue.'

Caren consulted her notes. She reeled off the names of the other girls that Mildred had given her and Tracy nodded confirmation of those that had been there.

'The place was packed.' Tracy began chewing a

fingernail on her right hand. She flicked back a stray lock of hair. Caren could see how young she looked.

'Did Jane have a regular boyfriend?'

'She'd just finished with Gwynfor Llywelyn,' Tracy continued. 'He runs that bakery. I was in school with his sister.'

'What happened?'

Tracy shrugged. 'He was just too intense. And he smelt.'

'Was there anyone special at the moment?'

'This boy had been after her all last year and then this year he was back. Llywelyn hated that she was going with him.'

'What was his name?'

'Julian Sandham. He lives in Birmingham, but the family has a fancy place in Rhosneigr. He kept bragging about it.'

Tracy made an unconvincing shrug.

'I need you tell me everything you know, Tracy.'

She looked away and then at her feet. 'She said she was going to the cottage with him. Said she knew where the keys were.'

Caren moved to the edge of her seat, her concentration heightened. 'What was happening in the cottages?'

Tracy stood up, a startled look on her face. 'I don't know. Really.' She stepped to the door. Caren and Drake exchanged glances, each telling the other that Tracy knew more, but for now they had a name. Enough to make progress.

By early afternoon Drake was looking at Superintendent Price scratching the top of his head with his fingernails. It made a dull rasping sound that Drake usually found reassuring; it had been a habit that he'd missed while Price had been on secondment to the West Midlands. Yet now, he was sure that flecks of Price's scalp would be floating down onto the desk and Drake tried to resist moving his chair back a few inches.

'Did you see the television news last night?' Price said.

'The reporter rang me as I was leaving the hospital.'

'He's a stupid young kid. I've already called the programme editor and played hell with him.'

'What did he say?'

'Not a lot; he told me it wasn't a police state.'

'How did you reply, sir?'

'Diplomatically.'

Drake paused. Price really had been learning from his work in England.

'The public relations department wants to organise a press conference this afternoon. Make an appeal for witnesses.' He drew a hand in the air. 'All the usual stuff. Somebody from the department will contact you about the details.'

Price looked over at Drake, his eyes focused and clear. 'Are the murders connected?'

'I have no idea, sir.'

'We need to establish that quickly.'

'The cottages where we found Jane's body are owned by a Somerset de Northway. And he owns the farm where the family live. And he was in the village very early on the morning Mostyn was killed. He collects a newspaper first thing.'

Price made a brief frown that curled the top of his eyelashes. 'Who did you say?'

'Somerset de Northway.'

'I've heard that name.'

Price reached for his mouse and then stared at

the screen until a glimmer of recognition passed his face. He sat back in his chair and rubbed a hand over his mouth. 'He's the deputy high sheriff. That means he'll be the next high sheriff.'

'I thought that was just a ceremonial role?'

'It is, but it means that de Northway is very well connected.'

Drake walked into the Incident Room and went straight up to the board. He stopped and stared at the image of Ed Mostyn, the three puncture wounds in his neck evident like a scene from a horror movie. He pinned up a sheet with the name of Jane Jones printed on it and made a mental note to get a photograph. He pondered whether there was a connection between the deaths and whether it was the same killer.

He stepped back just as a woman in high heels, wearing what appeared to be a designer suit, walked in. Her name badge hung on a lanyard, caressing her blouse, which had a long, deep neckline.

'I'm Mandy Finch, public relations. Just started last week,' she announced.

'DI Drake.'

'What can you tell me?'

Drake pointed to the board. 'Ed Mostyn was killed last week. His head was smashed in and then he was impaled to the sand with his fork.'

Mandy grimaced. 'I don't think we can release that image.'

'We've got another picture of him somewhere,' Drake said.

Mandy had opened a notebook. 'I need the details to build a press release.'

'Do you know that Calvin Headley?' Drake said.

'He's rung me a dozen times in the past two days.'

'What the hell is he doing?'

'Let me deal with him. Tell me about Mostyn.'

Drake led her into his office and pointed to the visitor's chair. 'Mostyn was a local fisherman. He was killed as he was digging for bait early one morning.'

'Any family?'

'Sister. He wasn't married and he didn't have any kids. Everyone in the village knew him. He was a bit of a character.'

Mandy scribbled the details into her notepad. 'And Jane Jones. Is she connected to Ed Mostyn?'

'Nothing to connect both deaths,' Drake said.

'So we can definitely rule out a serial killer.' Mandy didn't wait for a reply. 'I'll draft a press release.' She stood up, gathered her papers and made for the door. 'Press conference at 5pm, Inspector.'

Drake had an hour to spare and he sank into his chair. The photographs of his daughters needed the usual adjustment, and after running a finger over the top of the computer monitor he inspected the dust on his skin. He'd have to talk to the office manager about the cleaning staff.

Deciding that he needed to have a proper coffee, he trooped off to the kitchen and found a bag of finely ground Guatemalan beans. As the electric kettle purred into life he could feel the tension ebbing. He measured the grounds exactly and used his mobile to time the exact period that the coffee needed to brew.

Once the operation had been completed, he took the small cafetière and his cup and saucer back to his room. The words of the counsellor, warning him that his rituals would intensify after his father's death, had given him almost as much comfort and reassurance as the obsessions themselves. It had been difficult to explain all of this to Sian. She had frowned and when he'd said that his rituals might get worse her lips tightened until they'd lost their entire colour. He remembered that she'd said something about 'ridiculous counselling methods' and 'the green light to indulge' his 'habits'.

He plunged the coffee and filled his cup, letting the smell waft over his desk. He flipped open the box of Mostyn's belongings and extracted the first pile of files and papers. The first mouthful of coffee tasted nutty and strong.

An email arrived in his inbox and he clicked open the forensics report on the piece of timber found near Mostyn's body. Any optimism disappeared quickly when he read that the only DNA they'd found was Mostyn's. Slowly he turned his attention to Mostyn's papers. He found the photograph of the black-tie dinner still in its frame and he held it in both hands. Now he recognised Maldwyn Evans and Rhys Fairburn. The third man stood upright almost to attention, suggesting he had a military background. He opened up the back of the frame but the rear of the image was blank – no date or place. He stood up and walked towards the board where he pinned the picture below the image of Mostyn. Underneath he scribbled the names of Maldwyn Evans and Rhys Fairburn. Returning to his office he started on the piles of random papers; it filled him with disgust that anyone could be this disorganised. He pulled out annual accounts for Ed's business completed by Dafydd Higham with tax returns and letters from Higham about the tax and national insurance due. There were envelopes from investment companies with their annual reports, their envelopes torn open. A neat pile of papers grew on his desk and it surprised him that Mostyn had so many investments – reaching for his notepad he started a 'to do' list. They'd need to find out his net worth. He liked that phrase. It smacked of wealth and it reminded him of the session he and Sian had had with a financial adviser. He'd talked about their objectives for the next five and ten years and whether they wanted to save for university fees for the girls. The only thing that couldn't be timetabled was death itself, Drake thought morosely. Then he thought about his father, knowing he could never turn the clock back. There had been early morning wakefulness after his father's death, when he had stared at the ceiling, afraid to get out of bed and disturb Sian, when regrets about wasted opportunities and words unsaid had dominated his mind.

Then it struck him as odd that Mostyn still rented a property. Drake settled back to rooting through Mostyn's papers. There were envelopes full of circulars about broadband offers, catalogues from companies offering gardening equipment and plants. At the bottom of the box was a folder on which 'Land' had been scrawled in large letters. Drake blanked out the noise from the Incident Room, hoping he was making progress.

He flipped open the file and found various letters from solicitors and some correspondence from the nuclear power plant marked 'Strictly Private and Confidential'. Drake was going to be disappointed. The final letter was confirmation of a meeting with the representatives of the company – it used words like *constructive engagement* and *hoping we can make progress.*

Drake added the power company to his to-do list.

A second envelope had 'Cottage' scribbled on it. Drake piled out the contents and found an old tenancy agreement; he scanned the contents. Somerset de Northway was the landlord and Ed Mostyn was named as the tenant. At first Drake couldn't understand why the rent was a nominal sum of a hundred pounds every year until he read an exchange of correspondence about Mostyn having to rebuild and refurbish the cottage. Drake picked up the telephone and rang Andy Thorsen.

'Property law was never something I had any interest in,' he said, after Drake had explained the scenario. 'But it sounds like Mostyn had a full repairing lease while paying a nominal rent.'

'So what happens now that Mostyn is dead?'

'Depends on the lease, but it might revert back to the landlord.'

'Thanks.' Drake stared at the document, realising that he had another reason to talk to Somerset de Northway.

Everyone has a computer for emails, banking, buying gifts and Drake assumed that Mostyn would be no different. Somebody wanted the laptop badly enough to have killed him. It struck Drake that it must have been someone who knew his routine, which included everyone they'd spoken to so far. Mostyn's keys hadn't been found, which meant that the killer had taken them and used them, unless they were under a pot somewhere. And if they were, it would bring the killer much closer to home. Noticing that the time had passed more quickly than he had imagined, he cursed and left his desk, grabbing his suit coat from the wooden hanger. In the Incident Room he stopped by the board.

Drake pulled his arms through the suit sleeves and as he did so noticed an acrid smell like dead fish. He hoped it was his imagination, but to avoid it playing on his mind he made a detour into the bathroom and scrubbed his hands.

Caren sat back in her chair and thumbed through Jane's diaries. She blotted out the sound of Winder and Howick shuffling papers and tapping on keyboards as she took a step back into the world of a teenage girl with all its insecurities and uncertainties. Jane worried about who her 'best' friend actually was and recorded her disappointments when someone let her down. She acknowledged to herself – but probably not to the outside world, Caren guessed – how much of a 'cow' she could be during her period. Caren remembered her own teenage years and that aching certainty that sometimes the whole world was against her. There were unflattering comments about her mother and her appearance. Darker and more disturbing observations about her father but she kept her most acerbic remarks for her brother.

Drake was busy with the press conference and Caren could see her working day drifting on for hours. She texted Alun, telling him she would be late home. She stopped and looked down at the diaries on her desk. There was one for each of the last two calendar years. On impulse Caren flicked to the beginning of the first and read more intently. There was a rhythm and a confidence to the writing – not the prose of someone starting out as a teenage diarist. By the end of February Caren was convinced that Jane had earlier diaries. And the name of Aled Williams had been mentioned more than once in a tone that suggested he was special. She jotted down other names, knowing that they'd all need to be cross-referenced and investigated.

She scoured her notebook, found the contact number for Tracy and reached for the telephone. After it had rung out half a dozen times she almost hung up but then she heard a breathless voice.

'It's Caren Waits from the Wales Police Service. I need to ask you about Jane. Did you know she wrote a diary?'

'Yes. I never saw them of course.'

'How long had she been keeping the diary?'

'Years. Since she was at school. Four years ... maybe longer.'

'And Aled Williams, who was he?'

'He was one of her boyfriends.'

Caren thanked Tracy and finished the call before turning to Winder.

'We've got to investigate Jane's friends. I need you to ...'

He shrugged and rolled his eyes. 'I'm up to my neck in Ed Mostyn and his family.'

Caren looked over at Howick who had a resigned look on his face. 'Dave. The boss wants you to look at Jane's mobile telephones so maybe you can make a list of the people she called regularly against the names on this list.' She clicked her mouse and emailed him the list from the diary.

Howick sighed as he stared at the screen.

'Don't worry, Dave,' Caren added. 'I'll do half of the names.'

She settled down to more hours in front of the screen.

The rows of seats crossing the main conference suite were full of journalists talking to each other, notepads propped on their knees, ballpoints ready. The conversations hushed when Drake walked into the room with Price. Mandy stood at the back, chewing the top of a biro.

The lights from the television cameras clicked into life and Drake squinted for a moment. Price picked up the press release from the table in front of him and began reading. Calvin Headley sat in the front row and kept alternating hard intense stares between Drake and Price.

As soon as Price had finished various hands were raised and he pointed to a journalist in the second row. Price cleared his throat and gave a convincing if noncommittal reply to an innocuous question. After the second question from a local reporter Price was getting into a rhythm. Mandy had stopped chewing the top of her biro and had drifted down to the front of the room. She gave Price a brief nod.

'One more question,' Price said.

Calvin Headley had his hand in the air. He almost stood up out of his chair.

Price looked over his head towards the back. 'We'll take one more question from Terry.' He pointed towards an elderly hack with slicked-back hair, yellow with nicotine.

'Is there anything to suggest that both murders are connected?'

Price's reply had been rehearsed well in advance. Once he'd finished Price got up and pushed his chair backwards. As they left, Drake noticed Calvin Headley getting to his feet. 'Inspector Drake, is it true that you suspect there might be a serial killer loose in North Wales?' Drake darted a look at the young reporter. 'Can you reassure the public that they'll be safe in their beds?'

Price was already standing by the door. Mandy gave Drake a troubled look as he walked over towards the exit. 'Leave him to me,' she whispered.

'That went well,' Drake said.

'Mandy had everything organised,' Price said.

Drake's mobile bleeped in his jacket and he fished it out.

'DI Drake.'

It was Winder. 'Something you should see.'

Chapter 13

Gareth Winder was sitting at his desk when Drake strode into the Incident Room. Caren turned towards him, her hand on her mouth, a distressed look in her eyes. Howick stood behind Winder, chewing his lower lip.

'Something you should see on the Internet, boss,' Winder said.

Drake walked over towards him as he clicked refresh. A Facebook page appeared on the screen.

'This went live today,' Winder said.

The words 'Gone Fishing' dominated the title page. Winder then scrolled down before clicking on a photograph – the image of Mostyn's body lying on the sand was clear. It was early morning and there were still faint strands of fog still visible. What turned Drake's stomach was the sight of the fork impaled through Mostyn's neck.

'What the hell?' Drake said.

'Somebody must have been there first thing that morning to have taken these photographs,' Winder said.

'You mean there are more?' Drake said, hoping it wasn't the case.

Winder opened several more in turn. 'He was probably using the zoom on his camera.'

'For Christ's sake. This is one sad individual,' Drake began, until his mind focused. 'So, someone was there that morning. A walker, a cyclist.' Drake stopped abruptly. 'And Jane's body was found by a tourist out riding his mountain bike. We've got his contact details. I need him spoken to tonight. And I need more house-to-house completed near the beach.'

'Tonight?' Howick said.

Drake turned to him. 'Yes. As soon as.'

Nobody said anything for a few seconds. It felt like longer.

'I'll contact Facebook and get them to take down these images,' Drake said.

'It might not be that easy.' Winder sounded tentative.

'What do you mean?'

'They might not be against their rules.'

'The image of a dead body isn't against their rules? Caren, get hold of that cyclist. Dave and Gareth, find some uniformed lads from the local station to interview the householders near the beach. Somebody must have seen something. We need to know about anyone who uses the beach on a regular basis.'

Drake stormed off to his office just as his mobile rang.

'DI Drake.' Immediately Calvin Headley's voice put Drake on edge.

'I've told you not to contact me.'

'Can you give me an update. I was hoping—'

But Drake didn't hear anymore before he cut the call. Drake spent the next two hours getting more and more annoyed with the various Facebook employees who put one obstacle after another in his way. Eventually he found himself speaking to an account manager called Jason – no surname offered – with a North American twang that put Drake more on edge.

'There's nothing we can do, sir,' Jason said, almost apologetically.

'I'm investigating a double murder and the owner of this account clearly has crucial information that could help us.'

'Really sir. I wish I could help, but our rules don't give me any leeway.'

'What's your email address?' Drake said.

Jason hesitated, and then Drake jotted down the details.

It took Drake half an hour to visit the crown prosecutor's office and get the correctly worded warrant issued and emailed to Jason. Caren stood up as he came back into the Incident Room.

'Any luck?' Drake asked.

'The cyclist is back in Birmingham and I've got a DC from West Midlands going to see him.'

He called Sian who sounded vague, as if she didn't care what time he came home or indeed if he did. An hour passed. Drake read more of the statements from the house-to-house enquiries, before tidying the Post-it notes on his desk. He read through those that had already been actioned and then tore them carefully, before discarding them. Eventually he had three different columns of Post-it notes carefully aligned and he felt in charge again.

Eventually he checked his emails and saw a new message from Jason. His pulse thumped as he read the details, hoping that this was the breakthrough they needed. He shouted through at Caren. 'The account holder has an address in Bangor. Let's go.'

He left his room.

Caren was already on her feet.

'There's an address in Bangor. And a name – Osborne,' Drake said. 'Caren, get a couple of the uniformed lads from the local station to meet us there. We'll need stab jackets and batons for everyone. I don't want to take any chances. And I want to catch this bastard.'

Drake hammered the pool car down the A55 for the short journey to Bangor, Winder following behind him. The satnav took them off the A55 and past Penrhyn Castle until they reached the area near the bay. To the right was a new development of waterfront apartments and houses. Drake indicated left as instructed and found himself winding through a maze of narrow streets. He pulled the car onto the pavement a little way down from number eleven.

A minute passed and the car got stuffy, so Drake opened the window slightly. The shouts from children playing nearby in the warmth of the summer evening drifted in. Then the local patrol car arrived and immediately Drake got out and marched over to the front door, while Caren went round the back lane.

The net curtain moved slightly and then there was a shout from inside. Drake thumped on the door again. Nothing. And then it sounded like furniture was being moved inside and then more shouting. Drake fisted a hand and hammered on the door.

'Police. Open up. Now.'

Still the door remained firmly shut. Drake nodded to one of the officers holding a battering ram who steadied himself before swinging at the door. It gave way easily under the force and Drake rushed in.

The smell of cannabis was overpowering. In the first room a girl of around twenty was sitting on a couch. She had long hair parted in the middle and her eyes had a glazed expression. She smiled inanely at Drake. A second room was a bedroom, even though there was not a single square metre of carpet exposed amongst the piles of clothes and junk.

Two uniformed officers had gone upstairs and Drake could hear screams of protest. He went into the kitchen where the smell was stronger and, looking through the window, could see Caren handcuffing a tall thin man with hair to his shoulders and a beard to match.

'Which one of you is Osborne?' Drake said to the three occupants of the house, after they'd sat down in the front room. He was certain that the girl had no idea what was happening as she continued to smile at him in between scratching her face.

'Nobody of that name here, man,' one of the men said.

'Do you know anyone called Osborne?'

'Yeah. The Chancellor of the Exchequer.' The tall man wriggled in his handcuffs.

'And I'm sure the chancellor would want to know what you were flushing down the toilets,' one of the uniformed officers added before handing Drake various papers he'd found.

'It was just for personal use. And, hey, those are private papers. You can't take them.'

'Any computers or laptops?' Drake said to one of the officers, who nodded back.

'And some smartphones.'

'You'll go with these two officers to check your identity and for the time being we're confiscating the laptops and computers, as we suspect they were used for distributing malicious communications.'

It was getting dark by the time Drake stood outside the house with Caren. He flicked through the names in his notebook. There was a John Turville and a Sophie Elsworth and a Jeffrey Kernick, but definitely no Osborne.

The uniformed officers had driven away the occupants. The girl smiled at Drake from the back seat of the patrol car.

Caren looked up at the house number. 'Think it's a wind-up, sir?'

Drake looked at the number eleven and made the connection with Osborne and the current Chancellor of the Exchequer who lived at number eleven Downing Street.

'Of course. Fuck. The bastard.'

Chapter 14

'She's late.'

Price glanced at his watch after reading the briefing note Drake had emailed earlier that morning. He'd tugged at both ear lobes a couple of times and then rubbed his hands together vigorously.

'So, what happened last night?' Price continued, avoiding eye contact.

'House-to-house drew a blank.'

'Of course.' Price read the time again.

'I briefed one of the uniformed officers in Bangor to tell the students in the house that it was all part of a much larger operation against cybercrime and that they should all change the PIN numbers on their bank accounts and change all their important passwords.'

Price straightened his tie.

'The cyclist who found Jane Jones's body was in Birmingham when Mostyn died.'

Price's telephone rang and he grabbed the handset. 'Send her in,' he said, before checking his tie one more time.

The special adviser had a flat, round face, short hair and crystal-clear blue eyes. She wore a black pinstriped jacket over dark navy trousers and, for a woman who Drake guessed was in her forties, a very deep voice. 'Kate French.' She gave Price and Drake a politician's smile.

'Superintendent Price.' Price shook her outstretched hand.

Drake followed suit. She had a handshake to match the heavy make-up. 'Detective Inspector Drake. Pleased to meet you.'

'Let's get started shall we,' Price said. 'I'm sure we all have a lot to do.'

French sat down and turned to Price. 'You must think my presence is a little odd and probably unwelcome.'

She hesitated just long enough to give them an opportunity to disagree. They didn't.

'I have a role that involves coordinating policy between the governments of Wales and Westminster in the energy field. As you may know, there's a lot of conflict between the various political factions and my job is to ensure that things go *smoothly*. The recent death of Ed Mostyn is a concern, of course.' She corrected herself soon enough. 'And tragic for his family. His decision not to sell the land caused some problems. And the government, both governments, want to ensure that nothing prevents the development proceeding.'

'And the investigation is a potential problem? It could hold things up for months, maybe longer,' Drake said.

'While the proper course of events must take place and the investigation must leave no stone unturned, there is a certain *political* dimension to all of this.' She pitched her head to one side and looked at Drake. Her eyes said, *we're all in this together, aren't we?*

'Political dimension?' Drake said.

Price added, 'Kate, I'm sure that you want us to do our job without any interference.'

'Of course. Of course.'

'But you're hoping that the investigation can be completed as expeditiously as possible, thereby enabling the power company to proceed with its final land acquisition and removing any political dimension to the case.'

A masterly display of diplomatic civil service double-talk, Drake thought, rather surprised that Price had managed it without any show of emotion.

French blinked. 'I'm sure I can rely on you, Wyndham.'

By the end of an hour that had seen the best coffee served in china cups and some expensive-looking biscuits, French made her excuses and left, telling them both that she was visiting her elderly mother in a nursing home along the coast.

Price and Drake showed her to the main reception. They watched as she left. Price turned to Drake. 'That was a lot of fucking bullshit. Now we've got some spineless politician breathing down our neck.'

Drake swerved around some cuttings that had fallen on the tree-lined drive up to Crecrist Hall. A couple of hard-hatted tree surgeons hung from high branches, chainsaws hanging from straps. The drive had seen better times; the edges were crumbling and Drake had to keep a careful eye out for holes.

The road opened onto a circular parking area of fine gravel with a small ornamental pond in the middle, the tyres of the Alfa making a soft grinding noise. He parked near the main entrance.

The morning's newspaper was open at the Sudoku page on the passenger seat – he'd managed ten minutes on the puzzle first thing that morning, always had to be ten minutes. Any less and he'd feel cheated, any longer and he'd feel that he was cheating the WPS. Crecrist Hall had five Georgian windows on the first floor and four on the ground floor, two either side of the front door, its surface glistening from the recently applied gloss paint. He pulled the doorbell and listened for movement inside. Eventually he heard footsteps echoing through the hallway. The door creaked open. A man about the same height as Drake but several inches more around the waist stood in the doorway. He wore a long-sleeved pink shirt with a yellow cravat, the sort that Drake had only ever seen in period dramas on the television. His paunch quivered over the waistband of a pair of red moleskin trousers, held in place by a thick leather belt. After the first glance Drake had decided that de Northway was an impressive caricature of an English toff.

'Somerset de Northway?' Drake said.

'And who are you?'

Drake flashed his warrant card. De Northway pitched his head up slightly and peered at the card.

'I'm investigating the deaths of Ed Mostyn and Jane Jones.'

De Northway lowered his head and gave Drake a long, hard stare.

'May I come in and discuss the case?'

After a moment's hesitation, de Northway pushed open the door. 'Of course you may.'

The hallway was wide enough to hold a ceili and the supporting band. A couple of tapestries hung from high picture rails, but what struck Drake was the smell of slow decay that hung in the air. By a door in one corner Dafydd Higham stood, carrying a leather case in one hand. He gave Drake a hesitant smile.

'Good morning,' Higham said.

'Dafydd does the accounts for us,' de Northway said. He turned to Higham. 'Dafydd.' It came out like *Davyd* and the mispronunciation grated on Drake. 'Go and wait in the breakfast room.'

'We'll use the morning room,' de Northway said over his shoulder, as Drake followed him.

A large empty fireplace stood centre stage in the room, its surround populated with various companion sets that were very much in need of a polish.

'How can I help?' De Northway waved a hand over the sofas, as if it was beneath him to invite Drake to sit down. A long cord hung down by the side of the mantelpiece and Drake could imagine de Northway pulling it and waiting for a servant to appear, but his fortunes clearly didn't stretch to the indulgences his ancestors had enjoyed. And Drake guessed this was a disappointment to his host.

Drake sat down, de Northway opposite him. Drake noticed a hole in his shoe and the ragged seam on the turn-up of his trousers.

'I understand you were in the post office very early on the morning Mostyn was found.'

De Northway peered at Drake. 'Early riser. Always have been, ever since my days in the army.'

'What time do you get down to the post office?'

'It was just after six-thirty. I like to support the local shop. In fact I like to support as many local Welsh businesses as I can. I think it helps.'

'Did you see anyone?'

'Not a soul. Nobody much up at that time of the morning.'

'And what did you do?'

'Went to the shop but the place was deserted. I shouted for Hughes but the man didn't reply. So I picked up my *Telegraph* and then drove back here. I checked the livestock in the bottom field and spoke to the farm manager; then I had breakfast. Do you want to know what I had to eat?'

Drake stopped jotting in his pocket book and looked at de Northway, trying to fathom out whether he was being deliberately awkward.

'How well did you know Ed Mostyn?'

De Northway averted his eyes. 'Everyone knew him. He had lived in the village as man and boy.'

'I understand that he was a tenant of yours.'

'Is that a question?'

Drake squeezed the biro a little tighter. 'He was only paying a low rent for the cottage—'

'Look, if you're suggesting—'

'I'm not suggesting anything. I just want information.'

'Yes. Ed was a tenant of mine. He paid a peppercorn rent, but he had to maintain the property. When he took the place it was a wreck. Nothing really but walls and a rotten roof. He practically rebuilt it.'

'So what happens now?'

De Northway slanted his head again as if he was silently rebuking Drake, like a head teacher with a pupil who really ought to know better. 'The tenancy comes to an end.'

'So you get the property back.'

De Northway nodded.

'It must be very valuable then,' Drake said.

'That's a minor consideration. Ed is dead. It is a most fearfully sad business.'

'Do you own a lot of land?'

The question earned Drake another dark look.

'My family have been in Anglesey for four centuries.'

Drake felt like saying *and what good has that done?* 'Do you own the cottages near the sea where Jane Jones's body was found?'

De Northway sat back in the sofa and narrowed his eyes. 'Yes. We do. They're in a pretty bad state of repair. We did try to get consent to convert them years ago, but there were problems with access. One of them is let out to a local environmentalist charity.'

'And the others?'

'Empty.'

'Do you have keys?'

'Somewhere.'

'I'll need you to find them for me before I leave.'

'I'll try.'

'And you own the farm where Jane lived.'

'The family owns a number of farms which are all tenanted. All on a proper commercial basis. I hope you're not linking me to Jane's death because I own the farm where she lived.'

'I'm only trying to establish the facts. It's very early in the investigation.'

'Then I think your line of questioning is preposterous. I've been living in the community for all my life.'

And you still can't pronounce Welsh Christian names.

'The two recent deaths are as yet unexplained. Whether you like it or not I'm going to be asking a lot of questions. About a lot of people. And you happen to be linked to both victims.'

De Northway pursed his lips and gave Drake a sullen stare.

'Where were you on the night Jane Jones was killed?'

'I was here. My wife was poorly. I went to bed early.'

De Northway got up and glared at Drake as though he was daring him to ask another question.

'I'll need the keys,' Drake said.

De Northway left him without saying a word. Drake walked around the room. The curtains were frayed, the wallpaper yellow with age. No money had been spent on the place for many years and Drake wondered if the de Northways were really as wealthy as everyone imagined. On a round table were various family photographs and one of de Northway with Maldwyn Evans, Rhys Fairburn, and another man, that Drake thought he recognised, all looking much younger, beaming at the camera. It was similar to the one they'd found in Mostyn's cottage and then Drake at once knew that de Northway was the man they hadn't been able to identify in that photograph.

Eventually de Northway returned and, after giving Drake the keys, showed him to the front door, which closed with a loud thud behind him.

He walked over to his car, hoping he had enough on de Northway to make him a formal suspect. As he pointed his remote at the car, his mobile buzzed in his pocket and he saw the name of Dr Lee Kings.

'Ian, just thought you should know – Jane Jones was pregnant when she died.'

Caren sat next to Drake on a large L-shaped leather sofa. A couple of the panels of a wide expanse of tall folding windows were open, allowing a warm breeze to tug at the voile draped at the far end.The room overlooked a long beach flanked by dunes that stretched for miles out to the west. Small rocky islands jutted out of the surface of the sea and children with small dinghies and inflatables gathered at the water's edge. A couple of jet skis powered across the bay. A chilled glass of Pinot Grigio would make it perfect, Caren thought.

Julian Sandham had a pronounced Adam's apple and having to face two police officers on his own meant it was racing up and down his neck. Drake had been less tactful than usual as he dismissed the pleas from Julian's parents that they should be present when their son was interviewed.

Drake began. 'Let's start at the beginning. How long have you known Jane?'

'Three years. We always come to Rhosneigr for holidays in the summer. My mum thinks the place is *wonderful.*'

It was the second time that morning that he'd heard the mispronunciation of a Welsh word and he wondered whether Sandham had any real idea how he should pronounce the name of the village.

'Jane was fifteen then. And how old were you?'

'Sixteen.'

'Where did you meet?'

'At that place in the village. They have barbecues and parties in the summer. It's about the only place to go. Otherwise it's drinking on the beach or in some of the pubs, but then the local boys don't like us. She was just beautiful and so gentle.'

Caren wasn't going be the one to shatter Julian's image of Jane.

'That first summer we went swimming and we went sailing over the bay. We had picnics on the sand.'

'Did you go to the cottages near the pool where we found her body?'

Julian's head sank. 'Yes.'

'Did you have sex with her there?'

'Yes,' Julian spoke softly.

'And how did you get inside?'

'She knew where to find the keys. She said it was a special place and that it was her secret. And that I shouldn't tell anyone about it and that if we were caught then the owner would be sure to complain to the police. And that we'd be charged with burglary.'

'Which cottage was it?'

'We went swimming at night in that pool. We left our clothes on the sand.'

'Was it the middle cottage?'

Julian looked up at Drake. 'Yes, I think it was. It was the only one with any furniture.'

'Furniture?'

'Chairs and some cupboards and a bed.'

'Was it kept tidy?'

Julian gave Drake a puzzled look.

'You know, was it dirty or clean?'

'Clean, I suppose.'

'Tell me about the last time you saw Jane?'

Julian sat up on the sofa. 'It was Sunday. We'd arranged to meet. She was frightened of something but she wouldn't tell me. She was going to leave Anglesey and come and live with me in Birmingham. I was going to get a job and leave university. I …'

'Where did you see her?'

'On the beach … We …'

'What time was that?'

'I don't know.'

'Did you go the cottages that night?'

'No. She was going home. But she said she had something important to do.'

'Did she say what?'

Sandham shook his head.

'Did she talk about her family?'

Sandham managed a haunted look. 'There was something odd there. She didn't like her dad or her mum really. But she hadn't been herself in the last couple of months. I thought she was seeing someone else.'

'Were you jealous?'

'I just wanted to be with her.'

'Did you know she was pregnant?'

Caren saw the sadness in his face. There was something helpless there too. Drake had told her when they'd arrived at the house about his call from Kings and Caren had been surprised by the news.

'She didn't tell me. Why didn't she tell me …?'

'Did she tell you there was someone else in her life?'

Sandham brushed away tears. 'No, but

sometimes she didn't answer my messages and then she wouldn't answer the telephone.'

'Do you know Ed Mostyn?'

Julian's head sagged again.

'He was killed three days before Jane. His body was found on the mud near the bridge at Four Mile Bridge.'

Julian was nodding his head now. 'I know. I know. I didn't arrive in Rhosneigr until the day after.'

'Where were you?'

'At home in Birmingham.'

His alibi would have to be checked, but Caren had seen innocent men often enough to know that Julian hadn't killed Ed Mostyn. But Jane Jones? In a fit of temper ... Maybe.

Drake stood up and made to leave. Caren did the same and once they were outside she could smell the salt in the air and the sound of children's laughter drifting up from the beach.

'Organise for an officer to take his DNA,' Drake said as his mobile rang.

He rolled his eyes at Caren as he listened to the message.

'There's been a disturbance at Tyddyn Du. The local sergeant wants me to attend. I'll see you back at headquarters.'

Chapter 15

A patrol car was parked by the rear door of Tyddyn Du. Drake and Caren pulled up next to two other cars parked on a piece of gravel.

He strode up to the house and noticed Gwynfor Llywelyn sitting in the rear seat of the patrol car, his face a dirty grey colour, his eyes bloodshot. Drake recognised the uniformed sergeant from the scene of Mostyn's murder.

'The family's pretty upset, sir.'

'What happened?'

'Llywelyn arrived an hour ago. Off his head on something – booze and drugs at a guess. Kept shouting at the family that they'd killed Jane and that they were all evil. He was going to see them rot in hell. All that sort of stuff.'

'And has anyone been hurt?'

'No. They locked the house and he just kept raving outside.'

'Who's inside?'

'Mr and Mrs Jones and the local minister.'

Drake stepped up to the door, Caren following behind him. The parlour still had the same melancholic air that Drake recalled from his previous visits. Mildred was sitting quite separate from Ray on the couch. A tall man wearing a dog collar and an old black suit stood up. He had a noticeable stoop and he stretched out his hand. 'Reverend John Milburn.'

Drake shook his hand and noticed the man's intense stare.

Caren sat down on a chair near Mildred. 'It must have been very distressing Mrs Jones.'

She opened her mouth but said nothing, a bewildered look on her face.

Sergeant Watkins cleared his throat behind

Drake. 'I'm going to take Gwynfor Llywelyn to the station.'

Drake looked over at Ray and then Mildred. 'I'm sure you'll want to make a complaint about what happened.'

Ray shook his head slowly. 'We're fine, thank you.'

'It will be no trouble to take a statement.'

Mildred made a brief sobbing sound, as Ray Jones looked over Drake's shoulder before shaking his head again. Drake saw the troubled look on Caren's face.

'I'll go and talk to him,' Drake said.

He was followed through into the kitchen and then out through the back door by Milburn.

'I'm sure you must find this attitude very frustrating,' Milburn said quietly.

'I don't see what the problem is.'

'They are a very private family. Any invasion of their privacy is unwelcome. Ray is particularly old-fashioned and he's … how can I put this? Not the easiest of men. He has a very Calvinistic outlook – clear and positive about the right behaviour.'

Drake walked towards the car.

'Llywelyn can cool off in the police cells overnight.'

He yanked open the car door and looked in at Llywelyn, who swivelled his head around slowly. He moved to the edge of the rear seat and then leant forward, putting his head out of the car as he made a loud belching noise before vomiting all over the ground. Drake jumped out of the way a fraction too late, as bits of sick grazed his shoes.

The following morning Drake sat at the kitchen table as

breakfast happened all around him. Sian complained that he was miles away and glared when he ignored her requests to empty the dishwasher. He left the house and Sian gave him another wintry look that turned arctic when he said that he couldn't tell her when he'd be home that evening.

Headquarters was oddly busy, despite the fact that it was the height of summer. He navigated around three men delivering a new photocopying machine and headed for the stairs. The door of the Incident Room banged against the wall as he pushed it too hard. Winder and Howick looked startled as he walked in.

'Morning, boss,' Winder said. Drake heard Howick mumble something.

Drake headed for his office, where he booted up his computer. A text that morning had warned him to expect the full post mortem report on Jane Jones. Once he'd finished reading it he sat back and speculated who the father was and whether her family knew. His concentration was interrupted as he noticed Caren passing the door to his office. He rose and strode out.

Drake stood by the board, looking at the photograph of Jane Jones. 'I've just read her post mortem. She was three months pregnant when she died.'

'So we've got a father to trace,' Caren said.

Drake turned his back to the board. 'The CSIs are doing a DNA search. In the meantime,' Drake looked at Winder and Howick, 'I need you to concentrate on de Northway. He has the perfect motive for Mostyn's death. The house that he occupies is tenanted on a low rent and after his death de Northway gets the property back.'

'What about Jane Jones?' Howick said.

'De Northway owns the farm that her family

occupy ...'

Caren drew a hand through her mass of unruly hair. 'It's not enough to make a link.'

'And he owns the cottages near where she died.'

'Coincidences do happen,' Winder said.

'I don't like coincidences,' Drake said. 'And, Dave.' He turned to glare at Howick. 'I need results from Jane Jones's telephone.'

Howick gave an embarrassed look and averted his eyes down to his feet. 'Slow progress, boss.'

'Make it quicker,' Drake said, turning to Caren. 'Ready?'

From the car park of headquarters it was a short drive down to the A55, and once Drake was onto the dual carriageway he accelerated westward, passing caravans and trailers and motor homes heading for Snowdonia and the holiday destinations of Anglesey.

It was a journey of forty minutes to reach the police station in Llangefni in the middle of Anglesey. Drake drew up beside the barrier, buzzed the intercom and waited for the barrier to lift clear.

After parking he stood by the door, waiting for it to be opened, staring down at his clean shoes. The unlucky pair from yesterday had been cleaned, polished and stored away. There was a loud clunking noise as the door opened.

Drake peered through the small opening in the cell door at Gwynfor Llywelyn lying on the narrow bed, a grey blanket curled up at his feet. The custody sergeant drew out a handful of keys and heaved open the door. Drake led Llywelyn to an interview room.

'Don't I need a solicitor or something?' Drake could smell Llywelyn's rancid breath across the table.

'This isn't an interview under caution.'

'Why not?'Llywelyn put a hand to his mouth and pulled a face. He sipped some water.

'You're lucky. The Jones's haven't made a complaint.'

Drake couldn't make out the reaction on his face. It was surprise mixed with incredulity. 'But I still want to know why you were there?'

'They killed Jane. They're all weird, her father especially. She was terrified of him. He stared at her if he was angry and then said nothing for days. And her brother was a pervert. She complained that he'd be creeping around the house and be spying on her. I caught him once, when we were by the cottages swimming at night, just standing there, staring.'

'Going to the house isn't going to bring her back.'

Llywelyn was rubbing his temples.

"How long did you go out with Jane?'

'Almost a year.'

'Why did you finish?'

'She said I was too serious for her.'

'Is that true?'

Drake hesitated for a moment. He gave Llywelyn an intense look, wanting to gauge how he'd react. 'Did you know that Jane was pregnant?'

Llywelyn couldn't feign the surprise and pained expression. 'I had no idea,' he said, adding, 'She wanted to be with that English boy.'

'How did you feel?'

A muscle pulsed in Llywelyn's jaw and his eyes narrowed.

'Does this mean I can go?'

'One more thing. I need confirmation of your whereabouts on the night Jane died.'

'You cannot be serious.' Then the words tumbled out. 'I was at home. It was Sunday. I loved her. I would never have killed her.' His eyes filled with tears. 'I wanted her back.'

Chapter 16

Over a week had passed since the start of the investigation and Gareth Winder was pleased with himself for having got into work early every morning. His usual pattern of regular Internet gaming, often until the small hours, had been modified by the arrival of a new girlfriend and there'd been comments from Howick and Caren that he was looking healthier.

Once Drake had left that morning Winder sat back in his chair and looked over at Howick. He doubted that he'd ever want the promotion that Howick craved. Only another twenty-two years until he could draw a pension. He'd have all the time in the world then to play games and chill out. Howick was wearing a white shirt and a sombre blue tie. Winder glanced down at his own clothes and wondered if a smart appearance was the secret to passing the sergeant's exams. He hadn't worn a tie for months, or a suit come to that, and he was just coming to terms with the changes to his normal lifestyle that had meant less time checking Facebook every spare moment and having to think about the routine of a new girlfriend.

Jenny worked in the local council offices and kept pestering Winder with suggestions that she wanted to meet Howick and his work colleagues. She had given him a puzzled look as he explained the intricacies of the hierarchy in the Wales Police Service, before telling her that he couldn't imagine socialising with Inspector Drake. Maybe he'd suggest doing something with Howick and his wife.

Howick turned to look over at him. 'Busy Gareth?'

'Contemplating where to start.'

'At the beginning.'

'Very funny.'

Winder got up and walked over to the board. The image of Ed Mostyn had been enlarged and the puncture wounds on his neck made him look like an extra from a horror movie. Caren had pinned up an image of Jane Jones and Winder could see how she would have turned heads.

'So, what's the connection?' Winder wasn't expecting Howick to reply.

Howick's chair squeaked as it moved over the hard floor surface. Winder looked over at his colleague. Howick stared over at him, arms folded.

'Whoever killed Mostyn had a motive to kill Jane.'

Howick said nothing.

Winder had gathered momentum. 'And if Jane Jones was killed by this Somerset de Northway character, then what would be his motive? Maybe he was shagging Jane and Mostyn finds out and tries to blackmail him.'

'So he whacks him?'

'Dead right. Top of the class – *Sergeant* Howick.'

'So what would be his motive to kill Jane Jones?'

Winder hesitated. 'That's where …'

'He wouldn't kill Jane, his lover, unless she was trying to blackmail him too.' Howick stood up and walked over to Winder. 'And he admits to being around at the time of Mostyn's death.'

Winder returned to his desk. Howick was already staring at the screen. Winder glanced back at the board, pondering if Drake really was right to pursue de Northway. Winder had heard the name high sheriff and had a vague recollection of seeing photographs in the local newspapers of events where the name had been printed alongside the image of a well-fed man beaming at the camera. The morning passed quickly as he surfed through the various Google entries for the ancient role of high sheriff. Winder had dismissed this sort of pomp as a relic from history but as he searched he found frequent references to the present incumbent, a former diplomat who'd been posted to the US and then the UN before returning with a knighthood to the family home in a quiet corner of Snowdonia. De Northway stood alongside him in several photographs.

'De Northway seems well connected,' Winder announced, when Howick returned from the kitchen with two mugs of coffee.

Winder would have happily demolished a pastry with his coffee but Jenny had suggested he needed to watch his weight.

'Do you know what a high sheriff does?'

Howick sipped his mug and then shook his head.

'He or she is the queen's judicial representative in a county.'

'Bit like a governor general for a Commonwealth country.' Howick looked suitably intelligent.

'No.' Winder paused before correcting his friend. 'The queen's representative is the lord lieutenant.'

'So what does the high sheriff actually do?'

'He supports the judiciary and the emergency services in the county. And there's probably a lot of fancy dinners where they dress up in breeches and lace.'

'And de Northway is the deputy this year?'

Winder blew on the surface of his drink and then took a mouthful. 'De Northway will be the high sheriff next year. He'll get to meet all the local judges and the chief constable and the ACC in charge of

Northern Division and Super Price and—'

'So he's bomb-proof.'

'There was an article in one of the local papers a couple of years ago about the de Northway family. You know, the usual sort of stuff about their history and how far back they go.'

Howick had been back and forth to the forensics department during the morning until he'd announced that he had enough to work on in compiling a list of Jane's friends and contacts. He finished his drink and stood up, gathered his papers together and fished his jacket off the chair. 'I'm going to see one of Jane's ex-boyfriends. Maybe he'll have something constructive to tell me.'

Winder watched as Howick left the Incident Room. The website of the High Sheriff of England and Wales was one of the tabs open on the screen along the top of the browser and Winder clicked the one with the references from local newspapers. He found the names of various local historians who had commented about the de Northway family.

His mobile buzzed into life and he smiled as he read the message from Jenny suggesting they meet for lunch. Perhaps there was something to this sort of domesticity, Winder thought. He decided that he'd spend another half an hour on the Google search so he texted Jenny back – *forty-five minutes, usual place?x.*

He skimmed over the names of people working for the de Northway family, and disregarded the details of a book that had been published about them and their involvement in the abdication crisis of 1936 and, when his mobile warned him of another message from Jenny, he completely ignored references to Crecrist Enterprises.

As Howick drove towards the first address on his list, his mind wasn't on the deaths of Jane Jones or Ed Mostyn. He kept thinking that there must be some reason why the results of the sergeant's exams hadn't been published. All sorts of alternative scenarios were playing on his mind – but the worst always assumed that he'd failed and that the conversation with Drake afterwards would suggest that he should be looking elsewhere to pursue his career and that his talents weren't suited to CID.

He shuddered at the prospect of uniformed work in Wrexham or Rhyl, policing the pubs and clubs at closing time, hauling drunks into cells and chasing petty thieves. He pressed the accelerator a little harder. Then he noticed his speed and slowed. He'd have to make his mark: even if he failed, he would still want to stay in CID.

The satnav warned him that he needed to take the next junction. After negotiating his way through various villages he eventually parked in the forecourt of a garage. He left the car and walked over towards the ramps, where two men were working on an old Ford.

Howick carded both men, who gave him lazy, disinterested looks. 'Either of you Aled Williams?'

One of the men nodded towards the office. 'He's on his break.'

Howick pushed open the door. A woman gave him a toothy grin.

'I want to speak to Aled.'

'Aled,' she shouted down the corridor behind her. A door slightly ajar opened and a tall man with a shock of blond hair emerged. He was wearing a one-piece suit smeared in oil and grease.

Once Howick had shown him his card Aled relaxed.

'Is there somewhere we can talk?'

Aled motioned to the room he'd just left. Inside, another man – mid-fifties, greying hair and spreading paunch – was scanning the sports pages of a tabloid. He left when Aled said something in Welsh.

'I'm investigating the death of Jane Jones. You were her boyfriend at one time. How long did you go out with her?'

'Not long. I realised quickly enough what she was like.' Aled had a strong Anglesey accent.

'What do you mean?'

'All over me one minute. Especially if it was in winter when the rich visitors weren't here.'

'Did you meet her family?'

'Once or twice. They were odd too. I never could work out what her father was like. He'd stare at me as though I wasn't there. Weirdo if you ask me.'

The door burst open and two mechanics appeared, but left when Aled said something in a tone of voice that clearly meant they weren't welcome.

'You should go and talk to my Auntie Vera. She can tell you a lot about the family. Stuff nobody else knows. Look, I liked Jane. But she was bad news. She was playing every man she could get. I'd heard she had an English boyfriend. One of those rich families in Rhosneigr.'

'Where can I find Auntie Vera?' Howick's interest was piqued.

Without a postcode for the satnav Howick had to rely on the directions that Aled had given him. Howick had to reverse down narrow country lanes a couple of times on his way to the cottage where Vera Fraser lived. A small purple car was parked outside the garage alongside the house and there were neat flowerpots either side of the front door.

Howick heard the sound of chimes once he pushed the doorbell and moments later a woman appeared.

'Mrs Fraser?' Howick held out his card. 'I'm calling about Jane Jones. Aled Williams told me you might be able to help.'

It was difficult to guess the woman's age. Howick had expected someone in her mid-fifties from the implication in Aled's description. But Vera had few wrinkles and she was slim, neatly dressed and had lively, clear turquoise eyes.

'I don't know how I can help.'

'Aled thought you might know something about the family background.'

Vera ushered Howick into the house and he followed her into the small living room. It was perfectly decorated with pastel shades on the curtains and wallpaper to match.

'Aled told me that you might know something about Jane's family.'

'I was in school with Mildred. She had a difficult time of things when she was a girl. She lost her own mother when she was young – twelve, I think. And then she got in with Ray. I didn't think he was right for her. He was too like her father, overbearing and old-fashioned.'

'He's a lot older than her.'

Vera nodded. 'Well, she had Ellen and Huw when she was quite young. He's a strange one. Have you met him?'

'No.'

Vera settled back in her chair, as if it pleased her that Howick hadn't met Huw Jones. 'Well, Mildred left Ray when Ellen and Huw were young.'

Howick wasn't certain where the conversation was going but he doubted that he had the time to spend listening to the Jones family saga.

'Mildred had a pretty bad time of things with Ray.'

'He was violent?'

'I can't be certain, but she was frightened of him.'

'What happened that made her go back to him?'

'She became pregnant.'

At first it didn't sink in for Howick. 'So ...'

'Ray wasn't the father.'

'But why did she go back to him?'

'She had three children to raise. She didn't have a home. And he promised to change.'

Chapter 17

Drake found his way through the country lanes towards the cottages and parked near a small van. From the glove compartment Caren reached for the keys that de Northway had given Drake the week before. As they stepped out of the air-conditioned car Drake squinted at the sun reflecting off the sand. He loosened his tie and folded back the cuffs of his shirt.

It was a bright, clear day with the forecasters promising more warm sunshine well into September. He pushed a pair of sunglasses to the top of his nose. His shoes sank into the soft sand as he left the shingle and gravel of the car park. He laboured down towards the cottages. Caren took a few steps down the beach, but Drake stood, watching the sand stretch out in front of him. The pool looked wider now that the tide was in and he took a couple of steps towards the water. He contemplated taking off his shoes and paddling. The pungent smell of seaweed hung in the air.

He leant down and scooped up a handful of sand. He let it cascade through his fingers, watching the grains disappear back onto the beach. His thoughts turned to the investigation. There was still nothing to link the deaths together and if Drake couldn't get some hard evidence established, he was aware that each death may well end up being investigated separately – maybe even by different teams.

The cottage door opened easily once he'd found the knack of adjusting the key in the lock. Inside, the thick walls kept the cottages cool. How had the last occupants made a living, Drake wondered. A chimney breast dominated the room, but the fireplace had been brushed clean. Two old chairs had been pushed against one wall alongside an old, very scratched table. In one corner a narrow door was slightly ajar and

Drake could see the dark staircase beyond. Another door at the far end was firmly closed. The place had a damp smell. Caren kicked at the remains of the fire.

'I wonder when there was a fire here last?' she said.

Drake peered up the wooden staircase and beckoned her to follow. A small landing led into a bedroom at the rear of the cottage. It was clean and a lavender smell hung in the air, as though an entire can of air freshener had been emptied. A wooden bed dominated the room, but any mattress had long since disappeared. He stepped carefully back down the staircase, Caren following behind. It must have been a hard existence for a family living in such a place, Drake thought, recalling the simplicity of his grandparents' home. Through the door at the rear was the back kitchen. He pulled open the wall cupboards and gazed into empty shelves. Hoping that he hadn't wasted time, his train of thought was disturbed by the sound of movement from next door. He exchanged an inquisitive look with Caren.

After pulling the door closed behind them, they walked over to the adjacent cottage and nudged open the door that was already ajar.

'Hello?' Drake said.

A woman's voice replied. 'Who is it?'

A slim girl in her thirties, with thick red hair that cascaded over her shoulders, emerged from the back door.

Drake had his warrant card ready. 'Detective Inspector Drake. I'm investigating the deaths of Ed Mostyn and Jane Jones. This is Detective Sergeant Waits.'

'Rhiannon Owen.'

Inside, there were notice boards against all the walls with diagrams and illustrations and photographs of various birds. Tables covered with piles of paper and glossy folders lined the room. And, it was clean.

'Are you here every day?' Drake said.

'No. I'm one of the project officers for the Anglesey Environmental and Wildlife Trust. We've got a contract to monitor the wildlife along the coast.'

'How often do you visit the cottage then?'

'It depends. A few times a week.'

'Did you know Jane Jones?'

'No, but I saw her pictures in the paper.'

Owen read the time on her watch. 'I've got a group of students coming for a seminar. And ...'

'Does anyone else use the cottages?'

'I don't know, they all belong to the de Northway family.'

Owen had avoided any eye contact.

'Do you get on with Somerset de Northway?'

Owen gave him a sharp look. 'What do you mean?'

Drake moved towards the young woman, sensing uneasiness in her eyes. 'Well, he's quite a character.'

'He can be a difficult person.'

Drake's interest was aroused, so he stared at Owen. 'Do you have a lot to do with him?'

'As little as possible.'

Drake drew a hand over some of the folders on the table. 'You don't get on with him.'

'At the start, when we first had the contract, he'd make excuses about visiting when he knew I was here. Every time, he'd make suggestions that got more explicit. Until I reported him to my boss. Nothing happened of course, but de Northway stopped calling. He must have got the message.'

'What sort of *suggestions*?'

'He'd ask about my social life, did I have a

141

boyfriend, was I married.'

'How long did it go on for?'

'I can't remember. Then he asked how many boyfriends I'd had. And it all got very repulsive.'

She folded her arms together.

'Did you ever notice anyone in the other cottages?' Caren asked.

Owen straightened. 'I had to come back one night. I'd forgotten my laptop charger. And there was a light in the next door cottage and the sound of music playing, and voices.'

'What sort of voices?'

'There was a lot of giggling and laughing.'

'Did you see who it was?'

'No. And I didn't stay around.'

'When was that?'

'A year ago, maybe.'

Owen looked at her watch.

'When did you see de Northway last?' Drake said.

'This week.'

'What … I mean, when?'

'The day after Jane's death. He was moving stuff out of next door. I stayed in here until he was finished.' She gave a small shudder at the memory.

They left Owen and stepped out into the sunshine just as they heard young voices approaching along the sand.

Chapter 18

Drake made a concession to the informalities of working on a Saturday by not wearing a tie. His shirt had wide blue stripes and single cuffs. Sian's insistence that they had to talk privately, without the girls in the house, had filled him with an apprehension that focusing on work only partly obliterated.

When he returned to the Incident Room Caren had arrived. She had her hair in a tight knot behind her head. Her smart white blouse caught Drake's attention, it looked new or newly ironed certainly and was a welcome change from her usually crumpled appearance. Her jeans looked clean and she wore sensible flat-soled shoes. Winder sat alongside Caren, his feet on the desk, chewing something sweet judging from the sugar covering his lips. Howick straightened his loosened tie a fraction.

Drake moved the photographs of Mostyn and Jane together and stood back.

'Do you think they're connected?' Howick asked.

'Everyone is connected to each other in Anglesey, if you ask me,' Winder said, dabbing the forefinger of one hand on his lips.

'We keep an open mind,' Drake said. 'We haven't found anything yet to connect them.' He turned back to the board. Underneath Ed Mostyn were the photographs of Maldwyn Evans and Rhys Fairburn. He peered at them. 'They've both got perfect motives to kill Mostyn.'

'And their wives give them alibis,' Howick said.

'And then we have Somerset de Northway who keeps appearing on the scene,' Drake added.

To one side of Jane's image was the name 'Tracy' printed on an A4 sheet alongside the name

---

'Julian Sandham'. They were individuals from very different backgrounds, but the suspicion grew that each was hiding something.

Along the bottom of the board were thumbnail images of the items found near Ed Mostyn. They still had to find out who they belonged to and they still needed more intelligence on Evans and Fairburn and as this thought process developed the first edge of desperation sharpened in Drake's mind.

'Mostyn and Jane Jones,' Drake said out loud. 'We haven't got any details about Mostyn's friends. And I suggest you call Dafydd Higham – he did Mostyn's accounts so he's bound to know if he had a laptop. Mostyn must have gone to the pub sometime or done something. Gareth, go and talk to Richie Mostyn again. He was Ed's uncle and they lived near each other so he might be able to identify if the items the search team found belonged to Ed. And talk to John Hughes in the post office again. He likes the sound of his own voice.'

Drake looked over at Howick. 'Do some digging around into Maldwyn Evans. And then get finished on going through Jane's old mobile. And why would she keep an old mobile telephone?'

Nobody said anything.

'Let's go and see Tracy again,' Drake said to Caren.

It took them longer than Drake expected to reach the small housing estate. Three boys were playing football in the street, but they stopped and gaped at Drake and Caren as they parked and got out of the car. They walked over to the front door and Drake pressed the bell. A few seconds passed before the door opened. Tracy looked older somehow, her skin a mellow grey;

her eyes blinked hurriedly and she looked troubled.

'We need to ask you some more questions,' Drake said.

She stared over his shoulder towards the children before letting them in. She took them into the living room and stood, moving her weight from one leg to another while chewing the nail of the index finger of her right hand.

'Can we sit down?' Drake had already decided that a charm overload was needed, however difficult he may find it.

It was only after Drake and Caren had settled into the sofa that Tracy perched herself on the edge of a chair. Drake surveyed the crowded mantelpiece and cupboards, silently impressed that everything had such order.

'We've spoken to Julian Sandham,' Drake said. 'Had Jane told you about her plans?'

Tracy nodded. Drake waited.

'That Sunday night she was killed ...She was different – happy I suppose.'

'What time did you see her last?'

'I can't remember ... But it was late. I saw her arguing with her brother.'

Drake interrupted, his tone a shade too sharp. 'Her brother was there?'

'He's a right creep.' She shivered and ran her fingers up her forearms at the memory. 'Sometimes we'd go swimming by the cottages. And he would be there – hanging around.'

It might be nothing, but Drake recalled the statement from Huw that he'd last seen Jane at Tyddyn Du.

'She had savings that she bragged about. She was going away with him. She and Julian would have more than enough money, at least that's what she said.'

'Was she going somewhere on the night she was killed?'

Tracy shook her head, too quickly.

'Julian has told us she was afraid of something. He'd been very concerned about her. Do you know what that could be?'

Tracy shook her head in short movements, like a small child in trouble. Drake leant forward slightly. 'You know that Jane was pregnant, don't you?'

Tracy spluttered. 'Yes.'

Caren made her first contribution. 'Do you know who the father was?'

'She never told me...'

'Do you have an idea?'

Tracy shrugged.

Drake continued. 'It's very important that we try and find out what was happening in Jane's life. I'm sure there's more that you know that might help us find the person who killed her. Julian said that they regularly went to the cottages near where they found her body. Is that true?'

'Suppose.'

'What went on there, Tracy? Was Jane being harmed at all?'

Tracy looked over at him, her eyes wide. Drake gave a smile of reassurance. 'Who was harming Jane? Was it Mostyn or somebody else? If there was something going on, we need to know so it won't happen again.'

'It was supposed to be a secret.' Tracy swallowed hard.

'Tell me what was going on.' Drake kept his voice soft.

'It was the parties at the cottages a few years ago.' She was grasping her hands together. 'They

146

made us do things.' Tracy looked down at her feet.

Drake darted a glance at Caren – she frowned an encouragement.

'How old were you?'

'Fifteen.'

'Was it just you and Jane?'

'Sometimes Becky and Sue...'

'Do you have the contact details for both girls? I'll need their full names.'

'I might have Becky's mobile number.'

Drake continued. 'And who were the men involved?'

'Mostyn and a man called Mal – I can still feel his breath and his hands. He was a strange man.' Her eyes filled up.

'Can you describe him?'

By the time Tracy had finished, Drake knew exactly who she meant. 'And was there anyone else involved?'

Tracy stared at him. 'Not... with me.'

'But there was someone?'

A tear rolled down her cheek. Tracy ran out of energy and slumped back into her chair, clasping her hands over her face.

'Were there other men, Tracy?'

'Only voices,' she said. 'An English-type voice and another man, but I never saw them.'

Drake let out a long breath and hoped this was the connection they needed.

On the journey back to headquarters Drake detoured to a supermarket and parked while Caren bought lunch. She returned with two packs of sandwiches, crisps and bottles of soft drink. Drake found a packet of hand wipes from the storage compartment in the driver's

side door and wiped his hands. Caren passed over a
chicken and mayo sandwich and after breaking open
her BLT version began talking with her mouth full.
Luckily Drake didn't need to watch and he stared out of
the windscreen, half listening to what Caren was
saying but thinking that someone should have told her
as a child that making conversation and eating was
bad manners.

'We'll need to inform the Sexual Offences and
Child Protection team,' Caren said.

Drake had almost finished his first round and
was twisting the top of his drink bottle. He could always
rely on Caren to get the protocols right, even though he
thought it might be premature – he had a murder
inquiry to deal with first. He took a mouthful of the
orange liquid.

His mobile rang and he fumbled to close the
bottle before answering the call. It was Howick.

'I've been digging into the background of
Maldwyn Evans, sir. I just thought you should know
that there's some intelligence on him. Two complaints
relating to young girls.'

'Have you got the details?'

'I should have more in the next hour.'

'We're on our way.' Drake left the rest of his
sandwich and started the car. 'You'd better contact the
SOCP team,' Drake said before giving Caren a
summary of his conversation.

An hour later they were standing by the board in
the Incident Room. Drake looked over at Howick and
then turned back the cuffs of his shirt. The SOCP
officers had promised to be prompt but now they were
over ten minutes late. Just as he contemplated calling
them the door opened.

'Sorry we're late, Inspector.'

Drake knew Detective Sergeant Robinson who

was followed by a younger officer.

'This is DC Gregg,' Robinson said.

Drake shook the outstretched hand. 'This morning we interviewed a Tracy Newton as part of two ongoing murder inquiries. She identified the victim of the first murder, Ed Mostyn, as her assailant. It seems there was another man involved in the assaults some years ago. He is also known to us – Maldwyn Evans.'

'Was there anyone else involved?'Robinson said. She was a tall, thin woman with striking red hair, a long chin and enormous round earrings.

'Two other men. Not identified, other than by their accents, but also two other girls. All under fifteen at the time.'

Drake nodded to Howick. 'Dave has been digging into the background of Maldwyn Evans.'

Howick cleared his throat and struck a serious tone. 'There was a complaint five years ago about some fondling and inappropriate behaviour that would have justified a prosecution, but the complainant withdrew. And then ten years ago the family of a girl aged fourteen came forward, complaining that Maldwyn Evans had assaulted her. He was interviewed but never charged.'

'We'll need to interview the current witness,' Robinson said.

Drake straightened and folded his arms. 'Once we've traced the other girls involved.'

'But—'

Drake glared at Robinson. 'The murder investigation takes priority over any historic allegations of abuse.'

'There are protocols—'

'In the meantime, I'm going to arrest Evans on Monday.'

'I must protest. We'll need time to speak to the

witness first. And we'll need to talk to the other two girls involved.'

'Out of the question. I haven't got time. He might have murdered Mostyn and Jane and I need to interview him. You can always talk to him again.'

Robinson scowled and then left, taking Gregg with her just as Winder arrived. He flung his papers on his desk and looked up at Drake. 'Higham didn't remember the laptop. But a couple of his friends in the local pub remember him talking about getting it repaired and that it was very valuable. And Tom could identify the knife as a Gerber. Made in the US, it's a special design that fishermen use.'

'Good. Now all we need to find is someone who has lost a pair of Ray-Bans.'

Chapter 19

The car park in Llangefni was already half full when Drake arrived for the public meeting. He squeezed the Alfa into a parking spot next to a couple of vans, their bodywork streaked with mud. He got out and walked down to the town hall, passing a truck from each of the two Welsh television companies.

The entrance lobby was covered in dark mahogany panelling. The smell of polish hung in the air and Drake could hear voices beyond the double doors, which were flanked by two earnest looking teenagers. One of them thrust a leaflet into Drake's hand – *The Truth About Nuclear Power* – before asking him whether he'd like to sign a petition. Drake declined.

One of the doors in front of him opened and a woman with long flowing curls walked into the hallway. Behind her the door swung back and forth until eventually it came to rest. It had an ornate handle and immediately Drake thought about all the grime and dirt and germs that would be trapped in each little crevice. Door handles had become more of an issue recently, but he tried to shake off the urge to reach into his pocket and find a handkerchief he could use to yank the door open. But then the handkerchief would be dirty. Realising that the door would also open inwards, he pushed against it with his shoulder.

Inside, Drake stood and watched as people shuffled down the rows of chairs, mouthing apologies as they bumped into knees on their way to empty spaces. Immediately to his right a woman sat by a table littered with the earphones needed for simultaneous translation for those that didn't understand Welsh. She gave him an enquiring look but he walked past her. Luckily there were a few rows of empty seats near the back and Drake sat down near the aisle. He checked the time and waited. There was still another fifteen minutes before the meeting was scheduled to start. Gradually the seats around him were filled. At the front he spotted Gwynfor Llywelyn deep in conversation with Rhiannon Owen. Drake also identified the familiar faces of local politicians.

He wasn't clear what Gwynfor Llywelyn hoped to achieve; politics was all about sound bites these days, looking good on the television, and there seemed little possibility of preventing the nuclear power station development. Drake recalled the reminiscences of his father about the public meetings of the Welsh language campaign from the 1960s when road signs had been defaced and damage had been caused to public buildings: all in the cause of gaining equality for the Welsh language. Gwynfor Llywelyn's campaign struck Drake as futile.

The crackling sound of an amplifier being tested broke his concentration. He scanned the audience, noticing Joan and Dafydd Higham sitting upright two rows down from him. Rhys Fairburn sat on the opposite side of the hall. A little after seven-thirty an elderly man wearing an ancient suit over a white shirt, its collar frayed, rose to his feet. He made an announcement, but it did little to silence the chatter in the hall. Eventually he resorted to rolling some papers together and banging one end on the table.

'I think it is time we started.'

He had a broad singsong Anglesey accent that rolled out the vowels. Drake adjusted his position to catch a glimpse of the people sitting around the table. He could see Gwynfor Llywelyn, but didn't recognise any of the others.

'We all know that there are plans for a new nuclear power station and it's important for us all to have a say in whether it gets the go-ahead. Let me introduce the speakers.'

A woman with long, thin hair smiled broadly when she was introduced as an expert on the environmental impact of the new power plant. Drake didn't catch her name, but managed to remember that the expert on nuclear power was called Dr Woodward. Gwynfor Llywelyn was going to talk about the impact a new power station would have on the future of the Welsh language.

The environmentalist had sunken eyes, creating the impression of a fierce personality. She had been referred to as a doctor, so Drake guessed she was an academic of some sort. Barely pausing for breath, she turned her attention to the short-term economic impact that a large-scale development would have. After twenty minutes Drake looked at his watch. The speaker busied herself with an explanation as to how investing in green and renewable energy would create more jobs and be more sustainable environmentally.

Looking rather pleased with herself, she sat down after another ten minutes. The first contribution from the audience didn't wait for the chairman to invite comments.

'You're talking a load of rubbish.'

The chairman scrambled to his feet. 'There's no need to be like that.'

A man stood up from the middle of the audience. 'The nuclear power station has provided a generation of families on the island with great jobs. Good income, good prospects. And you want us to throw it all away in favour of protecting birds.'

'That's not what I mean.' The doctor raised her voice.

'That's what happened to those families in the south of England with all those floods. The government had spent millions on protecting birds, yet people's houses flooded. There's real jobs with the new power station.'

'Would anyone else like to make a contribution?' The chairman scanned the room.

Half a dozen more comments were made, all supporting the new power station and its promise of employment. The doctor answered politely and then crossed her arms and pouted when the chair moved on.

Dr David Woodward was another academic that Drake guessed was going to regret his decision to attend. He was only ten minutes into a detailed explanation of how the proposed reactor was unsafe before the heckling began. At first it didn't appear to faze him. He consulted his notes a couple of times, blinked heavily but carried on.

Once he'd finished, the chairman jumped to his feet. 'Would anyone like to ask a question?' He tried to strike a tone that implied rudeness would not be tolerated.

A man from the middle of the audience raised his arm. The chairman waved a hand towards him. 'Has Dr Woodward ever been unemployed?'

'Ah...' Woodward began.

'Because Anglesey has one of the highest unemployment rate in Wales. We need all the jobs we can get.'

A ripple of applause spread through the audience. Others weren't quite as sympathetic and there were several in the audience who wanted to know if it was the same reactor destroyed by the floods in Japan. A grim silence descended as Woodward explained how the reactor proposed was *more* dangerous. Once he'd stopped talking, the chairman turned to Gwynfor Llywelyn.

Drake noticed Joan and Dafydd Higham

adjusting their sitting position. Llywelyn looked over the audience before starting. He had a measured, reasonable tone and explained that the Welsh language had reached a crisis point and that in its heartlands, like Anglesey, there had been a critical decline that threatened the very future of the language. The audience listened to him in silence, some occasionally nodding.

Joan Higham stood up. 'What about the jobs for our youngsters? Without those jobs they will move away. And that means more decline in the number of Welsh speakers.'

'What I'm saying, Mrs Higham, is that jobs could be created on the island without having a nuclear power station.'

'Then why haven't they?'

'Because there hasn't been the political will.'

'That's rubbish.'

'It's only now with the debate around the nuclear power station that we are getting the opportunity to have our voice heard. This could mean the death of our way of life, the extinction of the language. Everything we fought for over generations gone in a few years. It's not something I'm prepared to see happen.'

'Even if it means we become one of the poorest areas in Wales?' It was a man's voice, loud and deep, three or four rows down from Drake.

Llywelyn turned towards the speaker.

'You've heard the evidence from the two experts tonight. The power station could have a profound impact on the environment, it could ruin Anglesey for years and we know that the technology isn't safe. The situation is desperate with our communities. If the power station gets the go-ahead, it's going to destroy our way of life forever. I'm going to

Stephen Puleston

do everything possible to protect our communities.'

The chairman rose quickly to his feet, sensing the opportunity to bring the meeting to an end. As the chairman thanked the speakers Drake got up and was one of the first to leave the hall. The audience began to stream out towards their cars, and a group of young men headed straight for a local pub. As he walked towards his car he heard a shout.

'Inspector Drake.'

He turned and saw Joan Higham walking up to him.

'Didn't I tell you? He's completely mad.'

'I'm sorry.'

'Gwynfor Llywelyn. He's an extremist. Like those terrorists who burnt the holiday homes years ago. We wouldn't have cars if it was up to him – or telephones. And look what he said.'

'I'm not sure I...'

'He's mad enough to murder. Surely you see that.'

Sian had warned Drake earlier that week that on Sunday morning they had to talk privately. She waited for her friend to collect the children and Drake set off for the newsagent. Apart from the occasional comment about Helen and Megan they had spoken little in the previous week and the distance between them had grown into a canyon that a conversation around the kitchen table was not going bridge.

It had irked him more than he cared to admit that her sympathy for the regular counselling had run its course. She had simply suggested that a course of drugs might be effective, and any reserve of patience and understanding that she had as a GP had evaporated long ago.

Sian was in the sitting room when he returned home from buying the morning newspaper, which he'd already opened at the Sudoku page. She had both hands placed carefully over one leg that she had crossed neatly over the other knee. He threw the newspaper down on the table and she gave the Sudoku a cursory glance, before sighing briefly. He sat down.

'There's no easy way to say this. Things haven't been right for a long time.'

Drake was perched on the edge of the sofa.

''Your obsessions are taking over everything. Absolutely everything. And I can't stand it. I just can't keep everything as neat as you seem to want it to be.' Drake wanted to say that Sian keeping things neat wasn't the issue – it was he who needed to do the tidying, the straightening. Sian's composure slipped a little. 'Half the time you're not listening to me and the girls because you're fiddling with the mugs, or the coffee, or the lights – or whatever.'

'But—'

'Let me finish.' Sian gave him a sharp look and lifted a hand to fix a loose hair behind her ear.

Drake stared at the Sudoku. He'd worked out one of the squares as he walked to the car from the shop, confident that it wasn't going to be a difficult puzzle.

'I'd hoped that after the counselling things might get better and that you'd get on top of these stupid obsessions. I wanted things to get back to normal. Whatever *normal* might be. I can hardly remember. And you're never here. The girls hardly see you.'

'Is this about your mother?'

She narrowed her eyes as she looked at him. 'You keep my mum out of this.'

'Only she—'

'I just don't think that our marriage is working anymore.' She was looking at the table top in front of her now. 'I want to separate. You need to move out and find somewhere else to live.'

The bald stark comment rammed into him like a thick cold icicle. For a moment he didn't know how to react. 'I do love you, Sian.'

From the moment he let the words fall from his lips he knew it had been a mistake. Slowly she turned towards him. 'I'm just not certain I love you any longer.'

Now the icicle was twisted, several times.

Chapter 20

Drake draped the jacket of his suit over the wooden hanger then brushed his hands lightly over the shoulders, clearing away some imaginary flecks of dust. His desk and office had the order and neatness that he expected for a Monday morning. The bin was empty, the carpet had been vacuumed and there was the faintest streak of cleaning fluid on the telephone and monitor.

He'd woken early, as he had the day before, his heart thumping and he'd decided that he needed to speak to Halpin. Seeking counselling again wasn't a sign of weakness, Drake thought, more of strength. The number rang out when he first made the call and Drake started to doubt the wisdom of contacting Halpin. He left it for a few minutes before trying again. He thought about Sian and her accusations over the weekend. And then he recalled the remarks from Price, who had hoped there wouldn't be *more difficulties.* Drake didn't want to think about the alternatives Price had alluded to darkly.

The second time he tried, the telephone was answered after the second ring.

'Is Tony Halpin available?'

'One moment,' the voice said without asking his name.

'Halpin.'

'Ian Drake. I need to speak to you.'

'Is it urgent?'

The old uncertainties filled his mind. 'It's just that …'

There was a rustling of papers and Drake could hear his breathing.

'I could see you first thing Wednesday morning, if that would be convenient.'

After agreeing a time Drake rang off. A feeling of relief washed over him and he slumped back in his chair. He settled into thinking about the day ahead. He read the post mortem report on Jane Jones. She'd been strangled, and the pathologist guessed that she'd fought with her assailant who must have been strongly built with large hands from the size of the bruises. Suede-like material, similar to garden gloves, had been found under her fingernails.

The telephone rang and he cursed silently, despite interruptions like this being commonplace. He grabbed at the handset. 'Drake.' It wasn't hard to sound severe.

'Detective Inspector Drake, good morning.'

Immediately, he recognised the voice of Kate French. His throat tightened. 'Good morning Mrs French.' But he had no idea if she was married.

'Call me Kate,' she said, solving his problem. 'Can you bring me up to date? Have there been any developments?'

'We're pursuing some current leads and we're building a much better picture of both victims at present.' There was a limit to how much he could tell her.

'Is there an arrest imminent?'

She really has no idea.

'Operationally we have a number of lines of inquiry ongoing this week—'

'But you can't tell me the details.'

'Ah …'

'I do hope that when the time comes we'll be fully informed. I would like to hope that you'd consider me as part of the team. Thank you for your time.'

Drake replaced the handset and stared at the telephone. He didn't need anyone – particularly Kate French – implying that he wasn't in charge; he was having enough trouble convincing himself that he was. Price had wanted to know how he was going to cope but that had been before his conversation with Sian, before his family began to fall apart. Telling Price about his marriage could wait; he wondered if there was any protocol in the WPS handbook about marital problems. How was he going to cope?

Caren appeared at his door. 'Good morning. How was your weekend?'

Drake looked up at her blankly.

Then Howick joined her. 'I thought you should know, sir, that I worked on Jane's old mobile over the weekend. The only number she called that I could trace belongs to Maldwyn Evans.'

'The old dog,' Caren managed through gritted teeth.

'Very good.' Drake sat back. 'I wonder what he'll have to say to that?'

It was a journey of no more than twenty-five minutes from headquarters to the home of Maldwyn Evans, but Caren could tell that there was something on Drake's mind. It had played on her mind that he'd been breaking protocols by ignoring the Sexual Offences and Child Protection team. She had wanted to say something, perhaps suggest he reconsider, but had decided against it.

Uneasiness that Drake's judgement was flawed crept into her mind. She indicated off the A55 towards Llanfairpwll, with Howick and Winder following behind her. They pulled up near the pavement by Evans's bungalow and got out. The housing estate was quiet, families at work, children on holiday.

Enid Evans opened the door. She narrowed her eyes, folded her arms and then stood in the doorway.

'I need to speak to your husband,' Drake said.

Enid Evans barely moved. 'He isn't well.'

Drake pushed past her and walked into the house, Caren behind him. She noticed the dark glare that Enid Evans gave Drake. It was still hot, although Caren noticed that one window pane was open a fraction. The piles of newspapers had gone and the room felt larger. Evans was already standing when Caren followed Drake into the room; he looked even shorter than Caren remembered.

'Maldwyn Evans, I'm arresting you on suspicion of murder and indecent assault,' Drake said before explaining his right to remain silent.

Evans had a lost look in his eyes, as though he had no idea what was happening. He followed Drake and Caren out to the car, passing his wife standing in the doorway of the kitchen as Winder and Howick began rummaging through cupboards.

Evans sat in the back seat behind Drake and they drove in silence. On occasions like this it was the power the police had over individuals that made the work so challenging, Caren thought. It never ceased to excite her when she thought that they were within touching distance of arresting a murderer. But there was something pathetic about Evans and that morning she had to smother a nagging sensation that they hadn't the clarity she wanted.

It was early afternoon by the time they were ready to interview. Caren had spent an hour with a bad tempered Drake, working out the questions they wanted to ask Evans and reviewing the evidence. By the end Caren was convinced that she had done something to upset Drake but, scanning her memory, she couldn't come up with anything.

The untouched remains of a dried-up lasagne sat in a container in the middle of the table in front of Evans. A plastic fork had been discarded to one side. The windowless room was stifling and Evans sipped slowly on a beaker of water.

Caren fumbled with the plastic wrapping of the tapes. Drake set out the papers in front of him in neat piles. Drake began once the formalities of introductions were over and the tapes were running.

'You know why you're here?'

Evans's eyes bulged slightly. 'Ah ... it's about Ed Mostyn.'

'Tell me about your relationship with him.'

'I hardly knew him.'

'That's not true, is it?'

Evans blinked hard now. Caren could see the fear in his eyes.

'Mostyn owned a piece of land that was preventing you selling your land. You went to reason with him, force him to sell the land. It was going to help you out of a massive financial problem.'

Evans drew his tongue over his lips. 'It wasn't like that.'

'How many times did you call to see him?'

'It was a couple of times.'

'When?'

'I don't remember.'

'What did you talk about?'

'I told him about the land. And about the money I owed to the bank and how they were threatening to repossess and that I'd lose the house unless I could sell. And that he was being completely unreasonable. And that everyone knew the power station was going to be built.'

'What did he say?'

'He said that it wasn't a decision he could make

lightly and that there was so much to consider and that he had an obligation to all future generations.'

'What did he mean?'

Evans looked up at Drake again. 'I didn't know what to think. I tried to reason with him but he wasn't having any of it.'

After an hour Drake had established that Evans had seen Mostyn three times and Caren was convinced that on each occasion Mostyn must have known Evans was more and more desperate. Mostyn must have derived some malign pleasure from seeing Evans's discomfort.

'He just laughed at me,' Evans replied to a question from Drake.

'How did that make you feel?'

'Sick … and angry.'

'Angry enough to kill him?'

Evans sat back in his chair and rocked slightly from side to side. 'Never. Never.'

'Did you know Jane Jones?'

Evans gave Drake a puzzled look. 'What do you mean?'

Caren thought about interrupting, but Drake was focusing on a sheet in front of him and had barely looked over at her during the questioning, which she'd taken as a signal that he didn't want her to interrupt him.

'Do you know the cottages near the beach?' Drake slid a photograph over the table.

'Sorry?'

'It's a local beauty spot. Have you ever been there?'

'No, why?'

'We believe that Jane had access to the cottages and that she may have taken men there. Let me ask you again. Have you ever been there with

Jane?'

Evans gave Drake a hard stare.

'Jane had a mobile telephone and your number is in it. How do you explain that?'

Another dark, intense glare.

'Do you know Tracy Newton?'

Evans jerked his head upright and opened his eyes wide. Drake waited, but he didn't reply. Drake stared back. 'For the purposes of the tape Maldwyn Evans makes no reply. Is it true that you had sex with Tracy when she was under sixteen in the cottage?'

Maldwyn's eyes settled into a frown, but still he made no reply.

'And that it happened on a number of occasions over a period of two years.'

No reply. Maldwyn moved in his chair, placed fisted hands on the table. 'I didn't kill Jane, if that's what you're driving at.'

Drake paced in front of the board in the Incident Room. He tugged at the cuffs of his shirt and turned the red elasticated links between his thumb and forefinger. Later, Maldwyn Evans would be released on bail; frustration gnawed at his mind. It was getting to the end of the day. Caren was sitting by her desk nursing a mug of tea. The remains of pastries lay on her desk.

Drake fiddled with his wedding band, but quickly stopped when he realised what he was doing. 'We'll bail Evans for him to return in a couple of weeks. At least we can go through all his records in the meantime.'

Nobody reacted. Caren said nothing. Drake didn't even invite her to make a contribution. He glanced over at the board and noticed the photograph they'd recovered from Ed Mostyn's cottage of the four men in dinner jackets smiling at the camera. There was still something familiar about the one face he couldn't identify, but before he could concentrate on it the telephone rang on his desk and he hurried over to his office.

'Get over here, Ian.' Price put the telephone down before Drake could reply.

Drake strode through the corridors and up the two flights of stairs to the senior management suite. Hannah pointed towards the door and even Drake could tell from the worry on her face that something was amiss.

Price was standing, legs apart, a television remote in his hand, staring at the screen on the table at the opposite end of the room. 'Press. I hate the lying toe-rags.' He didn't look at Drake. 'Just in time to see this report. We were only told about it ten minutes ago.'

The image of Calvin Headley appeared on the screen. He looked to be standing outside headquarters. '*It is understood that the Wales Police Service have today arrested a forty-eight-year-old man in connection with the murders of Ed Mostyn and Jane Jones. Local people have confirmed his identity as Maldwyn Evans. The police have refused to confirm what the present status of this inquiry is, although it is believed that the outcome of detailed forensic analysis is expected.*'

The reporter continued with a recycling of previous reports as the images on the screen showed the original crime scenes where the bodies of Mostyn and Jane had been found.

Eventually Price pointed the remote and the screen cut to black. 'If I ever meet that journalist I shall put his head in a fucking blender.'

Chapter 21

Drake was the first to arrive at headquarters and he stood before the board in the Incident Room thinking about Maldwyn Evans. He strode over to a window and fiddled with a catch until fresh air flooded in. He returned to the board, looking for inspiration. The date upon which Evans had to return to the police station was written underneath his name. Drake hoped that forensics would find something in Evans's computer or in his personal papers. He'd always distrusted fellow officers who boasted about their 'gut instincts', which he took as an excuse for not building a case from evidence, doing it the hard way. But now something nagged in his mind. Like a toothache that would inevitably get worse unless you saw the dentist.

He leant on one of the desks and stared over at the various faces. What was the motive for the deaths of Ed Mostyn and Jane Jones? There was always a motive. He stared at the unshaven face of Ed Mostyn. He decided that to make any sense of the connection to Maldwyn Evans they'd need to go back to the beginning. His concentration was interrupted as Caren walked in. She looked startled to see him.

'Good morning, sir. You're in early.'

'Caren.'

She moved nearer the board and stared at the image of Evans in the photographs from Mostyn's cottage, at the four middle-aged men in evening suits. 'The only thing they had in common was membership of the Cambrian Club.'

'There was a photograph of four men in dinner jackets in Somerset de Northway's morning room.'

'And one in Fairburn's study. It must have been some special occasion.'

Moments later Winder burst in, deep in

conversation with Howick about the latest managerial sacking from a Premiership football club. Drake got up and by the time he was standing by the board Winder had slumped into his chair, yet another bag of pastries on his desk – why did he always have to eat breakfast at work?

Drake scanned the faces of his team. 'Gareth, what did you find out about de Northway?'

'He's got lots of important friends. There are lots of photographs of him with circuit judges and men dressed in fancy clothes.'

'Anything else of relevance?'

Winder shook his head. 'I did find a letter from the power company to Mostyn. Looks like they were putting pressure on him. And there was a report of Huw Jones assaulting Mostyn but nothing came of it. It was no more than a pub car park brawl that got out of hand.'

Drake looked over at Howick who was shuffling through some papers on his desk. 'Dave?'

'I've been to see one of Jane's ex-boyfriends who sent me to see an aunt of his. And she gave me some background on Mildred and Ray Jones. Apparently they separated years ago and this woman, a Mrs Fraser, didn't think that Ray Jones was Jane's father. Nothing is secret on Anglesey. Everybody knows each other's business.'

'And how exactly is that going to help us?' Caren said.

Drake was thinking exactly the same. It was another piece of a complex jigsaw. 'We can never prove that, unless we've got some DNA. And find out if there's any progress with the DNA evidence from Jane's foetus.'

The telephone rang in his office but when he picked up the receiver the caller had already rung off.

Almost immediately Caren's telephone began ringing. Drake heard her usual introduction – name and rank. Then she went quiet. He'd sat down for no more than a few seconds before Caren shouted his name.

'You need to hear this, boss,' she said. 'It's about Maldwyn Evans.'

Drake strode out of his office. Caren pushed the handset towards him. A dark cloud enveloped his mind as he listened to the details. Caren reached for her jacket before he'd finished. He turned towards her. 'Let's go.'

Drake hammered the car down the A55 towards Anglesey, its hazard lights flashing. He shouted abuse at a car that was dawdling in the outside lane and nudged the speedometer to over a hundred miles an hour. Caren wanted to tell him that there was little point in rushing to the scene. Maldwyn Evans had died instantly when he'd thrown himself in front of the early morning express train from Holyhead to London.

'Has anyone been to see his wife?' Drake said.

'The sergeant didn't tell me.'

'What on earth drove him to kill himself?'

'The publicity, probably.'

'Or maybe guilt.'

'I was amazed that reporter mentioned him by name. I didn't think they could do that.'

Drake slowed at the Britannia Bridge over the Menai Strait and as soon as he crossed over onto Anglesey took the first slip road towards Llanfairpwll. In the village he pulled the car onto the pavement near some shops and they marched down towards a level crossing, its red warning lights still flashing, a patrol car parked diagonally in front of it, faces peering down from the train carriages.

Caren leant over the barrier and looked down the track. A small man with a swarthy beard, wearing a yellow high-visibility jacket with British Transport Police sewn into the left-hand breast pocket, eased himself between both ends of the barrier. 'Sergeant Wallbank.'

'DI Drake and this is DS Caren Waits.'

'We've almost finished. There wasn't much left of him. There was identification in one of his trouser pockets.'

'Where's the driver?' Drake said.

'He's with one of my officers.'

'We'll need to talk to him.'

Caren turned and saw a British Transport Police van slowing to a halt.

'Of course. Let me get organised with the relief driver first. There are passengers all over North Wales waiting for this train.'

'Who's been to speak to his wife?' Caren said.

Wallbank thrust his hands deep into his jacket pockets. 'One of my PCs went. She was in a hell of a state.'

Another transport police officer walked up to them, accompanied by a man that Caren guessed was the relief train driver. She watched them walking down the edge of the track.

Caren turned to Drake. 'Shall we go and see Mrs Evans, sir?'

Caren had worked with Drake long enough to understand his strengths as a detective, but small talk and comforting grieving relatives weren't his greatest skills. In fact, he could be downright rude and it occurred to her that it might be better if she saw Enid Evans on her own.

'I'd better check if family liaison has been informed,' Caren said.

She stood by the barrier contemplating how

she'd suggest that he didn't see Enid Evans. She fumbled for the mobile, hoping that making a call would give her time to think. She was halfway through a discussion with a civilian in headquarters when Wallbank returned.

'I'll take you to see the train driver.' Wallbank marched off down the road.

Caren took her opportunity. 'I'll go and see Mrs Evans while you talk to the driver sir.' She was convinced that she saw relief in Drake's eyes.

Drake had been pleased when Caren had suggested she speak to Enid Evans. Perhaps she knew him better than he guessed. It was just one of those situations where all that was needed was sympathy and reassurance.

Caren took a right turn at the junction. But as Drake and Wallbank turned left onto the main road they almost bumped into Calvin Headley and a television crew. Headley was wearing the same suit that he had worn on the bridge near the scene of Mostyn's death and the same virtuous attitude. The cameraman instinctively started filming, and Calvin Headley's mouth fell open slightly, clearly delighted to see Drake. The journalist came closer.

'Are you investigating this, Inspector Drake?' Headley managed to infuse both condescension and enquiry into his voice. It was a potent mix; Drake's face flushed and his chest tightened. 'What the hell are you doing here?'

'There's been a death on the railway. It will make the lunchtime news.'

Drake took one step towards the journalist and jabbed his forefinger into the man's chest. 'You're just a scumbag. I don't know how you live with yourself.'

Drake felt a hand on his jacket and, turning, saw the worried gaze of Wallbank. 'This way, sir.'

Drake left Calvin Headley with a self-righteous expression on his face.

By the time they reached the station car park Drake's equilibrium had returned. Wallbank pushed open the door of the mobile incident room and took off his jacket, which he threw onto a table. A man was sitting in the far corner, staring at the floor and clutching a plastic beaker.

'This is Harry Thomas. He was the train driver this morning,' Wallbank said, as though Thomas wasn't in the room.

'Can you tell me what happened?' Drake said.

Thomas looked up, his bottom lip quivered, his eyes filled. 'It's the first time it's happened to me.'

Two cars had been parked on the pavement outside Enid Evans's bungalow. Caren walked down the concrete drive towards the side entrance. She pressed the bell and waited. Moments later the door opened but she couldn't hide her surprise when Joan Higham appeared.

'And what do *you* want?'

Caren ignored the rudeness and used her most reasonable tone. 'Is Enid in?'

'Of course she is. She's hardly going to the supermarket.'

Caren crossed the threshold uninvited, catching Joan Higham by surprise. 'Are you related?'

'We've known Enid and Maldwyn for years. Dafydd does his accounts.'

'Is she in the sitting room?'

Joan gave a quick nod down the hallway. Enid Evans was sitting in the same chair that Maldwyn had occupied the week before. A man in his twenties stood up, who, from his pallid complexion and tapered chin, Caren guessed was Enid's son.

'Are you the police officer who was here last week?'

'Detective Sergeant Waits.' Caren turned to Enid. 'I'm very sorry for your loss Mrs Evans.'

'This is Iwan, my son.'

'I need to ask you some questions.'

'What? The bloody cops have done enough damage,' Iwan said, squaring up to Caren.

Enid spoke to him. '*Stedda lawr a bydd yn dawel.*'

Caren's Welsh was rudimentary but her understanding was confirmed when he sat down and pouted.

'That inspector not with you today?' Enid barely paused for breath. 'Maldwyn knew he was out to get him. Rotten to the core if you ask me. And that's what killed him. Couldn't stand the shame of being wrongly accused. Can you imagine what it's like having to face everyone in the village – looking at you and talking behind your back? When he knew that he'd done nothing wrong.'

Caren listened without passing comment. She kept her opinions to herself. It had been the press who reported Maldwyn's name. But it suited Enid to complain about the police.

'I need to ask you about Maldwyn.'

'Haven't you done enough damage?'

'What was he like last night and this morning?'

Enid frowned. 'He was quiet last night. He was so frightened and upset after the interrogation. He went to pieces, didn't say anything. He just sat in this chair, staring blankly into space. I've never seen anything like it. He didn't eat anything or drink anything and when I went to bed he was still there.'

'Do you know whether he spoke to anybody else?'

Enid clasped both hands tightly together. 'He spoke to Rhys Fairburn. They were in the Cambrian Club together.' She spat out the final words. 'And later, he spoke to Dafydd Higham.'

Iwan added. 'He spoke to him often. Dafydd was going to help with the land business.'

Caren turned towards him. 'What do you mean?'

Iwan pursed his lips. 'Dad should never have got Higham involved. He was going to fix things, speak to Mostyn. That's what Dad said …'He glanced over at his mother for approval. 'He should never have been arrested. He was an innocent man and you've killed him.'

Caren was uncertain whether persevering would achieve anything further. 'Did your husband sleep at all last night?'

'He came to bed but I was so tired …'

'What time was that?'

'I should never have gone to sleep.'

'Do you know when your husband got up?'

'It must have been early. He put the rubbish out and laid the kitchen table for breakfast.'

'Was there anything else, Mrs Evans? Did he say anything? Mention anyone's name?'

Enid clasped her hands again, and placed one on each knee. 'I think it's time you left.'

Drake ran a finger around his collar. Although it was early evening the video conference suite was stiflingly hot. He reached for a glass of water – it was tepid but at least it helped to moisten his lips. Superintendent Price sat across from Drake, both hands flat on the table in front of him. His mobile sat alongside a pile of papers that had an orange Lamy fountain pen perched on top. Price stared over at him.

'Before we speak to ACC Osmond I need to know all the details.' Price's slow, deliberate manner unnerved Drake.

'Maldwyn Evans was arrested on suspicion of indecent assault and murder of Ed Mostyn.'

'And your evidence for the murder?' Price had his chin propped on steepled hands now.

'There was direct evidence of Evans threatening Mostyn. And Evans was in dire financial problems that were made worse by Mostyn's refusal to sell the land he owned with his sister.'

Price curled up his eyebrows. 'And the evidence for the sexual offences?'

'A direct third party complaint that he and Mostyn had been involved several years ago.'

'And have the correct protocols been followed with the Sexual Offences and Child Protection team?'

'They have been informed—'

'Sergeant Robinson of the SOCP team has filed a memorandum that suggests the standard protocols weren't followed.'

Drake's shirt tightened around his neck.

'I wanted to give the murder investigation the highest priority.'

'Let's hope the ACC agrees. And how did the press find out?'

The image of Calvin Headley filled Drake's mind. 'I don't know. He must have spoken to neighbours.'

'No question of there being any leaks?'

A bead of perspiration gathered on Drake's forehead. 'Absolutely not.'

Price checked the time, stood up and fiddled with the controls for the video equipment. Moments later the screen filled with the image of the ACC Osmond in Cardiff.

'Good evening, Wyndham. DI Drake,' Osmond said.

The ACC was in his early fifties but the uniform and sheen of silver grey stubble made him look older.

'Sir,' Price acknowledged his superior officer. Drake followed suit.

'This is a mess. What the hell happened?'

Drake wanted to clear his throat but even swallowing was difficult.

'The arrest of Mostyn was lawful and justified,' Price continued.

After a few minutes Price had finished his explanation, interrupted by the occasional question from Osmond.

'Have all the protocols been followed?' Osmond said.

'The murder investigation is taking priority, sir,' Price said. 'The SOCP team haven't been fully involved yet.'

Even from the screen Drake could see the look of surprise on Osmond's face.

'For Christ's sake, Wyndham. I don't want there to be any room for the family to complain. That goes for you as well, Detective Inspector. Protocols are there to protect officers.'

'Yes, sir,' Price said. 'Is the force doing anything about the journalist?'

'We've made a complaint of course. You know, interfering with policing, prejudicing an inquiry etc. ... etc. ... But the man is dead. And we are getting the blame.'

Silence hung in the room for a moment.

'I need regular updates,' Osmond said. 'And remember the bloody protocols.'

The ACC nodded at someone in the room and then his image disappeared. The tension in Drake's chest subsided a fraction.

'We need progress, Ian,' Price said.

Drake let out a lungful of breath, hoping Price wouldn't notice.

Chapter 22

It was seven-thirty am when Drake arrived to see Halpin.

The mental health unit had a nondescript office in a side street. A sign with the name of the health board had been screwed to the door. He rang the bell and the intercom buzzed into life. He heard the sound of Halpin's voice and once Drake had introduced himself the door clicked open. He followed the counsellor through into a room at the rear of the building, which contained two armchairs and where he had seen Halpin before.

'How are things?' Halpin started.

Drake sat down and the soft cushion sagged under his weight. The room was cool. Halpin wore a brown herringbone jacket, the sort that Drake's father would have found fashionable, with an open-necked shirt and his usual neutral expression.

'You said I could contact you if things …'

'Of course. Tell me what's happened?'

'I'm involved in this case. A man and a young girl have been killed.'

'I read about it in the newspaper'.

'My superior officer has been asking how I'm coping.'

'And how are you coping?'

Drake propped a foot over one knee. 'Since Dad died it hasn't been easy. It's back to how it used to be. I can't get things done unless I've dealt with other things in a certain order. In a way, it's worse – I can't even touch a door handle now.'

Halpin ran a finger along his chin. 'Have you tried the coping strategies we discussed?'

Drake nodded. He took a deep breath and tried his best to blot out the comments from Price and Sian that were clouding his mind. After half an hour the concerned look on Halpin's face had intensified into a quizzical gaze.

Eventually Halpin said. 'How are things at home?'

The saliva in Drake's mouth had dried and he ran his tongue over his lips. 'Sian doesn't know if she loves me anymore.' It was easier telling Halpin than he'd expected.

'And is the feeling mutual?'

'No, of course not. It's just that sometimes I have to do the things she hates. And …' He wished it was as simple as giving up one thing for the sake of the other.

Halpin waited.

'Sian wants us to separate.' Drake stared at a brown stain on the carpet.

'Does she think it will be permanent?'

'She didn't say.' Drake looked up at Halpin, wanting to remember what Sian had actually said. If it was only temporary then she might have said so, Drake thought.

'Is separating from Sian something that you have been thinking about?'

'I can't say that I have.'

'Do you think the marriage is over?' Halpin said.

Drake stared at Halpin. It hurt to hear it in such cold objective terms. Sian had used a detached tone when she told him that a period apart might 'help to mend their relationship'. And she had made it clear that his failure to address the rituals that drove her mad was simply not acceptable. She had made it sound like a cold-hearted business decision.

'It's just not that easy …'

He'd agreed with Sian that they'd speak to Helen and Megan that evening. How do you explain to young children about their parents separating?

'How are your daughters dealing with it?'

Drake looked over at Halpin and knew then that he didn't want them to have to *deal* with anything.

The columns of multi-coloured Post-it notes had been moved strategically to one side. Open on Drake's desk was the local daily newspaper, its front page dominated by the tragic events from the day before. The train driver had been named and there was even an interview with a psychologist who claimed to be an expert in treating individuals who had suffered a similar trauma. Drake read the statement from Maldwyn Evans's family criticising the press but pointing the finger of blame directly at the Wales Police Service for having falsely arrested Evans.

Drake looked at the coffee granules descending slowly in the cafetière on his desk before pouring the coffee. A thin covering of creamy oil floated on the surface. He took the first mouthful and then carried on reading. He had tried being discreet when they'd left the house with Evans. But it was a small estate of bungalows and Drake imagined Calvin Headley flattering one of the neighbours into confirming the details.

Drake turned over to the second page of the newspaper and read with growing alarm an article on the ongoing investigations into Ed Mostyn and Jane Jones and how it was making no progress – 'politicians concerned' and 'local people worried' were comments frequently repeated. He searched for the name of the journalist responsible, suppressing the urge to pick up the telephone immediately and call the editor. He had little time, knowing that he had to leave for the meeting he'd arranged the evening before to see Joan and

Dafydd Higham.

He left his office, grabbing his jacket on the way out, but he stopped by the Incident Room board. A photograph had been pinned under the image of Evans. It was similar to the others he'd seen of men in dinner jackets smiling at the camera. It had in it Evans standing with Rhys Fairburn, Ed Mostyn and the same man that he'd seen in the image on the round table in the morning room of Crecrist Hall.

'Where did you find this?' Drake said pointing at the photograph.

Howick replied. 'It was with Evans's papers.'

Drake stared at the group and then at the similar photograph under Mostyn's details. Curiosity finally got the better of him so he unpinned both images and slid them into his papers – maybe Higham would know if something connected all these men.

Drake fumbled through the glove compartment until he had found the CD of Bruce Springsteen's *Working on a Dream.* He turned the volume up as he accelerated along the A55, hoping it would be a lucky day. On a whim he turned off the dual carriageway at the junction for Conwy and slowed as he negotiated various roundabouts until he was on the bridge crossing the estuary. To his right was an estate of houses in the marina development, the tips of yacht masts swaying gently. Ahead stood Conwy Castle, surrounded by the walls that had made the town such a fortress in the thirteenth century. Drake couldn't remember when he had last visited it but decided that this was the sort of activity a father should do with his children. At the beginning of the week Drake had seen a flat in the middle of Colwyn Bay that suited his needs – close enough to collect Helen and Megan and convenient for headquarters. The agent had sounded reluctant when Drake had said he wanted to move in the following weekend, mumbling excuses about the paperwork needed.

Pedestrians and traffic slowed his journey through the narrow streets until eventually he left through one of the ancient gates in the town walls.

He reached the Menai Strait and crossed over the Britannia Bridge, casting a quick glance at the fast-running currents. Plas Newydd, the ancestral home of the Marquess of Anglesey, shimmered in the sunshine. He accelerated off the bridge and within half an hour turned into the drive for the Higham farmhouse. It struck him that Joan Higham had shown little remorse at the death of her brother and that Dafydd Higham demonstrated an objectivity typical of accountants.

He strode over to the back door and heard the bell reverberating through the house, but the place felt empty. He peered in through one of the windows; the kitchen looked tidy, draining board clear, work surfaces spotless – the sort of order that his mother would have liked. He tried the doorbell a second time and stood back, this time looking around for any sign of life. Then he heard movement, a chair being moved perhaps and footsteps behind the door. It creaked open and he saw the drowsy face of Joan Higham.

'I'm sorry if I woke you.'

'I didn't sleep well last night. Recently I've been sleeping so much better, but last night I just couldn't get to sleep. Come in.'

Drake followed Joan into the kitchen. 'Is your husband in?'

'He's not here. He was at some accountancy dinner last night and stayed over at the hotel. I was expecting him back by now.'

Drake nodded – it explained her tentative tone

on the telephone the evening before. Joan busied herself making coffee for Drake and as she finished he heard the sound of a car coming to a stop. She poured the coffee and pushed a mug over the table towards him. Dafydd Higham walked in and dumped a small case on the floor. He wore a navy polo shirt and jeans. His hair had been cut more neatly than Drake remembered. He gave Drake a brief nod of acknowledgement.

'Inspector.'

Higham sat down next to Drake. 'How can we help with the investigation?'

'I wanted to ask you about Maldwyn Evans. How well did you know him?'

'We were good friends. It's tragic what has happened to him. I don't think Enid will recover.'

'Did you socialise regularly?'

'We were in the Cambrian Club.'

'I understand you spoke with Maldwyn on the night he was arrested, the night before he killed himself. What did you talk about?'

Higham fiddled with the bone china mug on the table and shrugged.

'Did he mention the reason why he'd been arrested?'

'I don't remember much about the conversation.'

'What did he say? Did he mention Jane Jones or Mostyn?'

Higham avoided any eye contact with Drake. 'As I have said, I don't remember much about what he said.'

'Did you discuss the sale of the land?'

'He was very upset, almost incoherent ...'

Higham folded his arms and glanced over at his wife. Drake found the photograph from Evans's house and showed it to Higham. 'This is a photograph we found with Maldwyn's effects. Do you know when it was taken?'

'It was at one of the Cambrian Club dinners.'

'Who is the third man?'

'That's a friend of Somerset de Northway. I'm surprised you don't recognise him.'

Drake took back the photograph and looked at the face again.

'It's Judge Hawkins.'

Immediately Drake saw the resemblance. Hawkins was leaner but Drake could see the narrow sharp eyes he'd noticed in court. Drake took a mouthful of coffee. It was fresh, a welcome change from the instant most people served.

At least they had the identities of all the men featured. Now they had seen four photographs of the Cambrian Club dinner although Fairburn and de Northway still had theirs on display. It was a small community where everyone knew each other but were the photographs merely coincidence?

Drake's mobile rang and he fumbled in his pocket. He recognised Caren's number and pressed the handset to his ear.

'We've found an address for Becky and Sue, the girls named by Tracy.'

Chapter 23

Twenty minutes later Drake indicated left into a small housing estate in Cemaes and read the text message on his mobile with the address. Number thirty-three was a semi-detached house with wooden window frames that needed replacing and an overall tired feel that properties acquired as a result of landlords who were disinterested in improvements.

Drake left the car and strode over to the front door. There was no car in the drive and nothing to suggest any sign of occupants. There was no bell, so Drake hammered on the door. Immediately he heard muted voices, and moments later the door opened.

He flashed his warrant card at the young girl standing in the doorway. She was no more than eighteen, but the defiant look in her eyes suggested she wanted to be a lot older. Drake looked over her shoulder.

'I'm looking for Becky Jackson and Sue Pritchett.'

'Why?'

'Are they here?'

'No.' The girl angled the door towards Drake. 'Becky's at work. And I haven't seen Sue for ages.'

'Where does Becky work?'

'In the bakery in the village.'

Drake hesitated. 'Is that the place owned by Gwynfor Llywelyn?'

'Yeah, that's right.'

'Where does Sue live?'

The girl shrugged. Drake turned on his heels and left, guessing that as soon as the door was closed she would be texting a message to Becky. Drake drove down into the village and after parking walked down towards the bakery. All the loose ends and various threads intertwined in Drake's mind as he faced the real possibility that the investigation was failing. Everyone was connected or it certainly appeared that way. And despite the billion-pound investment in a modern nuclear power station, the local community of Anglesey still wanted to keep its secrets.

A thin veil of flour and a strong smell of yeast hung in the air inside the bakery. Gwynfor Llywelyn gave Drake a wary look as he finished serving the only customer. 'What do you want?' he said once the shop was empty.

'I want to speak to Becky.'

Llywelyn scowled. Then he raised the flap on the counter and Drake followed him through to the office.

He recognised the girl he'd seen on his first visit. She was stick thin but that morning she had her hair, a deep scarlet, gelled to look like a spike. She still had the nose rings and callow, restless eyes. Drake had mulled over how he'd start the conversation – is it true you were abused? Who was involved? He'd never really ascribed to the touchy-feely, considerate school of police interrogation. He had a job to do, questions to be asked and he expected answers. But even so, a degree of sensitivity was required.

'I'll need to speak to Becky on her own,' he said to Llywelyn, who gave the young girl a fierce look and left.

Drake drew up a chair and sat down.

'Becky, I know this could be difficult. I'm investigating the death of Jane Jones and Ed Mostyn. We've spoken to Tracy.'

Becky swallowed hard. She tried to find things for her hands to do. Drake continued. 'She's told us about what went on in the cottages near where Jane was killed. She said that you and Sue Pritchett were involved.'

Becky stared at her hands curled up on her lap. 'They always liked Jane better than the rest of us.'

'Can you tell me who was involved?'

She shook her head slowly. 'I only ever saw two them. That creep Ed Mostyn was one of them. He came here sometimes. Made my skin crawl.'

'And the other one?' Drake reached into his shirt pocket and found the photograph. 'Do you recognise any of these men?'

She put her hand to her mouth, caught her breath. 'It's that one in the middle,' she said, pointing to Rhys Fairburn.

Drake had expected her to identify Evans. 'Are you certain?'

'Of course.'

'How old were you …when …?'

'Fifteen.'

'Why didn't you make a complaint?'

'At the time we were frightened. Then later Jane didn't want to. She wanted to go away and make a new life. She had money. I saw it, she had lots of it.'

'How much?'

Becky looked at Drake wide-eyed. 'Thousands, I saw it all in bundles.'

'Where did she get it?'

'She wouldn't tell me. And anyway, nobody would have believed us.'

'Where did she keep the money?'

'How would I know? She's dead.'

Becky choked back a tear. Drake sat back, thinking to himself that once he found the answer to how Jane had acquired lots of money he'd probably find the answer to her death. And maybe even the death of Ed Mostyn.

'Do you know where Sue Pritchett is?'

Becky shook her head. 'She worked here for a while. But I don't know where she is now.'

Drake thought about the possibility that the bakery might have some record he could use to trace her. 'You do the accounts here, don't you?'

'Yes. Why ..?'

'Do you have the national insurance number for Sue?'

Becky folded her arms severely. 'I can't give you that information. He'd go mad. I'd lose my job.'

Drake glanced back over his shoulder. The door to the office was firmly closed. There was a crowd in the shop, Llywelyn was busy. 'He'll never find out. And I'm sure you want me to find Jane's killer.'

Becky stared out into the shop. Then quickly she drew her chair nearer the desk, opened the bottom drawer and drew out a file suspended inside. Quickly she skimmed through the documents and then jotted a set of numbers on a Post-it note that she folded and handed to Drake.

'Thanks,' Drake said.

She even managed a brief smile. He left the office, and as soon as he was outside dialled Caren's number.

By mid-afternoon Howick had scanned dozens of folders with articles about the latest trends in farming and photographs of Evans and his wife in happier times, before deciding that he'd benefit from a brisk walk, so he grabbed his jacket from the back of his chair and left headquarters. He returned half an hour later but his mind was now more dominated than before about his promotion.

Howick had arrived at work that morning, convinced that the reason for the delay in the publication of his exam results meant only one thing: failure. Every day for the past week he'd pondered the possibility of calling and asking about the results. But each time he'd lost his nerve. It had actually occurred to him a couple of times to go home at lunchtime to check whether the results had been sent by post instead of the email that had been promised.

The morning had been spent digging around in the private life of Maldwyn Evans. With their only tentative suspect mashed to a pulp by a speeding express train, Howick's motivation to build a picture of Evans had flagged. Everything that Evans had told them about his financial position had been confirmed by the bank statements and the results of standard financial checks. Howick had little sympathy for the farming community that he saw on the television regularly complaining about their incomes and standard of living. They all appeared remarkably well fed. It became clear by the middle of the morning that Evans had been a disaster at farming. Letters from the business relationship manager of the bank criticised his business decisions and suggested that he should be looking for alternative sources of income.

Howick stared towards the board and looked over at the names under the words 'Persons of Interest' printed in bold font. He doubted whether Evans could seriously be considered as a person of interest any longer. He turned his attention back to the papers on his desk and realised that he hadn't seen a copy of the accounts for Evans's business. But he didn't have the patience to get the paperwork he needed for the Inland Revenue so he left it – promising himself to go back to it later. In any event, he still had more of Evans's files to read.

The file open on his desk contained the results of house-to-house around Evans's home. He thought again about the sergeant's exams. The promotions board would surely be able to tell him by now. He found the number on his mobile telephone and pressed the handset to his ear, clearing his throat at the same time.

'It's DC David Howick. I sat the sergeant's exams some time ago. I was just enquiring about the results.' Howick tried to eliminate any criticism from his tone.

'Let me check.' The voice sounded uninterested.

As the silence continued, he tried not to think about how his entire future could turn on the conversation he was about to have. Maybe he should have waited. There was rustling sound. He watched Winder mouthing excuses about something, which Howick couldn't interpret, before leaving.

'I'll need to get back to you. I don't seem to be able to find the records.'

Howick's mouth dried; something invisible caught in his throat. 'Thank you,' he managed.

More doubts crept into his mind as he got back to work. Maybe he should be looking for a transfer to traffic. He found it hard to concentrate, but turned his attention to Evans's computer. He managed to boot it up without any trouble and spent the rest of the morning trying to put to the back of his mind the ever-increasing conviction that he had failed.

Evans had various files that he'd marked 'personal' and 'financial'. Howick clicked them open in turn. Eventually Howick spotted a folder marked 'miscellaneous'. Inside it were more files with innocuous-sounding names. Howick clicked them open. Each in turn had more files, some occasionally with only a single document. He looked at the time on the clock at the bottom of the screen, wondering how long he could reasonably leave it before he called the promotions board again.

Then he found a file called 'various'. In it were folders, each protected by a password. Howick hesitated. He found Evans's date of birth and punched the number in. No luck. Then he tried a variation of the same digit until he thought he'd exhausted all the various alternatives. He drew a blank again. Then he used the numerals from Evans's telephone and his house number. Another dead end.

This was a futile exercise, he decided, and settled back into his chair heavily, realising that soon he'd have to involve the forensics team but that would mean delays. So he tried to picture Evans using a computer and whether he'd keep passwords in a folder somewhere. His father had a moleskin notebook with all his personal details: bank account number, password for internet banking and all his pin numbers. Howick had warned him frequently that he might lose the notebook but his father was afraid of hackers extracting the information from his computer.

So Howick rummaged through Evans's papers until he finally found a small notepad with a ring spine. The first pages listed addresses for family and colleagues but by the final few pages expectation had built in his mind until he read the details he needed and his pulse beat faster.

He typed in the password and pressed 'enter'. He did a double-take, scarcely believing what was on the screen: dozens of thumbnail images of young naked girls. Then on impulse he went back to Evans's emails and searched for the name of Ed Mostyn. After half an hour his patience was rewarded.

Howick's constant fussing about his exam results was

getting on Winder's nerves. Even when Howick wasn't saying anything Winder could tell that his mind was distracted. There were regular glances at his watch and occasional sighs of irritation, and the lapse in his concentration had made it hard for Winder to work effectively. The promotions board need to put Howick out of his misery, Winder thought.

By mid-morning Winder was halfway through the box of papers relating to Somerset de Northway that he had put to one side the previous week. He read the name 'Crecrist Enterprises', knowing it had been a thread he'd ignored. The possibility that he had missed something of relevance began to play on his mind. He typed the name of the company into a Google search, hoping that the results would be irrelevant.

By the middle of the first page a spasm of guilt jolted into his mind. As he read a newspaper article he hoped that it didn't have any relevance to their inquiry, but the more he read the more he knew he was going to have to find an explanation for his delay. He read the article a second time before deciding to double-check the facts. He needed a map, and the location of both Tyddyn Du and Mostyn's cottage. It was another ten minutes until he had found the location. He chewed one of his nails, imagining Drake's reproach when he explained himself.

Then he remembered the accounts for Crecrist Enterprises.

It was time for a visit to the economic crime department, Winder concluded, reaching for the telephone.

Howick could barely contain his enthusiasm. The answer machine had clicked on as soon as he rang Drake's number. Then he tried Caren but all he heard was her voice inviting the caller to leave a message and if there was anything urgent to ring headquarters. He had more luck with Winder.

'Gareth, where are you?'

'In economic crime. What's wrong?'

'Get back here.'

Howick tossed the mobile onto the pile of papers on his desk just as Drake and Caren pushed open the door. 'I've been trying to call you, sir,' he said.

'Anything urgent?'

'I've been working on Evans's computer. You need to see some of these photographs.'

'What photographs?'

Howick sat down by his desk and Drake and Caren stepped over towards him, leaning over his shoulder. He'd only managed a couple of clicks of the mouse when Winder barged in. Howick found the file that he'd analysed. He clicked on the slideshow button and the images gradually appeared. The girls were teenagers with narrow waists and young faces that stared into the camera apprehensively. The occasional image had them fully clothed, pouting or caught mid-twirl but most were of the girls naked, their breasts undeveloped, small round lumps of flesh with erect nipples. One of the girls tried to give a seductive look to the camera. When the screen filled with the first of a series of images of the girls lying on a bed, their legs spread in the air, Caren gasped. Howick glanced up and saw the dark, troubled look on Drake's face and the horror on Caren's.

'How many different girls are there?' Drake said.

'I've counted four, sir,' Howick said. 'And they were sent to Evans by Ed Mostyn.'

'So Joanna Barnes was right. Did he send them on to anyone?'

'There's only a passing reference in an email from Mostyn to the photos. Evans must have deleted them.'

'Stop,' Drake said as Howick clicked on one image. He leant forward. 'That's Becky. I saw her today. She named Fairburn and Mostyn as her abusers.'

'Is Jane Jones one of them?' Caren said.

Howick found another image. 'She looks a lot younger. But I'm sure it's her.'

Caren stared at the monitor. 'Where were these taken? Only it looks like the bedroom at that cottage. Go back to some of the other photographs.'

Howick did as he was told and scrolled back until Caren stopped him. 'Look, I told you,' she said. 'See that ceiling is curved? It's definitely that cottage.'

'That certainly makes sense with the comments we've had about what took place there,' Drake said.

Howick shifted his position in his chair. 'There's more, sir.' He clicked back to where he'd stopped the slideshow before. Soon enough there were various grainy images of men sitting around a table, a bottle of wine and various glasses in front of them, and a young girl sitting on each knee. 'These pictures must have been taken with a very old camera phone. But that's Maldwyn Evans, Ed Mostyn and Rhys Fairburn right enough,' Howick said.

'I wonder who took the photographs?' Drake said slowly.

By late afternoon Drake stared at the Incident Room board, not really focusing on the faces or the details, uncertain whether he had learnt anything from speaking with Dafydd Higham. The images of the girls and the details from Becky meant evidence. The sort that any prosecutor would relish.

Caren joined him and he turned towards her; she had a determined look on her face. He tapped on the dinner party photograph.

'I spoke to Higham and he confirmed that the name of the third man in the Evans photograph as Judge Hawkins.

'What!' Caren said.

Winder whistled. 'Not Hawkins, the Hangman?'

Howick left his desk and joined them at the board. He stared at the image. 'I can see the similarity now.'

'He's a friend of de Northway,' Drake said. 'And there's a similar photograph in de Northway's place that included Hawkins. And Rhys Fairburn had a framed photograph but I don't remember it featuring de Northway or Hawkins.'

'Do you think there's a connection, boss?' Caren said.

'Somebody took the photographs ...'

'Do we arrest Fairburn?'

Drake didn't respond. Howick piped up. 'And do we inform Sergeant Robinson in the sexual offences team?'

There was a brief silence as Drake hesitated. 'We'll wait until we've traced Sue Pritchett. She could be the corroboration we need.'

'Should have the result soon,' Caren said.

'I've been doing some more digging around into de Northway's background,' Winder announced.

Drake didn't answer. His mind was already thinking about the right protocols and that he had to make the right decision. He turned and stared at him. 'And?'

Winder stepped over to the board and pinned up a form he'd printed with the words 'Crecrist

Enterprises' on it, and below it a plan with three areas each marked in a different colour. 'Somerset de Northway has plans to develop an enormous solar farm between Tyddyn Du and Mostyn's place.' Winder tapped on an area edged red.

'So if de Northway can get his hands on both those extra pieces of land—' Howick said.

'It would be an enormous solar farm. And therefore very profitable.' Drake said.

'But even more interesting, boss,' Winder said. 'It looks like de Northway could well be bankrupt. I had a DS from the economic crime department look at his accounts. The business has made a loss for the past three years and there are lots of debts.'

'And why haven't you found this before now?'

'I…'

'We can't afford to miss anything. So we need to pay de Northway a visit,' Drake said. 'There was something happening in those cottages that links everything together.'

'We'll need to speak to the fisherman who was there when we found Jane's body, too,' Caren added.

Drake nodded. 'I'll see him tomorrow while you talk to more of Jane's friends. Gareth, first thing tomorrow I want you up in Cemaes checking out Llywelyn. Do it discreetly. And Dave, get over to Rhosneigr and talk to the witnesses from the night Jane was killed. We know that Huw lied to us about when he saw Jane. We might need to interview him under caution. And then we get started on Rhys Fairburn. We know he had a motive to kill Mostyn.'

Drake read the time. Usually he would have gone back to his office and worked for another hour, maybe longer, before tidying and rearranging his desk. Instead he strode back to his room, picked up the telephone and called Sian to arrange to take Helen and

Megan out for pizza.

Chapter 24

Before leaving headquarters that morning Drake read an email from Price arranging their third weekly briefing since the death of Mostyn. It clashed with the arrangements he'd made to collect the keys for his new apartment that Friday afternoon. The new meetings had been a recent management innovation followed by regular minutes that always needed to be read and replied to. Anxiety tightened in his mind at the prospect of having to spend more time on paperwork and he hoped he could reschedule the meeting with the letting agent.

Driving past the junction for Llanfairpwll he thought about Maldwyn Evans and contemplated whether he could have done anything differently. Perhaps he should have asked Evans to call in at the police station, avoiding inquisitive eyes and indiscreet neighbours. Calvin Headley is the one that needs to explain his actions, Drake thought, not the WPS, and he got more annoyed just thinking about the journalist.

Drake presumed that the dirty grey clouds hanging in the air satisfied the forecaster's prophecy of 'murky conditions'. The weather would often remind him of his grandfather who didn't need any predictions to know when it was likely to rain. Then he let his thoughts drift to his father and to the last time that he'd seen him. He'd looked sallow, the will to live extinguished, a man in the last waiting room of life. Drake was pleased that his father wasn't alive to see the problems between him and Sian. There would probably have been sharp words. The car touched eighty miles an hour down a hill so he slowed, knowing it was a favourite place for traffic cops to catch speeding drivers.

Twenty minutes later he parked in front of a row

of terraces. He checked his notebook again and read the name of the house that he needed. He left the car, pressed the remote and stared over towards the end house, trying to spot the name – Bryniau. There were numbers but no names so he strode over to the end property. Weather and neglect had left the dark blue paint peeling off the surface of the front door in long shards. The knocker was stiff but he heard its sound reverberating inside, as though the house was empty of furniture. After a few seconds there was movement and soon enough the door creaked open.

Drake had his warrant card ready. 'Detective Inspector Drake, Wales Police Service. Do you know where Eifion Cooper lives?'

The man had a few strands of white hair and several days' stubble to match. His cheeks were sunken but the whites of his eyes had an intensity unusual for a man of his age. Drake guessed he was in his late seventies, perhaps a few years older than his father, if he'd been alive.

'Come in.' The man turned on his heels and walked through into the back kitchen. Drake followed, noticing the confident, purposeful steps.

'I was making porridge for breakfast. I don't need to get up so early these days.'

An old Aga warmed the kitchen and the man stood, slowly stirring a saucepan.

'Do you know Eifion Cooper?'

'Are you Tom's son?'

For a moment Drake hesitated. 'Yes, I …'

'I knew him years ago. He was a good man. Decent and honest. I was sorry to hear of his passing.'

Drake just looked over at the man, not really knowing what to say.

'I dealt with him quite a few times when I had the farm. I'm sure he was very proud of you. He would always do the right thing. I remember once someone cheated me out of some money. But your father helped me and I got it all back.'

The man finished turning the porridge, poured it into a small bowl and then sat down. He looked up at Drake. 'I met your grandfather as well. You were very lucky to have known him.' His sprinkled some sugar onto the porridge.

'My grandfather died when I was a teenager.'

The man took his first mouthful of breakfast.

'I really need to know where Eifion Cooper lives.'

The man looked at the mantel clock. 'He'll be home by now. It's next door. And it's easier for you to go round the back.'

Drake pulled the door closed behind him and, spotting the rear lane, walked behind the terraces until he reached a tall gate. From behind he could hear the sound of activity in the small yard.

'Eifion Cooper,' Drake shouted. The noise stopped abruptly.

The gate opened and a flicker of recognition crossed over Cooper's face. 'I've been half expecting you.'

The yard that was full of lobster pots and fishing gear. Cooper wore the same red fleece, both knees of his dark jeans were frayed and his T-shirt was almost transparent. Cooper made for the back door. The kitchen stank of fish, Drake's flesh tingled and he hesitated on the threshold, convinced that all his clothes would stink for days if he had to sit down. Cooper kicked a chair to one side as an invitation for Drake who stood, clasping his hands together. Cooper ignored him and flicked on the electric kettle. Drake declined the offer of coffee, the prospect of drinking from the dirty mug too gruesome to contemplate.

Eventually Drake sat down. The sooner he got this over with the sooner he could leave. 'I'm investigating the death of Ed Mostyn and Jane Jones.'

'I knew Ed well.' Cooper put a teaspoon of granules into a mug.

'And Jane Jones?'

'Not really. Some of my friends talked about her. She was really fit.'

'And Somerset de Northway?'

Cooper poured water over the coffee. Then he dribbled milk into it, followed by two teaspoons of sugar.

'Everyone knows the de Northway family. They own a lot of land. Can't stand the man personally, he's a bumptious English toff.'

'Do you fish a lot near the cottages where Jane's body was found?'

'Yes, all the time. I can land my pots there.'

'And have you seen anybody in the cottages?'

Cooper took a long noisy slurp of the coffee. 'And what if I have?'

'It might be relevant.' Drake hoped that lowering his voice would make it sound more important.

Cooper looked down at the table. 'All I can say is that late at night there could be a light on and the sound of voices. And there were always young girls. Judith can tell you all about Somerset de Northway.'

'Judith?'

'Judith Farnwood. She had invitations years ago to some of his *parties*.' Cooper began assembling a roll-up cigarette. 'I say parties but it was more like orgies really. If you're into that sort of thing, strap-ons, wife swapping. I missed out on it at the time. Too young.'

'Where can I contact Judith?'

Cooper ran a finger along one length of the

cigarette before reaching for his mobile.

Judith Farnwood had a young voice, but the wrinkles around her mouth and the crow's feet that creased the skin around her eyes couldn't disguise her age. She was still slim for a woman that Drake guessed had to be in her fifties, but she moved with the ease of a person half her age.

'What did you say your name was again?' she asked, as she led him into the kitchen.

'Ian Drake.'

'How can I help?'

She reached a pine table that had a vase of mixed flowers in the middle, recently bought, healthy looking. Drake pulled out a chair as Farnwood sat down.

'I'm investigating the deaths of Ed Mostyn and Jane Jones.'

'I read about it in the paper.' She gave a slight frown.

'I've just spoken to Eifion Cooper. He was landing his fishing boat when we were at the scene of Jane's death near the cottages owned by Somerset de Northway. He tells me that you know the de Northway family.'

Drake could see the realisation in Farnwood's eyes, that now she understood why he was there.

'And Eifion told you I could help?'

Drake decided it really wasn't a question.

Farnwood continued. 'It was a few years ago but I was in a circle of people who were invited for *adult* parties at Crecrist Hall. I was single, no commitments and I was flattered. There were lots of other people there. And Somerset could be a congenial host.' She paused and looked at Drake. 'And there was a lot of casual sex, Inspector. All between consenting adults.'

Drake gazed over at her. Was there disappointment in her voice or regret? He couldn't quite tell, but there was definitely a challenge for him to be disgusted. 'Who else was there?'

'Somerset's friends mostly.'

'And the cottages?'

She dipped her head slightly. 'I never went there, but I heard things.'

'What sort of things?'

'It's a while back now so I couldn't be certain. I heard one of the men joking about young girls, but when they knew I was within earshot they quickly shut up. It was probably nothing.'

Drake spent the next half an hour clarifying and cajoling further details from Farnwood until he asked her to confirm if she'd provide a statement.

She paused before answering. 'It's a long time ago.'

Drake stood up to leave and walked over to the door.

'I saw one of the men who went to the parties in the paper recently.'

Drake turned to face her.

'He was in the army when I met him. One of Somerset's pals. Loud booming voice.' She shuddered at the memory.

Drake waited for her to finish although he already guessed who she meant.

'He's a judge.'

Winder was pleased to be out of the Incident Room and away from Howick's company and his fluctuating moods. His colleague had to get on with life, Winder thought, hoping that his friend would see sense and concentrate on work. Not every officer was destined to make sergeant or inspector or superintendent and Winder was perfectly content to see out his career as a constable.

He had been mulling over Drake's instructions to be discreet. He had the images of Jane and Mostyn in the papers on the passenger seat and he'd decided to try the general approach in the hope that witnesses near Llywelyn's bakery would be talkative.

He pulled up at the car park in the middle of Cemaes and after paying for a few hours' parking set off towards the shops and houses. On the journey from headquarters he had been rehearsing how he'd ask questions about the death of Ed Mostyn in a way that might not have all of Llywelyn's neighbours telling him that the police were investigating him. He had settled on the simple subterfuge that Mostyn and Jane had been seen in the pubs of Cemaes on the evening before their deaths and that the police were following usual lines of enquiries. It had produced wide-eyed astonishment from the elderly women he spent most of the morning interviewing and any attempt to lead the questions into asking about the artisan bakery of Llywelyn had been a dead end.

By lunchtime Winder had realised it was a complete waste of time. He sat in one of the cafés nursing an enormous scone he'd lathered with jam – the café didn't do Danish pastries. He finished his coffee and decided that he ought to start on the shops in the village.

He sat looking out of the window and saw a small van pull up on the pavement opposite, its rear covered with empty milk cartons. Winder had a vague recollection that milk had once been delivered door-to-door to his grandparents' house. A milkman must start his round early, Winder thought.

A man in a pale white T-shirt marched round the back of the van and dropped empty bottles into crates. Then it dawned on Winder that he needed to talk to the driver and that he had to hurry. So he pushed the plate with the last of his lunch to one side and stood up. He glanced over at the young waitress mouthing that he wanted the bill. She was tall with long blonde hair and attractive eyes that lit up as she smiled at him.

Momentarily distracted, Winder heard the van's engine starting and he made for the door. He raised a hand helplessly as the milkman drove down the street. Winder went back inside. The waitress had a relieved expression on her face when she saw him re-enter the café. It soon turned serious when he produced his warrant card.

'Do you know the name of the man who delivers milk?'

'Sorry. I've got no idea.'

'Is there someone else that might know?' Winder said, looking over her shoulder towards the kitchen.

'I'll go and ask.' The girl went through into the kitchen, returning with an older woman.

'You want to know about Sam Underwood?'

'Where can I contact him?'

'I've got his number somewhere.'

Winder let out a long slow breath of irritation as he watched the woman fumble in a drawer.

'Here it is,' she said, reading a number to Winder from a notebook.

'Do you know where he lives?'

'Sorry.'

Winder tapped the number into his mobile and headed for the door before he remembered his bill. He left the change on the counter and walked onto the pavement. The call rang out – not even a voice mail message.

Winder banged on the door of the house opposite. A man in his seventies with a grey shirt and an old polyester tie opened the door.

Winder flashed his warrant card at the man. 'There was a milkman here just now. Do you know where he lives?'

'No idea but he was going to Amlwch when he left here.'

Winder frustration boiled over. 'For Christ sake. Why the hell …'

'No need to swear.' The man closed the door on Winder who jogged back to his car.

The text arrived just as Caren left the last address on the list of Jane's friends. She'd had futile circuitous conversations with one disinterested young girl after another, none of whom had any time for her, making Caren half-wish for a desk job. And each conversation took her no further, adding to the sense that her efforts had been pointless. She hoped that the meeting with the de Northways would prove more constructive.

She grabbed the mobile from the bag on the passenger seat and read Drake's message while trying to steer the car simultaneously. She pulled into a nearby farm gate and tapped out a reply. The traffic was light as she drove down the western side of Anglesey. The sun broke through the dense cloud and cast a pallid shroud of light over the port at Holyhead. She dawdled, admiring the view, and within twenty minutes was pulling up alongside Drake's Alfa Romeo in the car park he'd suggested as a meeting place.

'Any luck?' Drake said once she'd sat by his side in the passenger seat.

'Nothing. They had nothing to add. And only

one of them seemed remotely upset.'

It was nothing more than he'd expected. 'I've just spoken to the fisherman who put me in touch with a Judith Farnwood. She told me all about the adult parties at the hall and that she remembers Judge Hawkins being present.'

'What!' Caren spluttered.

'When he was in the army. Apparently he served in the same regiment as de Northway. But even then there was talk about young girls in the cottages.'

After Caren returned to her car he fired the engine into life and started the brief journey towards Crecrist Hall. A few minutes later they indicated for the entrance and passed the lodge cottage. The borders still needed attention but the grass near the main door had been cut. Caren parked alongside him and left her car.

'This must cost a pile to maintain.' Caren looked up at the main building of the hall.

'De Northway will go out of his way to tell you that his family has been in this area for three thousand years. And even so they can't pronounce the simplest Welsh name.'

Drake strode over to the front door and pulled on a knob set into the middle of a recess sculpted from the stone pillar. Caren could make out a booming voice inside and then a shout. She half expected to see a butler open the door wearing a stiff white shirt and tails ready to announce that his lordship was indisposed. Instead de Northway appeared. The red trousers he wore had lost all sense of shape and he had a bold Tattersall checked shirt with a brown woollen tie.

'Inspector Drake. And what can I do for you today?'

'This is Detective Sergeant Waits.'

De Northway scanned Caren slowly from head

to toe, as though he were licking her and it made her skin crawl. He turned back into the hallway. Caren followed Drake inside. It was cold and barren. The atmosphere was oppressive, similar to Ray and Mildred Jones's farmhouse, but a world apart. A world separated, not only by money but by culture. It would have been impossible to imagine Mildred and Ray being comfortable in the company of Somerset de Northway.

'Somerset, I need you at once.' The voice sounded feminine, just.

'Let's go through into the library,' de Northway said, without hiding the irritation in his voice. As they left the hallway Caren heard the source of the booming voice.

A tall woman with a flowing skirt that billowed around wide hips appeared through an open doorway. The skin around her chin was loose but Caren could tell she had been fine boned once. Her steely grey hair brushed her shoulders. She stood looking at Drake and Caren.

'I didn't know you had company. There's a problem with the water main.'

'This is Detective Inspector Drake. They're here about that ghastly business with Mostyn and Jane Jones. My wife, Catherine, Inspector.'

'Ah, yes, dreadful. How can we help?' Catherine said. It was more of an order than a question.

'We're going into the library. Are you going to join us, darling?' de Northway said.

'Of course, of course.'

Drake skirted around the room deliberately idling alongside the photograph on the tabletop still covered in fine dust. Casually he paused. 'That's Maldwyn Evans, isn't it?'

'Cambrian Club do a few years ago. The club celebrated thirty-five years. Wonderful dinner. One of the best.'

'I should recognise the others. But ...'

De Northway caught the bait easily enough. 'That's Rhys Fairburn.'

Drake had already recognised him.

'And who is the other man?'

De Northway was enjoying himself. 'And that's Aiden Hawkins.' He pointed to the man at the end of the group with a stern look. 'He was in the regiment with me. Of course, you should know him – recently appointed to the bench. Damn fine judge too.'

Drake glanced over at Caren before mumbling. 'Of course.'

Caren sat alongside Drake on an old sofa. The edges of the rug in front of the large open fireplace were frayed, the material lying in curling loops. Catherine found a packet of cigarettes from a box on the coffee table and after the first lungful let out a deep crackling cough.

De Northway sat down next to his wife and announced, 'Inspector Drake suspects I killed Ed to get the cottage back.'

Catherine took another drag of her cigarette and blew a mouthful into the air. 'It would give us the most perfect motive for his murder.'

Drake stared at her.

'But I'm afraid we disappoint you. We have nothing to do with his death, especially if it's linked to that poor girl,' de Northway said.

He sat back, looking down his nose at Drake.

'And I understand you have a planning application on land adjacent to Tyddyn Du and Ed Mostyn's property for a solar farm.'

'It's the way of the future. Green energy. Gets

my vote all the time.'

'I need to ask you about the cottages. Are they used regularly?'

'Of course not.'

'We have eyewitnesses who told us that they've regularly seen people use the cottages, nearly always at night. Who has keys apart from you?'

'The keys are kept here and there's only one set. What are you alluding to?'

Caren cleared her throat, uncertain whether she really should contribute.

'We have one witness who tells us that the cottages were used for sex.'

Catherine snorted, then her whole torso shook before a cough rattled free.

'And I must ask you about another allegation about parties that you hosted here over the years.'

Catherine blew out another lungful of smoke. 'Nothing like that going on any longer. Not since poor Somerset had problems with his prostate. Whatever you've heard is probably absolutely true. I had a very powerful libido years ago, Inspector and Somerset and I understand each other fully.'

Caren darted a glance at Drake. There was a mixture of disgust and then surprise in his expression.

'And why did you move furniture out of one of the cottages the day after Jane was killed?'

De Northway stood up abruptly. 'What do you mean? What on earth are you insinuating?'He walked to the end of the sofa and turned to Drake. 'Well, you can go and rot in hell. It's types like you that's the cause of this country going to the dogs. We haven't got a police state.' He lifted an arm and pointed towards the door.

Winder spent the rest of the afternoon chasing round the side streets of Amlwch, the town nearest to Cemaes, in a vain attempt to find a milkman. He tried the number repeatedly but eventually gave up, convinced that he had the wrong number. Visiting various shops drew a blank and calling at the police station and asking very officer if they knew the identity of the milkman earned him odd stares.

He called at bed and breakfast premises and then at one of the hotels that finally gave him a business card for Underwood's business. Winder almost screamed out of frustration when he noticed that the number he'd been given earlier was wrong. He scrambled for his mobile and punched in the correct number.

Then he cursed out loud when a voice began, 'I'm not available. Please leave a …Hello, who is this?'

For a moment Winder thought it was part of the message. 'It's Detective Constable Gareth Winder, Wales Police Service. I need to talk to you.'

'Why?'

'I need to speak to you, Mr Underwood.'

Winder jotted down the address and the post code that he punched into the satnav. A few minutes later he was parking behind the milk van. He almost ran up the drive to the front door of Underwood's home.

The door opened without Winder having to ring the bell. 'What's all the panic about?'

Underwood was still in the pale white T-shirt. He had deep brown bags under both eyes that Winder put down to sleeping at odd hours. The prospect that Underwood had nothing constructive to add would mean the complete waste of a day. Winder didn't relish explaining that to Drake.

'I'm investigating the death of Ed Mostyn and

Jane Jones.'

'What's that got to do with me?'

'You have a regular milk round in Cemaes?'

'Yes. But I don't …'

'Can I come in?'

Half an hour passed as Winder asked the same questions he'd asked all morning. Underwood was yawning frequently by the time Winder got to his last question.

'We know that Ed Mostyn was friends with Llywelyn who runs the bakery—'

'He's a jerk.'

'I'm sorry?'

'He doesn't like me. Doesn't like anybody who's English if you ask me. But I still take him milk every morning.'

'I'm just wondering if you saw Mostyn there the night before he was killed.'

'No, sorry mate. The place was all closed. Usually I see a light in the morning or something but the place was dead so I left the milk outside.'

Winder took in a long breath, wanting to hide the eagerness in his voice. 'Can you be certain?'

'I'd recorded the first Manchester United game of the season the night before. I was going to watch it before getting some sleep. All this working nights buggers up your life.'

Chapter 25

The following morning Drake arrived early at headquarters after a stilted conversation with Sian when she had asked him, with typical objectivity, about the arrangements for 'the move'. He had reassured her that he was collecting the keys to his flat that afternoon.

He dragged a chair over to the board and stared at the photographs of the Cambrian Club dinner. Rhys Fairburn, Somerset de Northway and Judge Aiden Hawkins all looked jovial, probably drunk, Drake thought. He wanted to convince himself that it was only a matter of time before he could find the right motive for one of them to have killed Jane.

Fairburn and de Northway had a motive for the death of Mostyn, but then Drake faltered with nothing to implicate Judge Hawkins. And there'd be other Cambrian Club members, all well respected in the community. He looked over at Gwynfor Llywelyn's image and the certainty that the killer was among the dinner-suited men in the photographs evaporated. He stared at them, wondering what secrets they could share. Back in his office he opened a notebook and made four columns. At the top of the first he wrote the name 'Mostyn' and beneath it the names of the men in the photograph found in his cottage. Then he repeated the exercise for Evans and Fairburn and de Northway. He sat back and rubbed his eyes, as though that might help him see some hidden meaning. He doodled wavy lines between the names of all the men involved. It was the sort of gesture designed to help him think. They'd have to interview Fairburn and he would have to notify the sergeant in the SOCP team. And maybe de Northway was the 'English voice' Tracy had mentioned. Despair crept into his mind that they might never find

Stephen Puleston

the killer.

Caren was the first to arrive and she peered into his room. He waved a hand and she pushed open the door.

'I want to review everything before we interview Fairburn.'

'Have you thought that there might be two killers?'

'It's possible but for now let's concentrate on Fairburn.'

He looked again at the names on the paper. Two of the men were dead and there was enough evidence to charge Fairburn with historic sex offences but this time he wasn't going to take any risks.

Drake sat back and decided that the rest of the morning had to be spent reviewing everything. Caren drifted back to her desk.

He opened a new page on his notepad and scribbled means, opportunity and motive under Mostyn's name. There was a clear list of people with a motive, some easier to add to the list than others. After scribbling the names of Evans and Fairburn he stopped, ballpoint poised ready. He simply wrote *somebody else* but it made no sense, so he scribbled it out and added *girls* and then the word *laptop*. Then he added *Cambrian Club?*

He googled Cambrian Club and wasted enough time to make himself feel guilty. Then he found Dafydd Higham's number and made the call.

'Is Mr Higham expecting your call?' the receptionist cooed.

'No, but I'm sure he'll speak to me.'

Soothing music played in the handset before he heard Higham's voice. 'Inspector Drake, how can I help?'

'You're still the secretary of the Cambrian

Club?'

'Yes.'

'I need a list of the Cambrian Club members.'

'Of course. Can I send them to you by email?'

'Thanks.'

Once Drake had given him the right email address he rang off, dismayed that Higham seemed so disinterested in the murder inquiry into his brother-in-law's death. Winder appeared at his door and Drake waved him in.

'You won't believe this, sir. I found a milkman in Cemaes who delivers to Llywelyn every morning and guess what, on the morning of Mostyn's death the bakery was empty first thing.'

'Can he be certain?'

'It was the night after a Manchester United game on the television, which he'd recorded. I did double-check.'

'Well done, Gareth. That puts Llywelyn back in the frame. We'd better talk to that girl who works for him. Where is Dave?'

'He went back to Rhosneigr. He still had a couple of witnesses to see.'

'Good, good. Review later then, once he's back.' His mind was already computing what else needed to be done.

Drake then started a Google search.

Judge Hawkins produced a lot of entries, mostly summaries of his career with references to his army service before his elevation to the bench. An image of Hawkins, dressed formally in breeches and holding white gloves with his wife alongside the high sheriff, was the first search result Drake found.

Then he imagined what Price would say if he suggested interviewing Judge Hawkins. What possible justification do you have? Drake could almost hear the incredulity in Price's voice. He'd be right of course. He stared again at the word *laptop*, deciding that starting at the beginning was as good a place as any. Mostyn's girlfriend had alleged he had photographs of young girls on his laptop. They'd been sent to Evans but seemingly no further. Drake shook off the feeling that it was impossible to think of Evans and Mostyn being the only two involved in the paedophile ring.

He walked through into the kitchen, flicked on the electric kettle and reached for the ground coffee granules from the cupboard. He had the container in his right hand. He thought about his rituals. Then about Sian and the girls. He replaced the tin and made instant instead.

Returning to his office, he knew the specialist officers would have to take over the historic sex abuse allegations, but for now it was his case. It made him realise that he should discuss the protocols with Price, but a nagging doubt pushed it to the back of his mind as he turned to the box of papers belonging to Evans on the floor of his office.

It was full of bank statements and piles of correspondence with the bank. He tried in vain to find the accounts for Evans's business, realising that after his death the inquiry into him had fizzled out, his concentration suddenly focusing on the possibility that they might have missed something. He was certain that Howick should have been responsible for getting the records.

Glancing at his watch, he realised he was late, so he grabbed his jacket and strode out of his office. Caren was poring over the computer on her desk. 'We need the accounts for Evans's business. I'm going out for couple of hours. Check with Dave and then contact Inland Revenue and get them to email copies.'

'Of course, boss,' Caren said, as he turned and

left.

It had been years since Drake had rented a flat and his recollection of the formalities bore no resemblance to the mountain of paperwork that the agents insisted was necessary. He sat on the visitor's chair as the lettings manager tapped away on her keyboard. The name badge pinned to the lapel of her navy jacket said Jackie P. Hallam alongside the corporate logo of the estate agency office. What did the P. stand for – Paula or maybe Patricia? On the other side of the office two women sat by desks, both busy on the telephone, both explaining about various available properties in loud and positive terms. They all had the same navy blue jackets, white blouses and name badges.

'I'm really sorry about all this paperwork,' Hallam said.

Drake folded his arms and adjusted his position on the chair, uncertain whether she really was.

'The credit reference search is fine. And we've had all the necessary references from your employers.'

Hallam gave him a brief smile and for the first time he thought about what exactly the reference would have said. Had it said something about his personal circumstances? He recalled the inquisitive look from the human resources manager when he'd given her the necessary form to complete.

'I have the paperwork from the deposit company.' Hallam tucked an A4 sheet into a plastic folder and handed it to Drake. Then she began a long explanation of how the deposit would be held by a third party until the tenancy was at an end. 'I'll need to go around the property with you so that we can check the inventory.'

Hallam reached into a drawer, found two sets of

keys and left her desk. Drake followed her out into the afternoon sunshine. It was a short drive to the block of purpose-built flats in the middle of Colwyn Bay. Hallam walked around the flat with Drake, ticking off all the furniture and appliances that had been included. She hesitated by the door.

'When are you moving in, Ian?'

'Tomorrow, I hope, if I can get everything organised.'

'Where are you from originally?'

'Near Caernarfon.'

'That's a lovely part of the world.'

Drake checked his watch; he was late for a meeting back at headquarters. 'Are we finished? It's just that ...'

'Of course.' She held out the keys. 'Where were you stationed before you moved to Colwyn Bay?'

Drake took the keys. 'I've been based here in Northern Division for over ten years.'

Hallam stood for moment as though she were expecting Drake to continue. 'If you have any queries, please give me a call.' She smiled as she left.

He walked through each room of the flat wondering how his life had come to this, debating the practicalities of where Helen and Megan would sleep when they came to visit. Eventually he closed the door behind him and drove to headquarters, trying to refocus his mind on the investigations.

The first thing Drake noticed was the image of Catherine de Northway pinned to the Incident Room board. He guessed that Caren was responsible, just as she had been in sharing the details of de Northway's social life with Howick and Winder judging from the smirk on their faces.

'Any progress in Rhosneigr?' Drake said to Howick.

'There are lots of witnesses who saw Huw Jones. And some who saw him arguing with Jane.'

Drake raised an eyebrow. 'So Tracy's evidence is corroborated. At least that helps.'

'Is this taking us anywhere, boss?' Howick added. 'Can't help but think it was a waste of time.'

Drake needed no reminding that the inquiry wasn't making progress, certainly not from a junior officer. He had Price to see and he desperately wanted something to report. He repressed the desire to reply with some sharp comment, so he turned to the board.

Winder gave Howick a surreptitious glance.

'Dave's got some news.' Caren smiled as she looked towards Howick.

Drake looked over at a beaming Howick. 'The results came through this morning, sir. I got the promotion.'

'Congratulations, well done.' Drake stepped over to Howick's desk and extended a hand. 'Sergeant Howick. It has a good ring to it.'

Back in his office Drake clicked into his inbox. A dozen emails had arrived since he'd left earlier that day and carefully he opened each in turn, checking for anything of value. He deleted most but the final email was from Inland Revenue, attaching the accounts for Maldwyn Evans. He opened the first of the three documents and stopped at the second page. His stared at the details; his jaw tightened and a muscle twitched under one eye. He shouted for Howick, who moments later appeared at his door.

'Damn it, Dave. Why the hell did you miss this?'

Howick gave him an odd look. The printer on the table whined and spewed out various sheets of paper.

'Maldwyn Evans had a partner in the business.' Drake gathered the pages from the top of the printer and pushed them at Howick. 'Catherine de Northway.'

Before Howick could say anything Drake's mobile rang. He recognised Price's number. 'I need to see you now.'

Drake didn't have time to reply before the line went dead.

'He is the undersheriff for Christ's sake.'

Price leant towards Drake, palms flat on his desk. Drake stood, waiting for the invitation to sit down.

'I've had that idiot of a judge on the telephone already.' Price's South Walian accent was more pronounced the angrier he became.

'Judge?' Drake said.

'Judge Hawkins. You know, the one who was in the army. How the hell they made him a judge is beyond me.'

Drake's throat tightened.

'He wanted to be kept informed about the inquiry. He reminded me, in that upper-class accent, that Somerset de Northway would soon be the queen's judicial representative.'

Price waved a hand towards a chair and then stroked his forehead with the fingers of his left hand. If it was intended to soothe his temper it didn't succeed. 'He must be completely fucking mad if he thinks I'm going to tell him anything. I'm sure he thinks, because he's English, he can throw his weight around.'

Price slumped back in his chair. 'What can you tell me about Somerset de Northway?'

It's more what I can tell you about Hawkins, thought Drake. 'Judge Hawkins appears in a photograph of Cambrian Club members in de

Northway's morning room.'

Price's mouth fell open slightly. 'What are you trying to suggest?'

'We've got two other similar photographs and three of the men featured are involved with a paedophile ring. Mostyn was killed, Evans threw himself under a train. And one of Jane's friends has told us she was abused by Rhys Fairburn – who is one of the men in the photographs – and another man with an English accent.'

Price blew out a lungful of breath. 'And de Northway?' An edge of despair had crept into Price's voice.

After fifteen minutes Drake had managed a detailed explanation but from the lack of eye contact he was convinced that Price had paid little attention, except for the part where he'd described Catherine de Northway's admission about her sexual proclivities when Price had opened his eyes wide and stared intently at Drake.

'Do you have any *realistic* suspects?'

'I'll need to speak to Catherine de Northway about the Evans accounts.'

Price curled his hands behind his head and, leaning back in his chair, propped his shoes on the desk.

'And how do you suggest we discuss this with Judge Hawkins?'Price added.

Drake opened his mouth as if to say something but Price continued. 'It's a mess. We'll arrange to discuss it with Andy Thorsen first thing in the morning.'

Chapter 26

Sian narrowed her eyes and folded her arms severely. She even managed to flex the muscles of her jaw as Drake told her that he'd have to postpone the arrangements she had so carefully choreographed for him to leave the house the following morning.

'What am I supposed to tell my mum?' Sian said through gritted teeth.

Drake wanted to suggest that she ought to make clear to her mother that killers had a habit of ruining the best-laid plans. But it wasn't a question that needed a response, despite Sian's stare. Helen and Megan could go and stay with *Nain* tomorrow night instead. He could imagine her delight in participating in the planning for him to leave the house.

Drake spent a sullen evening sitting by the kitchen table watching various television programmes. He heard Sian in the sitting room talking occasionally on the telephone. He slept fitfully in the spare bedroom, dreaming about attending a Cambrian Club dinner and having to make a speech and endure the stares of elderly members who failed to laugh at his jokes.

The following morning Sian was up earlier than he'd expected.

'And what time are you likely to be back tonight?'

It was a question she had asked a dozen times, maybe hundreds of times. That morning there was finality in her tone as though she took pleasure in knowing it was the last time she'd ever have to ask.

'I'll send you a text later,' Drake said, as he left the house without breakfast.

Outside he stood next to the Alfa parked on the drive. The smell of frying bacon from an open window drifted through the morning air. He smiled briefly at one of the neighbours leaving for his regular Saturday morning slot on the golf course.

He sat in the car clutching the key, suddenly feeling sad and uncertain about the future. He fired the engine into life and started the short distance to headquarters, stopping to buy a newspaper as he did every day, which he folded open at the Sudoku puzzle.

He was still parked outside the newsagents when his mobile bleeped. He recognised Winder's number– *please make contact – urgent.* It was less than a five-minute drive to headquarters, so he slammed the car into first gear and made it in under four, parking next to Price's BMW.

He found his mobile under some papers on the passenger seat and dialled Winder's number. 'What's up?'

'Where are you, boss?'

'Just parked.'

'Something you need to see.'

Drake reached reception and, ignoring the lift, he took the stairs two at a time to the Incident Room. Winder was huddled over a computer screen, Howick sitting alongside, Caren nowhere in sight.

The light glistened off Winder's recently shaved head and, when he turned, Drake could see the worry etched in his eyes. Howick stood up, straightened and looked down at his colleague.

'There are some photographs that have appeared on Twitter overnight, sir,' Howick said.

Drake joined both officers. 'Show me.'

Winder clicked a couple of times and the top of the screen filled with an attractive early morning image, harsh shadows, the last vestiges of the early morning fog trailing in the distance. Drake noticed the narrow channel of water lying almost stagnant, waiting for the tide to turn. Then he saw the fork, upright in the sand

and the outline of Mostyn's body.

Bile gathered in his throat and he drew his right hand into a fist. He picked out the words *gone fishing* and *latest tourist attraction.* 'Can we trace the bastard who did this?'

'We've already started enquiries with Twitter,' Howick said.

'It must be the same sick individual who put up that Facebook page,' Drake added, still staring at the screen. 'We need to find him. Now. He could be our best witness.'

'Or the culprit,' Winder said.

Somehow Drake couldn't imagine de Northway or even Llywelyn being twisted enough to display a photograph of Mostyn pinned to the mud. Experience told him that he should keep an open mind and never dismiss the possibility of human beings being capable of anything. He was still staring at the screen when he remembered his meeting with Price and Thorsen. He cursed silently. He was already late and his pulse pounded.

'I've got a meeting with the superintendent,' Drake said, wagging his finger at Winder and Howick. 'I want a full report from Twitter by the time I'm back.'

Drake arrived at the senior management suite and Hannah, Price secretary, glanced at her watch and frowned. He pushed open the door and two sets of eyes darted a look at him.

'You're late,' Price began.

'I'm sorry, sir. Something came up this morning—'

'Sit down.'

Drake mumbled an acknowledgement at Andy Thorsen. The crown prosecutor simply nodded back – no good mornings or even the barest of smiles.

Price made an exaggerated gesture of checking

the time on his watch. 'I haven't got much time, Ian. I'm travelling to Cardiff this morning. There's an important dinner this evening.'

Price sat back in his chair. The light-blue shirt had the Gant logo on the breast pocket and Drake noticed the chalk-coloured chinos that looked expensive.

'Are you making any progress?' Thorsen said.

'Mostyn, Evans and Fairburn were in a paedophile ring. We're still trying to trace one of the victims.'

'Is there any direct evidence?' Thorsen said.

'Two girls willing to give evidence. And we've got photographs—'

Thorsen continued in the same deadpan manner. 'Do you have *any* suspects for the death of Ed Mostyn? Anybody we can put at the scene at the time of his murder?'

Drake glanced over at Price who stared at him, an inscrutable look on his face. 'This morning a Twitter account appeared showing a picture taken at the time of Mostyn's death. We're urgently trying to find the person responsible.'

Thorsen curled up his mouth. 'You'll have to do better than that. And Jane Jones?'

'She was linked to a paedophile ring. But we can't—'

'So, another dead end.'

Price was tapping a fountain pen on a pile of papers on his desk. 'Get to the point, Ian.'

'Catherine de Northway is in some way involved with the business affairs of Maldwyn Evans. I'll need to interview her.'

Thorsen rolled his eyes as Price propped both hands behind his head.

'Be careful. Follow every protocol to the letter,'

Thorsen said.

The saliva in Drake's mouth had nearly all disappeared. He dampened his lips. 'We found a set of photographs. All taken at a Cambrian Club dinner. Mostyn is included, Evans is pictured as well and Rhys Fairburn.' Drake curled his fingers around the edge of the desk and squeezed hard. 'Another guest at the Cambrian dinner was Judge Aiden Hawkins.'

'And you're trying to make assumptions that they're somehow implicated?' Thorsen said, raising his voice slightly. 'So far as I'm aware the legal system hasn't developed into guilt by association, just yet.'

'Nothing wrong with being a member of a Cambrian Club,' Price said.

Thorsen nodded his head slowly.

'I wasn't suggesting there was,' Drake said.

Thorsen glared at Drake. 'You have absolutely nothing to justify speaking to Hawkins. I suggest you concentrate on your present lines of enquiry.' He fumbled through the papers on his lap. 'And remember, there is every possibility the deaths are unrelated.'

Price was staring at some papers on his desk.

'Are we finished?' Price stood up. 'Keep me posted, Ian.'

Drake got up and left the senior management suite. He made his way back to the Incident Room, hoping that Winder and Howick would have some progress to report but the dismay on their faces made clear he was going to be disappointed.

'Twitter need a warrant,' Winder said.

'And then?'

'They'll consider the request,' Howick added.

'For Christ's sake!'

Another hour elapsed until the necessary warrant was emailed to a senior account manager at Twitter. It was almost lunchtime by the time he sat back in his chair and thought about Catherine de Northway and what the connection to Evans could be. He tapped her name into a Google search. A couple of articles appeared from a local newspaper referring to her support for various local charities and then glamorous images of her at important local functions. He requisitioned a financial assessment, hoping there'd be something different from the result on her husband

After lunch he got back to the notes he'd made the previous day. They looked a mess and all the wavy lines seemed to merge into each other. Through the open door of his office he heard the telephone ringing in the Incident Room and then Winder's voice whooping with delight.

'Found him, boss,' Winder shouted.

Drake was on his feet, car keys at the ready.

An hour later Drake dawdled around a council estate in the middle of Holyhead, a few miles from where Ed Mostyn's body had been found. The block of flats had five storeys with views over the harbour and the middle of the town. The police national computer check had produced a list of previous convictions for Dylan South, which included indecent assault and various convictions for drug-related offences.

Drake pulled up behind a white van covered with the livery of a plastering company and rang the local sergeant who snorted when Drake asked about South.

'He's a weirdo. He'll come in here all times of the night making complaints. He's a constant pain in the neck.'

'Any family?'

'Don't think so …'

'Is he working?'

'You're joking, of course. He lives on benefits, but that doesn't stop him having a top-of-the-range mountain bike.'

'A bike?' Drake immediately knew how idiotic it sounded.

'Yes, you know, two wheels and pedals.'

Drake peered through the windscreen, scanning the pavement and looked up towards the fourth-floor flat. Net curtains had been drawn on two of the windows; another had a casement slightly ajar. His mobile rang. It was Winder, who had parked a little way behind him.

'Any sign, boss?'

'Let's go and see if anyone's at home.'

Drake left the car, Winder and Howick following behind. They reached the main entrance and faced a bank of entry buttons. Drake pushed the light-blue button next to the number eight and the loudspeaker made a brief crackling sound. He waited for a few seconds and tried again but there was no response. He tried the next button down. A few seconds later they heard a timorous woman's voice. 'Who's there?'

'I'm trying to find Dylan South, who lives in number eight. Could you open the door please? It's important police business.'

'What's that got to do with me?'

'Nothing madam. Could you open the door?'

The loudspeaker went quiet and then the lock buzzed. Drake pulled back the door and led the other two up the staircase to the fourth floor. Number eight was at the front of the building; a mountain bike was chained and padlocked in the hallway. He hammered on the door. Then he shouted, 'Dylan South. Open up. Police.'

Behind the closed door there was shuffling, as though someone was dragging their feet on the floor.

The door opened but caught on a chain and a woman's face appeared.

'What do you want?'

'Is Dylan South here?'

Drake pushed his warrant card towards her. She eased the door closed and let the chain fall back.

'I don't know where he is.'

'Can we come in?'

'Suppose.'

The woman had long matted hair draped over her shoulders and a colourless complexion to her skin. Two small crosses were pinned to either side of her nostrils. Drake marched past her and into a lounge, which was dominated by a large television. To one side a bookcase was stacked with DVDs. Back in the hallway he peered into the empty kitchen, before walking towards the bedrooms. At least there was one tidy bedroom, Drake thought, as he looked at the bank of monitors and a table next to a PC. He turned to Winder

'We'll need to seize all of this.'

'Yes, sir.'

'And do a search of the rest of the flat.' Drake marched back to the lounge where the girl was now sitting on a sofa.

'What's your name?'

'Cathy.'

'Any ID?'

Cathy shrugged.

'Have you got a driving licence?'

She shook her head.

'Anything to confirm who you are?'

The girl sat back in the sofa.

'You live here?'

'Sometimes.'

'So where is Dylan?'

'I don't know.'

It took all of Drake's self-control not to shout. 'When was he here last?'

'Dunno.'

'What the hell do you mean?'

Howick piped up behind Drake. 'We need to know where Dylan is, Cathy. He's in big trouble. Have you got a mobile number for him?'

'No. Sometimes he stays with his mates.'

'Where?' Drake spat out the question.

'Dunno. Out in the country.'

Drake stood, leaning against his car, watching Winder and Howick hauling various bits of equipment from South's flat. He'd already left detailed instructions with area control about the apprehension of South. It's impossible for a man on benefits and known to the police to simply disappear, Drake thought. It would only be a matter of time.

Driving back over the island Drake decided to detour to see his mother. After crossing the Menai Strait he indicated left off the A55, drove through Caernarfon and then onwards to the farm. He reached the turning for the lane down to the smallholding and parked. He could just make out the towers of Caernarfon castle. A thin veil of white cloud stretched over the sky. In the distance he watched a couple of microlights travelling slowly towards Anglesey. It was a view he had taken for granted as a boy, but one that he now valued more than ever. He felt guilty that he hadn't made an effort to visit his mother more frequently. There were always lame excuses, busy at work, having to spend time with the family.

He drove down towards the farmhouse, reassured by the sound of car tyres crunching on the slate waste. By the time he'd left the car Mair Drake was standing by the door.

'You got here quickly,' she said. 'Supper won't be long.'

Force of habit made him point the remote at the car. He kissed her on the cheek and followed her into the house.

'You're working too hard,' she said eventually. 'You shouldn't have to work on a Saturday.'

Drake mumbled a reply. He had mulled over how to tell his mother that he was moving to a flat that weekend. He could have told his father easily enough, or was he just thinking that because Tom Drake was no longer with them?

'I've got some news,' he said, sitting down by the kitchen table.

His mother gave him a stern look. 'I don't know what to expect any longer,' she said.

'I'm moving out tomorrow. I've got a flat in town.'

'I see. Is it big enough to have Helen and Megan stay?'

'Yes, of course.'

Mair Drake narrowed her eyes. 'I never really thought that Sian and you were suited.'

Momentarily stunned, Drake looked at his mother. 'You never said anything.'

'What could I have said? You'd never have listened.'

A cloud of resentment hung over the meal as Drake thought that hindsight was the most useless emotion known to man. It was getting dark by the time he left.

Chapter 27

Drake woke early and stared at the ceiling. A gloomy light filtered through the curtains. He had barely spoken with Sian for several days and their conversation earlier that week with Helen and Megan had been the most painful experience of his life. How do you explain to young children that their parents are splitting up? He didn't have the answer and he'd stumbled over things that he should have said, forgotten others and wanted everything to be back to normal.

Helen had given him a look that reminded him so much of how Sian could challenge everything he'd say with a simple turn of her head and a raised eyebrow. 'There are lots of my friends in school whose parents are divorced,' she had said, as though separation was an everyday occurrence.

He knew from his counselling that an emotional crisis in childhood could have a profound effect. He wanted to insulate Helen and Megan from any fallout, build a bubble around them so that he could protect them. A sense of guilt kept telling him that the demands of his work were the source of the guilt. Sian had thought it best that both girls stay with her mother the night before. 'I don't want the girls to see you packing.' She had made it sound distant and remote.

A small part of him blamed her decision to work fulltime in the practice, as once she'd started that, the reproaches about his rituals and his absences had intensified. The house was still quiet when he left the spare bedroom and padded downstairs. He turned the volume of the television to low and switched on the kettle. He flicked through the channels without paying any attention to the various programmes, his mind distracted by Ed Mostyn. His killer had obviously been somebody who knew his movements, Drake thought.

His concentration was broken as Sian entered the kitchen, already dressed.

'I need to do some shopping.' She made the announcement sound faintly regal. 'Are you going to be long?'

'I'll text you when I'm finished, if you like.'

'Yes, thanks.' Sian turned on her heels and left. Although he had never admitted to Sian about the cannabis he'd smoked as a student, it struck him that smoking a joint later that evening might well appease the creeping loneliness.

He drank coffee without enthusiasm, ate a couple of pieces of toast and then showered and dressed. It took him a couple of hours to pack his belongings but he was distracted by finding old shirts and crumpled ties in the back of drawers. He agonised about which of the old clothes he should discard.

He filled the boot of his car with cases. The stereo system was wedged carefully on the rear seat between piles of clothes. Finally he loaded the car with the boxes of cutlery and crockery that Sian had put to one side in the garage. She had reminded him that he'd need to buy washing-up liquid, cleaning fluids and bleach.

Once the car was full he went back into the house, knowing that the neighbours would be intrigued. He walked around the house one more time, checking for things he might have forgotten.

Outside, he stood for a moment by the front door, before pulling it shut behind him and he rattled the door three times, always three times, just to make certain. He scanned the street; it was unusually quiet, nobody washing cars despite it being Sunday. He climbed into the Alfa and drove away.

It was the end of the afternoon by the time Drake parked outside the superstore. The electric kettle in the flat didn't work, the toaster he'd seen on his first visit had disappeared and he also needed a television. He couldn't remember ever shopping alone for domestic appliances. Drake declined the offer of help from an energetic assistant, probably no more than eighteen, who came bounding up to him as he entered.

He walked around the various counters looking at different colours of kettles, some with matching toasters. After deciding on a dark purple one he paid and took the purchases to the car before returning to choose a television.

A long row of screens showed short clips of various films and it surprised Drake how quickly technology could move on.

'Do you play games?' an assistant asked. His name badge said 'Pete'.

For some reason Drake immediately thought about Kevin Spacey as an American congressman who relaxed by playing with an Xbox in the drama series *House of Cards*. Perhaps he should think about gaming as a hobby.

'No, I don't.'

'Have you thought about the possibility of 3D?' Pete pointed towards a bank of expensive-looking televisions. Drake occasionally watched Blu-ray films but when he saw the price of a 3D set he shook his head and walked back towards the row of gleaming screens. Pete's tone of voice indicated that Drake was a dinosaur. Eventually, he made a decision and Pete gave him an insipid smile before trooping off towards a door that said 'Staff Only/Stockroom'. He returned moments later carrying a large box that he took to the counter. His smile was more sincere by now.

'Would you like an extended warranty? They

are very good value for money and protect you for up to five years.'

Drake shook his head.

'Would you be prepared to take part in a short survey? You'd have the opportunity of winning a thousand pounds.'

Drake narrowed his eyes. 'No, thanks.'

Drake headed for the door but before he reached the exit he saw Caren walking towards him. She smiled briefly. 'Hello, sir.' She looked down at the box he was carrying. 'On your own?' She looked around for Sian.

'Ah … Yes.'

'Did you find what you are looking for?' Caren sounded like one of the assistants. 'I thought I saw earlier, when we were looking at the washing machines.'

Drake knew he should tell Caren about what was happening at home but the foyer of an electrical store hardly seemed appropriate. Over Caren's shoulder he noticed Alun approaching. 'I'll see you tomorrow.'

'Of course.'

Drake gave Alun a brief nod as he arrived by Caren's side and then made for the door.

Alun had finished unloading the car by the time Caren had boiled the kettle. She filled an old-fashioned red teapot and placed it on the kitchen table to brew. She shouted at Alun who was still fussing in the utility room. She sat by the table, a packet of biscuits open in front of her. She had decided that they needed to continue their last conversation about starting a family. It had been something occupying more and more of her thoughts recently. And now Alun had settled into a regular full-time job with a local company, and with her body clock ticking more loudly, she had to discuss it again.

Alun closed the door and walked over towards her. 'That Ian Drake is a strange one.'

Caren poured tea over the milk in the mugs.

'He saw me coming over towards you in the shop. And just buggered off.'

Caren reached for a biscuit. 'He's been a bit odd the past week or so.'

'He could have stayed to say hello.'

'He was looking at the kettles and toasters earlier. Bit odd seeing him there on his own.'

Caren took a mouthful of digestive.

Alun continued. 'I'd say he was odd all the time.'

'He does have his good points.'

'And they are?'

'Well …'

Alun laughed and then slurped a mouthful of tea.

Caren tried not to sound serious. 'I wanted to talk to you about …'

'What?'

'You know, about starting a family.'

Caren paused.

'Last time we didn't come to any decision. It just … I don't know, it just sort of petered out. But now with you back working fulltime, I thought … And I know that there might be problems. And we would have a lot to plan.'

He reached a hand over the table and held hers.

'My parents could help and I want to have children whilst we're still young enough,' Caren said.

She stopped and stared at Alun. He smiled

back. 'I'm sorry things haven't worked out over the past couple of years—'

'And the WPS are very flexible about working arrangements.'

'Caren.' He squeezed her hand. 'I agree.'

'Things might not work out anyway.'

'Let's not waste any time,' Alun said, smiling broadly.

Chapter 28

An unfamiliar sound drifting up from the street outside woke Drake early and for a moment he couldn't place his surroundings. He got up, showered and dressed. The flat was quiet and he missed the noise from Helen and Megan eating breakfast, preparing for school. Deciding that he'd call them tonight didn't make him feel less lonely, but lessened the guilt marginally.

Leaving the flat, he smiled briefly at a smartly dressed young couple on the stairwell. The man gave him a brief nod of acknowledgement. He walked the short distance down a side street to his car and then drove to headquarters. It unsettled him to take an unfamiliar route so he made an unnecessary detour to the regular newsagent, where he bought a paper.

He had decided after seeing Caren the day before that he needed to tell her about his personal circumstances. Only the barest details of course. And he'd need to speak to Superintendent Price.

Drake wanted that Monday morning to feel like a new start. At least now they had the name of Dylan South and it would only be a matter of time until they'd find him. And he hoped that would be true for Sue Pritchett as well. Perhaps she would know how Jane had come by fistfuls of money and, more importantly, where it had gone.

No sooner had Drake arrived at his office and put the newspaper, folded open at the Sudoku page, on the corner of his desk, than the telephone rang. The voice immediately frayed his nerves.

'Good morning Ian,' Kate French said. 'How are you this morning?' The question was full of implications and immediately Drake thought that she knew about his personal circumstances; perhaps Price had shared a confidence with her at the dinner on Saturday night–

needed counselling after a difficult case– not certain he's got over everything yet.

'Good morning.'

'Wyndham tells me you're making some progress.'

Drake's jaw tightened. Speaking to French was the last thing he wanted on a Monday morning.

'I hear there might be some *challenging* lines of enquiry.'

What the hell did she mean by that?

'Challenging,' Drake repeated. 'Building a picture of the victims is an important part of our job. Unless we've got that we can't start on identifying possible perpetrators.'

'I'm sure you appreciate the sensitivities of this case. Mr and Mrs Higham have made contact with the power company. It seems that Ed Mostyn hadn't made a will, so his sister is entitled to his estate.'

'And that means she can sell the land.'

'Yes, of course. And the adjacent owners will then be able to sell their land. I'm sure Mrs Enid Evans will be very pleased.'

Drake was a fraction of a second from saying something he'd later regret about how pleased Mrs Evans would be to have lost her husband.

'So the nuclear power station will proceed according to plan. But all of this is very confidential. There's been no public announcement. They've got to wait for the lawyers to draw up the papers.'

Drake's grip was tightening around the handset. He wanted to know exactly what this woman knew, exactly what she wasn't telling him.

'Do keep me posted,' French said cheerily before finishing the call.

Drake stood up in a temper. A murder investigation can't take second place to the sale of piece of land, Drake thought, getting angrier by the minute.

He refocused his mind on the tasks in hand as the telephone rang again, breaking his concentration. He didn't hide the annoyance in his voice. 'Drake.'

It was Caren. 'We've traced Sue Pritchett.'

Parking on the promenade in Llandudno would be difficult so Drake found a side street with no restrictions. Caren had kept up a regular commentary on the investigation as they drove the short distance from headquarters. It meant he had little need to contribute to the conversation and for that he was grateful. He nudged the car into a space and they headed on foot towards the seafront. Walking past the entrance to the Great Orme tramway, they passed a queue of families with young children. Drake made a mental note to add the attraction to his to-do list with Helen and Megan.

They reached the end of the street and looked down towards the water's edge. It was a glorious, hot late-summer afternoon; Drake squinted against the sun reflecting off the sand and the wide expanse of the concrete boulevard. Elderly couples ambled hand in hand, disabled scooters threaded their way through the tourists and young families with children thronged the beach.

Briskly they strode towards the hotel where Sue Pritchett was working. A discreet telephone call before they'd left headquarters had already established that she was working that morning. The website had said it was a boutique hotel and there were photographs of luxurious bedrooms, expansive bathrooms and a small opulent dining room.

The receptionist gave Drake a broad perfect-teeth smile, after she peered at his warrant card and then at Caren's. She disappeared into an office and moments later returned to reassure him that Sue would be with him shortly.

A couple in their fifties with healthy tans, generous waistlines and expensive-looking luggage arrived in reception to check out. Drake and Caren moved down towards the entrance door where he read the room rates, realising that guests would need deep pockets.

A young woman emerged from the office behind reception and Drake saw her mumbling apologies to the departing guests, as she looked over in his direction. Her make-up was precise, her hair drawn back into a bun and she had orange-framed glasses. She was tall with broad shoulders and a narrow face.

'Sue Pritchett,' she said, holding out a hand after reaching Drake.

'Is there somewhere we can talk in private?' Drake said.

'Of course.' She knows why we've called, Drake thought and a glance shared with Caren told him she agreed. Pritchett led them into a small office at the back of the building.

'We are investigating the death of Jane Jones,' Drake said, sitting down.

Pritchett said nothing, giving them both a wary gaze.

Drake continued. 'And we have spoken to Tracy and to Becky.' He looked over at Pritchett, but the expression on her face hadn't changed.

'Both of your friends are prepared to make statements that could result in prosecutions. It's important that we have a complete picture. Becky says you were involved as well.'

Pritchett sat upright, her hands folded neatly on her lap. 'Jane never wanted to complain. She wanted to hide it all away. And now maybe I want to do the same. I hate those men for what they did to me and to the others.' She had a cultured accent, crisp vowels, almost elongated, certainly not the average product of a Welsh education.

'Who was involved?'

'That's where they were clever. We were kept apart, at least most of the time. But I know that the Evans man who killed himself was involved. They liked me because I spoke differently from the other girls who'd been brought up on the island. When my parents split up my mother came to live on Anglesey. I hated the place, still do.'

'Can you remember any names?'

Pritchett folded her arms, crossing one leg over the other. 'Of course. There was a slob of a man called Somerset de Northway but I only knew his name after I'd seen his picture in the paper. The others were local.'

'Would you remember their faces? Caren made her first contribution before reaching into her bag for the photographs.

'Maybe.'

Caren handed her the Cambrian Club images and they watched as Pritchett scanned each in turn. 'That's de Northway. And this other man was involved,' she said, pointing to Fairburn's face.

'When did you see Jane last?' Drake said.

'Last month.'

Drake hesitated, nonplussed by the answer. 'Where did you see her?'

'She came to town. I told her I was going to go to the police. But she pleaded for me not to do so. She said she had money, over ten thousand pounds, and then she offered me some of it to keep quiet.'

Drake glanced at Caren, an anxious look on her face.

'Did she tell you where she got the money from?'

'No. And I didn't ask. Then she said she was going away. Leaving Anglesey – she had a boyfriend. They were going to start a new life together.'

'How did she seen?'

'What do you mean?'

'Was she frightened?'

'I don't think so ...'

Drake leant forward in his chair, stared at Pritchett and then spoke slowly. 'I need you to remember everything about your discussion with Jane.'

An hour later Drake and Caren sat in a café in the middle of Llandudno, coffees on the table in front of them in round mugs emblazoned with a fancy Italian-looking logo.

'So where did Jane Jones get all that money from?' Caren said.

Drake stirred a spoon through his Americano. 'We'll need to go back through the bank accounts of Mostyn and Evans. And then those belonging to Fairburn and de Northway in due course. Somebody paid her off.'

'And then had a change of heart?'

'Looks like it.'

'Where's the money gone?'

'Back to its source I'd guess.'

The new evidence from Pritchett would make the investigation even more *challenging*. They had the corroboration they needed. Fairburn could be interviewed – Drake would notify Price as soon as they were back in headquarters before calling Sergeant

Robinson of the SOCP team. And telling Price that they had direct evidence to implicate de Northway in historic sex offences was on the top of Drake's list. That prospect brought a smile to his lips. Caren took her first noisy mouthful of coffee; usually it would have grated but that lunchtime he sat back, unaffected.

'So what next, sir?'

'We get Fairburn in for an interview under caution and search his house.'

'And de Northway.'

'Fairburn first.'

Getting Price to sanction arresting de Northway might have to wait.

Their lunch arrived and Caren smothered her plate, full of fish and chips, with tomato ketchup. Drake had settled on a tuna sandwich with a side salad littered with red and green peppers. The café was full of retired couples eating food without saying anything to each other, staring blankly into space. Caren made the occasional comment through a mouthful of food, the habit that Drake hated. Although he thought that his personal circumstances were nothing to do with Caren, he judged that it would be sensible to tell her; he waited until she'd finished.

'Just thought you ought to know that Sian and I split up.'

Caren blinked a couple of times, but there wasn't surprise or shock at the revelation on her face. 'I'm sorry,' she said eventually.

There wasn't much more that she could say. They finished the rest of their coffees in silence until Drake's mobile rang.

It was headquarters. 'There's someone in reception for you.'

'Who?'

'Asked for you. Said it was about the inquiry

into Ed Mostyn.'

'I'll be there as soon as I can.'

They paid and left the café and returned to headquarters. Drake made his way over to the reception desk where one of the staff read from her screen. 'It's Mr Jessop. He's sitting over there.' She gazed over towards a faux leather sofa. Drake walked over and extended a hand.

'Mr Jessop? Detective Inspector Drake. How can I help?'

'Daniel Jessop. Are you in charge of the Ed Mostyn investigation? It's just that I might have something of relevance.'

Drake led Jessop into a small conference room and force of habit made him put his mobile on the table. Jessop was about five foot six with a strong jaw and an athletic build. His hair brushed his ears and he had a deep tan.

He sat down and drew an envelope from the inside pocket of a jacket which had a padded fleece around the neck. 'I've had this letter,' he said, holding it up in his right hand. 'I know it was written a couple of weeks ago. But I've been away. I do a lot of professional sailing.'

'What letter?'

'The one from you asking about a will for Ed Mostyn. It was signed Detective Constable Howick. I'm sorry, I should explain. I run a small legal practice. I do non-contentious work mostly. Some property work, but mostly looking after people's affairs once they've died. It leaves me enough time for my sailing. And I write the occasional will.'

Drake moved nearer the table and focused on Jessop.

'And last year Ed Mostyn instructed me to prepare a will for him.'

'Have you got a copy?' Drake sounded impatient.

'That's the odd thing. I can recall making the will. He was going to leave everything to a charity. One of those environmental lobbying outfits. And he was very specific about leaving a legacy of £5,000 to a man called Eifion Cooper. I remember it quite distinctly because he gave me a long story about how Eifion Cooper had helped him out years ago and he'd never properly repaid him.'

'Where's the will now?'

'I sent the will to him for signature. I'm sure I sent all my usual forms, telling him how to have the will signed.'

'Did he confirm that the will had been signed?'

'I never heard from him. I know that he paid my bill.'

Drake fiddled with his mobile. 'Do you have a copy? I'll need your original file of course.'

'That's the other odd thing. I can't find it.'

'What do you mean?'

'I can't find it anywhere. We had a break-in recently but I didn't think any files had gone missing. After all, who would want to steal clients' papers?'

'But you must have records on your computer.'

'I've looked there too. The file has gone.'

'Did anyone else have access to your office?'

'Apart from my staff, no. Our auditors have been in and we've had an inspection by the Solicitors Regulation Authority.'

'I'll need a list of all your staff. And did you report the burglary?'

'Of course. A Detective Constable Adam Jones dealt with it.'

Drake scribbled down the details; one of the team could retrieve the papers.

Jessop promised to email a list of his staff and left Drake thinking about Eifion Cooper and the smell of raw fish, Catherine de Northway and how everything fitted together.

Chapter 29

The following morning it wasn't the smell of raw fish that hit Drake's nostrils but the smell of newly cut grass. It always brought back such strong memories of childhood that he idled by the turning for the lane leading to Tyddyn Du and watched the reed bed swaying gently in the late summer breeze. To his left a man sat astride a tractor lawn mower, circling a large meadow.

It was the regular changes of the seasons that reminded him of his grandfather and the patterns of his life. There was simplicity to the farming life that appealed to Drake, especially when he thought about the certainties that his grandparents had. He wondered how they had dealt with estrangement or bereavement, before realising that if he had learnt anything in the police force it was that human nature never changes.

Tyddyn Du still looked a miserable place to live. A permanent cloud of despondency seemed to hang over the place. He powered the car ahead and made for the turning up the lane to the farmhouse. He spotted Huw Jones tramping the fields in his purposeful lopsided gait. Caren was back at headquarters although Drake had arranged to meet her later in Crecrist Hall, and in an odd way he had missed her conversation on the journey over the island.

He parked the car and got out. His skin tingled in the warmth of the sun after the air-conditioning of the car. He glanced over at the house but saw no movement. He strode out in the direction that Huw had been headed. Drake could see that the field was badly maintained from the little he remembered of his father's farming. The ditches were choked with weeds and Drake imagined that in winter the land could be waterlogged. Fences topped with barbed wire needed repairing, long lengths offering no protection for livestock. The Jones family was making it easy for Somerset de Northway to make a claim for possession.

Drake clambered over a rotten wooden gate to reach the field where Huw was working on some of the fences. Looking down the field, Drake saw the sea beyond the field boundary. He had assumed that the murders were linked but the possibility became very real that Jane and Mostyn had been killed by different people. And was he now looking at her killer? He walked down to Huw, who noticed Drake when he was within a few yards and stopped working, stood up and stretched his back slowly. He took off a pair of suede working gloves that he stuffed into a pocket.

'What do you want?'

'It must be a lot of work, repairing all these fences.'

'Yes. I suppose it is.'

'Does your father help?'

'Not much. Not any longer. And the de Northways' land agent is here all the time. Interfering.'

In the distance he could faintly make out a chimney of Crecrist Hall. Drake could easily imagine how poor land like Tyddyn Du could be turned into one giant solar farm. What did de Northway say? – *Green energy. Gets my vote all the time.* And he was planning to get a lot of cash as well, Drake thought.

'Why did you lie to me?' Drake said. 'You told me that you had last seen Jane here in the house the night she died.'

Huw stared back at Drake.

'You were in the club in Rhosneigr. That's where you saw her last. And you had an argument with her.'

Huw stiffened.

'What did you argue about?'

249

'She was running around with lots of men. She was nothing more than a whore.' He spat out the last words.

The words sounded old-fashioned, more likely to have come from Ray Jones.

'Why did you argue with Julian Sandham?'

'He wouldn't leave her alone. They're all the same, lads like that. She just couldn't see it.'

'There was an incident earlier this year with Ed Mostyn, when you assaulted him.'

'I wasn't charged.'

'Come on. You know that was a technicality.'

Huw folded his arms tightly and stared at Drake.

'So why did you lie to me?'

Huw jolted his head towards the farmhouse after a moment's delay. 'He doesn't know I go there. He'd make my life hell if he ever found out.'

For a moment it occurred to Drake that Ray Jones had already made Huw's life wretched. He looked over at Huw – there was something unbearably joyless about him. An interview under caution in the police station would have to wait for another day.

Catherine de Northway tilted her head upwards, blew out a long plume of cigarette smoke and then coughed loudly. She held the hand that was holding the cigarette in an exaggerated pose that reminded Caren of an actor from some vintage film. But what Caren also noticed were her large hands. Not only were her fingers long but her hands were broad and chunky. The flesh of one finger had expanded around a wedding band. Caren couldn't remember the exact words in the pathologist's report on the death of Jane Jones but it had made quite clear that Jane's assailant had strong hands.

Caren had been pleased when Drake had agreed that she conduct the interview with Catherine de Northway and it had been lucky that they had arrived when Somerset de Northway was out.

'We need to speak to you about Maldwyn Evans,' Caren said.

De Northway drew heavily on the cigarette. Two columns of smoke poured out of her nose and Caren resisted the urge to waft her hand in the air.

'Poor man. Terrible way to go.'

'How well did you know him?'

She shrugged. Noncommittal, good sign of a lie coming, Caren thought.

'Did you meet him socially?'

'I can't remember. Somerset would know – shall we wait for him to get home?'

Caren noticed Drake fidgeting with a file of papers by her side.

'Did you meet him professionally?'

Caren sat back a fraction, gauging how de Northway would respond. She is calculating what we know, Caren thought.

'What do you mean?'

'Tell me about your relationship with Maldwyn Evans.' Caren's voice was a little too direct.

'He came to one or two of our parties.'

Drake adjusted his position and let out a brief cough. Caren stared at de Northway, reading every movement of her eyes and face. It wasn't the answer they expected and Caren's initial reaction was to doubt that Evans had been anywhere near any of the de Northway 'parties'.

'When was that?'

Another shrug. Another deep drag on the cigarette followed by another relieving cough.

'Is this helpful? Only I'm very busy and I've got

a thousand and one things to do.'

Caren sat back. This was her interview; she would conduct it in any way that she wanted and Catherine de Northway wasn't going to irritate her anymore.

'Catherine, have you been completely honest with us about your relationship with Evans?'

Using her Christian name caught de Northway off guard and she frowned briefly then rearranged the material of her skirt lying on her knees, avoiding eye contact.

'It's very important for our investigation that we have all the information we need and that we get the background relationships between everyone quite clear. Individuals who fail to cooperate only raise suspicions in our mind. And all of that points to guilt, of course.'

Caren had got into her stride now. Catherine de Northway was guilty, she just knew it. She reached into the folder.

'And we know that you had a business relationship with Maldwyn Evans. You were a partner in his business or you invested money into the farm as your name is mentioned in the accounts for his business.'

'Am I a suspect?'Her voice was slow and full of contempt.

'Are you prepared to answer my questions?'

De Northway took another pull of her cigarette and looked down her nose at Caren. 'I want my lawyer to be present.'

Drake's desk had all the usual Post-it notes in their neat and tidy order when he arrived back. He looked over at the photographs of Helen and Megan. He reached over to adjust the position of each but instead of moving them a few millimetres he picked each one up and looked at them carefully in turn. He smiled to himself as he recalled the holiday in France where the images had been taken.

Caren had been delayed by traffic and arrived a few minutes after him. Drake replaced the frames and sat back as his colleague came into the office.

'She's hiding something.' Caren sat down in one of the visitor chairs.

Drake nodded.

'She's lying and she's devious,' Caren continued.

'She could have killed Jane. Did you see the size of her hands? Somerset de Northway is near the scene of Ed Mostyn's death. So it would have been easy for Somerset to have killed him. They get the cottage back and with Tyddyn Du likely to be empty their plans for the solar farm can proceed.'

'And in the meantime Jane tries to blackmail Somerset de Northway.'

'Catherine de Northway has a business relationship with Evans.'

'Just business?' Caren had a questioning look in her eyes.

'With Mostyn out of the way she can collect on her investment. All very convenient. In the morning I want as much information on Catherine de Northway as we can get. Everything. Then I'll go and get authority from Superintendent Price for an arrest.'

'Two arrests, boss?'

Drake looked over at Caren. 'That's right.'

Drake stayed at his desk for another hour reviewing the paperwork and rehearsing the various arguments he'd put to Price that would justify the arrest of Somerset and Catherine de Northway. As a precaution he rang Hannah to check the superintendent's diary.

'It'll have to be early afternoon,' she said.

They fixed a time and Drake left headquarters.

He collected shopping on the way home to his flat and made a meal without much enthusiasm. Then he rang Helen and Megan and spoke to both girls. He wondered how long it would take him to become accustomed to monosyllabic answers to his questions about their day and their friends at school. He watched the evening news but afterwards he didn't feel like sleeping so he left the flat and drove down to the beach. He parked near the promenade. He drew a fleece tight up against his chin as he walked towards the old pier. The moonlight was a dim reflection off the surface of the flat, calm water and in the distance the blades of the wind farms were silent. It was quiet and Drake hoped that with the investigation coming to an end he could plan to do more with Helen and Megan. After half an hour he shivered before returning to the car. Back in the flat he fell soundly asleep as soon as his head hit the pillow.

Chapter 30

Drake spent the following morning reading reports that included the house-to-house enquires near Ed Mostyn's cottage and misleading statements from well-intentioned members of the public until he couldn't justify to himself that the evidence existed to arrest Somerset and Catherine de Northway. He spent an hour sitting in front of the board, looking at the smiling faces from the formal Cambrian Club dinner, and listening to Howick and Winder and Caren discussing how they all fitted together. Even the burglary at Jessop's office wasn't going to help: there were no forensics, a window had been broken and an entry forced. Money had been taken from a petty cash box as well as an antique corner clock but nothing else had been reported stolen. Drake stared at the face of Gwynfor Llywelyn – and where did he fit in?

Drake was polishing the last paragraph of his memorandum to Price when the telephone rang. He was accustomed to interruptions but this one didn't fray his nerves, as he'd reached the stage where Price would have to make the decision. He might even include Thorsen.

'Area control. We have a report of a fatality. A Mr Fairburn was found dead this morning.'

Drake was still half-reading the memorandum on the monitor on his desk.

'I'm sorry,' he said, recognising a familiar name.

'A Mr Fairburn has been killed.'

Drake stood up; the chair behind him tipped up and finished up on the floor.

'What the hell do you mean?'

'Do you need the address, sir?'

'No, of course not,' Drake replied.

Then he shouted. 'Caren. Fairburn's been

killed.'

He rushed for the door, grabbed his jacket from the stand and headed for his car. They raced over the car park and Drake pointed the remote at the car.

'Get more of the details,' Drake said as he accelerated hard through the gears until he was in the outside lane of the A55, almost reaching a hundred miles an hour. He slowed as he approached the tunnel under the estuary, but once he was clear he pressed his right foot to the floor. The traffic was light in the tunnels through the mountains, but slowing for the roundabouts at Penmaenmawr and Llanfairfechan only added to his frustration. A white delivery van delayed his progress and he pressed the car horn hard and cursed. Eventually the driver pulled into the nearside lane and Drake raced ahead.

Drake paid no attention to the traffic police who passed him on the opposite carriageway and within a few minutes had left the A55 and was slowing to a roundabout at the top of the exit slip. The journey dragged until eventually he drove up the lane leading to the farmhouse and parked alongside two marked police cars. A uniformed sergeant stood by the back door.

'Where's the body?' Drake said.

The police officer dipped his head towards one of the outbuildings. 'The workshop behind the black door over there, sir. Alys Fairburn, the widow, is in the house, hysterical.'

A Mercedes 4x4 screamed to a halt just behind Drake's vehicle. A woman in her thirties jumped out of the passenger seat, followed by the driver, a man about the same age.

'His daughter,' the sergeant said. 'And son-in-law.'

Drake noticed the woman's tear-filled eyes and

puffy cheeks as she raced past him towards the door, followed by her husband.

'Let's have a look at Fairburn,' Drake said to Caren.

A young constable guarding the entrance to the outbuilding stiffened as Drake and Caren approached. Inside, the air was thick with the smell of peat and manure. A single wooden enclosure was the only thing that suggested the building had once been used as a stable. Various implements were propped up against one wall and bags of agricultural lime had left a white trail along the cobbled floor.

'He's in the next section,' the officer said, nodding his head into the main part of the building.

Drake pushed open the door. The afternoon sunlight streamed through the wooden casement windows. He stood, staring at the body of Rhys Fairburn lying on his back. Force of habit made him snap on a pair of latex gloves. He gazed down at the body – a white shirt was blotched with dark stains and his hair was thickly matted from the blood covering his face. A pair of dark navy trousers was covered in dust and dried-up mud. Just behind and above his left ear was a large gaping wound. Instinctively Drake looked around for the weapon. He would have to leave the search to the CSI team. Fairburn's visit to the workshop was unplanned, Drake thought, as he looked at the shine on the dead man's brogues.

Drake recoiled as he took in Fairburn's neck and the two clear punctures wounds. Looking around, he noticed a workbench, its top littered with tools and various empty plant pots. Moving over the recently brushed floor, he knelt down by the body. He reached over and touched the dead man's trousers. The deep throaty sound of a van engine drifted in from the farmyard and he guessed that the crime scene investigators had arrived. At least this time the crime scene investigators won't be working against the tide, Drake thought. There was a chance for forensics. Behind him he heard voices entering the stable.

'Where's Ian?' Foulds said.

'In here, Mike.'

Moments later Foulds stood by Drake's side. 'Jesus. It's exactly like Ed Mostyn.'

Drake turned to Foulds. 'I'm going to see the family. Let me know once you've finished.'

Drake moved past him, back into the stable and then out with Caren. He stood for a moment in the sunshine, taking a few deep breaths. He wanted to be certain that his emotions could never become accustomed to such horror; he had to sense the rawness of death.

'Let's go and see the family.' Drake started walking over to the farmhouse.

In the kitchen two women in their mid-fifties turned and stared at Drake and Caren. The taller one opened her mouth as if she was about to say something, but then Fairburn's daughter strode in. She stood for moment and then blew her nose.

'Detective Inspector Ian Drake. I am very sorry for your loss.'

'Ann Parry. Can we see my ...?'

'Not at the moment.'

She gave him a rather pleading look.

'Once the crime scene investigators have finished we'll arrange to take your father to the mortuary. There will be some formalities of course.'

Ann opened her eyes wide. She had probably seen a dozen television crime dramas where the next of kin have to make a formal identification, but it was never the same in reality.

'I'll need to speak to your mother.'

She shook her head slowly. 'She's in no fit state.'

'I really must insist that I speak with her.'

Caren smiled at Ann. 'It's very important for us to be able to speak to the person who saw him last. Your mother might be able to tell us what his movements were immediately before he was killed.'

Ann's lips quivered and her eyes filled with tears.

Caren continued. 'I know it will be difficult but it's something your mother will have to face.'

Drake looked past Ann. 'Is there someone with your mother?'

'Peter, my husband.' She turned and walked out of the kitchen, Drake and Caren following behind her.

She led them through a newly carpeted hallway, heavy with the smell of fresh paint. There was the sound of movement behind a stripped pine door, which was slightly ajar. Ann pushed it open and Drake saw Alys Fairburn sitting on a sofa, despair and disbelief competing in her expression.

'This is Inspector …'Ann sat down by her mother but struggled to remember Drake's name.

'Detective Inspector Drake and this is Detective Sergeant Caren Waits. My condolences. I need to ask you some questions.'

Alys Fairburn stared at him. Her mouth fell open slightly. 'There's nothing I can say. He's dead. I don't know what to do.'

'Was Mr Fairburn due to see somebody today?'

Alys Fairburn shook her head, grasping the handkerchief between both hands.

'Does he have a mobile telephone?'

'In his study.'

'My dad has an office at the bottom of the hall,'

Ann said.

'And a computer?'

Alys Fairburn blew her nose loudly. 'He spent hours on the computer.'

'Did he have a meeting with anybody?' Drake persisted.

'It was like any other day, I suppose.' Alys Fairburn lifted her gaze and stared at him blankly. 'We're ordinary people. And now he's ... gone.'

Drake looked over at Ann. 'I'll need to see his office.'

She touched her mother's arm and then left taking Drake and Caren down the hallway.

Drake was surprised at the modern feel to the room, its computer set up with two monitors and a large printer on a shelf behind the desk. It had a neatness he admired. Caren stepped towards the bookcase and picked up a photograph in a glossy black frame. She tilted it and offered it to Drake – he nodded his recognition.

'Do you know anything about your father's movements today?' Drake said to Ann, who was standing by the window with her arms firmly folded together.

'Not really. It was another ordinary day. He visited the shops he runs as he always does. Mam said he had some meetings with some suppliers but ... I don't know. Who would want to kill him?'

'Does your father keep a diary?' Drake asked.

Ann pointed at the PC. 'He did everything on that.'

'Did he have more of these photographs of the Cambrian Club dinners?'

Ann looked at her blankly. 'I really don't know.'

Drake sat down by the computer, pressed the 'on' button and stared at the screen. 'I'm sure we'll manage,' he said to Ann.

She glared at Drake before leaving.

'Better get started on his paperwork,' Drake said to Caren. 'I'll see if there was anything on his PC.'

Caren pulled out the top drawer of the filing cabinet and began sorting through papers. Once the computer had booted up Drake clicked on 'My Documents' and found dozens of folders, all neatly tagged with names and dates. He clicked on one entitled 'Property' and began opening the first of a dozen folders with addresses in different parts of the island. It struck Drake that Fairburn was very different from Maldwyn Evans. There were assets and a regular income that supported the lifestyle that Fairburn obviously enjoyed, judging from the file 'Holiday', which had hundreds of photographs of various destinations across Europe.

Drake clicked open the Outlook icon and found the calendar. A box opened with reminders – the first read *year-end figures, urgent* and another said *contact cheese supplier.* He clicked it closed and it occurred to him that Fairburn may have noted down any meetings he had for that day in his computer system. The first entry immediately grabbed Drake's attention. It read '2.30 Gwynfor Llywelyn'. He sat back, tugged at his nose and then glanced at his watch, knowing they had another visit to the bakery to make.

He scanned the various entries in the online diary but nothing else of relevance was obvious. Hours of work were needed on the computer so he found his mobile and called Howick, giving him instructions on how to find the farmhouse.

Ann appeared at the door. 'Do you want coffee or something?'

'No thanks,' Drake said, answering for both of them. 'Did you know that your father was seeing

Gwynfor Llywelyn today?'

'He's been pestering my dad to sell his bread. Dafydd Higham advised him against it. He said Gwynfor Llywelyn had a bad reputation. I always thought he was harmless enough.' Ann rested on the doorframe.

Caren had reached the second drawer and pulled out a folder. 'More photographs,' she announced, stepping towards the desk.

Drake watched as she drew out of the folder images of the black-tie dinner. Now that a second Cambrian Club member had been killed, the inquiry had changed. Judge Hawkins will have to be interviewed, no matter what Thorsen says, Drake thought. But first he had to see Gwynfor Llywelyn.

Drake rattled the door to the bakery but there was no response from inside. He strained to hear the sound of a radio but the place was silent. Finally he knelt down and peered in through the small windows but inside the glass was covered with grime. Caren returned from the back of the building.

'No sign, boss.'

Drake reached for his mobile and rang headquarters. He barked instructions for Gwynfor Llywelyn's address to be texted and moments later his telephone bleeped. 'Let's go.'

It was a short drive to Llywelyn's home, a terrace house with a neat front yard. A large blue-glazed pot stood alongside a terracotta planter, both filled with lavender by the front door. Drake hammered on the door.

'*Iawn. Pwy sydd yna?*'

Llywelyn's voice sounded slurred as he asked who was there, even though he opened the door without waiting for a reply. His eyes looked glazed. Drake wanted to smell cannabis but the house was odour free – maybe he was sitting in the back garden, Drake thought.

'I need to speak to you about Rhys Fairburn.'

Llywelyn gave him a puzzled look. 'Why?'

Drake barged into the house and walked through into the kitchen, a bemused Llywelyn following behind him. He stood by an old table covered in crockery and empty bottles of beer.

Drake looked intently at Llywelyn. 'He's dead.' Drake focused on the reaction. Llywelyn let his mouth fall open, his eyes wide. 'Rhys is dead?'

'Where were you this morning?'

'At his place. I was supposed to meet him.' He drew a hand over his mouth. 'When was he killed?'

'Did you see him?'

'He wasn't there. I waited around and tried his mobile and then I left.'

'Did you see anybody else?'

'Shit, this is terrible. He was going to sell my bread. He was a nice bloke.'

If only you knew, Drake thought.

'Funny thing was, I saw his car when I arrived and I thought he was at home.'

The mobile in Drake's pocket buzzed and he reached in and sent the call to voicemail.

'Did you see anyone else?'

'No.'

'Any other cars?'

'The farm tractor was outside, as well as a motorcycle.'

The mobile rang again; the screen said 'Unknown'. He pressed to decline the call and turned to Llywelyn again.

'Can you account for your movements for the

rest of the day?'

'I went to see my mam.'

'We'll need the details in due course. In the meantime don't go anywhere near the Fairburn family.'

'Why?'

'Because I bloody well say so.' Drake turned and strode out towards the front door, Caren behind him.

They stepped out into the sunshine as Drake's mobile rang again. 'For Christ's sake.' Drake hit the accept button.

'Can you confirm that there's been another murder? I understand Mr Rhys Fairburn has been killed.' The voice sounded authoritative, even calming.

'Who is this?'

'Calvin Headley.'

'No comment.'

'But I'm sure the Wales Police Service would like to comment on a story that we're running in tonight's news.'

Drake said nothing.

'Is it true that you think a serial killer is at work?'

Drake didn't bother even saying 'no comment': he killed the call, and then glared at the mobile before realising he was squeezing the handset tightly in his right hand.

Chapter 31

'Who's going to be next?'

Drake stood by the board, quietly suppressing a yawn – he had woken at six am, his mind racing with possibilities. He turned to look at the team.

Howick stood by his desk, legs slightly apart, powder-blue shirt, tie neatly folded. Winder sat at his desk, shirt open to two buttons, a couple of days' stubble on his head. Both men shared a dark, hard intensity in their eyes as they looked over at Drake standing by the Incident Room board. Caren leant on her desk, her hair pulled back into a rough knot. He didn't need to tell them that things had changed. The photographs of the smiling Rotarians had taken on a new significance with the murder of Fairburn.

'Did you see the television last night, boss?' Winder was the first to say anything.

'Yes, of course.'

'Press is mad to run scare stories like that,' Howick said.

Caren nodded enthusiastically.

'I've got a list of the members of the Cambrian Club. We need to go through all the names and see if any of them have come up in the investigation so far.' Drake hesitated. 'And then we need to dismantle Fairburn's life. I want you to go through everything. And it needs to be done today. There has to be a connection between Fairburn and Jane Jones and Mostyn.'

'And Evans, sir?' Caren said.

'Maldwyn Evans,' Drake said, turning to look at Caren. 'Let's assume that someone wanted both Fairburn and Mostyn dead and that the same motive exists for others in these photographs; Evans killing himself must have been convenient for the killer.'

'Stretching it a bit, boss,' Winder said.

Howick added, 'So it puts de Northway and Judge Hawkins in the frame as possible victims.'

'Or perpetrator,' Drake said.

There was an awkward silence, as Drake looked around the team. He returned to his office, knowing he had to gather his thoughts before seeing Price.

He worked on his notes for Price, noticing an unusual silence in the Incident Room. Initially he found it unnerving until he was reassured by the team's palpable concentration.

An hour had passed when he saw Flanagan, a civilian computer geek, walk past his door. Drake guessed that one of the team was making progress. He got up and walked through to see Winder standing over Flanagan, who was staring intently at Howick's screen.

Howick looked up. 'Could be nothing, sir. But there are passwords on these files.'

'This won't take long.' Flanagan's fingers flew across the keyboard. Drake stood and waited. Flanagan muttered occasionally, as it obviously took longer than he expected. Then he stopped and leant forward in his chair, both elbows propped up on Howick's desk, chin resting on his hands. Winder gave Drake a brief shrug of his shoulders. Flanagan settled back to tapping away on the keyboard, until he shouted like an impassioned football supporter. 'Yes.'

He double-clicked on the various folders and then into the files.

'Is this what you're looking for?' Flanagan said quietly, as the images of young girls filled the screen.

By the time Flanagan had finished there were several dozen photographs of young girls. Some they'd seen before, others not. And then Flanagan clicked open the images of Maldwyn Evans and Fairburn with young girls on each knee and another man with his back to the camera.

'Hold it,' Drake said, voice raised. 'Who's that?'

Howick leant towards the screen. 'It's difficult …'

'Then solve it and quickly. I need to know who else was there.'

'Looks like they were taken in the same place as the others,' Caren said.

Drake sounded breathless as he recognised the scene. 'It's the de Northway cottage. It comes back to *that* man every time.'

'These men are sick bastards,' Caren said slowly.

Howick and Winder nodded.

'I need all these images cross-referenced to the ones from Evans.' Drake checked the time and cursed under his breath. 'I've got a meeting with the super. And get a photographer to look at all of them. If it's the same cottages I want to know. I need progress by the time I get back.'

A bead of sweat formed under both armpits as Drake entered the senior management suite. Hannah examined his shirt and tie carefully as he stood by her desk. 'You're a minute late.'

Drake sat down to wait. All he could think of was the practical difficulties of tracing the girls in the photographs on Fairburn's computer. Each of them had mothers and fathers, maybe sisters and brothers. There were young lives that had been corrupted. It might take them days or weeks to trace all the girls. The enormity of the task began to overwhelm him and they still had no clear motive for the murders.

'Ian.' Price stood in the doorway and waved a hand over at Drake.

Drake got up and followed the superintendent

back into his office. Price had the local newspaper open on his desk; its headline proclaimed – *serial killer loose on holiday island*. 'The press are having a field day. You'd better have something positive to tell me.'

Price waved to one of the visitor chairs as an invitation for Drake to sit down.

'We've found dozens of photographs of young naked girls on the computer owned by Rhys Fairburn.'

Price raised his eyebrows.

'There's a photograph of Rhys Fairburn and Maldwyn Evans. And another of a man we can't identify. He had his back to the camera and he was moving out of the shot.'

'So who took the photograph?' Price said eventually.

'That's what we need to find out. I'm convinced that Somerset de Northway is involved. We have an eyewitness who saw him move furniture out of the cottage the day after Jane was killed. And his wife had lent money to Maldwyn Evans. We're almost certain that these photographs were taken in one of his cottages.

'Well, you had better be really careful. You know how well connected de Northway is.'

Drake paused. 'We'll need to speak to Judge Hawkins.'

'What!' Price snorted. 'You must be joking.'

'Two men in the Cambrian Club photographs have been killed and another kills himself. There are two other men in the pictures – de Northway and Hawkins.'

'But that's too random,' Price said. 'You can't go around questioning all the members of the Cambrian Club.'

'Evans and Fairburn are pictured with the girls.'

Price shook his head, exasperation evident in

268

his eyes. 'You've got nothing to suggest de Northway or Hawkins could be the perpetrators. Nothing at all. You haven't given me one shred of credible motive.'

Drake hesitated for a moment. 'I was thinking of them as possible victims too.'

Drake fiddled with the air conditioning in the Alfa, cursing its unreliability, which meant occasionally he had to turn it to maximum before it would engage. Superintendent Price had his jacket and cap laid over his knees in the passenger seat. A film of perspiration gathered on Drake's forehead, but by the time he pulled out onto the A55 the air conditioning was blowing a stream of cool air into the car. Apprehension filled his mind as he powered the car eastwards.

During the half-hour car journey Price rehearsed aloud all the matters he wanted to raise with Judge Hawkins and hearing them out loud only exacerbated Drake's anxiety. Prosecutions for historic sexual offences and child abuse could be difficult; abusers close ranks, protect their own, knowing that the girls would want to move on, forget about the past. And how did the abuse link to the murder of Mostyn and Fairburn? Maybe they had missed something, and perhaps it was all linked to the sale of the land. Money can be a strong motive, Drake thought.

He pulled into the car park at the rear of the crown court building. After pressing the intercom a voice crackled and Price asked for the judge's clerk. The door buzzed open and a thin woman in her mid-fifties held out her hand. 'Francis Wadham,' she said. 'I'm Judge Hawkins's clerk.'

Price shrugged on his uniform jacket and tucked his cap under his arm. Drake fastened both buttons of his suit. Despite the warmth outside, the building was cool. Two flights of stairs later Wadham pointed to a couple of chairs and they sat down as she punched a code into the security pad.

Moments later the door opened. 'Judge will see you now,' Wadham said.

They followed her towards a door with the notice 'Judge's Chambers' screwed to the middle. Judge Hawkins sat by a large oak desk, a tray with a stainless steel teapot and a china tea set having been pushed to one corner. The red gown of a circuit judge hung on a wooden coat stand, his wig placed in an oval tin box on top of a nearby cupboard. Wadham directed them towards the chairs at the conference table, which were at right angles to the desk.

'Good morning, Superintendent.' Hawkins sounded affable.

'Good morning, Your Honour.' Price put his cap neatly on the conference table in front of him. 'This is Detective Inspector Ian Drake.'

Hawkins gave him a brief nod. The judge's face looked older than in the photograph Drake had in the folder he was holding. There were pouches either side of his chin and the hair was grey, less healthy.

'I hope this won't take long. I'm needed back in court.'

'DI Drake is the SIO in three recent murders. Ed Mostyn was killed four weeks ago and yesterday a man called Rhys Fairburn was found dead. Exactly the same MO and both men were members of a Cambrian Club.'

Drake thought he caught a glimmer of recognition crossing the judge's eyes.

'Both dead men had photographs of a Cambrian Club dinner taken several years ago.' Price nodded at Drake. He opened the folder and pushed one of the photographs towards the judge.

'I believe, Judge, that you were present at the same dinner.'

Hawkins pulled himself nearer the desk, threaded the fingers of both hands together and dropped them onto the desk with a thump. 'Let me be absolutely clear as to what you're suggesting.'

The superintendent ran his tongue over his lips and blinked repeatedly before asking, 'How well do you know the men in these photographs?'

'I'm sure you know full well that I was in the army with Somerset de Northway.' The judge's cut-glass accent reminded Drake of the documentaries from the 1950s. He gave the photograph a cursory examination. 'And I was certainly at that dinner. But as for the other men ...' He shook his head.

'Apart from this dinner, did you ever meet Ed Mostyn or Maldwyn Evans or Rhys Fairburn?'

Hawkins sat back in his chair. 'No, I don't believe I have.'

'Between both murders a young girl was killed. And it's become clear that she was abused in a paedophile ring when she was under sixteen.'

Hawkins raised his voice. 'Are you suggesting that I might—'

'If there's a link, Judge, then you might be a target,' Price said.

Drake saw the aggression on Hawkins's face evaporate as he frowned.

Drake switched on the lamp and slumped into the chair by his desk. Until the previous weekend it was the time of day when he'd be leaving headquarters for home. He reached for the handset and dialled home, at least what he still considered to be home.

Sian sounded distracted. 'How are you coping,

Ian?'

'Okay. I was ringing to talk to Helen and Megan.'

'Give me a minute.'

Drake flicked through the emails his inbox as he waited. A memorandum of the conversation with Price caught his attention, as did various emails from Assistant Chief Constable Osmond in Cardiff asking for the latest developments. He scanned a dozen emails that had no relevance for him. It always struck him that it was far too easy to c.c. irrelevant recipients in the vain hope that nobody would be left out and therefore complain.

Helen's voice broke his concentration and he asked about her day. After a couple of minutes of stilted conversation she passed the handset over to Megan, who sounded more relaxed. He rang off, promising to see her on Saturday.

A tranquil silence from the Incident Room seeped into Drake's office. He fired off emails to Winder and Howick about the house-to-house enquires they needed to coordinate next to Fairburn's farmhouse. Occasionally a telephone rang somewhere in the building and then the dull humming of a vacuum signalled the cleaners starting their nightshift. He turned his attention back to the emails in his inbox. Then it struck him: would Rhys Fairburn have been comfortable using emails and the Internet?

It took him almost twenty minutes to find the right computer, the one that held Fairburn's data. There were two email addresses, one for Fairburn – *RhysFairburnfarmwr@gmail.com* and another for his wife, both linked to a Microsoft Outlook account. Drake scanned through the various emails, not certain what should be catching his attention. There were emails from members of the Cambrian Club about social events and then emails from friends and his children. Fairburn had booked a holiday in Spain the following Easter and there was a flurry of emails confirming the arrangements.

After an hour Drake rubbed his eyes vigorously but the tiredness remained. He found an old Filofax-style notebook in a box of battered files and old magazines that one of the team had removed from Fairburn's house. He flicked through the various pages. There were contact names, telephone numbers and the occasional address, including Dafydd Higham's business and Somerset de Northway again. Someone in the team would have to construct a matrix of all the people involved in the investigation and how they were linked. This was a small community, where people would know each other, and their secrets. How many scandals were buried in the pages?

By the time he reached the final page Drake had a troublesome sense that he'd missed something. But it was late and he needed to sleep. He went back to the beginning and he turned the pages more slowly this time. If he had missed something he needed to spot it quickly, otherwise Winder or Howick could check everything again tomorrow.

By the second page he'd found a list of email addresses. He paused. There was an address for *sden@gmail.com*, which he knew he'd missed and it gave him a brief sense of achievement. Further down Drake read *rjf@gmail.com*. He checked all the records relating to Fairburn and smiled to himself when he discovered that Fairburn's middle name was John. If it was Fairburn's email address, it hadn't been linked to the Outlook account and Drake began to feel his pulse increasing.

He accessed the Internet from Fairburn's computer and then found Gmail. He typed in the email address and held his breath. The box marked 'password' was automatically populated with a line of asterisks. Drake hesitated and then clicked 'OK', praying the computer would have been programmed to remember any password.

'Yes,' he said out loud, as the monitor screen opened in a new page. He made a brief tapping motion with a clenched fist like a tennis player pleased with the outcome of a difficult shot.

He moved nearer to the monitor and paid far more attention to these emails than the ones in the Outlook account. He didn't keep track of time until he read one very clear, very specific email. Then he knew that tomorrow would be another long day.

Chapter 32

'He gave me the morning off.'

Drake stared at Becky, who was fidgeting in the chair and checking the time on her watch repeatedly. There were loose ends that he had to check that morning and he'd arrived at her home before she was properly awake.

'Are you certain?'

'Of course. It was the day that Ed Mostyn was killed. I got to work at lunchtime. Everything seemed normal.'

'Does he give you time off regularly?'

Becky yawned and patted her hand on her mouth. 'Not really. Look, I'm late already.'

Drake stood up, thanked her and left, pleased that another small part of Llywelyn's life had fallen into place.

Drake drove through the narrow country lanes to the home of Eifion Cooper, hoping that his second meeting that morning would resolve another loose thread. Mostyn had made a will, even though all record of it had disappeared, and the possibility that Cooper knew something had preyed on Drake's mind.

That morning's Welsh language news programme was playing on the radio inside the yard at Eifion Cooper's house. Drake recognised the voice of the Welsh government's health minister complaining bitterly that the criticism by the London government of the health service in Wales had everything to do with party politics and nothing to do with the correct statistics. At least it was a change from the regular criticism of the policing powers that had been devolved from London to Wales.

Drake banged on the door before undoing the latch.

Eifion Cooper squinted as the smoke from the cigarette clasped between his lips crawled up his face. He sat on an old box fiddling with the bottom of a lobster pot. Cooper took the cigarette from his lips. 'I didn't expect to see you back so soon.'

Drake took a couple of steps into the yard. 'Did you know that Ed had made a will in which you were given a legacy?'

Cooper threw the remains of the cigarette onto the concrete by his feet and rubbed the butt with the sole of his boot. 'And you think I killed him because of that?'

'I'm asking whether you knew about the will?'

'He mentioned that he was going to look after me, but I didn't pay it much attention. He could be full of bullshit.'

'Did he say anything else about his personal affairs?'

'What do you mean?'

'Did he ever mention financial problems?'

Drake could see from the look in Cooper's eyes that he had something to add.

'What did he tell you?'

'It's nothing.'

'Let me be the judge of that. We're talking about a man's life here.'

'It must have been about a year ago when he said that de Northway had offered him a lot of money for the house. Ed couldn't make out what was going on. Apparently de Northway used a load of bollocks like "family land", and that for centuries they'd owned Ed's place – even though Ed had a secured tenancy. He'd spent thousands on the cottage over the years. And he always paid his nominal rent on time.'

'How much money did de Northway offer him?'

Cooper shrugged. 'He didn't tell me.'

'How much did you think it was?'

'Ed never told me. He had so much fishing gear, he didn't think he could find somewhere else suitable.'

Cooper rolled another cigarette and, as Drake gathered his thoughts, he wondered how Somerset de Northway with an ailing business could afford to buy out Ed Mostyn. Somewhere in the middle of this investigation he hoped that he could pull together all the right threads.

'I'll need a statement from you.'

It took three sparks from an almost empty lighter before Cooper could draw on the next cigarette. 'Yeah, whatever.'

Drake drew the door closed behind him and retraced his steps to the car. He'd parked in exactly the same spot as he had done before, opposite the terraced houses. The car had been sandwiched tightly between a large estate car and a small hatchback. He checked that the bumpers front and back had not been damaged and then calculated that one of the cars would have to move for him to manoeuvre. He looked over at the terraces and noticed that the door of the end house was open. A woman's voice floated out from inside and then a man appeared in the doorway. Drake walked over. 'Is that your estate car in front of my Alfa? Only it's in my way.'

The man glanced over Drake's shoulder. 'It's my wife's.' He shouted into the house. 'Nerys, you'll need to move your car.'

He turned to Drake. 'Sorry about that. We're just sorting a few things.'

'Is it your father who lives here?'

'I'm sorry?'

'The elderly gentleman who lives here. I spoke to him last week when I called to see Eifion Cooper.'

'I think you're mistaken.'

'No. We had a chat. He was making porridge in the back kitchen. And he knew my father – quite a coincidence really.'

'Look. I don't know what you're talking about. My father died three months ago. The house has been empty ever since.'

Drake drove back to headquarters, his mind a complete daze. At first all he could think about was the last time he had spoken with his father and his eyes filled with tears as he recalled that conversation. It had been forced, almost unreal, an exchange of platitudes and assurances and false smiles.

He drove on autopilot, keeping to the speed limit by some instinct. That morning he had intended to make progress with investigating de Northway; the photographs Fairburn had emailed de Northway completed the corroboration they needed for the historic sex offences. And his wife's involvement with Evans gave him more than enough to arrest de Northway. A search of Crecrist Hall would inevitably produce some forensics.

His mobile rang as he was on the Britannia Bridge. He fumbled for the handset but there was no easy place to park so he juggled driving the car and pushing the mobile to his ear.

'They've found Dylan South,' Caren said.

'Where?'

'Bangor. I'll text you the address.'

Drake slapped the steering wheel in excitement, and indicated left at the next junction.

The text arrived on his mobile with the address and he made his way through the town to the old port area that shimmered in the late afternoon sunshine.

Drake parked behind a car from the local station. The front door was already ajar, so Drake pushed it open and, noticing that the small lounge was empty, headed down the hallway.

South sat by the kitchen table, an enormous mug with 'Keep Calm I'm A Terrorist' printed in bold letters. He had a centre parting with hair that draped his shoulders. A pair of small oblong glasses had been pushed to the top of his nose.

'This is police intimidation.'

'Are you Dylan South?'

'And who are you? Special Branch? MI5? MI6?'

Drake pulled up a chair, sat down and looked at South. He fished out his warrant card. 'Detective Inspector Drake.'

'I've got human rights. I'm entitled to a solicitor. I can make one phone call.'

Drake waited. 'I haven't arrested you. Yet.'

It had the effect of lessening the hostility in South's eyes.

Drake moved his chair towards him. 'I'm investigating the murder of Ed Mostyn. You were the first on the scene. We know that because you took photographs that you posted on a Facebook page and on your Twitter account. Now unless you tell me exactly what I want to know, I'm going to assume you killed Ed Mostyn before taking photographs of his body for your personal gratification. Then I'm going to arrest you and you'll be remanded in custody to a prison where human rights come a poor second to survival.'

South swallowed hard and grasped the mug with both hands.

'I was cycling, it was very early in the morning. It's something I do quite often. I just saw him there. There was a fork through his neck. I just took some photographs and buggered off.'

'Did you see anyone?'

'It was early, there was nobody else around.'

'Did you hear anything?'

South blinked furiously. 'No …'

'Any traffic?'

'It was early …'

'What's your connection with Mostyn?'

There was panic on South's face. 'I didn't know him.'

'Why did you kill him?'

South's left knee began to twitch. 'I didn't kill him. You can't say that.'

Drake glared at South. 'I need you to remember very carefully everything about that morning. Every sound, every movement. Tell me exactly what you did after you left the beach. You might have seen the killer, heard him.'

'I don't know … It was early … I was just … riding my bike. I cycled up to the bridge. There was nobody there, no traffic, except …'

'What?'

'There was a sound of a scooter. You know that sort of pop-popping sound.'

'Anything else?'

'I remember now. There was a dog yelping, jumping around the place.'

'You didn't think to call the police?'

South didn't reply.

The Incident Room was quiet and Drake slumped into the chair behind Winder's desk, before staring at the board. He leant back slightly and hoped that the silence might be conducive to clear thinking. He couldn't escape from the image of the old man stirring porridge and he shook off the recollection. Pressure of work had played on his mind, making his imagination work overtime.

Back to basics, Drake thought, trying to remember which politician had used the phrase. They had to get back to what they knew about Ed Mostyn and Jane Jones. There had to be a connection between both deaths and he had to find it. He wanted to ignore the foreboding pulling at his mind that more of the paedophile ring were going to die. And one of them might have killed Mostyn and Jane. But Fairburn?

He stared at the name 'Jane Jones'. There was something immensely sad about her life, her family. She should have been protected; her father should have been there to look after her. Briefly he remembered his rebellious teenage years and those of his sister, but his father had been present. Resolving that he had to be a better father for his own daughters, he had to make finding Jane's killer a priority. It was time to recheck everything; he walked back to his office and started work.

Among the emails he hadn't read from the day before was the DNA report on Jane's unborn child. It confirmed what he suspected – that Julian Sandham was the father. An hour later he had a mind map on a notepad with the name 'Julian Sandham' underlined and circled with a red highlighter. Underneath Jane's name he'd written '£10k' and given it the same highlighter colour as Sandham's name.

He recalled Caren speculating in one of the briefings that she thought some of Jane's diaries were missing. They weren't with her belongings and her friends didn't know where they were. He sat back and rubbed his face – it was getting late, his shoulders ached. Julian Sandham might just know something about them.

It was time for another visit to the Sandham

home, Drake thought, before deciding to leave for the
night.

Chapter 33

The following morning Drake was back at his desk before the rest of the team arrived. He had woken early thinking about Somerset de Northway, who appeared at every turn in the investigation. Even in the photograph pinned to the board he had a patronising air that matched the rich vowels and condescending manner. He should have guessed that middle-aged men might have fallen under de Northway's spell and become involved with a paedophile ring. Maybe it was de Northway that took the photographs and the more he thought about the possibility the more it dominated his mind.

The Post-it notes straddled his desk like a short colourful chain of Christmas decorations. Each colour had a specific designation and he'd made certain that the edges of each note had been carefully placed under another, thereby achieving uniformity. It usually gave him order and restfulness. But now he plonked them one on top of another and put them on top of a cupboard in the far corner of his room.

He reached for the telephone handset and punched in the number of the forensics department. After a couple of rings he heard the familiar voice of the crime scene manager. 'Foulds.'

'Did you have any luck with the photographer?'

'I spent an hour at the cottage. We both think you're right. The photographer found the exact location where the photographs of Fairburn and Evans were taken.'

Another link in the thread towards Somerset de Northway.

A couple of other administrative telephone calls took Drake's time, until eventually he could turn his attention seriously to Somerset de Northway. He reached down to a box file on the floor by his desk. He flipped off the cardboard cover, deciding that he'd go back to the beginning and look again at Somerset de Northway. Even his name made him sound like a villain from an Ealing comedy. De Northway was the only person of interest who was near the bridge where Ed Mostyn was killed. But it would have been odd for him not to have been there. Perhaps de Northway was counting on that as the perfect cover. But what stopped Drake developing this line of thought with any enthusiasm was the murder several days later of Jane Jones. Along with every other potential suspect, Somerset de Northway's wife would confirm that he was safely tucked up in bed at the time she was killed. But it might mean that both Catherine and Somerset were involved.

He read the forensic report on their finances and knew it would take no more than a barrister of average competence to outline to a jury that Somerset de Northway was well and truly bankrupt.

From a drawer he pulled out a notepad and scribbled the name 'Ed Mostyn' and underneath it – 'means, opportunity and motive', as if reminding himself about the basics might help. It had to be Somerset de Northway, Drake concluded. So he turned his attention back to the box. He pulled out another file from the box marked 'planning'. It amazed him how a planning application for a solar array could produce such a whirlwind of paperwork. Various shades of memoranda filled the file, from the highways department, the water board, Natural Resources Wales and internal departments of the council. A dozen different plans had been produced by the agents retained by Somerset de Northway. Drake opened each in turn over his desk, studying the demarcation between various plots. To satisfy himself he photocopied a larger scale drawing and then coloured in the area farmed by Jane's family at Tyddyn Du and the cottage occupied by Ed Mostyn. It certainly made a larger unit and was probably far more profitable.

He read the various notes from officials. Mostly they were routine, referring to statutes or current regulations. A long memo from an official recorded their advice and guidance. Its terms had been shrouded in obfuscation, so he re-read the memo, convincing himself he had to understand it. It was in the pre-penultimate paragraph that Drake's attention suddenly focused. There were references to a preliminary meeting, *outline plans* and *sizeable development.* A buzz of anticipation dominated his mind as he scoured the rest of the file for references to a meeting predating the memorandum he was reading. After a fruitless half hour he gave up and then stared at the name of the planning officer.

It was another half an hour before he tracked down the right official.

'Is that Gail Jones?'

'Yes, who are you?'

'My name is Detective Inspector Ian Drake, Wales Police Service. You're the planning officer that dealt with the solar array for Crecrist Enterprises? There's mention in your file of a preliminary meeting. I'd like to know what that was about?'

'The application that we are dealing with now is much smaller than what we originally discussed.'

Drake's chest tightened. He warmed to the prospect of Somerset de Northway sitting opposite him in the interview room.

'Have you got plans from that discussion?'

'Yes, somewhere.'

'Email them to me as soon as you can.'

Drake sat staring at the plan on his desk,

struggling to make the connections as he had throughout the case. Somerset de Northway wanted Tyddyn Du back, but why kill Jane Jones unless she'd blackmailed him?

Howick knocked on his door, interrupting his train of thought. 'I thought you should know, boss. We traced one of the staff members of Daniel Jessop's law firm. One of the secretaries is Somerset de Northway's daughter, Judy. I didn't recognise her at first because of her married name – Somerville.'

'She might have removed Mostyn's file.' Drake sat back in his chair. 'But the will has gone missing ...'

Howick moved nearer his desk. 'Why would she want to do that? No reason for de Northway to remove the will. I did some research, boss, and apparently the charity that was supposed to benefit could go to court about the will. Something about reconstructing a will from written records.'

Drake noticed an email in his mailbox and double-clicked on it, ignoring Howick. Then he opened the attachment and his pulse beat a little faster.

Chapter 34

Drake returned from a meeting with Price in which he had dissected every line of the memorandum Drake had prepared on the justification for arresting de Northway. It was a relief when the superintendent had given his consent. He watched as two civilians struggled to erect another board in the Incident Room. Once they'd finished he pinned up the plan that confirmed Tyddyn Du and Mostyn's cottage had been included in the de Northway plan for an enormous solar panel farm.

'He was going to make millions,' Howick said.

'It might give us a motive for de Northway killing Mostyn. But Jane Jones and Rhys Fairburn?' Caren offered.

Drake had been thinking exactly the same thing.

'She must have been blackmailing him,' Winder said. 'Suddenly she has lots of money. There's no way she's earned all that cash. We'll probably find lots of cash withdrawals from his bank account.'

Drake turned to Howick and Winder. 'Get started doing banking enquiries. We're going to see Sandham on our way to see de Northway.'

The caravans and summer tourist traffic delayed their journey to the Sandham holiday home, which aggravated Drake's impatience. He parked the Alfa next to an Audi 4x4 and a new BMW in the small driveway near the front door. They walked over to the house where Mrs Sandham opened the door, peering at Drake and then at Caren as though they were doorstep salesmen.

'I need to speak to Julian,' Drake said.

'He's sailing. And I don't know when he'll be back.' She glanced at her watch. 'Call back in a couple of hours.'

She gave them a brief, insincere smile and edged the door closed.

Drake walked around the village, squinting against the summer sunshine. He watched as a group of youngsters, about Helen and Megan's age, gathered for a sailing lesson. They wore wetsuits, a buoyancy aid and listened intently as the instructor began the course. Drake noted down the contact details for the sailing school into his mobile telephone, resolving to book a course for the girls before the end of the summer. Then they killed time, sitting in a café drinking Americanos and watching the tourists passing in the street.

After two hours they returned to the house to find Julian's kit piled outside the garage door, with the sound of a shower inside. His mother waved them into the south-facing sitting room, its windows open and allowing a gentle summer breeze to drift inside with the last of the afternoon sunshine. Drake stood for a moment, enjoying the view over the beach and bay. A few minutes later Julian appeared, wearing expensive leather loafers – no socks – and a plain white T-shirt and Levis.

'Mrs Sandham. I'd like to speak to Julian on his own.'

She pouted, before giving Julian a stern look, and left.

Drake was sitting at the edge of one of the leather sofas, nursing a coffee mug in both hands and hoping he could make the youngster feel at ease. 'Julian, I don't think you've told us everything you know about Jane.'

Julian darted a nervous glance at Caren.

'We've had a chance to interview some of her friends and they've all mentioned that there were some bad things going on in the cottages with older men. Did Jane ever mention anything?'

Julian blinked, and then let out a long breath.

'If there's anything you know about what was going on, you owe it to Jane to tell us so that we can find her killer.'

Julian glanced over his shoulder towards the door.

Caren made her first contribution. 'Is there something you don't want your parents to know?'

'They never knew her.'

Drake and Caren said nothing.

'They would have liked her, I'm certain.'

Drake decided on a shock tactic. 'Did she ever mention Somerset de Northway?'

Julian's eyes opened wide.

'Did you ever meet him? We know all about him, of course.'

Julian twisted and turned and then stood up. 'There's something you should see.' He left the room, returning a few minutes later. From a rucksack he produced two small diaries, which he handed to Drake, and then a plastic bag, the contents of which he began to empty over the table. Wads of carefully wrapped twenty-pound notes cascaded over the top, some falling onto the floor.

'It's all in there,' Julian said. 'The dates of when she met him and the others. He gave her all of that. To keep her mouth shut.'

'Why didn't you mention this before?'

'He was here in the summer. I got really scared.'

Drake turned the papers through his fingers. He had decided that Sandham needed to know that he was the father of Jane's child, but now he wasn't so certain.

'Julian. We've also had the result of the DNA analysis. The child was yours.'

The boy's lips quivered and tears poured down his cheeks.

A red band of dying sunshine narrowed slowly over the horizon. By the time they reached Crecrist Hall it would be dark. Idly he speculated about de Northway's evening routine. Pink gins in the drawing room? A three-course dinner served in the draughty, cold dining room and then brandy in the library. But the hospitality that the Wales Police Service could offer would be quite different.

'How many men were actually involved?' Caren was scanning the pages of Jane's diary through the protective packaging of an evidence pouch.

'Let's hope we find something linked to de Northway,' Drake said.

'What if the killer is another member of the group?'

Drake slowed and indicated as he reached the junction for the turning off the A55 for Crecrist Hall. It was another few minutes before they turned into the hall's long drive. Drake flicked his sidelights to dipped full beam. Clumps of turning leaves glistened along the tarmac and shrubs and bushes appeared as ghostly silhouettes. He slowed as he approached the house. It was in complete darkness and although Drake knew that the dining room was at the rear of the house overlooking a large paddock, the place felt empty.

Drake dragged on a fleece from the back seat of the car and stood looking at the imposing facade as Caren joined him. De Northway's Range Rover was parked by the front door, dirty wellingtons and waxed jackets thrown into the rear.

'Nobody home?' Caren said.

'Let's find out.' Drake yanked the door bell. It rang out. He pushed the handle gently. Nothing happened. So he rattled it and the sound of wood against metal echoed through the tiled hallway beyond. He turned to Caren. 'You go and find the back door. I'll go around the side.'

Caren walked off down the drive. Drake looked up at the first-floor windows. They were all closed, a couple heavily curtained. He strode over to the downstairs windows and peered in. A table and chairs were laid out in the middle – perhaps it was the breakfast room.

He moved around to the next window and as he peered in a brief blast of moonlight broke through the clouds and shone through into the library beyond the glass. Drake recalled sitting in the room previously, but it was empty now. Skirting around the gable, he found himself at the rear of the property. Looking up, he noticed a curtain flapping at a first-floor window, even though it looked closed, and his pulse beat a fraction faster.

He checked all the windows, a feeling of urgency invading his thoughts. Hoping that he might see Caren, he glanced over towards the far end of the property. Reaching an old-fashioned metal-framed French door, he turned the round porcelain doorknob and as the door opened a heightened anticipation filled his chest.

For a couple of seconds he allowed his eyes to acclimatise to the blackness inside the building. He tried to remember the layout of the house that he'd seen with de Northway and then he listened for any sound. Outside an owl hooted and Drake turned sharply to look through the windows into the paddock and then the trees beyond.

Deciding against exploring the ground floor,

hoping that Caren would soon find the open French door, he headed for the staircase. It was a stone cantilever one and he could hear his footsteps reverberating through the stairwell. He stopped a couple of times and let the silence engulf him. He was halfway up the final flight when he heard movement ahead.

He reached the landing. To his left was a long corridor; to his right he noticed two doors, both slightly ajar. Deciding against the darkness to his left, he pushed open the first door. Through the uncurtained windows he saw the moonlight flickering over the trees surrounding the paddock. From the damp, musty smell in the bedroom he guessed it hadn't been used for months, maybe longer. And the second bedroom was much the same, with the smell of mothballs and dying flowers clinging to the air.

He heard a metallic click, as though a window was being opened, so he stepped out onto the landing and stared down the corridor. He let out a long, slow breath, hoping he could quell his apprehension. His black brogues weren't suitable for walking on the balls of his feet, so he stopped when he reached the first door and gently pushed it open with his right foot. The heavy curtains hung over the window; a small lamp sat on the bedside table next to single bed.

Down the corridor a door rattled and Drake heard footsteps. Stepping back onto the landing, he noticed a light seeping under the door of one of the bedrooms. He drew his tongue over drying lips, his pulse thumping in his neck. After a moment's hesitation he tiptoed down the hallway and stared at the light before pushing open the door.

Inside, he took a few steps before he saw Somerset de Northway lying on the floor. There was movement to his right and he made to turn around, but suddenly there was a clap of thunder from inside his head. And then the floor raced towards his face.

Chapter 35

Somebody was using an electric hammer drill and Drake wanted them to fucking well stop. He was lying on his back but the surroundings were unfamiliar. Opening his eyes, he saw Wyndham Price's pained expression. The daylight streaming in through the window only intensified the throbbing in his head.

'You're in hospital,' Price said.

'What happened?'

'Caren found you with de Northway.'

Drake raised a hand to his forehead and rubbed his temples, but the drilling continued.

'Is he …?'

'No. Unconscious but he's alive. It looks like your presence saved him.'

'What time is it?'

'Just after seven.'

The drilling stopped for a moment when the realisation dawned that he'd been unconscious for hours.

A nurse came in with a beaker of water and a plastic container with some pills. He downed half in one swallow. Price waited until the nurse had left, pushing the door closed behind her. 'There was no sign of his wife at the time. She turned up later.'

'Has she been interviewed?'

'Not yet.'

'I'll do it later,' Drake said, wanting to believe that the painkillers would soon eradicate the pounding.

'We rang Sian after you'd been brought in here. I think you should call her.'

Drake slumped back against the pillow and cast a glance out through the window. Somebody had wanted de Northway dead, so Drake had to face the reality that de Northway wasn't their killer.

'I've got to get back, Ian. Call me when you've been seen by the doctor.'

As soon as Price had left one of the nurses came in carrying a tray of breakfast. He prodded the porridge with his spoon. The smell reminded him of the old man again so he pushed the bowl to one side. His imagination had to stop playing tricks on him so he demolished the dried-up rubbery toast and the watery coffee. Even the drilling began to abate. He got up and found the toilet a few yards down the corridor and, thankful that he hadn't fallen over, decided that he couldn't wait. So he dressed and walked briskly out of the ward, telling a bewildered-looking nurse that he was discharging himself.

Drake stood outside the main hospital entrance and called Sian. He reassured her that it was no more than mild concussion and that two paracetamols from the hospital had been effective. He made excuses as he saw Caren turning into the short-stay car park, promising to call her later. Seeing Caren sitting in the driver's seat of his Alfa Romeo immediately struck him as odd. He strode over as she got out and gave him a warm smile.

'How are you feeling?'

'I've been better.'

'I'll drive if you want, boss.'

Drake's first instinct was to insist he drive. It was his car after all. But now he looked over at Caren. 'Thanks.'

Drake sat back and nursed his temple as Caren drove out of the car park. 'Dave and Gareth are at Crecrist Hall.'

'And Mrs de Northway?'

'She's at the hall too.'

'We need to question her. Has she said where she was last night?'

'Nothing. She's barely said a word.'

En route to Crecrist Hall Drake called Price, who sounded mildly surprised to hear his voice. 'I'm fine sir.' Drake tried to get as much confidence into his reply as he could. Although the headache had abated, a wave of exhaustion washed over him as Caren drove.

A Scientific Support Vehicle was parked alongside de Northway's old Range Rover, a marked police car alongside it and two unmarked cars. Drake didn't bother with tugging the bell; the door opened easily and he strode in with Caren behind him. He began to take the stairs to the landing two at a time but a pinprick of pain pierced both sides of his forehead with each step and he hesitated.

'Are you all right, boss?' Caren was a couple of steps behind him.

'I'll be okay.'

Drake surveyed the landing. This time light was flooding down the corridor. There were voices in various rooms, furniture being moved and Caren pointed towards a door.

'Dave and Gareth are in here, sir.'

They entered what looked like an office. There were shelves full of storage and old-fashioned ledgers. A computer screen hummed on an antique kneehole desk. Howick and Winder looked up and each enquired about his health, but Drake reassured them that he was well enough to be on duty.

'We'll need to get as much of this back to headquarters. Give operational support a ring if you need any help.'

Winder and Howick returned to trawling through

a mound of paperwork. Drake strode down the landing towards de Northway's room. Mike Foulds emerged, followed by a white-suited crime scene investigator.

Foulds did a double-take as he looked at Drake. 'I didn't expect to see you here today.'

'I'm all right. Bump on the head.'

Foulds stood to one side as the CSI passed him and walked down the corridor. Drake looked into the room. Foulds moved to one side. Drake had little recollection of the room from the night before. The ache in his forehead returned and with two fingers he rubbed a spot on his right temple, hoping it would help. The room was an odd mixture of bedroom and sitting room. It had a comfortable chair, a single bed pushed into one corner and a large television propped on top of a sideboard. An ancient wardrobe dominated one wall. It had large doors with a sweeping curved top and Drake could imagine it in some French country château. The Tattersall shirts and bold checked jackets hanging over cord trousers of varying colours confirmed that Somerset de Northway slept alone.

He turned to Foulds who was standing by the door. 'Where's Mrs de Northway?'

'Downstairs in the kitchen.'

Drake stepped out of the bedroom and turned back towards the staircase.

'There's another way, boss.' Caren was walking towards the end of the corridor. She opened another door, revealing an enclosed narrow staircase. 'Servants access. In the days when they could actually afford servants to run up and down with breakfast, do the cleaning, etc. It leads down towards the kitchen. The killer must have used it last night, to avoid meeting me on the main staircase.'

'So the killer knows the property?'

'Could be. Or he's just lucky.'

They walked down, their feet echoing against the bare timber of the risers. At the bottom a narrow hallway led off towards the back door and Drake noticed a heavy door in front of him and the sound of murmured conversation from behind it.

A woman officer that Drake recognised from the family liaison team sat with Catherine de Northway, a plate of fruitcake and empty cups on the table.

'Morning, sir. You all right?'

Drake nodded. 'I need to talk to Mrs de Northway.'

'Of course.' She reached for her bag and rolled her eyes, as she exchanged a look with Caren that Drake completely failed to notice.

Drake pulled up a chair and wasted no time with pleasantries. 'Does your husband have any enemies?'

'He can be a bit of an arse.'

'Has anybody threatened him?'

'Not that I'm …'

'Has he been behaving oddly?'

'No more than usual.'

Drake narrowed his eyes, uncertain whether she was serious. 'What happened yesterday?'

'What do you mean?'

'What were your husband's movements yesterday – did he go out? Did anyone call to see him?'

Catherine de Northway swept her hair back with a flourish and summarised the activities of the day, apologising occasionally for her uncertainty. 'The high sheriff rang, asking if Somerset would deputise for him at some function next week. After he'd finished Somerset complained like hell. He couldn't abide the man.'

'Did anyone call?'

'That accountant man. He was here in the afternoon.'

'Who?'

'Dafydd Higham. But Somerset didn't have the time to see him. He had another meeting with those *consultants* about the solar business.' She fluttered a hand in the air, as though the subject was beneath her. 'I'm awfully sorry. Frightfully rude of me. I haven't offered you coffee.' De Northway made to stand up.

Caren was on her feet first. 'There is no need, Mrs de Northway.'

'No, I insist.'

'Please sit down. Caren will make coffee.' Drake managed a sympathetic tone. 'Where were you last night?'

'Why do you need to know?'

'It's important that we build a complete picture.'

'I was with a *friend.*'

Caren glanced at him abruptly as she plonked an old-fashioned whistling kettle on the Aga.

'Can you give me her name?'

'I really don't think this is relevant.'

'Mrs de Northway, let me be the judge of that.'

'It's … not what you think.'

Drake frowned. The kettle made a gurgling sound.

'It's just that ever since Somerset had his prostate op things haven't been, well … back to normal, so to speak.'

For the first time Drake noticed her crystal-blue eyes. They had a hard edge that matched the steely grey hair. A pinch of pain flashed behind his eyes and he guessed that he needed more paracetamols. His irritation at Catherine de Northway and her *so to speak* was compounded as he thought of how little progress they'd made in wading through the secrets of rural

Anglesey.

'Are you suggesting that your husband had erectile dysfunction?'

Drake didn't think he'd ever used the last two words in conversation. He'd heard them in the cinema during an advert for Viagra and he just hoped that he'd understood Catherine de Northway correctly.

'Somerset knew all about us.'

'I'm sorry.'

'As you put it so quaintly, Somerset couldn't get an erection, poor thing. And over the years we've always had this sort of *understanding*.'

'*Understanding* – what on earth do you mean?' Drake's patience with Catherine de Northway's coded language finally snapped.

'Well, until the operation, Somerset often entertained in the cottages with some of his friends.'

The kettle gurgled.

'And I have certain *needs,* Inspector.'

Caren cleared her throat. Drake got the message: even he could understand what she meant by *needs*.

'And tell me, Mrs de Northway, who exactly is your friend?'

She sat back and gave a long, deep sigh. 'Aiden Hawkins.'

Drake and Caren stared at each other simultaneously as the whistle on the kettle pierced the silence.

Chapter 36

On their way back to headquarters Drake had insisted on a detour for a shower and a change of clothes. Caren sat in the car and waited. There was a faint smell of mint on his hair when he returned and she guessed that he was using one of those bright green shower gels. Back in headquarters Drake stood before the Incident Room board, turning two fingers round the wedding band on his left hand. Caren had noticed him fidgeting like this before.

'Catherine de Northway,' Drake announced. 'She's the only person we haven't looked at.'

Nobody moved in their chairs. Howick gave Drake a quizzical look.

'Judge Hawkins satisfies her *needs* and she gets him to try and kill poor old Somerset who can't get it up any longer.'

'And you interrupted him, boss,' Winder piped up.

'So why would she and Hawkins kill Fairburn and Jane Jones?' Howick added. 'Every time we focus on a suspect the less likely they seem.'

'I know, I know.' Drake raised his voice a fraction too loudly. He looked over at Howick. 'Was there anything from de Northway's computer and papers?'

'He had the same stack of photographs on his computer. And they were sent to him by Fairburn.'

Winder shifted in his chair. 'We removed a huge pile of paperwork about solar power. And there are dozens of spreadsheets and projections about the profitability of the project on his computer.'

'I wonder if there might be more than one killer,' Drake said.

There were unconvinced glances around the

room.

'Somerset de Northway kills Ed Mostyn in order to be able to expand his property and develop the solar farm. He had the opportunity because he's in the village every morning. Mrs de Northway is on his scheme. But unknown to him she has a scheme of her own.'

'But what about Jane Jones?' Caren said.

'She's the one who pays her off. Maybe she has the money and she knows all about de Northway and his *pals*.'

'It's disgusting,' Caren said. 'They were a bunch of sick old men.'

Drake turned towards her. 'But something goes wrong and they argue and Jane is killed.

'Still doesn't explain the link to these paedophiles,' Caren said.

Drake ignored her. 'Question is, how many of them are still alive? And who's killing them?'

Winder pushed a chocolate bar around the top of his desk. 'Maybe we'll find something in de Northway's papers. Emails and contacts. There could be others.'

'And I need a photograph of Catherine de Northway,' Drake said, tapping the board. 'And then we've got Gwynfor Llywelyn. He's got the motive to kill Mostyn and Fairburn.'

'Is he really mad enough to kill both men to stop them selling the land?' Caren said.

Drake drew a hand over his face and pulled at his lips. He didn't say anything for a moment. 'We'll start again in the morning.'

Caren heaved a sigh of relief, pleased that she'd avoided having to make excuses for leaving early. She'd already planned the evening meal – chicken stew with roast potatoes and mashed swede. It was one of Alun's favourites and she'd found that the old cliché as to the way to a man's heart being through his stomach was just as true for the bedroom.

Drake went back into his office. Howick and Winder milled around, exchanging banter about the prospect of an evening in their favourite pubs before dragging on fleeces and leaving. Caren waited until they'd left and then found her coat. She stopped at Drake's door. He was staring at his desk and gave her a weary look as she left. If I ever make detective inspector I'd get a proper work–life balance, she thought, as she pondered how long he'd stay behind his desk.

It was over two hours before Drake finally satisfied the instinct that kept him at his desk. Before he left he picked up the telephone and called Sian.

'What did the consultant say?' Sian asked when he told her he'd discharged himself that morning.

'It was mild concussion, that's all. I slept all night and they gave me some painkillers.'

'No tests?'

'What for?'

'Look, I can't talk, Ian. I'm going out.'

'Going out?' the question came out before he had time to think. 'Who's looking after the girls?'

'Helen is staying with one of her friends and Megan is with my mother.'

'They could have stayed with me.'

'Ian.' It always annoyed him that she succeeded in getting far more meaning into a single word than anyone else he knew. This time there was a rebuke and exasperation. He didn't know which was worse.

'I mean next time. When things settle down. You could call me …'

'You don't answer the telephone.'

The silence that hung between them tightened like a violin string until the tension snapped. 'I spoke to your mum today. I think you should call her. I've got to go.' Drake stared at the handset for what felt like minutes, different questions coursing through his mind, but uppermost – where was she going? And who with?

She hadn't even suggested that he telephone either of his daughters, so after replacing the telephone he found his mobile and called Helen. The conversation was stilted until eventually she rang off and then he tried Megan. He could almost smell his mother-in-law down the telephone and he sensed the force of her presence, like a female Darth Vader.

'Mam said you were busy with an important case.'

'I'll arrange something for next weekend, *cariad*.'

'*Nain* has got a DVD for me to watch. I'll have to go.'

It's probably a cartoon that will be completely unsuitable for her age, he thought, before wishing her goodnight.

An hour later he'd bought some ready meals, ice cream and fruit, mainly because he could hear Sian's voice telling him he had to have a healthy diet. He dumped his shopping onto the table in the kitchen and transferred the contents of the bag into the fridge. Without much enthusiasm he read the instruction on the ready meal and placed it into the microwave. After a couple of minutes experimenting he managed to get the machine to whirl and buzz. Socialising at the weekend was overrated, he persuaded himself, avoiding the painful truth that he had no social life to speak of in any event. He drank a glass of wine while he waited and got the television to work. Flicking through the channels, he eventually found a programme following a building project in Italy. It must have been the vicarious effect of the stupefying heat from the scenes on the television, but he yawned violently. From the kitchen there was a pinging sound.

Once he'd heaped the steaming pasta onto a plate, he picked up the salad bowl and sat in front of the television. He drank more wine and watched as an elderly English couple with accents like Catherine de Northway directed the Italian workmen who were finishing their swimming pool. His eyelids sagged and another yawn gripped his jaw. Deciding he had to sleep, he left the dishes on the worktop, resisting the temptation to clean them immediately.

Chapter 37

Drake slept well and woke feeling that progress would at long last be possible. Somerset de Northway would be well enough to interview and forensics would be certain to pick up something from Crecrist Hall. He arrived at headquarters and headed for his office but as soon as he sat down the telephone rang.

'Area control, sir. We've had a call from Holyhead police station. You need to attend urgently.'

'For Christ's sake. What the hell is it?'

'A Mr Dafydd Higham wants to see you. Apparently he's quite distressed.'

'About what?'

The voice hesitated. 'The desk sergeant reported that Higham thinks he's the next murder victim.'

An hour later Drake propped his chin on steepled hands and looked over at Dafydd Higham, sitting on the opposite side of the table, who shifted his position on one of the uncomfortable rigid plastic chairs. Two days' worth of stubble covered his chin and it made him look older than Drake remembered. And dirtier somehow, as though the silvery grey stubble needed scrubbing clean.

Caren entered the interview room and slid three plastic beakers full of weak-looking coffee over the table. Higham reached over and grimaced as his fingers touched the hot rim.

'You might have some information for us?' Drake said.

Higham moved his chair nearer the table.

'It's about these murders.' He stumbled as though something heavy was caught in his throat. 'I know I should have come sooner. Ed didn't get on with Joan. In fact they pretty much hated each other.'

'Go on.' Drake folded his arms, turned up his nose at the coffee and stared over at Higham.

'He spoke to me quite a lot recently. He'd been thinking about the land. And about whether to sell. I'd been trying to persuade him that he should agree. Joan would get very angry with him. Shout at him, call him all sorts of names. She can be very abusive when she puts her mind to it.'

'When did you speak to him?'

'If I was visiting clients nearby I'd often call in.'

'Were you on good terms with him then?'

'Yes. I suppose.'

'So what else did you discuss?'

Higham reached for the coffee and, after blowing on the surface, took a brief sip. 'Ed knew all about those men. Rhys Fairburn, Evans, and Somerset de Northway. They were all in this together.'

'What exactly?'

'They were involved in having sex with young girls. It's what turned them on. I think it's disgusting.' Higham looked up at Drake and curled his lips into a frown. 'I couldn't sleep last night. I kept hearing things. I was certain there was somebody outside.' He stopped, swallowed hard and gave Drake and Caren a pleading, rather pathetic, look. 'It was Gwynfor Llywelyn.'.

'What makes you think that?' Drake measured his words carefully.

'Ed told me that he and Llywelyn had blazing arguments. Llywelyn had been able to persuade him to make a will leaving everything to some charity. He's got a hell of a temper and sometimes he'll be nice and friendly and then others fly off the handle like a madman.'

'What did they argue about?'

'Ed threatened to sell the land. And I was

outside his cottage one day when Llywelyn was there.'

Caren changed position in her chair and drew her hair back behind both ears. 'Did you actually hear what was said?'

'Of course.'

She scribbled his replies on the legal pad on her lap and looked up at Higham. 'We'll need a statement in due course, but tell me in your own words exactly what you can remember him saying.'

Higham let out a long sigh. 'It was a while ago. I can't be certain of the exact words.'

'Do your best.'

'Jane had been one of the girls involved and Llywelyn was in love with her – obsessed in fact. I heard him tell Mostyn never to touch her again or he'd kill him.'

'How did Llywelyn know about Mostyn and Jane?'

Higham shrugged.

Caren occasionally held a hand up to pause Higham as he recalled the argument. He had walked up the drive to Mostyn's cottage so that both men would have been oblivious to his presence outside. Once Higham had finished his tale, Drake leant over and scanned the notes that Caren had prepared, as the accountant sat silently finishing the last of his coffee.

'Did Ed Mostyn tell you he was involved in the paedophile ring?' Drake said.

Higham put the plastic beaker back onto the table. He covered his mouth with both hands and avoided eye contact with Drake and Caren. 'He didn't admit that to me directly. He just made comments. It was disgusting.'

'And why are you frightened now?'

Higham opened his eyes wide and stared at

Drake in astonishment. 'I took the photographs in the Cambrian Club dinner. And he might think that I was involved too.'

Caren had fixed Higham with an intense glare.

'Thank you, Mr Higham, for coming in.' Drake stood up, pulling his jacket from the back of his chair. 'Sergeant Waits will arrange to take a detail statement from you in due course.'

'Aren't you going to arrest Llywelyn or something?'

'You've been very helpful.' Drake reached over and shook his hand. They led Higham out of the interview room. Caren punched the security code into the keypad near the door and after Higham left she turned to give Drake a troubled look.

Drake reached for his telephone as soon as the door closed.

'Get here as soon as you can.' Drake mouthed the name 'Gareth' at Caren.

'What did you make of that?' Caren said, once he'd finished.

Drake was already walking towards the main stairs. On the first floor he found an empty room. He sat down by the table and rubbed his eyes and then his temple. His skin was greasy and he wanted to clean, but first he had Caren staring at him, an excited look on her face.

'It's not enough to arrest Llywelyn is it?'

'Higham's reference to a slanging match?' Drake spread his hands flat over the table. 'Nothing circumstantial about that. Llywelyn is on a mission to stop the nuclear power plant and we know he has a hell of a temper.'

'But the other deaths?'

'He's on a mission to kill the men involved with the paedophile ring because he loved Jane. You know the saying – love is blind.'

Caren sank back in her chair. 'And Jane?'

Drake hesitated. 'Fit of temper?'

Caren puckered her brow.

'We'll need to plan an arrest.'

Drake reached for the mobile and called Price. It was a short monosyllabic conversation and ended with Price grunting confirmation. 'Just arrest the toe-rag and do a full forensics on his place.'

Another hour passed until Winder and Howick arrived. Drake waved them to chairs around the table and summarised the interview with Higham. 'We arrest Llywelyn on suspicion of murder and take him back to area control. Caren, you and Dave get to his home address while Gareth comes with me to the bakery. I'll call the CSI team to meet us there in half an hour. And, Caren, get the search warrant sorted. Dave and Gareth, get some of the uniform lads organised.'

'To ride shotgun?' Winder said.

Nobody laughed.

Drake parked at the end of the village, a little distance down from the patrol car that had followed them to the north of the island. Behind them he saw the Scientific Support Vehicle slowing to a halt. He dialled Caren. 'Where are you?'

'Outside his house.'

'Any sign of the girlfriend?'

'None. It's all quiet.'

'Good. Let's go. I'll call you once we're by the door.'

Drake slipped the car into first gear and drove slowly down the high street. He drew to a halt next to the bakery entrance. He pressed 'send' on his mobile as he entered the property.

Inside baskets were piled on the counter with white loaves, large sourdough and dark rye bread. Gossamer-thin mists of flour drifted in the air. A radio played in the office beyond the counter. Drake lifted the flap and walked to the rear. He recognised the sound of The Flaming Lips asking the listener if they realised that someday everyone must die – appropriate enough, Drake thought.

Llywelyn was sitting in the rear room with his feet propped onto a table, drawing deeply on a joint. A puzzled look crossed his face, like a man who couldn't remember where he'd parked his car. He took the joint out of his mouth. 'What the fuck are you doing here?'

'Gwynfor Llywelyn.' Drake held up his warrant card. 'I'm arresting you for murder.'

Chapter 38

'Your client is under the influence of drugs so he's not fit to interview at present.'

It was going to be late in the evening before Llywelyn could be interviewed and by then the custody sergeant would want him to have eight hours' sleep. All of which would give them valuable time to search the bakery and the house.

'He seemed perfectly coherent to me.' Matilda Spencer was one of those lawyers who attempted to distil the wisdom of the entire legal profession into everything she said.

'We'll do a drug test tonight and aim to interview in the morning.' Drake forced a smile.

'What's your evidence?'

'I'll discuss everything fully in the morning.'

'You haven't got enough to charge him, have you?' Although Spencer was clever, she needed to learn discretion. 'And you're doing a search at the moment.'

'I can't discuss the nature of our inquiries.'

'So you *are* searching his property. Desperate, I'd say.'

Irritation at Spencer was quickly turning into annoyance.

'Seven-thirty am. We'll even provide coffee.' This time he didn't even try to smile.

Drake returned to headquarters and went straight to the forensics department. He had a few hours to get the search finalised and everything in the bakery and Llywelyn's home dusted and examined. Foulds looked up at Drake as he entered and then nodded at the garden fork laid out in the middle of the table in front of him. Alongside it stood a pair of wellington boots.

'Is that ... ?' Drake began.

'Found in the shed at the back of the garden. On the outside it's an ordinary garden spade, but if you look a little more closely, then ...' Foulds reached for a switch behind him and dimmed the light. He picked up a handheld device that Drake had seen operated before. A thin band of translucent red light shrouded the handle and stem of the fork. Small dark blotches appeared and Foulds stopped and peered at them, a narrow grin forcing itself through his lips. Then he moved onto the wellington boots.

'Looks like the fork has been cleaned thoroughly. But even if you clean something really carefully blood will have a nasty habit of leaving a stain that this beauty will pick up.'

'Is there enough to—'

'Sure is. Samples are on their way to the forensic science lab as we speak.'

'How long?'

'I've told them it's top priority.'

Drake waited.

'First thing in the morning, hopefully.'

Drake could see that Foulds was pleased with the results so far.

'Good work, Mike.'

'Thanks. I've emailed you a list of the exhibits recovered from the bakery and the farm.'

Drake walked back to the Incident Room, his step a fraction lighter than it had been earlier. He hoped that by now the team would have made some progress. The hubbub of broken conversation and chatter gradually died as he entered. From the half-grins on their faces he guessed that Foulds had shared the details of the discovery.

Winder was chewing a doughnut, a fine residue of sugar coating his lips. Howick stood by the board and Caren was nursing a mug of coffee. Drake looked around. 'You've heard about the fork?'

Heads nodded slowly.

'Anything else turned up from his house and the bakery?'

Howick pointed to the computer on a spare desk. 'Llywelyn was running a massive campaign against the nuclear power plant. It'll take us years to go through all of his emails. He sent them to every politician you could name. He was making a right nuisance of himself.'

Winder dabbed a handkerchief to his lips. 'There's a mobile telephone, boss. We found it in a kitchen drawer. It's one of those pay-as-you-go handsets. There are calls to Rhys Fairburn and Evans.'

'Really. Get a list of all the calls made.'

'His girlfriend got hysterical when we were at the house,' Caren said, turning an elastic band through her fingers. 'She said it was a conspiracy by the English state, which was all part of the subjugation of the Welsh people started by King Henry VIII.'

Drake raised an eyebrow. 'Carry on going through all his papers. There must be something.' Drake walked back to his room.

He sat down and for a moment he couldn't remember which day it was. He glanced at the time and date on the screen of his monitor. Over a week had passed since he had moved into the flat although he had barely spent any time there. And in reality he didn't want to spend time there. Then the remains of the brief telephone conversations with Helen and Megan came flooding back to him, along with a guilt that tugged heavily on his conscience. So he got up, walked around the desk and closed the door before calling Sian.

'Are you still at *work*?'

'It's a complex investigation ...'

'Aren't they all?'

'I'd like to speak to Helen and Megan.'

'It might be nice if you arranged to see them. You know, things that fathers do.'

Drake heard Sian's raised voice and then, through the sound of muffled conversations, Sian telling both girls not to be long. Talking to Helen and Megan felt unnatural, as though he were talking to his nephews in Cardiff. After he'd finished he found the door into a dark space in his mind and he settled in, happy to stare blankly at the order on his desk. Eventually the noise from the Incident Room broke his concentration and he looked over at the monitor screen, forcing himself to think about Gwynfor Llywelyn.

'Do you know why you're here?'

Every interview opened with that question, but it struck Drake as absurd, bearing in mind that Llywelyn had already spent over twelve hours in custody. Drake had listened politely when Matilda Spencer gave him her usual grilling before the interview started, reminding him about the latest Court of Appeal guidelines about police interrogations. The polka dot blouse she wore under her navy jacket contrasted sharply with the un-ironed top that Caren wore underneath a light green fleece.

Drake tugged at the elasticated links holding the double cuffs of his white shirt in place. That morning he had chosen a solid blue tie. It was a formality that somehow told the suspect, his or her lawyer and any colleague present that he was in charge. A quiet satisfaction buzzed in his mind as he flicked through his papers on the table. The interview wouldn't take long; they had enough to charge on at least two murders but he still had to go through the formalities. He might even have time to see Helen and Megan that afternoon.

Yesterday's stubble had thickened into a dirty grey mass on Llywelyn's chin and Drake caught a slight musty tang from old clothes, sweat and the remains of the joint from the day before.

'Yes. You've told me a dozen times.'

'How well did you know Ed Mostyn?'

Llywelyn shrugged.

'Can you explain, for the purposes of the tape?' Drake tilted his head towards the cassette machine on the table.

'I got to know him because of the nuclear power station.'

'When did you learn that he and his sister owned a strip of land important to the development?'

Llywelyn rolled his eyes. 'How the hell would I remember?'

'But you admit that it was something you were aware of?'

'Of course. Look, everyone knows that Joan Higham and Ed Mostyn had a piece of land. Everyone knows each other's business.'

'Did you and Mostyn ever discuss the nuclear power plant?'

'Of course. He wanted to do everything possible to stop it.'

'Just as you do.'

'Yes. I think it will destroy this part of Wales. It will ruin centuries of culture and be the final nail in the coffin for the Welsh language.'

'Would it be right to say that you would do anything to stop the development?'

'I wouldn't kill, if that's what you mean.'

Drake hesitated, glancing over at Caren. She had a determined look on her face and Drake went back to the interview plan they'd finalised the night before. 'How often did you visit Ed Mostyn?'

'I never kept a record.'

'Well, you must have some idea. Was it every week?'

'No, of course not.'

'Every month?'

Llywelyn shrugged again.

'Answer the question.'

'Sometimes we'd go out for a drink. Other times I'd see him at his cottage.'

'Where were you on the morning Ed Mostyn was killed?'

'Working.'

'What time did you arrive at work?' Drake flicked through his papers to the statement from the milkman.

'The usual time.'

'And when did Becky arrive that morning?'

'Usual time.' Llywelyn managed to sound impatient.

'That's not true is it? We had an eye witness that says the bakery was closed first thing. Just about the time Mostyn was killed.'

Llywelyn straightened in his chair.

'Okay. I was late in that morning. I overslept.'

'Why did you give Becky the morning off?'

Llywelyn folded his arms. 'She only works part-time. There was nothing for her to do. I really need to cut her hours.'

Drake looked over at Llywelyn. 'Were you aware that Mostyn had made a will?'

Llywelyn shifted his position on his chair. 'He mentioned it.'

317

'What did he tell you?'

'He said he was leaving everything to charity.'

'And it would be fair to say that if Ed Mostyn died they wouldn't agree to the sale of the land to the nuclear power company.'

Llywelyn stared at Drake. Drake stared back. 'So it would be in your interests to make certain that Ed Mostyn never changed his will.'

'I don't know what you mean.'

'If Mostyn had threatened to sell the land straightaway, there would have been nothing you could have done to prevent the development of the nuclear power station.'

'There's so much more we can still do.' Llywelyn leant over the table towards Drake. 'We haven't started with public opinion and getting everybody on the island to oppose this development.'

'Do you accept that the land owned by Mostyn and his sister is crucial?'

Llywelyn sat back and hesitated. 'I don't know,' he said. 'I don't know enough about it.'

Trying to be clever, good sign.

Drake flicked to his notes of the conversation with Higham and then looked directly towards Llywelyn. 'Did you have an argument with Ed Mostyn in which he threatened to sell?'

Llywelyn blinked and then averted his eyes. 'Ed could be an obnoxious bastard. He thought he could control everybody. And, yes, one occasion he did say something like that. He often said things that he didn't mean.'

'But if he had agreed to sell the land that would have ruined all your plans.'

Matilda Spencer plonked her notepad on the table. 'Is that a question, Inspector? Because it seems to me that you've got very little *evidence*.'

Drake gave her a brief glance, toying with the possibility of telling her that this was his interview and he would conduct it in any way he saw fit.

'If Ed Mostyn had agreed to sell the land with his sister it would have ruined your life's work. Destroyed everything that's important to you. Would you agree?'

'I wouldn't kill if that's what you mean.'

Drake extracted a forensic report from his file. 'We found a fork at your property. A normal garden fork.' He pushed over a photograph. 'Does this belong to you?'

'Looks like mine.'

Drake looked over at Spencer and thought he detected a worry pinching at the crow's feet around her eyes. 'Do you use the fork regularly?'

'Occasionally.'

'You remember when it was last used?'

'How the hell would I?'

'Is it used for gardening?'

'It's a garden fork, for Christ's sake.'

'Can you remember when you last used it?'

Spencer interrupted again. 'I hope this is relevant, Inspector.'

'I can't remember. No idea.'

Drake turned to the papers again. 'And can you confirm you own the wellington boots we recovered from your property?'

Llywelyn stared at the photograph. 'Never seen them before.'

'The fork and the boots have been recently cleaned, wouldn't you say?'

Llywelyn peered at the image. 'If you say so.'

'Have you cleaned the fork recently?' Drake raised his voice.

'I'll wash it after it's been used, if that's what

you mean.'

Drake sat back and took his time composing the next question. Then he glanced at Spencer and Llywelyn. 'We've had a forensic analysis of the fork and boots completed. There are two areas of bloodstains. The blood on the wellingtons matches Ed Mostyn's blood type and the blood on the fork is a match to Rhys Fairburn. Can you explain how their blood found its way onto your garden fork and boots?'

Chapter 39

'He denied everything.' Drake stroked the handle of the china cup with his thumb and forefinger. Although he'd had heard dozens of denials during his career, sometimes a shred of doubt managed to wriggle its way into his mind. It was like an itch at the bottom of his back, difficult to reach but demanding attention.

'There is first-hand direct evidence. And he had a clear motive for killing Mostyn,' Andy Thorsen said in his usual deadpan manner.

Price sat next to Thorsen around the conference table, nodding severely. 'It's only a matter of time before he coughs.'

Drake didn't share the superintendent's optimism. Llywelyn's denials had been genuine enough and vociferous. And there had been what appeared to be real shock and disgust when Drake had challenged him about the death of Jane Jones.

Drake reached over and poured himself another coffee from the cafetière on the tray.

Thorsen replaced his cup on the saucer and pushed it towards the middle of the table. 'We've got the mobile telephone that connects him to Fairburn so we'll charge him with the murder of Ed Mostyn and Rhys Fairburn.'

'And Jane Jones?' Drake said.

Price spoke first. 'I want you to go after all of her friends again. We know that she jilted Llywelyn for Julian Sandham. That must have been difficult. Sandham is everything that Llywelyn hates. He is English, wealthy and privileged – probably supports the nuclear power station. And we know that Llywelyn has a violent temper. So when she confronts him – tells him it's over, the red mist descends.'

'That's how I see it too, Wyndham,' Thorsen

said, tidying his papers and readying to leave.

'It's only a matter of time, Ian,' Price added. 'Once he realises that he's going down for two murders he may as well cough to the other. It might not even add to his sentence. And his brief can at least say that he cooperated.'

Thorsen stood up and reached for a linen jacket folded over the back of the nearby chair. 'Thanks, Wyndham. Good work.'

Price turned to Drake. 'I've arranged sandwiches and a round of drinks for your team in the Ship and Anchor.' He looked over at Thorsen. 'Are you going to join us, Andy?'

'No thanks.' Thorsen left without further explanation.

'Mr Personality, eh?' It was the first time that Drake had heard Price criticise the Crown prosecution lawyer.

During the brief journey from headquarters he had decided to keep his visit to the public house brief. The paperwork could wait – now he could spend more time with his girls. He strode over to the entrance, passing a group of young girls tottering on high heels.

He heard his mobile ringing and dipped a hand into his jacket pocket.

'DI Drake.'

'Is it true, Inspector, that you've made an arrest today?'Headley said.

Drake hesitated. He should have pressed 'end' immediately.

'It's people like you who give journalism a bad name.'

'I've had it from a very reliable source.' Drake turned on the 'record' function of his handset as

Headley continued. 'Is it true that it's all connected to the power station? This will be an enormous story. Any chance of an off-the-record chat? I'll make it worth your while.'

Drake smiled as he pressed 'end', certain that Headley's editor would have something to say about the journalist's last remarks.

Inside the pub he made his way to the end of the bar and found Winder sitting by a table, already halfway through a pint of lager. Howick was eyeing the clingfilm-covered sandwiches and bite-sized pork pies that a young waitress had delivered. She gave him a brief smile and then disappeared back into the kitchen, returning moments later with a container full of crisps. Caren walked up to them as Drake dialled Sian's number. He walked away from the table a couple of metres.

'I'll call round later and take the girls out.'

'What's that noise?'

'I'm in the Ship and Anchor.'

'Celebrating?'

'Sort of. I'll take the girls to see my mother later.'

He heard a sharp exhalation of breath. 'Don't be late bringing them back.' She rang off just as Drake saw Price striding into the bar wearing a blue fleece over his uniform, the regulation tie discarded. They sat down around the table.

Caren had already pulled back the clingfilm and started eating a ham sandwich. Price lifted a glass by way of a toast. 'Well done. At least Llywelyn is behind bars.'

The superintendent demolished a round of sandwiches, finished his pineapple juice and then left, allowing the conversation around the table to relax. Drake excused himself, fished the mobile out of his pocket and called his mother. She sounded delighted with her unexpected visitors and Drake was equally pleased with her offer of a meal. It was a short drive to the house that he had called home for many years. Helen and Megan were excited at the prospect of an evening with their *nain* but seemed less so at spending time with their father. The journey passed slowly. Questions enquiring about what they'd been doing in the holidays were met with monosyllabic replies, and a sullen mood overtook him. What did fathers do with their children on access visits? Where did they go? What did they talk about? An improvement in his father–daughter skills was badly needed, Drake concluded.

He reached the top of the drive to the smallholding and hesitated for a moment, looking down at Caernarfon Bay and beyond towards Anglesey. Thickening grey clouds passed over the island onto the mainland, promising rain. He pulled the car to a stop outside the backdoor and watched his mother emerge, hugging Helen and Megan as they ran over.

'You look tired,' Mair Drake said, kissing him lightly on the cheek.

'I've been very busy.'

'How are things?' She cupped his chin with both hands.

'It's been so busy at work. I haven't had time to think.'

Inside, the smell of rosemary and sage filled the warm kitchen. Immediately Drake found himself relaxing and he yawned. It was a familiar aroma that took him back to the certainties of childhood. It had taken him several visits before he'd become accustomed not to expect his father to be there.

'You go and sit down,' his mother said. 'Helen and Megan can help me with supper.'

He walked through into the sitting room and lifted the supplement of an old Sunday newspaper. He had no idea what was going on in the outside world, hadn't seen the news for days. He sat down and tried to read but his eyelids were heavy. Within seconds he was fast asleep.

Chapter 40

Drake returned to headquarters after watching Llywelyn leering at him from the dock as he was remanded in custody by the magistrates' court. A nagging worry still tugged at his mind, which he put down to tiredness and the knowledge that he had a mountain of paperwork to complete.

He stared at the chaos on his desk. There were overtime logs that needed to be signed off, reports to the finance department about the budget for the investigation. He hadn't read any of the fifty or so emails from the Police Federation, mostly related to the ongoing campaign about the latest *threats to police pensions.* Price had sent him an email from the Independent Police Complaints Commission asking for their formal response to the treatment of Somerset de Northway's daughter Judy Somerville, who worked for Daniel Jessop.

Drake printed off the various forms and began searching for the notes that had been made during the interview. Howick could be overzealous and, with his impending promotion, perhaps he'd been rather too enthusiastic. He picked up the telephone and punched in Howick's extension.

'I need a word,' Drake said.

Moments later there was a knock on the door and Drake waved the young officer in. Drake motioned to one of the visitor chairs. 'I need to talk to you about Judy Somerville. She's made a formal complaint about the nature of your interview.'

'I thought she might.'

'I've got to respond to the IPCC in Cardiff.'

'There are only two members of staff in Jessop's firm. So it's really odd that a file went missing.'

'They must know everything that goes on.'

'All Jessop does is sort out the affairs of dead people. And he writes wills. But mostly he goes sailing.'

'It must have been a bit chaotic for them to have lost a file?'

Howick pursed his lips. 'It all seemed well organised.'

'What did she say when you challenged her about the file?'

'She just repeated what Jessop told you. There had been a break-in and the alarm had failed. Money had been taken from the cash box and files had been strewn all over the floor.'

'Had any other files been taken?'

'Not so far as they were aware. The accountants had just finished an audit.'

Drake read again the complaint form completed by Somerville that was flickering on his monitor. 'She says you were aggressive and grossly rude. Specifically, she says you made her feel like a criminal.'

Howick raised his hands and then opened up the palms in despair. 'You'd told me to be careful. I went round and round in circles asking whether she had been involved in making the will, whether she'd ever met Ed Mostyn. I don't think I was aggressive or rude.'

It was shaping up to be a complaint that would take a disproportionate amount of his time. He began composing bland phrases that might satisfy the IPCC without being an open admission of guilt.

Howick stood up. 'Anything else, boss?'

Drake looked at the notes again. 'Who were the accountants by the way?'

'Dafydd Higham's firm. Small world.'

'Yes, I suppose it is ...'

Already Drake was beginning to think that it was too small for another coincidence. His throat tightened slightly and he focused on the initial conversation with Daniel Jessop. He didn't recall the reference to accountants and certainly no mention of Dafydd Higham. He put Judy Somerville's papers onto the far corner of his desk and reached for his notebook. Flicking through the pages quickly, frustration built when he couldn't find his notes of the discussion with Jessop. He was rushing – that's when mistakes happen, he thought, so he slowed until eventually he found the relevant record – *auditors*, Jessop had said auditors. He gripped the notebook tightly, cursing to himself.

The earlier reservations about everything he had done in the case resurfaced. It struck him that Higham had been a ghostly presence throughout the case: related to Ed Mostyn, the accountant for Rhys Fairburn, Maldwyn Evans and Somerset de Northway. What other connections exist that we haven't discovered? Drake wondered. Perhaps Higham was even involved with the others and the young girls in the cottage. Drake fisted his right hand and banged it on the table very slowly.

Motive. There always had to be motive – money or revenge or hatred.

Drake stood up abruptly, walked over to the door of his office and yanked it open. Three sets of eyes turned to face him. 'Who saw that woman who suggested Mildred Jones had an affair?'

'It was me, boss,' Howick said.

An idea was forming in Drake's mind. 'What was her name again?'

'Fraser.'

'Did she tell you who the other person was?'

'No.'

'Did you ask?'

'Not at the time.'

'Send the address to my mobile.' He turned to Caren. 'You drive.'

Drake punched the postcode details into the satnav and watched as the machine told him the journey would take fifty-three minutes.

'Dafydd Higham gets everywhere in this inquiry. Even into Jessop's office. So, what if it suits him to make certain that his wife inherits after Mostyn?'

Caren was in the outside lane touching ninety miles an hour, the lights flashing on the car. 'So he had to get rid of the will.'

'Exactly.' Drake dialled a number into his mobile. 'We need to check a couple of things.'

The call rang out far longer than he expected. Every unanswered ring pulled on an already heightened tension until very soon he might curse. But then he heard Enid Evans's voice.

'Detective Inspector Drake, Mrs Evans. I need to ask you something.'

'What?' There was an angry edge to her voice.

'Your son mentioned that Dafydd Higham was helping your husband with the land.'

'Yes.'

'What did he mean?'

She paused. Drake could hear her breathing. 'Maldwyn was going to give him some money.'

The tension pulling at his chest subsided. It was exactly what he'd suspected.

'Thank you.'

Drake looked over at Caren. 'Higham had done a deal with Maldwyn Evans for a slice of their proceeds. And he probably did the same with Fairburn.'

Caren blasted the horn at a car dawdling in the outside lane.

Drake found the number for Rhys Fairburn and a brief three-way conversation between him, Ann and her mother told him what he had already guessed.

'Crooked bastard,' Drake said.

'But why did he kill them – well, Fairburn anyway?'

'He has access to all their computers. He's their accountant. So he sees all their personal papers. And the photographs of all the girls involved. And that included Jane.'

'But the files were password protected.'

'I know, I know. But ...'

Drake's mind raced. 'Mostyn had the images on his laptop; we know that much, even though we don't have the computer itself. Higham must have seen them – they probably weren't protected.'

He slammed an open palm against the dashboard as he thought how the investigation had been sidetracked into focusing on the activities of Somerset de Northway and his cronies with the young girls in the cottage. And all the time the answer had been right under his nose.

It took them forty-five minutes to reach Vera Fraser's house. He jumped out of the car and ran up the concrete drive to the front door, noticing movement behind the net curtains. He reached the bell just as Vera Fraser opened the door.

He flashed his card so quickly that Fraser had little chance to read the details. 'DI Drake. I need to ask you about Jane Jones.' Drake didn't wait for an invitation, barging directly into the hallway and through into the sitting room.

'You told my officer David Howick that Mildred Jones had an affair. Are you certain?'

Fraser sat down and curled one leg over the other knee. 'Well ...'

'Do you know who she had the affair with?'

Fraser gave him a guarded look. 'I can't be certain ... But a cousin of mine ... She saw Mildred with Dafydd Higham.'

'So Jane must be his daughter.'

'I don't know about that ...'

Chapter 41

Drake sat in the car, knowing he had to find Dafydd Higham. Quickly.

He dialled the office number, breathing slowly, his thoughts dominated by the Cambrian Club dinner photographs taken by Higham. If it was true that Jane was his daughter it must have sickened him every time he saw one of those images. The men who had abused his own daughter, smiling at the camera, sharing jokes.

'I'm afraid Mr Higham isn't here at the moment,' the receptionist said. 'Can I take a message? Can I tell him who called?'

Drake rang off.

'He's got an alibi,' Caren said. 'His wife confirms that he was in bed all night …'

And before she finished another piece of the jigsaw fell into place.

'Richie Mostyn said Joan Higham had trouble sleeping; apparently it was common in their family. And then when we saw her the first time she told us she had no trouble sleeping. The night Dafydd Higham was away she couldn't sleep. So what does that tell us?'

Caren crunched the car into first gear and accelerated towards the main road, towards Dafydd Higham's house. 'He's probably got a supply of sleeping tablets.'

'And we've got to find them.'

'But it's all circumstantial. Nothing that will get the CPS to drop its case against Llywelyn.'

It wasn't long until they turned into the drive for the Highams' property. The sun was warm as they left the air conditioning of the car. Drake strode over to the rear door, looking around for signs that Dafydd Higham was present, but the yard was empty. For the first time he noticed the outbuildings that had been refurbished, a new roof, new guttering and mahogany windows. He hammered on the door, giving Caren an apprehensive look. Her jaw was tight, her eyes small but focused.

Drake peered through a couple of windows but there was no sign of movement.

'Let's go and have a look at these outbuildings,' he said eventually.

Drake tried the first door, but it was locked and, leaning down, he was able to see inside what looked like a converted workshop. Various tools were scattered on the surface of a bench. Caren had walked ahead and opened a set of double doors without difficulty. Drake followed her inside. In the middle of a makeshift partition of unpainted plasterboard was an unlocked door that Drake nonetheless struggled to open. When he did, he saw what looked like an artist's studio, canvases stacked against a table and various cupboards screwed to the wall. Drake opened each in turn, examining various pots of paint and artists' accessories until a white bag caught his attention. He snapped on a pair of latex gloves and dipped his hand inside, where he found blister packs of prescription medicine. Quickly he scanned the leaflets, realising that the powerful sleeping tablets had been bought on the Internet.

'You were right Caren,' Drake said, turning towards her and holding the bag with two fingers. 'Enough sleeping tablets for an army.'

They retraced their steps and stood outside on the remains of old cobbles, in the cool shade of the midday sun. Drake looked over towards the end of the outbuildings, its door hanging off old hinges. He walked towards it and stepped into the gloom. A couple of quad bikes had been pushed into one corner, and various pieces of garden equipment dropped into an old dustbin. In the far corner the frame of an old garden cloche and stacks of timber stood against the wall, but underneath Drake spotted a piece of tarpaulin. Then he noticed the faint outline of a tyre track in the mud. His pulse beat a little faster, the anticipation building as he yanked the tarpaulin away and spotted the Vespa.

'We need to find Dafydd Higham now,' Drake called over at Caren.

He reached for his mobile telephone. He barked instructions to Winder. 'Get a warrant issued for Dafydd Higham.'

'Sir?'

Drake had already finished the call.

'Where could he be?' Caren said.

Drake immediately thought about the dinner jacket images. Only two of the men involved were still alive – Somerset de Northway and Aiden Hawkins. Then it struck Drake that it must have been Dafydd Higham in Crecrist Hall the evening de Northway was assaulted. He jogged back to the car. 'We need to contact de Northway and Judge Hawkins.'

Caren gave him a puzzled look. 'I thought de Northway was in hospital.'

They reached the car, Drake's breathing heavy. They jumped in and Drake powered down the window. Caren accelerated away from the farmhouse, skidding to a halt by the main road.

Drake fumbled with his mobile telephone, scanning the Internet for the hospital's number. Pressing the handset to his ear, he muttered an encouragement for the call to be answered.

'This is Detective Inspector Ian Drake of the Wales Police Service. I need some information urgently. Do you still have a patient called Somerset de Northway?'

Drake could hear voices in the background at

the hospital reception. He didn't have to wait long; a woman's voice sounded reassuring, informative. 'That patient was discharged yesterday.'

Drake didn't bother thanking her before he finished the call, repeating the details to Caren who was trying to overtake a tractor. 'We should be there in fifteen minutes.'

Drake dialled Price's number, but his direct line was engaged. Drake cursed, and tried Winder instead. 'Get an armed guard to the crown court to protect Judge Hawkins. There is every reason to believe that Dafydd Higham will try and kill him.'

'Have you spoken with the super?'

'Line's engaged. Just do it. Tell him what we know. Speak to Judge Hawkins's clerk and make sure he doesn't leave the building.'

Caren was already nearing the lane to Crecrist Hall by the time Drake finished. His heart pounded in his chest as the car raced past the small lodge cottage and skidded to a halt outside the front entrance. Drake ran over to the door but it was locked. He pulled the bell violently, but it made no noise.

They ran together towards the back of the house, but the French doors he'd used before were locked. The grass around the house had been recently cut; fresh clippings were scattered over the sandstone paving slabs.

'The rear entrance is over here,' Caren said.

A large oak door was ajar and Drake hesitated. He pushed it open, and rushed into the kitchen followed by all the ground-floor rooms in turn. He shouted de Northway's name but there was no response. He ran up the stairs, Caren behind him, both looking into each room until they were satisfied the place was empty. The noise of his leather shoes reverberated against the servant's wooden staircase and seconds later he stood outside.

In a copse he saw the line of chimneys and the sagging slates of an old roof and set off towards it. Caren's laboured breathing was noisy by his side; Drake wiped away the sweat from his brow but could do nothing about his sodden armpits. He undid his tie while running. The buildings looked like old stables – a couple had large doors, and from the furthest he heard a dull thud before the sound of a door squeaking open.

He speeded up and, reaching the first window, peered through it, with Caren doing likewise. But the glass was thick with grime and dust. He tugged at the main door but it barely moved, simply rattling the attachments on the inside. He took a step back and thought about smashing a window until he saw a stone staircase leading to the first floor around the gable. Hoping he could get access from the top, he took the stairs two at a time. Fighting to keep his balance on the small platform at the top, he aimed a kick at the door. It fell away easily against his weight.

Inside there was a wide mezzanine floor; below him, he saw de Northway. Drake tumbled down a wooden staircase, at the same time shouting at Caren to follow him, before jumping on the table and taking the weight of de Northway's body hanging limply from a noose.

Seconds later Caren appeared and helped Drake remove the noose while they both held de Northway's body. As they laid him flat on the table, Drake pressed two fingers hard into his neck.

'Call an ambulance. There's still a pulse.'

In the distance the faint sound of a motorcycle broke the silence.

'You stay here; I'm going after that bastard.'

Drake grabbed at the piece of old timber holding the door closed. It gave way easily under his weight and Drake made for the car. He pressed on, despite the pain of a side stitch.

He jumped into his car, keeping the nausea at bay. The engine screamed as he accelerated in low gears down the lane to the main road. He could hear the approaching ambulance siren and looked right and left, trying to decide which route to take. He indicated right. He reached the next village and scoured the car parks for any sign of Higham. Reaching a crossroads, he accelerated through the traffic lights just as they turned to red. He called the local station on his mobile, requesting assistance, insisting they get all available traffic cars to the west of the island.

He accelerated along a straight stretch of road, and in the distance caught sight of helmeted figure riding at a steady pace. Drake pressed the accelerator hard to the floor and the car hurtled forward. He switched on the police hazard lights and reached the motorcyclist within seconds. He got his car alongside Higham, before nudging him into the side of the road. Higham braked and when the motorcycle stopped he jumped off, leaving the scooter to fall into a ditch.

Higham ran towards a farm gate and scrambled over it, falling flat onto the ground on the other side. Drake pulled the car nearer to the side of the road and headed off in pursuit. Higham was making good progress along the edge of a field sown with sugar beet. Drake's brogues were uncomfortable as he slipped and banged against the dried-up tracks of tractor wheels. He started breathing deeply, blowing out deep lungs of breath.

Higham fumbled over another gate and now Drake was within a few yards.

Drake watched as Higham wrested his head free of the helmet, which he discarded into the brambles. He gained a few yards on Drake, until he fell headlong.

Drake arrived seconds later, and leant down, hands on his knees, gasping for breath. He looked down at Higham who was wincing in pain. 'My leg,' he said.

Drake took a few seconds to allow his breathing to return to normal. 'Dafydd Higham. I'm arresting you for murder.'

Chapter 42

When Drake returned to Dafydd Higham's home a Scientific Support Vehicle and several marked police cars were parked in the yard. The Vespa, a neutral teal colour, stood outside the outbuildings, a couple of crime scene investigators working inside. Routine house-to-house enquiries and an appeal to the public would probably find an eyewitness who'd seen Higham's Vespa travelling near Fairburn's house on the day he was killed. And with South's and Llywelyn's evidence, any denial by Higham would be futile. Drake saw Mike Foulds emerging from an outbuilding and walked over towards him.

'We found Mostyn's laptop in the house,' Foulds said. 'Lots of pictures in files with no passwords. And pictures of Higham with Ray-Bans that his wife says he lost on holiday last year.'

'Good.'

More evidence.

'And Higham's been stockpiling sleeping tablets.'

'I thought so,' Drake said.

A patrol car pulled into the drive. Caren emerged from the passenger side and Drake walked over. 'How is Somerset de Northway?'

'He'll live. We got there just in time.'

Drake worried that he had allowed an innate dislike of Somerset de Northway to cloud his judgement even if focusing on him at the time was logical.

'Have you heard about the suicide note, sir?'

Drake frowned and shook his head.

'Higham forced de Northway to write out a note explaining what he had done with the girls in the cottages. How he was overcome with guilt and grief.

And that killing himself was the only honourable thing left to do.'

They both turned towards the rear door of the house as they heard a woman's voice. 'You can't take that,' it shouted, and Joan Higham appeared.

Drake and Caren walked towards the house. Joan spotted them and marched over. 'You've got no right taking my personal possessions.' She raised a hand out towards the boxes being removed from the house by the crime scene investigators.

'You should leave Mrs Higham,' Drake said.

'How dare you! This is my home.'

'We've arrested your husband for multiple murders. We have to go through all his papers. If you've got a complaint, take it up with Superintendent Price or the chief constable or your MP or anybody else you want. But if you get in our way I'll arrest you.'

Drake turned away, leaving Joan Higham, hands on hips, glaring at him.

By early evening Drake sat with Caren in the interview room looking at Dafydd Higham. His small dark eyes peered unblinkingly at Drake. To his left Don Hart, his solicitor, looked uncomfortable in the narrow plastic chair and no matter how he moved his substantial frame, he wasn't able to find the right position.

'Don.' Drake glanced over at the lawyer, who was a regular in the area custody suite.

'Bloody hot in here,' Hart said, undoing his tie, jowls flapping over his open collar.

Drake sat down and, once he'd completed the formalities, looked up at Higham.

'You've been arrested for the attempted murder of Somerset de Northway. I'll read his preliminary statement.'

It was no more than a few sentences but Drake looked up regularly, trying to gauge the response in Higham's eyes. Whenever he thought he saw a reaction, Higham's black lifeless eyes snuffed it out.

'Dafydd. Why did you try to kill Somerset de Northway?'

Higham shook his head slowly.

Drake ignored him again. 'You and your wife stood to make a lot of money once the land had been sold. Is that why you killed Ed?'

Higham crossed his arms, pulled them tightly to his body and smirked at Drake.

'Now is your opportunity to explain everything,' Drake said. 'Did Ed discuss his private life with you?'

'You've got no idea.' Higham spat out a reply.

'Did he invite you to join their little *parties* at the cottage?'

'What's this got to do with the attempted murder of Somerset de Northway?' Hart interjected.

Drake turned to him abruptly. 'I'll conduct this interview anyway I choose.' Higham sneered at Drake when he looked back at him. 'After you'd killed Ed Mostyn, you decided to set up Gwynfor Llywelyn. He was the natural scapegoat, had a motive for killing Mostyn and you knew that he was in love with Jane. The murder of Rhys Fairburn just made it easier to create a picture that Llywelyn was the guilty party.'

'And why exactly would I want to kill Rhys Fairburn?'

Drake hesitated and pressed the small of his back against the stiff plastic chair. A person's natural instinct was to engage and Higham was the sort to believe he was cleverer than any policeman.

'You were aware that Rhys Fairburn and Somerset de Northway had a liking for young girls. In fact, the younger the better, mostly under sixteen.'

Higham rolled his eyes.

'For the purposes of the tape, can you confirm that you were aware of their activities?'

Higham coughed briefly. 'Yes. Ed Mostyn told me. He'd been involved. I thought it was disgusting. They were paedophiles taking advantage of young girls. They should have been locked up.'

'Can you help us with the names of the girls involved?'

Drake watched as Higham tried to work out exactly what was going on. He pushed over the table a photograph of Tracy sitting on Fairburn's lap. 'You know who this girl was?'

Higham shook his head.

'Did Ed Mostyn ever mention Tracy?'

'Not that I remember.'

'And there are three other girls that we can't trace.' Drake pushed over three more photographs.. 'Do you recognise any of them?'

'Of course not.'

Drake paused, staring over at Higham. 'Did Ed Mostyn mention to you that Jane Jones was one of the young girls targeted?'

Higham swallowed hard. Drake had his answer.

'He might have mentioned her name.'

'How did you feel about that?'

Higham gave a puzzled look. 'I don't know what you mean.'

'Well, you've told me that you thought what they were doing was disgusting and that they should be locked up. I want to know how you felt, knowing that these middle-aged men had been having sex with Jane, your daughter.'

'You should have seen the look on his face,' Caren

said, putting down the pre-packed sandwiches and soft drink onto her desk. Howick and Winder had already finished their lunch; a mug of coffee sat on the desks in front of each of them.

'What did he say?' Winder said.

'His mouth fell open. I could almost see his tonsils.'

Howick grunted a brief appreciation of Caren's comment.

'Denied killing her of course. Said it was nothing to do with him. Once he thought we were going to charge him with killing Jane Jones he began to talk.'

'Did he cough?'

'He denied having anything to do with Jane's death.'

Winder stretched an elastic band and then aimed it at Llywelyn's photograph on the board. It flew across the room once he'd released it and fell onto the floor. 'The boss was right about Somerset de Northway,' Winder said. 'His fingerprints are all over the twenty-pound notes you recovered from Sandham.'

Caren stood up and began to walk for the door.

'So, did Somerset de Northway kill Jane Jones?' Howick said.

Caren stopped, then turned around. 'That's what we have to work out.'

Drake returned to his office and slumped into the chair behind his desk. He wanted to switch off from the inquiry; he wanted to feel satisfied that Dafydd Higham was locked up. He didn't envy the officers in the SOCP having to deal with these kinds of offence every day. They were always painful for the victims involved, reliving the mistreatment, and with the passage of time memories faded. It would probably take the Crown Prosecution Service days, maybe weeks, to decide if Somerset de Northway would be prosecuted. And he couldn't think how he'd explain to Tracy, Becky and Sue if the decision was not to prosecute. But it wasn't his decision to make or to influence.

He got up and stood by his window, looking out over the parkland surrounding headquarters. It was dusk; the occasional car drove on sidelights. A jogger weaved between two men walking their dogs. How would he feel if either Helen or Megan had been abused? There would be rage, anger – he decided that he had to talk to Andy Thorsen and tell him that they owed these girls a duty. They would have to do the right thing.

He strolled out into the Incident Room and stood before the board, looking at the image of Jane Jones. She should have been protected, safe from abusers. From the moment he'd known that Higham had killed Mostyn and Fairburn, the identity of Jane's killer had been foremost in his mind. Perhaps it had been Llywelyn all along. For now he could focus clearly on who had killed her.

He returned to his desk and read the notes and statements again, forcing his mind to picture her killer by the cottages late at night. There had to be a motive, simple or complex. He sat back, recalling everything about Tyddyn Du and Jane's family. Then he read his notes of Julian Sandham's interview and pictured the face of Tracy as she spoke about her friend.

He read the forensics report and when he read the section with the results, sadness filled his mind, as well as clarity. It was another hour before he had finished all his notes and constructed the basis for an arrest.

Chapter 43

Drake woke after another uncomfortable night in unfamiliar surroundings with no dreams that he could recall. Checking the time, and knowing that Helen and Megan would be having breakfast, he rang and spoke to them.

'Do you want to speak to Mam?' Megan said as their conversation faltered.

'No. I wanted to speak to you. We'll go out this weekend.'

'Okay.'

'I'll ring again tomorrow.'

Drake rang off. He finished his breakfast, dumped the crockery in the sink and left the flat. He went straight to headquarters, ignoring his usual routine of collecting the newspaper and doing a couple of squares of the Sudoku. Speaking to his daughters was a much better ritual than being enslaved by numbers.

The late summer sunshine was gradually giving way to autumn coolness. He buttoned his jacket as he left the car and strode into headquarters. He was the first to arrive and he draped his jacket carefully over the wooden hanger – some rituals were still worth keeping. He called Mike Foulds.

'I need a CSI team this morning.'

'We are really shorthanded. I've had a couple of CSIs on holiday, another on maternity.'

'It's a simple job. Won't take more than a few hours.'

'Is it urgent?'

'It's linked to the death of Jane Jones. It'll complete the inquiry.'

'What time and where?'

Drake gave the details and rang off just as

Caren entered the Incident Room. He called her name. She appeared at the door and waved her in.

'Jane Jones,' he said simply.

There was a tinge of sadness in his voice as he explained his conclusions to Caren and once he'd finished she nodded her head slowly. They left headquarters. Drake drove at a pace that was certain not to attract the attention of any sharp-eyed traffic officers. The person he was going to see wasn't going anywhere so he didn't need to rush.

Another forty minutes passed before Drake drove up the lane for Tyddyn Du, the Scientific Support Vehicle following behind them. He parked and Caren left the car without a word and walked over to the house.

'This way,' Drake said to the two CSIs, before striding towards the barn.

Inside, Drake headed over to the cupboard and pulled open a door, taking in the overalls and heavy-duty gloves that would fit the hands of both Huw Jones and his father. Hands that would have been large enough to squeeze the life out of a young girl.

'I want everything in here catalogued and photographed. You know the drill.'

He left to walk over to the house, just as Caren emerged from the back door and came to meet him.

'They're in one of the fields by the sea,' Caren said, pointing towards the cottages where they'd found Jane's body.

Drake saw the outline of Mildred standing just inside the door.

'She knows,' Caren said simply.

Drake glanced over towards the house, but Mildred had gone back inside.

'You stay with Mildred,' Drake said, setting off down the lane with the morning sun warm on his back.

The lane led down towards a grassy track surrounded by blackberry and sloe bushes. After a few minutes Drake found himself in front of a gate. In the field beyond he heard voices and the occasional thumping.

He undid the catch on the gate and at the bottom of the field he saw Huw and Ray Jones working by a ditch, a pile of fence posts perched on the back of a quad bike. The ground was hard beneath Drake's shoes as he walked down towards them.

Huw turned as he approached and tightened his grip on a long-handled lump hammer. He picked it up off the ground and Drake hesitated. Huw motioned to his father and said something Drake couldn't make out, before he squared up to Drake.

'Put it down, Huw.'

Huw made another move towards Drake, but stopped after a couple of steps. He straightened, pushed out his chest and gave Drake a defiant look.

'Huw, put the hammer down.'

The young man sagged, loosening his grip. Drake moved the short distance towards him and put his hand on the wooden handle before stepping away. He turned towards Ray Jones, who'd thrust his hands deep into the pockets of his overall. Over his shoulder Drake heard distant conversation and, turning, saw Caren and a uniform officer standing by the gate behind him.

He moved away from Huw and over to Ray. 'Ray Jones. You know why I'm here.'

Chapter 44

It was another early meeting organised to accommodate the diary of Andy Thorsen. Drake sat in Price's room opposite the superintendent and the crown prosecutor. It had been over a week since Ray Jones had been remanded to the vulnerable prisoners' unit of the local prison.

He cupped his fingers around a mug of coffee. It smelt fresh and strong. Drake pursed his lips and stared over at the prosecutor. The interview with Ray Jones had been the oddest that he'd ever encountered in his career and had left him uncertain what really went on in Ray's mind. His insistence that the local minister be present with his solicitor had been unusual, putting Drake on edge.

'Do you think he's fit to plead?' Andy Thorsen's voice was devoid of any emotion.

'I really don't know.'

'We'll need a psychiatric report, of course.'

'It was as though he couldn't bring himself to admit he'd killed her. I'll never forget his stare. There was a deep hatred right through every part of him. When I put the forensic results to him he just sat back and grinned, sort of smirked really, as though I was talking rubbish.'

'But the evidence of Jane's DNA from his clothes and from the gloves makes it an open-and-shut case.' Thorsen flicked through the papers in his hand. 'Defence might try and argue that her DNA could have got there some other way. Contamination because she was family.' Thorsen leant forward, tilted his head and looked at Drake. 'How are you certain it wasn't Huw Jones?'

'He was out in Rhosneigr the night Jane was killed.'

'But he could have got back.'

'I know, but Ray Jones has a hell of a temper. And he knew Jane wasn't his daughter. It was the sort of thing that would have eaten at him, until the hatred would have been too much. And the minister described him as Calvinistic. Once he knew Jane was pregnant, that would have been enough to tip him into madness. And Mildred said something that struck me as odd from the start – implying that she should have stayed at home. She must have known from the beginning.'

Drake continued. 'There's sadness at the heart of that family. As though they couldn't function in the modern world.'

'He's a killer. End of.'

Drake wished it were that simple. Ray had killed his step-daughter and he'd have to live with that for the rest of his life. The courts would decide if Ray was mentally fit enough to plead to a murder charge or whether it would be manslaughter.

'We've been reviewing the evidence about Somerset de Northway.' Thorsen interrupted Drake's thoughts. 'We've decided to prosecute for the historic sexual abuse charges. Forensics found some old furniture in one of his barns that the victims have identified. But it was Jane's diary and his fingerprints on the money that were the clincher.'

'Good. Very good.' Drake sounded more enthusiastic than he intended. Price and Thorsen gave him a wary look.

Thorsen continued. 'Judge Hawkins will have to excuse himself from dealing with that case.'

Price interrupted. 'And he rang me the other day, wanted me to pass on his thanks for sending armed officers to the court.'

Drake wasn't certain how he should respond. Thorsen collected his papers together and stood up.

'Good work. Ian.'

Price nodded his agreement.

When Drake returned to the Incident Room two civilians were dismantling the boards. The photographs and paperwork that had dominated the inquiry had been piled on an adjacent table ready to be filed away in the flat-packed storage boxes lying on one of the desks.

The door opened and Mandy Finch strode in. She gave the activity in the room a cursory glance. 'Thanks for that voice recording– you know, the one from Headley.'

'Of course. He was an unprincipled journalist.'

'Not any longer. That's why I called in – I thought you might like to know personally. The editor sacked him yesterday.'

'Not before time.'

'He did name his source, which is helpful.'

'You had better notify professional standards.'

'Been done.'

The room had the feeling of the morning after the night of a heavy party. It was odd seeing Howick's desk empty, knowing that he wouldn't be back. He wasn't just on leave or away sick: he was now a custody sergeant in Wrexham. Neither Caren nor Winder were at their desks and he stood for a moment, realising that they didn't need to be there. The civilians stopped and gave him a curious look.

Back in his office someone had left the local newspaper on his desk. It was open on a page that had an image of Llywelyn smiling at the camera. Drake winced at the headline – *Campaigner Sues for False Arrest*. It would mean more meetings with lawyers and more time away from policing. He read the long article that gave Llywelyn an opportunity to tell the readers about his crusade. He pondered for a moment whether they'd actually had an alternative at the time. There had been a credible motive – but his train of thought was interrupted when the telephone rang.

'Drake.'

'Ian.' Drake recognised the sound of the special adviser's soothing tone. She probably rehearsed every morning before a mirror. 'I wanted to thank you for all your efforts with the inquiry.'

'I don't think Llywelyn would agree.'

'Minor problem. The lawyers will sort him out. A small payment no doubt that will help with his overdraft and a confidentiality clause so tight he'll be afraid to fart.'

Drake thought he heard a brief giggle.

'And Aiden Hawkins was most impressed and he's not the most affable of men.'

She made it sound as though she was on first-name terms with Judge Hawkins. He would never know how much of her special advising had been needed, because someone somewhere suspected the judge might be involved. Above my pay grade, Drake thought.

'Good,' Drake said.

'I suppose you've heard about the sale of the land?'

'No?'

'The charity that should have inherited the land has agreed a generous settlement with Mrs Higham and the power company.'

'So the development proceeds smoothly.'

'Yes. Of course.' French sounded contented. 'Thank you again, Inspector,' she said, before finishing the call.

Drake saw Caren walk past his door quickly,

followed by Winder. The civilians had finished when Drake walked back into the Incident Room. Winder was chewing hard on some gum and looking very bored. Caren sat by her desk sorting papers. They looked over at Drake.

There was still a file to prepare for the crown court. Every statement had to be cross-referenced, every exhibit numbered and every photograph logged. But for now it could wait.

'Take the rest of the day off, both of you.'

Back in his office Drake sent a couple of texts before taking his suit jacket and heading for the car.

Later that afternoon he sat in his car waiting for Helen and Megan. He left the car when he saw them walking out of the school gate. They ran over to him.

'Where's *Nain*?' Helen asked.

'I told her I was collecting you today.'

Drake had received a simple '*Okay*' from his mother-in-law to his text telling her that he'd collect the girls from school that afternoon. The local mountain zoo was quiet as Drake parked and then paid for three tickets. He had forgotten how much the girls enjoyed visiting the various enclosures, but he hadn't forgotten how much he enjoyed being with them.

It was late in the afternoon when Sian called his mobile.

'Where are you?'

'In the zoo with the girls.'

'Oh ...'

'Do you want to have a meal with us later?'

There was silence for a moment.

'Yes, I suppose ...'

An hour later they were sitting reading menus in a pub with a sprawling garden area and a large conservatory.

'I want to work in the zoo when I leave school,' Helen announced.

Sian smiled. 'You've got lots of time before you have to decide anything like that.'

'Really, Mam, I am going to do it.'

Helen had the determination Drake had seen in Sian and the stubbornness of his own mother.

'What sort of exams are there?' Helen asked.

Sian was fiddling with the menu card; a waitress hovered around their table. 'We need to order,' Sian said.

Helen decided upon pizza and Megan soon followed suit.

Sian turned the conversation away from animals and the zoo, wanting to hear about their day in school. One of the other girls had been taken ill and Megan wanted to go and see how she was, only to be told by Sian that her friend would probably be back in school the following day.

Two large pizzas arrived with glasses of soft drinks for the girls and lasagnes and salad for Drake and Sian.

'How was your day?' Drake asked Sian.

'I saw thirty-five patients today. That's a record.'

The bags under her eyes evidenced that Sian was working long hours. After two large ice creams for the girls and coffees for Drake and Sian, he paid. They left the pub, Helen and Megan running out to the car as Sian touched Drake's arm, before kissing him lightly on the cheek.

Epilogue

It had been two months since Drake had last visited Cemaes Bay. A new sign in the main street pointed potential customers towards Llywelyn's bakery. A van less than three years old, with *Becws Cemaes Bakery* in a bold red logo, emerged from the side street, Llywelyn at the wheel, and drove away.

Drake fastened the zip of his Barbour against the autumn chill and walked past the shops. The interview he had that morning at the home of an officer badly beaten in an assault late one night had ended sooner than he'd anticipated, with the man experiencing a coughing fit that meant his wife had ushered Drake out of the house as she called an ambulance.

He found a small café and sat drinking watery coffee.

'Did you hear about Dafydd Higham?'The voice came from the adjacent table. He jerked his head around and looked over at two women, each with a blue rinse and full, round faces.

'He'll be out in twenty years.'

'They should lock him up and throw away the keys for what he did.'

'And poor old Joan.'

'I heard she's going to live in Spain.'

Drake finished his drink, got up and went over to the counter to pay.

'And that Ray Jones is completely off his head apparently. He's in a prison for mad people.'

Ray's plea to manslaughter on grounds of diminished responsibility had been accepted and he was starting a twelve-year sentence in a specialist prison unit, but Drake wasn't going to explain the intricacies of the legal profession to the women. He heard them talk about the cakes that Llywelyn's bakery had just started selling as he left.

The WPS had still not appointed a successor to Howick and the previous week Caren had announced with a broad smile that she was pregnant. There'd be a temporary appointment while she was on maternity leave; it would be odd having to work with new members of his team.

Then he realised it would only be a short detour to the terraced property where he'd seen the old man making porridge.

He parked in the lay-by and looked over to the front door. It still looked weather-beaten. He left the car and crossed the road. The windows needed painting and, for the first time, he noticed a stone set into the wall above the door with a date, 1874, with some letters that he could only just make out – *Hapusle*.

He smiled to himself. The old man was contented, happy with himself and with life. What made a person christen a house 'happyplace'? Drake thought. It didn't have the same warmth in English as it did in Welsh. He peered through the windows. The front room was empty apart from an old chair upended onto its side.

He wondered if the old man would have understood his world. If his father ever did. There was a certainty to life in the country, a rhythm and Drake knew then that he had to live his for his own family. He walked back to his car. His mobile rang.

'Area control sir. I've been trying to get hold of you.'

'There's poor reception here.'

'Superintendent Price wants you as the SIO on a burglary in Llandudno.'

'On my way.'

Made in the USA
Coppell, TX
02 October 2023

22303481R00197